LAST EVENINGS WITH TERESA

Juan Marsé

LAST EVENINGS WITH TERESA

Translated from the Spanish by
Nick Caistor

Copyright © Juan Marsé, 1966, 2003, and Heirs of Juan Marsé

The right of Juan Marsé to be identified as the
Author of the Work has been asserted by him in accordance with the
Copyright, Designs and Patents Act 1988

Nick Caistor asserts his right to be identified as the translator of the work

Originally published in Spanish as *Últimas tardes con Teresa* in 1966 by Seix Barral

First published in the English language in 2025 by Mountain Leopard Press
An imprint of Headline Publishing Group Limited

1

Apart from any use permitted under UK copyright law, this publication may only be reproduced, stored, or transmitted, in any form, or by any means, with prior permission in writing of the publishers or, in the case of reprographic production, in accordance with the terms of licences issued by the Copyright Licensing Agency.

Excerpt from 'Promenade du soir' by Nazim Hikmet © Nazim Hikmet
Translation rights arranged through Vicki Satlow of The Agency srl.

Excerpts from English language translation of 'Right-Wing Thought Today' by Simone Beauvoir, translated by Veronique Zaytzeff, Frederick M. Morrison, Sonia Kruks and Andrea Veltman in *Political Writings* (2012), reprinted with kind permission from University of Illinois Press.

All characters in this publication – apart from the obvious historical figures – are fictitious and any resemblance to real persons, living or dead, is purely coincidental.

Cataloguing in Publication Data is available from the British Library

Trade paperback ISBN 978 1 03543 905 8

Typeset in Sabon LT by CC Book Production

Printed and bound in Great Britain by Clays Ltd, Elcograf S.p.A.

MIX
Paper | Supporting responsible forestry
FSC® C104740

Headline's policy is to use papers that are natural, renewable and recyclable products and made from wood grown in well-managed forests and other controlled sources. The logging and manufacturing processes are expected to conform to the environmental regulations of the country of origin.

HEADLINE PUBLISHING GROUP
An Hachette UK Company
Carmelite House
50 Victoria Embankment
London EC4Y 0DZ

The authorised representative in the EEA is Hachette Ireland,
8 Castlecourt Centre, Dublin 15, D15 XTP3, Ireland
(email: info@hbgi.ie)

www.headline.co.uk
www.hachette.co.uk

Prologue

They walk slowly across a bed of confetti and streamers on a starry September night, along a deserted street covered by a canopy of garlands, bunting and torn paper lanterns; the final night of the Fiesta Mayor street festivities (the farewell confetti, the last waltz) in a working-class district on the outskirts of Barcelona. It's four in the morning, everything is coming to a close. The stage where, until a short while before, the orchestra was playing requests, the piano under in its yellow dust sheet, the folding chairs stacked on the pavement. The street reflects the desolate feeling at the end of celebrations in garages or on terrace roofs; a new day is crouched, waiting for dawn, in doors and windows, a day that will bring its monotonous tasks, the sad dealings of hands with iron, wood and brick. The melancholy braggart, the shadowy local youngster who all summer long has been in search of an alluring adventure, the besotted companion of the beautiful stranger, is as yet unaware of this: to him, the summer is still a green archipelago. Glittering coils of streamers hang from balconies and streetlamps whose yellow-tinted light (even more indifferent than that of the stars) falls like weary dust on the thick carpet of confetti that has turned the street into a snowy landscape. A slight breeze stirs the paper canopy in a cool whisper of reed beds.

The contrast between the solitary couple and their surroundings is as stark as their clothes are from each other: the young man (jeans, trainers, black polo shirt with a striking wind rose printed on the chest) has his arm around the waist of the elegant girl (flared pink dress, smart high-heeled shoes, bare shoulders and straight, thick blond hair); she leans her head on his shoulder as they step into the distance, casually trampling on the white flakes as they head for a gleaming shape visible on the corner: a sports car. The way the couple move has something of a solemn wedding rite about it, that ideal slowness we enjoy in dreams. Gazing into one another's eyes, they have almost reached the car, a white Renault Floride, when suddenly a damp gust of wind swirls round the corner towards them, raising clouds of confetti: the first wind of autumn, the rain-laden slap in the face that confirms summer is over. Caught out, the young couple laugh as they separate and raise their hands to protect their eyes. The eddying confetti is stirred up again, and rustles beneath their feet, unfurling its snowy-white wings as it envelops them; for a few seconds they are completely obscured. They reach for one another as if they're playing blind man's buff; they laugh, call out, embrace, let go again, and finally stand back to back like statues, waiting for this commotion to abate; momentarily lost, nowhere to be seen in the storm of white flakes whirling around them.

Part One

Some nicknames illustrate not only a way of life but also the nature of the society in which we live.

On Saint John's Eve, the night of 23 June 1956, the Interloper stole out of the shadows of his neighbourhood wearing a brand-new, cinnamon-coloured summer suit. He walked down the main road from El Carmelo to Plaza Sanllehy, jumped on the first motorbike he saw that seemed to offer little risk (not to steal this time, simply to use and abandon when he didn't need it any more), and sped off in the direction of Montjuich. That evening he was intending to go to the Pueblo Español, where foreign girls joined the celebrations, but he changed his mind halfway and instead headed for the upper-class San Gervasio district. He rode along slowly, breathing in the fragrant June night, full of misty promises, down deserted streets flanked by railings and gardens, until he decided to abandon the motorbike and smoke a cigarette, leaning against the bumper of a flashy sports car parked outside an imposing detached house. His melancholy, brooding face, sallow-skinned and stern-looking, was reflected in the shimmering mirage of the car's bodywork as he listened admiringly to the gentle music of a foxtrot: opposite him, in a private garden festooned with paper lanterns and streamers, a party was in full swing.

The lively atmosphere of the festivities was not the sort to make anyone nervous, still less in a neighbourhood such as this, and yet a group of elegant couples who happened to pass by the young man couldn't help feeling the mild sense of unease that an out of place detail can create. What caught their eye was the harsh beauty of the Interloper's southern Spanish features, together with an unnerving stillness that bore a strange relation – or more precisely a suspicious incongruity – with the marvellous automobile he was standing next to. But this was all they perceived. Their antennae were alert to any small thing that seemed not quite right, and yet they could not detect in his strong brow that subtle impassivity that precedes drastic decisions, or spot in the furious stars of his eyes that vaguely glazed look indicating troubled thoughts that might even portend crime. His dark, olive-skinned hands, trembling imperceptibly as he lit a second cigarette, marked him out like a stigma. And there was something about his black, slicked-back hair, apart from its natural appeal, that the admiring females noted with a shiver: his elaborate hairstyle betrayed a vain, concealed effort, a hope still intact despite being repeatedly frustrated – the unmistakable evidence of a daily struggle with poverty and oblivion, the desperate coquetry typical of great loners and the highly ambitious.

When finally he made up his mind to push open the garden gate, his hand stopped trembling, as with some alcoholics when they pick up their second drink; his body straightened, and a smile came to his eyes. He was striding along the gravel path when suddenly he thought he saw a shadow moving in the bushes on his right: among the greenery in the almost complete darkness, two shining eyes were peering at him. He came to a halt and tossed away the cigarette. Two yellowish, immobile dots were openly staring at his face. The Interloper knew that in cases like this it's best to grin and brazen things out. But as he drew closer, the luminous dots disappeared; he saw an indistinct female silhouette scurrying off towards the house, carrying what looked like a tray. Off to a bad start, kid, he said to himself as he made for the dance floor, improvised on a roller-skating rink. Hands in pockets, assuming a nonchalant air, he headed first for the buffet set up beneath a tall willow tree, shouldering his way through a solid mass of backs to serve himself a brandy and soda. No one seemed to pay him the slightest attention. As he turned to make way for a girl heading for the dance floor, he accidentally elbowed a young man and spilled some of his drink.

'Sorry,' he said.

'Don't worry about it,' said the other man with a smile, before moving off.

The calm, almost disdainful indifference and self-assurance he read on the youngster's face restored his own confidence. Under the willow tree, glass in hand, he felt momentarily safe; a few moments later, moving stealthily so as not to draw attention to himself, he searched for a suitable dance partner – someone not too striking, but not too modest either. He noticed that all the people at the party, about seventy of them, were very young. Many of the girls were wearing trousers, the men coloured sports shirts. When he realised he was one of the few in a suit and tie, he felt ridiculous. They're richer than I thought, he told himself, feeling stupid for looking elegant at the wrong moment, like someone dolled up in their Sunday best. A few couples were sitting by the side of a swimming pool; a toy boat was bobbing on the transparent pale-green water. Under the leafy trees strung with coloured lights and loudspeakers, he also noticed some bored-looking guests sitting around tables, conversing listlessly and exchanging sleepy glances. Up at the house, a little girl in pyjamas was seated at one of the ground-floor windows, while inside a group of older people were drinking around a low table.

A record of classic rumbas dragged on endlessly. The Interloper's eyes fastened on a girl seated at the edge of the pool. Dark-haired, wearing a simple pink skirt and white blouse. Head down, apparently not interested in dancing, she was amusing herself tracing imaginary lines on the reddish tiles. She looked curiously shy and lost, as if she too had just arrived and didn't know anyone. He hesitated: if before I count to ten I haven't gone up to that girl, I'll chop it off and throw it to the dogs. Clutching the tall glass and feeling surer of himself – why did its purple colour make him feel like that? – he made his way towards the girl through the dancing couples. A violent light and a sound like the buzzing of bees cascaded on to his head and shoulders. As he advanced, his determined profile, resolutely focused on a dream, stirred a troubled blue sprinkling of furtive glances (like his own, in more torrid climes, when a smart convertible roared past, inside it a beautiful girl, hair streaming in the wind). For a few brief seconds an imaginary network of secret, unconfessed desires was created. These glances also had less pleasant undertones: he knew his appearance betrayed his Andalusian origins – a *xarnego* or immigrant from Murcia (used as a racial description rather than a geographical one – another Catalan eccentricity), a son of distant, mysterious Murcia ... As he strolled towards the pool he saw another girl sit down next to the one he had picked out and speak affectionately to her, slipping an arm round her shoulders. He studied the two of them carefully, weighing up his chances of success with one or the other: he had to make up his mind before he accosted them. The face of the blonde girl in trousers who had just arrived was almost hidden; she seemed to be confiding in her friend, who was listening to her silently, eyes lowered. When she raised them to look at the approaching newcomer, a smile appeared on her lips. Without hesitation, he chose the blonde one: not because she was more attractive – he had barely seen her face – but because he was taken aback by the other's unexpected smile. Just as he reached them and bowed – maybe a little too ostentatiously, you dolt, he thought – the blonde suddenly stood up and went to sit further away with a young man who was trailing his hand in the water. For the fraction of a second, the Murcian caught a glimpse of a pair of blue eyes behind the straight, golden hair that partially concealed the girl's face; they were like a blow to his heart. He considered following her, but changed his mind and instead asked her friend to dance. It makes no difference anyway, he told himself.

The girl was already on her feet, standing quietly and hesitantly in front of him, glancing shyly at her blonde friend, who was now a couple of metres away and had her back to them, oblivious to what was going on. No longer trying to attract her attention, the dark-haired girl held out her hand to the stranger in a surprisingly determined manner, once again flashing her enigmatic smile. Instead of allowing him to lead her to the dance floor, she pulled him towards the darkest and most remote part of the garden among the trees, where two couples were smooching in each other's arms. The Interloper was in a dream. The girl's hand, whose soft, moist touch seemed strangely familiar, gave him an uncannily cold sensation, as if it had been in the water. Putting his arms around her, he gave her his best smile, and peered deep into her eyes. He was a good deal taller than her, and she had to tilt her head back to see his face. The Interloper began to speak. His voice was his great attraction: gravelly, with a strong southern accent, persuasive. His splendid eyes did the rest.

'Tell me something: do you need your sister's permission to dance?'

'She's not my sister.'

'You seem afraid of her. Who is she?'

'Teresa.'

The girl danced clumsily, as if unaware of her own body. She was about to turn nineteen and her name was Maruja. No, she wasn't from Andalusia, even though she looked it: she was Catalan, like her parents. Bad luck, we're stuck with a frumpish Catalan *noia*, he thought.

'Well, it's not obvious – you don't have a Catalan accent.'

She did pronounce her words carefully, in a monotone whisper. She was very shy. Her slender but surprisingly vigorous body was trembling in his arms. By now, a bolero was playing.

'Do you go to the university?' he asked. 'I'm surprised I've never seen you.'

The girl didn't answer, but simply smiled her mysterious smile once more. Steady on, you brute, steady on, he told himself. She lowered her head and asked:

'And you? What's your name?'

'Ricardo. But my friends call me Richard . . . the stupid ones, that is.'

'When I saw you, I thought you must be one of Teresa's friends.'

'Why?'

'I don't know . . . Teresa is always turning up with strange boys; nobody knows where she finds them.'

'So I look strange to you.'

'No, I mean . . . a stranger.'

'Well, I feel as though I've known you all my life.'

Pulling her closer, he brushed her forehead and cheeks with his lips, searching for a kiss.

'Do you live here, Maruja?'

'Close by. On Vía Augusta.'

'You're very tanned.'

'Not as dark as you . . .'

'Actually, that's how I always am. You're tanned from going to the beach, but I've only been three times this year, actually,' he replied, repeating the adverb, fascinated by it and a way of using the word that he considered appropriate to this rich kids' party.

'I haven't had the time, I'm studying for the exams . . . Where do you go, to S'Agaró beach?'

'No. To Blanes.'

The Interloper was expecting it to be S'Agaró. But Blanes wasn't bad either.

'Hotel . . . actually?'

'No.'

'Your family villa?'

'Yes.'

'You're a good dancer. Here I am, asking you all these questions, and I was forgetting the most important one: do you have a boyfriend?'

All of a sudden Maruja bowed her head and pressed herself against him, body trembling. He was surprised by the insistent pressure of her thighs and stomach. She again transmitted that lost, abandoned feeling he had noticed when he saw her sitting with her friend. He dismissed the thought. She's getting turned on, he said to himself. He began kissing her top lip, and finally directly on her mouth. He was unsure whether it was a rich, spoiled girl's whim, or a natural instinct for survival, but he was taken aback when he heard her say, 'I'm thirsty . . .'

'Shall I bring some champagne? I suppose every couple has the right to a bottle.'

The girl laughed shyly.

'You can drink as much as you like here.'

'I was saying it on your behalf. You girls get tipsy over nothing. Well, shall I bring you a glass?'

'I prefer a *Cuba libre*.'

'So do I. Good idea. Wait here for me.'

Rockets whistled through the sky. The sound of firecrackers going off in the distance gradually diminished; the vast hum of the sleepless city lent the night a profound sense of magic that other summer nights lacked. As he sauntered towards the buffet, the garden gave off different aromas – oily, damp and slightly rotten. He pushed past golden shoulders, the sweet perfume of perspiring young bodies and tanned necks, bare armpits and jiggling breasts. The dancers jostled against him while he prepared the drinks. Never before had he experienced being so close to the odour of firm, fragrant arms, the confident gleam of bright-blue eyes. He felt safe, so pleasantly surrounded that he was no longer even worried by a group of young men who seemed to be in charge (doubtless the party organisers) and were keeping a close eye on him. He added a good shot of rum to Maruja's glass and went back to her, proposing a toast . . .

'Here's to tomorrow,' he said cheerfully.

The girl drank slowly, staring at him. He led her to a swing chair in the middle of the lawn. They sat and kissed each other tenderly. By now, though, they were no longer protected by darkness. He checked his watch: it would soon be four in the morning. Behind them, the house's flamboyant outline was beginning to show against the reddish dawn sky, where the stars were melting peacefully like ice cubes in a glass of Campari left forgotten on the grass. Some of the guests were already taking their leave. He had to hurry. Three young men were staring at him from the brightly lit buffet; their expressions left no room for doubt: they were wondering who the devil he was, and what he was doing at their party.

Now the fun starts, he thought, as he bent down to pick up his glass. He whispered in Maruja's ear:

'Another *Cuba libre*? Stay where you are, I'll be right back.'

She smiled sleepily.

'Don't be long.'

As he was carefully and slowly preparing the drinks – waiting for the rich kids to confront him – he weighed up what there still remained for him to do. Very little in fact: get rid of them, agree on a date with Maruja for the following day, and say goodbye. He heard the young men approaching.

'Hello there,' said a nasal voice with a slight ironic quaver to it. 'Do you mind telling us who you are?'

The Interloper turned slowly to face them, a glass filled to the brim in each hand. He smiled broadly, casting in their faces like a challenge the blatant evidence of how calm he was. And as though more than willing to let an innocent joke bounce off him, a show of a camaraderie that deep down he would have liked to be real, he nodded in a friendly way and said:

'My name is Ricardo de Salvarrosa. How are things, lads?'

The youngest of the three, a white jersey tied round his neck, let out a giggle. The Interloper suddenly turned serious.

'You think there's something funny about my name, do you, kid?'

The Interloper shut his eyes with an unexpectedly pained expression. When he opened them again, he couldn't avoid looking down at the drinks in his hands, as if that was the only thing preventing him from throttling the person in front of him. Perhaps that was why, although they didn't really understand what he meant, none of them doubted his word when he added softly:

'You're in luck.'

'We don't want a scandal here, do we?' the youngster said.

'Who's saying we do?' he replied, his voice still neutral.

'All right, so who invited you to this party? Who did you come with?'

Abruptly, the migrant from the deep south assumed a dignified air, lifting his chin proudly. Over the shoulders of the three youngsters he had just spied a woman staring at him, standing, arms folded, with a chilly, solicitous look on her face that barely concealed her annoyance. She must be the lady of the house. Determined to get this over with, he pushed past the young trio. A dazzling smile lit up his face once more as he bowed lightly to her, and with a tranquil self-assurance that emphasised his youthful charm, he said:

'My compliments, *señora*. I'm Ricardo de Salvarrosa; you must know my parents.' Evidently despite herself, this gave the woman pause for thought, which allowed him to pile on his trademark gallantry. 'I'm so sorry not to have had the pleasure of being introduced to you . . .'

He went on to praise the party and how convenient it must be to have a garden large enough for this kind of event, expounding at length in pleasant, jocular terms on how everyone that night was one big family, despite the new faces; the quiet of a residential neighbourhood such as this; how wonderful it was to have a swimming pool in summer, how much better that was than the beach, and so on. The *señora* smiled sweetly and agreed that possibly the music was too loud, but apart from that rarely interrupted him. There was a veiled arrogance in the Murcian's voice that occasionally undermined his obvious attempt to sound respectful. His accent was another thing that clashed; at times it could sound South American, but when you listened closely it was nothing more than a simple distortion of Andalusian, combined with Catalan from the outskirts of Barcelona – the lilting vowel sounds, an abundance of 's' and a very special turn of phrase – together with a vocabulary sprinkled with fashionable frivolity and copious adverbs the Interloper was proud of, even if he was uncertain as to where exactly to place them, which he muddled up and used in an unexpected and fanciful manner, but always politely, with a real desire for dialogue, demonstrating that unshakeable, moving faith some illiterate people have in the redeeming virtues of culture.

LAST EVENINGS WITH TERESA

The woman's face remained a blank. She naturally forced herself to meet the gaze of the intruder – this impertinent upstart whose ridiculous speech immediately gave away his origins. She held his gaze with the intention of crushing him, but didn't take the precaution of gauging the rival forces in play, or the depth of their reciprocal mistrust. The result was a disaster for the good lady (the only satisfaction it brought – assuming she was able to appreciate it – was to sense a slight quiver she had not experienced in years in a part of her being she thought was long since dormant). She preferred, somewhat hastily, to direct her gaze towards one of the young men:

'What's going on, son?'

'Nothing, Mama. I'll see to it.'

The Interloper had an idea.

'Señora,' he said unctuously, 'since I am being insulted, and wishing to spare you such a disagreeable spectacle, I should like to speak to you in your office.'

This left the lady dumbfounded. She was about to tell him that naturally they had nothing to talk about in her office, and that besides she didn't have any such thing, but by then he was already launched on another tack.

'Very well,' he said gravely. 'For some reason I was asked to keep it a secret, but the moment has come to speak out.' He paused and added: 'I came with Teresa.'

What induced him to shield himself behind the name of Maruja's friend, that beautiful blonde girl? Not even he knew for certain; perhaps because he was hoping she had already left, which would prevent the truth from emerging, or at least postpone it until the next day. Also because he had just recalled what Maruja had said about her friend: 'Teresa always invites strangers.' Either way, there was no doubt that by mentioning Teresa's name he had hit the target; a total silence ensued. The woman smiled, sighed and rolled her eyes up to the heavens, as if calling on God as her witness. One of the young men began to laugh, which took the Interloper completely aback. What is it with these people, he wondered.

'Do you mean to say,' another of the rich kids asked, 'that Teresa invited you?'

'That's right.'

'I could have sworn it,' said the first youth, glancing round at his friends. 'Her latest political discovery.'

'Where's that silly girl got to?' asked the son of the family. 'Where's Teresa?'

'With Luis. They took Nené home. She won't be long.'

'Tere gets crazier by the day,' added the boy who had laughed at the Interloper. 'Completely crazy.'

'She's a baby, a spoiled brat.'

'Carlos . . .' his mother admonished him.

'She goes too far. She can invite whoever she likes, but she should tell us. I'll give her what for.'

'Well, children,' the lady of the house concluded, noting that the Murcian was still gazing at her devotedly, even though by now he hadn't the faintest idea what they were talking about.

Now that the matter had been resolved, for the moment at least (she knew how difficult and impetuous the Serrat family's daughter was), she said goodbye with a weary smile and turned back to the house. The party was almost over. As the three young men wandered slowly back to the dance floor, the hostess's son could be heard saying to his friends in a forlorn, reproachful tone:

'When that stupid girl arrives, tell me.'

Maruja had not budged from the spot. Standing there pensively, slightly disconcerted, she looked like one of those unfortunate creatures who at some point in their lives decided to be respectable only to discover that now, for reasons they don't fully comprehend, being respectable doesn't suit them at all. Her face and stubborn smile conveyed the touching but completely futile piety of those who advise the rich and poor to love one another. Throwing herself into the Murcian's arms, she exuded a kind of deep-seated moral weariness that now emboldened and betrayed her: all that was left of her former respectable front were her natural shyness and a sweet, helpless quality that the Interloper would not have been able to put his finger on, but which seemed very familiar and disturbing, as if he sensed in it a danger he knew only too well.

They danced and kissed in the darkest, dampest corner of the garden, startling the birds beneath a sky that seemed to glow red through the acacia branches. The young *xarnego* stopped pretending: all of a sudden words of love came pouring from his ardent lips, and he was overcome with a febrile sincerity. Even in situations where, thanks to his scheming, boastful temperament, he put himself at most risk, and however far his capacity for lies and cunning took him, deep down the Interloper retained a curious conception of himself, his own worth and spiritual standing – a view that obliged him to play by the rules. Almost despite himself, his mouth inevitably met the girl's with a real awareness of his role in an amorous ritual that required faith and a willingness to surrender oneself, a candour originating in heroic childhood dreams which now represented far more than a pastime and demanded greater dedication, more fantasy and courage, than any flaunted by the most conceited adolescents at this party.

The music had ended. He made a date to meet Maruja the following day at six in the evening in a bar on Calle Mandri. He politely offered to see her home, but she said she had to wait for her friend Teresa, who had promised to take her in her car. He didn't insist, preferring to leave things as they were.

There in the garden, under the acacias tinged with pink and with the early-morning breeze awakening new fragrances, the young migrant embraced and kissed the girl one last time. Despairingly, as though he were off to the wars.

'Until tomorrow, my love . . .'

'Until for ever, Ricardo . . .'

As he passed the lady of the house, Ricardo de Salvarrosa said farewell with a discreet and courteous nod of the head.

Monte Carmelo is a bare, arid hill to the north-west of Barcelona. Their invisible strings pulled by the expert hands of children, brightly coloured kites are often to be seen, buffeted by the wind as they rise above the hill like banners heralding a warlike dream. In the grey post-Civil War years, when empty stomachs and typhus created a constant yearning for a fantasy to make reality more palatable, Monte Carmelo was the favourite, mythical field of adventures for the ragged children of the Casa Baró, El Guinardó and La Salud neighbourhoods. They would climb to the windswept summit and launch crude kites they themselves had fashioned from reeds, rags, flour paste and sheets of newspaper: for a long while, high in the sky above the city swooped photographs and news articles about the German advance on European fronts, cities in ruins, and the black mushroom rising over Hiroshima. Death and destruction reigned, together with the Spanish people's weekly dose of rationing, poverty and hunger. Today, in the summer of 1956, the kites above El Carmelo no longer carry news or photos; they're no longer made from newspaper, but from thin, shop-bought sheets of tissue paper, and their colours are brash, strident. And yet although they look much better, many are still home-made; their frames are rough and ready, and they climb the sky only with difficulty. They continue to be the neighbourhood's warlike banner.

El Carmelo rises alongside Parque Güell, peering sceptically over its shoulder at the park's green leafiness and fairytale architectural fantasies, and forms a chain with Turó de la Rovira and its densely populated slopes, as well as the Montaña Pelada. Over fifty years have passed since it was an isolated island on the outskirts of the city. Before the war, this district and El Guinardó were filled with chalets and single-storey houses: back then, they were still the choice as weekend retreats for prominent businessmen from Barcelona's middle class, fake peacocks who have left traces here and there of their presence – an ancient house or abandoned garden. But these people are long since gone. Who knows if in the forties when they saw the tattered gypsies arriving, gasping for breath like shipwreck survivors, skins burnt not only by the merciless sun of defeat in war but from a whole lifetime of failures, these earlier inhabitants finally became aware that their nation was foundering, their island flooded for ever and Monte Carmelo, their former paradise, now lost. Very soon, the tide of the city also lapped at its southern flank, slowly flowed around its slopes, and swept on to the north and west, towards Valle de Hebrón and Los Penitentes. Stepped like an amphitheatre, the hillsides are covered in dark green grass, dotted here and there with cheerful splashes of yellow broom. An asphalted snake, pale in the harsh dawn light, black, hot and strongly smelling in the evening, skirts the side entrance to Parque Güell as it climbs from Plaza Sanllehy up the eastern slope, across a hollow full of time-worn carob trees and wretched allotments with wooden huts, until it reaches the first houses. At this point its exhausted flat head sighs and gives out; dirt roads branch off it: twisting, dusty streets, some of which point higher, while others descend, spread in every direction and rush down the northern slope to the plain leading to Horta and Montbau. Apart from the old chalets and an occasional more recent one built in the previous decade when land was cheap, the upper slopes are covered with low red-brick houses built by migrants, with flaking, rusty iron balconies and tiny interior verandas creating a make-believe floral atmosphere, where women water plants grown in wooden crates, and young girls peg out the washing with a song on their lips. At the foot of the steps up to the Carmelitas chapel, a public fountain stands in the middle of a big puddle where barefoot children splash about, purple iodine on skittish tanned shins, sullen knees, olive faces with snub noses, prominent cheekbones, and eyelids of Asian tenderness. Above them, dust, wind, dry slopes.

The people of the neighbourhood are easy-going, a spicy mix of many of Spain's regions, especially the south. Occasionally you might see an old man seated on the chapel steps or taking his rural nostalgia for a stroll across the waste ground. Hands behind his back, wearing a countryman's grey jacket, a striped shirt with the neckband buttoned under his Adam's apple and a wide-brimmed black hat. This man's life has two stages: one when before going out into the fields he needed to think, and the present one, when he goes out so as not to think. The same thoughts, the same frustration he once felt, now underlie the gestures and expressions of the young people on El Carmelo as they peer down at Barcelona from on high. They also share the same dreams, not born here but travelling with them, or in the hearts of their migrant parents. Impatience and dreams that at first light each morning flow once more down the hill, rolling over the roofs of a waking city, towards the buildings slowly emerging from the mists. Indolent, dark, undefeated eyes with suspicious, half-closed eyelids warily survey the vast blanket of blue-tinged mist and lights that, seen from above, promises a vaguely nuptial welcome, a physical sensation of being united with hope. On luminous summer mornings, when swarms of children roam the slopes, raising clouds of dust, Monte Carmelo is like a shimmering screen. But on Sundays it is barely touched by the atmosphere of universal reconciliation, of plenary indulgence, that permeates the city below like the fragrance of fading roses. This is not simply a question of altitude: it's as if up here they still worship the smile of Baal, that pagan god Jezebel worshipped, who was driven from the original mountain in Palestine. Baal's smile flexes itself like a muscle, a blend of lewd cunning and irony that defies the empty promise of the Lord's Day creeping up the hill to anoint the inhabitants with heaven knows what wretched acceptance of hopelessness and of Nature. It is not yet time for that: dogs and men have been seen crossing El Carmelo like shipwrecked sailors on an island, and sometimes the streets are shaken by an aimless, raging wind, its angry, indignant gusts carrying away the ignoble voices of radio presenters, tear-jerking songs, the crying of children, sheets of newspaper, the smells of burnt stubble, wet grass, cat excrement, cement, hay and resin. Persistent flies buzz around, while on the ground a cardboard box, with printed on its side in a language soon to become familiar, *Dry milk – Donated by the people of the United States of America*, is bowled over and over until it reaches the feet of a figure standing motionless: a young man with a dark-skinned face and hair the colour of a raven's wing who is gazing at the city from the roadside as if staring into a muddy pond.

It's the Interloper. He has sent a young boy to the Bar Delicias for a packet of Chesterfields. While he waits, he straightens his tie and shoots his white shirt cuffs. He's wearing the same suit as the night before and canvas shoes; his tie and handkerchief are a matching light blue. He hears muffled laughter behind his back; on the corner of Calle Pasteur a group of lads his age is staring at him, whispering and making jokes. When he turns to look at them, all their heads swivel away, as if blown by a gust of wind.

He has just left home, one of a cluster of low buildings built below the last bend on a spur overhanging the city. Approaching them from the main road, it's as if you are walking into a ravine, until you catch sight of the single-storey brick houses. Their tarred uralite roofs are dotted with stones. Painted in soft colours, each scarcely taller than a man's head, the houses are lined up in rows pointing seawards, forming narrow dirt streets, carefully swept and cleaned. Some have a small patio with a vine. Far below, Barcelona stretches to the vast azure Mediterranean, while out of the fogs and dull echoes of weary industry rise the grey bottle shapes of the Sagrada Familia, the blocks of the Hospital San Pablo, and further down, the black spires of the cathedral and the old quarter: a thicket of shadows. The port and the sea's horizon close this hazy panorama, together with the metal towers of the cable car and Montjuich's aggressive silhouette.

The Interloper's house is the second in the right-hand row at the edge of the hill's upper slopes. He lives with his elder brother, his sister-in-law and four impish young kids. The house once belonged to his brother's father-in-law, an elderly mechanic from the El Perchel district in Malaga, who arrived here in 1941 in one of the first waves of immigration, after losing his wife and managing to rescue his tools and some savings. He built the house with his own hands and bought a small shack at the top of the road, between a baker's and what is now the Bar Pibe, turning it into a bicycle repair shop. From the outside, it seems the business couldn't fare any worse. The old man died after marrying off his daughter, a plumpish Malaga woman with a warm, docile look, and after teaching his trade to his son-in-law, originally from Ronda, who had met the girl working on the bumper cars during the Fiesta Mayor in Gracia. The son-in-law inherited the modest business and together with it a big surprise: in reality, the takings didn't come from the workshop, but from a distinguished-looking individual who had the smooth talk of a priest and was known in the neighbourhood as the Cardinal. He was the purchaser of all the motorbikes that a taciturn, prematurely aged youngster from El Guinardó brought to the shop at night: motorbikes whose origin and subsequent destination, after being dismantled and handed over to the Cardinal, were revealed by the mechanic the day before he gave away his daughter to his son-in-law, with the embarrassed smile of a person offering a wedding present clearly beyond his means. With many ups and downs, including periods of inactivity that threatened the closure of the tiny workshop, as well as others of great euphoria (four of which led to the four children), the stolen motorbike business survived, despite never being successful enough to allow the mechanic and his family to change houses or neighbourhoods. Those were hard times. Other slender, delicate petty thieves (selected by the Cardinal) took over from the lad from El Guinardó after he emigrated to France. They were from distant neighbourhoods that were part of the city's sprawl: Verdum, La Trinidad, Torre Baró. The Cardinal only ever took on two boys at a time. In the autumn of 1952, when the Interloper unexpectedly turned up in Monte Carmelo demanding his brother's hospitality, the business suddenly took off, thanks to a purely personal form of seduction the Cardinal was especially susceptible to. None of this was to become clear until much later.

'Here you are, Manolo,' said a childish voice beside him.

Giving the kid a cigarette as a tip, the Interloper put the packet of Chesterfields in his pocket. As he made his way down the hill, he could hear rockets left over from the previous night's festivities whistling and exploding in the clear blue afternoon sky.

By six o'clock he was in the Bar Escocés on Calle Mandrí. Hardly anyone was there. He waited three hours for the girl, then, dejected and disappointed, returned home.

In mid-September that same year, he and an associate from El Carmelo went for a swim one Sunday with two girls to a beach near Blanes. They set off very early on motorbikes and with picnic baskets. For the first time in his life, the Interloper was allowing himself a fling with a girl from his own neighbourhood: something his friends saw as the start of his downfall.

They left the main highway four kilometres beyond Blanes and followed a track down to the beach through a private property. They were riding slowly, gliding along the dusty path. The Interloper ignored a sign that read: PRIVATE PROPERTY. NO ENTRY.

'Fuck their signs!' he shouted. 'How do they expect us to get to the beach? By helicopter?'

'You tell 'em!'

Following some way behind, his friend Bernardo Sans was laughing to himself. A short, thickset youth with small, lazy eyes set close to a bulbous nose, he had a prominent, slightly lopsided jaw that lent his face an amiable, slightly sad air. Sans looked up to his friend; he would have given his life for him. The seventh child of a Catalan gypsy, he had become very popular in Gracia thanks to his skill at grooming horses. The passenger on his pillion seat was Rosa, his girlfriend: chubby and short-legged, a moon face and voluminous breasts.

The track led them to the rear of an enormous, silent old Villa, where they had to turn left. Kicking down part of the fence around a pine wood, they chose a shady spot not far from the shore. At first they couldn't stop gazing at the big, ivy-covered red-brick Villa that rose majestically some two hundred metres away. Built in the early twentieth century, it had been partly renovated, but its two towers topped by slate turrets gave it the air of a medieval castle. A terrace added on one side led to rocks jutting out of the sea; steps had been hewn out of the cliff, leading to a jetty where a motorboat was moored.

They soon saw that they weren't the first to trespass on the property: the fence was flattened in other places, and in among the pines lay strewn the remains of food and grease-stained wrappers. But there was no one to be seen, and the excitement at finding themselves in the private domain of a fiefdom created a wave of nervous exhilaration that led them to push down several more metres of fence.

'*Collons*, Manolo, let's destroy the lot,' said Sans.

The Interloper didn't reply. The two girls, who had already stripped to their bathing gear, eventually managed to stop the destruction by laughing and jumping on the boys' backs, demanding attention. After breakfast, they all bathed in the sea, played football and ran along the deserted beach. Every so often the breeze wafted a distant music towards them, no doubt coming from the Villa. The Interloper quickly grew bored: he wandered along the shore or suddenly plunged into the wood without warning, not reappearing for a long while. His attitude was upsetting rather than surprising: for some time now he had been easily irritated, lost in his own thoughts. Every so often he would throw himself down on the sand away from the others, hands behind his head.

His partner Lola only succeeded in worsening his mood with her friendly questions and exaggerated wish to please and be useful, employing not her physique (which, according to the Interloper, was the only thing girls from El Carmelo could and should offer if they really wanted to help) but her limited intelligence. As if that wasn't enough, he had already guessed he wouldn't get anywhere with her. She was a friend of Bernardo Sans's girlfriend and also lived in El Carmelo, but he had hardly ever noticed her. He didn't even like her, and had only agreed to bring her at the insistence of Sans, who had said she was ripe for the picking. But when after lunch the two couples chose a quiet spot under the pines and he lay down next to her, his suspicions were confirmed that he was up against an ingrained, ancestral resistance, inherited convictions steeped in the bottomless abyss of insuperable mistrust, the obscure denial shown from time immemorial by most of the girls he knew: the fear of bodies.

Added to which, Lola never stopped talking.

'No, it's not that I don't want to,' she was saying in her squeaky voice as she lay beside him, keeping a watchful eye on his hands caressing her. 'It's not that, it's just the way I am. Don't think I don't like you, I always have done ... I would see you pass by the house every night, especially this last winter, when you were heading for the bar, and I always thought you were different from the others, not just handsomer ... I don't know, different, even if you also play cards with the old men in the Bar Delicias on Sundays rather than go dancing, and in spite of everything they say in the neighbourhood about you and your friends, Sans and others, that you sell stolen motorbikes and break into cars and that your brother helps you in the bike workshop. You'll see what happens to all of you one of these days, you'll see, they say, because where else do you get the money from? I don't care, but that's how it is, it's not easy to make money, and as far as I know you've never worked apart from a while after you arrived from your village, in your brother's workshop, and as I say, it's not as if I care ... No, please, not that, not there, it's not nice ... You have lots of money sometimes, you can't deny it, and nobody earns so much working honestly ...'

She fell silent for a while as he sighed with boredom and pulled up her swimsuit straps. He waited ten seconds, then tugged them down again, without any great hope. Lola was one of those girls with a soft, sad, hypochondriac body – one of those bodies that seem accustomed to being pawed over, even though in fact they never have been; their puffy, beatific faces looking disgusted not from making love too often, but precisely from never having done so. It is a look that combines distaste, sweetness and prudishness, as if their noses were constantly being assailed by a pestilential stench that at the same time somehow underlined their dignity, their convictions, or simply their delicate, soft skin – or whatever it may be that keeps them mired all their lives in this animal loneliness.

'It's not that I want to pry into your affairs, Manolo, seriously, I'm no gossip, you can ask anyone, but there's talk of you and that nasty girl Hortensia, the Cardinal's niece. You're always in her house – what is it they give you? Though I reckon it's not because of her but her uncle, and the business you're mixed up in, he's such a weird one as well. It's obvious something went on between him and Luis Polo, that kid from Galicia who was in your gang and who they say got nabbed by the police stealing from a foreigner's car while by some miracle you managed to escape. That's what they say in the neighbourhood. One Saturday I went to the pictures with Rosa, after she had quarrelled with Bernardo: all she could do was weep, and she told me everything . . . Ow! Don't be so rough, you're hurting me . . .!' She covered her breasts with her hands, saw his gleaming teeth but didn't pay any attention to his longing look or the gentle way he was stroking her hair, and so went on: 'See? You're all the same, and then what? You get tired of that as well . . . what are you doing? Please don't . . .' Her voice faltered and turned deliquescent: 'Not that, I knew this would happen . . . What will you think of a girl who lets herself be . . . But tell me, are these motorbikes stolen as well? Even though at least I never see you drunk and creating a ruckus in the neighbourhood, and that's a fact . . . Not that, I'm telling you. How could you think that I . . . what about my honour?'

Her body was so dead and fearful, her groin so frozen . . . Manolo angrily pulled away, rolled off her and lay on his back on the pine needles. Above his head a sparrow was singing on a branch. What a place to preserve your honour, he thought. The sun was shining directly on his face, and he half closed his eyes, determined to resist the blinding light until tears came. It's a dog's life, he reflected sourly. All money, money, and I've no more than ten miserable pesetas in my pocket, all that's left from the last transistor. The worst of it is Bernardo hasn't a clue, he's well and truly stuck this time. Rosa has got more balls than him, she's completely changed that kid. She gets him to tell her everything, then goes and blabs to this tart who keeps her legs crossed, so now the whole neighbourhood knows. Wait till I get hold of them – fuck the lot of them . . .!

He sat up and took an orange from one of the girls' baskets.

'Where are you going?' asked Lola, an apprehensive look in her eyes. 'What are you going to do? Are you mad at me . . .?'

Manolo walked away through the wood to where Sans and his girlfriend were lying. He heard them laughing. Sans was face down, and Rosa was tickling his back with a sprig of rosemary.

'Bernardo!' he shouted. Leaning against a tree trunk, he began to peel the orange. 'Come here, I need to talk to you.'

'Right now?'

'Yes, right now.'

Reluctantly, Sans half sat up. His girlfriend pouted irritatedly, but didn't dare look at the Interloper: an obscure fear, rather than shame at being seen naked, made her quickly cover herself. This wasn't the first time the Murcian had caught her out like this, and of course he wasn't exactly a stranger, but Bernardo's best friend, even if he sometimes looked at her as if he didn't know her. Although she couldn't see his eyes now (she didn't dare lift hers), she could tell he was studying her body – not admiringly, still less with desire, but more like disdain, a reproach at what this nakedness meant for Bernardo. Rosa had always disturbed him, above all because of something harsh about her mouth, a hint of rapaciousness; a sour, colourless mouth as sinewy as a muscle. She had veiled, smoky eyes; her shoulders were milky white and covered in freckles. Her body looked good in a swimsuit, with a surprisingly graceful waist, but it was too soft and pale, with the sticky whiteness of a peeled potato: it seemed to offer nothing more than a short-lived, fleeting attractiveness that was undermined by a more or less imminent collapse due to her growing fat, a sense of virtue, or the wretched way of life she was trapped in. She muttered a protest:

'You could at least warn us, couldn't you?'

But the Interloper carried on peeling the orange without a word. He had always known that those huge, round, blind breasts, with their two purple, almost metallic painted flowers staring at you like sunglasses, contained some terrible, secret, destructive power: a vague, deadly, annihilating threat that left you as defenceless as if you were in the sights of an infernal war machine sowing chaos and destruction as it advanced. By now Sans was sitting up, leaning on one elbow and looking at him, head twisted to one side and his lips painfully curled; it was as if he was already mortally wounded.

'What do you want now?' he said, a lopsided smile on his gaping monkey's mouth. 'Where's Lola – have you got what you were after yet?'

'Stop talking shit and come with me.'

Rosa muttered something unintelligible and rolled over on to Sans, squashing her left breast against his shoulder and laughing with a nervous clucking sound. Manolo had an intuition that one of these days the deadly machine would open fire, and leave him without a friend.

'Didn't you hear me, Bernardo?' he called out. 'Come on, wake up!'

Straightening up from the tree, he cast one final glance at

Rosa and walked off towards the beach. Sans had finally got to his feet and was grudgingly following him. Rosa collapsed on to her back: for the moment, her formidable armoury, her fatal attraction, was left wobbling like a pair of jellies on her chest.

As they were walking along the beach, the Murcian suddenly turned and hurled the orange peel in his friend's face.

'You're a piece of shit, Bernardo. One day I'm going to smash your face in. I warned you not to take that tart seriously, remember? She's made you spill the beans, and now the whole neighbourhood is talking about us.'

'What's that?' Sans didn't seem to comprehend. The sun was shining in his face, so he shielded his eyes with his hand, hopping up and down at the same time because the sand was burning the soles of his feet. 'Hang on a minute, what's got into you? There's always been talk in the neighbourhood, but it never bothered you before, nor me either. So why are you so upset now?'

'You'll end up sending us all inside. What exactly did you tell Rosa?'

'Me? Nothing . . . the thing is, you're scared.'

'Scared? Go fuck yourself. You didn't want to do the job last night, although the car was on its own and all I asked was for you to keep a lookout while I did everything, but you refused. The same last week, and the one before that. What's wrong with you? She's got you by the balls, hasn't she? Go on then, get married so you can rot in a stupid workshop like my brother – that's all you're fit for!'

'Don't be like that, Manolo.'

'And early this morning, after we snitched the bikes, instead of taking them to the workshop you came snivelling to me, begging for us to go to the beach with the girls, and how Rosa and you . . . and how great Lola is . . . It's so ridiculous. You've got to be joking, you hear me?'

The sun was blazing down. They stood without moving on the sand, sweat pearling on their foreheads. Sans looked at the ground.

'It's not that, Manolo. The thing is . . . I told you last night, she's different . . . I love her.'

'You love her. She jerks you off. And you love her.'

'Take care what you say. Besides, it's not that, it's just – look, the life we lead . . .'

'Better than a lot of others, asshole.'

'They could nab us any day, like they did Polo. The Cardinal is always up to something, you can't trust him . . .'

'You're an idiot.'

Sans bent down to pick up a handful of sand.

'Want to know something? Rosa thinks she's going to have a baby.'

The Interloper looked at him without a word. Rosa had fired the death ray.

'Bah, it's bound to be a lie,' he said after thinking it over. 'Don't trust her, Bernardo, don't even trust God . . . When did she tell you?'

'I have to marry her, don't I?'

'You're a sad case. I pity you. Come on, when did she tell you?'

'A few days ago. She burst into tears. But it's still not definite.'

'Okay, so you play dumb . . .'

'But she says . . .'

'It's a lie, a stinking great lie. You'll see what happens to you! You're all the same. The first slut who strokes your damn dick gets you in the bag. You'll never have a fucking cent, I'm telling you. It's not going to happen to me, I swear on my mother.'

'You'll be the same, you'll see,' said Sans, smiling slyly, trying to be conciliatory. 'What about the Syringe, that Hortensia, eh? So serious . . .'

'Shut it. What would an idiot like you know? It beats me how I could ever be your friend.'

The Murcian took a few steps round Sans, the peeled orange still in his hands. He looked down at it for a few moments, then split it and began silently to eat the segments. Sans peered at him: all of a sudden, with the sun beating down, there was something sad about his friend's rhythmical chewing, his crestfallen appearance, the bewildered eyelids, the long eyelashes blue-tinged in the sun.

'I know you're just talking for the sake of it, Manolo,' Sans said. 'You're a good guy. You're the best friend I've ever had.'

The Interloper turned his back on him.

'I swear on my father, Bernardo, that one day you won't see hide or hair of me again. I gave all of you in the gang the chance to earn good money.'

'That's finished, Manolo, but you refuse to see it. The Cardinal is done for. He's a drunkard and he's scared, he's an old man. Everyone is leaving him, and you ought to do the same.'

'That's not true. And shut your trap. Let's get out of here.'

He had begun to walk slowly towards the pines, wiping his sticky, juice-stained fingers on his front. 'Come on, you old man, let's get back to the girls,' he said. Sans was trotting along behind him like a prancing, high-stepping foal, head nodding and knees up to his chest as though treading on hot coals.

It must have been about five o'clock when they heard a car brake sharply and a woman's voice shouting insults. The girls barely had time to cover themselves. Manolo was the first to sit up. Next to the two motorbikes leaning against the broken fence, a woman of around forty stood cursing, arms akimbo. She had on a pair of spotless white slacks and a coffee-coloured blouse knotted at the waist. She was wearing sunglasses, her eyes fixed on the damaged fence. Manolo, bare-chested and bathed

33

in sweat, headed through the wood towards her, doing up his trousers as he went, Sans following a few paces behind. The girls stayed where they were, tugging their tops over their breasts. The woman was struggling as hard as she could to push the motorbikes over with her foot. The Interloper glanced at the car parked on the track to the Villa; at that moment a young dark-haired girl emerged from it, wearing a pleated blue skirt and a tight, long-sleeved purple blouse. She was carrying a missal and a mantilla. The older woman was furious:

'This is the limit! It's the same every Sunday! Didn't you see the fence? Get out of the wood this minute . . .! Pigs! Filthy swine!' she added when she saw the half-undressed girls. 'Or I'll call the Civil Guard!'

'Now listen here, *señora*,' said the Murcian slowly, confronting her as he finished doing up his jeans. He put all his body weight on one leg, assuming his favourite indolent posture. At last he had the chance to let off a bit of steam, get rid of all the bad feelings building up inside him for days. He shook his head, pushing his long, unkempt hair back off his forehead. 'What's wrong? The fence was broken when we got here, so don't screech so loud.'

'You're nothing but a bunch of louts! What about showing some respect? You break in wherever you want, eat like pigs, make everything filthy, tear down the fence, and to top it all behave like animals with these girls . . .! How dare you speak to me like that, you shameless creature!'

'Watch what you say, lady, or I'll smash your face.'

He took a step forward. Things had been going so badly for him lately he was desperate to take it out on someone. But suddenly, as if struck by lightning, he came to a halt. The colour drained from his face and he kept staring a few metres beyond the woman: the girl, who was standing motionless by the open door of the car, was looking straight at him.

Instantly, the Interloper's attitude underwent an astonishing change. Adopting his most dazzling smile, he bowed in front of the raging woman and spread his arms in a gesture of abject apology.

'Madam ... the fact is, you're quite right. As you know, we young ones like to have fun ... Actually, I can't find the words to express how sorry I am.' He turned to Sans, who was staring at him in frank amazement. 'Come on, don't stand there like a booby, apologise to the lady!'

Sans managed to stammer something. After a few moments, the woman went back on the attack, simply to set things straight.

'Look how you've left everything! I'm sick and tired of having to clean up all this paper and rubbish. This isn't a place for picnics, go somewhere else ...' Then, slightly confused by the unexpected turn the argument had taken and suspecting the two youths were making fun of her, she turned back to the car and got in.

'I hope you're gone within half an hour ... Come on, child, this is the last straw!' She switched on the ignition.

Manolo stepped closer to the car, desperate to make eye contact with the young girl again, but he didn't succeed: she seemed to have completely forgotten him. He saw her sitting next to what must be her mother, eyes on the floor, cheeks flushed, and he thought of how rude he had been. What a spectacle for a well-brought-up young woman. Doing up his flies and then threatening to punch her mother. I'm a swine, he thought, watching helplessly as the car moved off towards the Villa.

The rest of that evening, the Interloper wandered like a sick dog along the beach and in the pine wood near the house. There was nothing Lola could do to win him back. Her repeated pleas of a woman rejected but now submissive, as she begins to understand that the male sex is far more honest, dreamy and romantic than she has imagined, fell on deaf ears. When she saw the infinite sadness veiling her companion's eyes, she guessed at something dark and difficult, dimly aware of why love-making can occasionally be not simply the perverse, animal rubbing together of skin, but also a tortuous effort to give palpable form to certain dreams, to some of life's promises. By now, though, it was too late, and all she received in return was a distant look and careless, cold and distracted hands that explored her body for an instant and then fell still. The Interloper's thoughts and desires were roaming far from her.

For the rest of the evening, Manolo went on walking round the Villa, hoping to see the young girl again. Just once, and before he had time to react, he spotted her: a fleeting instant when she appeared at a ground-floor window on the ivy-covered back wall, and thrust out her arms to close the shutters so rapidly he couldn't fail to notice. This brief glimpse of her was enough to unleash the dazzling array of his fantasy, as yet again his imagination took over from reality. He pictured himself running to the window, which was open, allowing him to see the defenceless young girl struggling in the arms of a drunken, fair-haired upper-class man in a tuxedo ... But however long he stared at the window, he never saw it open again. Sans didn't know whether to wait for him or leave with the girls, because whenever he had pointed out how late it was growing, his friend told him to go fuck himself.

Finally, as night was drawing in, the Murcian caught sight of the girl as she was leaving the Villa, heading towards the jetty; she was walking quickly, and turned two or three times to glance back at the terrace. The Interloper nudged his friend, took him by the arm and led him a few steps off.

'Time for you to get the girls out of here ... '

'What? And what about you?'

'I'm staying.'

'What's wrong? You're crazy, it's almost dark ... And anyway, you're a real bastard – with the two girls on my bike I'll get a fine!'

'Then pay it,' said Manolo, tapping his friend's head in a friendly manner. 'Come on, you spend less than Tarzan does on neckties. Don't be a spoilsport, take them with you.'

Patting Sans on the back, he strode off along the beach, close to the pine trees. A breeze had arisen, and the pink moon was beginning to be reflected in the sea. He passed by some fifty metres from the Villa just as two windows were lit up, one after the other. Above the murmur of the waves he thought he could dimly hear violin music.

The girl was in the motorboat moored to the jetty. She was squatting down barefoot, a pair of flippers hanging over her shoulder, searching for something among a pile of bathing towels. She was wearing a skimpy yellow skirt and a T-shirt so tight it looked as if it was too small for her. The boat, its sides licked at by long, gentle waves, was rocking softly. Climbing across the rocks, the Interloper jumped down on to the jetty, and stood for a minute studying the girl, who was not yet aware of his presence. Bent over like that, head sunk on her chest and engaged in her task with the seriousness of a child absorbed in a private game, she looked defenceless and fragile alongside the sea's immensity – and another fantasy flitted through the Murcian's mind, a residue from his heroic childhood dreams. A dreadful typhoon was raging, the girl lay unconscious in the bottom of a canoe, exposed to the wild waves and the wind, while he was struggling, bare-chested. Now he held her in his arms, still semi-conscious, moaning, her soaked clothes in tatters (wake up, my love, wake up!) with blood on her sun-tanned thighs, and a puncture on one blond breast, a snake bite. Quick! He had to suck out the poison, treat the wound, light a fire and remove her wet clothes to prevent her from catching cold, the two of them wrapped in a blanket, or better still carry her up to the Villa. The fact that he had respected her nakedness promised a glittering welcome that would give him access to luminous regions from which he had until now been excluded ('*Papa, et present el meu Salvador . . .*' Papa, may I present to you my Saviour . . . '*Jove, no sé com agrair-li, segue, per favour, prengui una copeta . . .*' Young man, I don't know how to thank you. Go on, please have a drink . . .), while he, wounded in one leg as he climbed the rocks with the girl in his arms (or had he twisted his ankle playing tennis?) limped, elegantly and melancholically, as everyone looked on admiringly and expectantly towards the big, comfortable armchair on the terrace, towards a future of hard-won peace and dignity.

'*Xarnego, no fotis!*' the monotonous lapping of the waves against the sides of the motor launch seemed to be saying mockingly – *Xarnego*, don't shoot! – and of course there was no hope they would be whipped up to the heroic hurricane the occasion demanded. The Interloper cleared his throat, the mists in his mind now dispersed, and he strode to the end of the jetty.

'You ought to take the outboard motor as well, Maruja,' he said, smiling. 'There are suspicious people prowling around here.'

She raised her head calmly. A hint of surprise showed on her face, and then she returned his smile.

'Is that so?' she said, concentrating once more on her task.

'Small world, isn't it?' he said. 'I was wondering, as I was on my way to apologise for what happened earlier – a joke in poor taste, I admit, but a joke nonetheless – I was wondering if you would remember me.'

Maruja didn't reply, although she continued to smile and glanced at him out of the corner of her eye as she rummaged among the towels. It seemed to him she wasn't really doing anything, merely trying to play for time. As she bent over, her

T-shirt had ridden up, revealing a strip of very dark, firm flesh and prominent vertebrae.

'Well, practically speaking,' he added, 'those people with me weren't my friends. I met them by chance in Blanes . . . When you arrived with your mother, I was saying goodbye, practically speaking.'

Maruja said nothing. She straightened up and, with some towels under her arm and the pair of flippers over her shoulder, jumped from the launch to the jetty. As she did so, the flippers slid off. The Interloper quickly picked them up and replaced them on her shoulder, taking advantage of the situation to leave his hand there for a moment.

'Why didn't you come on our date?' he asked, his voice softening as he drew closer. 'Or don't you remember any more?'

'Yes, I do. I couldn't go.'

She pulled away from him and began to climb the first steps in the cliff, but with a couple of strides he was in front of her, blocking her way. He smiled.

'Wait, sweetheart. You don't think I'm going to let you get away like that now I've been lucky enough to find you, do you? I've spent months and months desperately looking for you. And I've been thinking of you day and night. Tell me, did you know that?'

'No.'

They were very close to each other. By accident, her knee brushed against his leg. At that moment, someone in the Villa switched on the terrace lights, and a luminous glow spread across the rocks above their heads. At the same time, the sound of muffled female laughter could be heard and the music suddenly became louder. To the Interloper at least – because for Maruja these unremarkable events must have lacked any symbolic value – this seemed like an agreed signal, linked to who knew what distant dream. Still leaning back casually against the rock, he stretched out his arm and pulled the girl towards him, just as the flippers were starting to slip off once more. Before his mouth had time to cross the small gap to hers, she pressed her own lips against his. As on the night of the party in the garden, he noticed she was embracing him with a strange intensity and determination. It wasn't exactly as if she were struggling against her own impulses, but rather as though she was obeying an obscure need for protection, only then relaxing and giving free rein to her desire, the imperceptible ebb and flow of her blood, movements of the female body that he recognised and was able to control at will. This was a language he understood more readily, and it calmed his anxiety.

Years later, he would recall the smell of pine resin, the murmur of the waves, the gentle lapping of water against the sides of the motorboat; he would forever remember the Villa's imposing turrets lit up against the starry sky, and how through the French windows came snatches of music, light and intimate conversation, fragrances of married life, the echo of footsteps and laughter, while on high shone the moon, as weightless and solemn as the host at Mass. Pouring out from his agile serpent's body, the heat and yearning for the absolute passed to the young girl's belly, which blossomed like a thirsty plant receiving rain, so forcefully and with such a daring thrust that for a moment he couldn't help doubting she was someone brought up believing in prudence and self-control. All of a sudden, she lowered the T-shirt over her chest and shifted back, dropping her head on to his chest.

'They're waiting for me for dinner,' she murmured. 'They're waiting for me . . .'

He didn't think twice.

'Maruja, tonight I'll come to see you,' he whispered in her ear. 'When everyone's asleep, I'll come in through your window . . .'

'Don't say that. You're crazy.'
'I swear I'll do it. Tell me which one it is.'
'Let me go, let me go . . .'
But the Interloper wouldn't release her.
'Not until you tell me which is your bedroom.'
'What do you mean? Who do you think I am . . .?' she protested, her voice unsteady.

He silenced her with another kiss, an extremely gentle one this time, a despairing, tender kiss, the kind intended to demonstrate a wish to atone for all one's sins apart from the one about to be committed. And yet he didn't have the slightest hope she would tell him which was her room.

'Is it the window I saw you at this afternoon?'

Maruja gave him a rapid, fearful look. She squeezed his arm and gazed at him, eyes moist. 'Please . . . I'll call out if you come, I swear I'll call out.' With that, she ran up the steps and disappeared at the top.

For the next four hours the window remained shut. A few metres higher up, the lights on the terrace continued to celebrate the night, while it seemed to the Interloper, sitting on the stump of a pine tree, chin in hands and eyes fixed on her window, that these were the most painful hours in his entire existence. His back was cold, and somewhere deep within him he felt once more the sadness that had run through his veins as a boy. She doesn't want to, he told himself. She doesn't want to. He heard music on a record player, youthful voices on the terrace, and saw a car arrive with a man in it – a distinguished-looking, grey-haired gentleman who was welcomed joyfully. Then the depressing silence of the dinner hour, followed by a farewell to some female friends, then again some discreet, pleasant conversation, and finally complete, definitive silence. He no longer even looked towards the window; his forehead lay sadly on his arm as the last lights in the Villa went out one by one. It was all over. She doesn't want to, dammit, she doesn't want to.

No one ever had such a hangdog look, such a forlorn expression, an instantaneous, animal awareness of the vastness of the night, the senseless vehemence of the waves. The sensation of being abandoned kept the Interloper there, robbed of all strength or desire, hunched on the tree stump, eyes open wide in the darkness, in the same foetal position he had adopted in his mother's womb. He sat there for hours, hugging his knees, the indifference of the firmament high above him acting like a drug: his face was so perfectly rigid, his mouth slightly open, his gaze so petrified it seemed to fuse with that same cosmic emptiness that is beyond all frustration. *Aaah!* came the sound of the top of a pine tree swaying in the breeze.

It took him some time to react. First there was a strip of light filtering through the shutters, which immediately went out; then the thud of wood against the wall. The Interloper was already on his feet, trembling, racing in his mind towards the Villa when in reality he was still rooted to the spot, quickly smoothing down his hair and checking the state of his clothes. As he drew closer to the ivy-covered wall, he could make out the open window and shadows inside that were denser than those of the night. He had to cross a flower bed against the wall. He came to a halt. The window was at shoulder height. He couldn't hear any sounds. Before hoisting himself up, he peered inside: nothing, apart from the white blotch of a sheet on the bunched-up silhouette of a body. He slipped in through the window without a sound, and went straight towards the bed.

Maruja appeared to be sleeping soundly, face down and with the sheet wrapped round her body, arms by her sides and the top half of her suntanned back left uncovered. Her head was outlined prettily and clearly on the pillow. He hesitated a few seconds at the foot of the bed, listening to his own heartbeats, then drew closer and bent over her. The warm smell of the bed and female skin, the perfume of her hair, enveloped him: his fear evaporated. He whispered her name several times, his lips against her ear, and gently took her by the shoulders, but immediately had to restrain her when she sat bolt upright, clutching the sheet to her chest.

'How dare you . . .! I told you I'd call out!'

'And I told you I'd come. We need to talk, Maruja. There's only one thing I want to tell you, and I won't leave here until I've done so . . .'

She leapt out of the far side of the bed, and stood there, wrapped in the sheet. He straightened up and walked towards her as she protested: 'My God, I can't believe it!' She was trapped behind the bedside table, her face and tanned shoulders merging with the shadows in the room.

'I'll shout if you don't leave at once,' she said, on the verge of tears. 'Do you hear me? I'll shout!'

The Murcian halted. He had noticed something that removed any doubt he still might have had about his chances of success. It wasn't the tone of her threats – a tone close to tears, it was true, but which had seemed half-hearted from the outset – but a gesture she made that he could clearly make out even in the darkness: she patted the nape of her neck to straighten her hair, tilting her head slightly to one side with that air of tranquil nonchalance that surfaces at even the most inopportune moments, the spontaneous reflex action of feminine wiles. And so, obeying the dictates sometimes imposed by his instinct, the Interloper advanced towards Maruja, hand outstretched, completely sure of himself.

'You can't fool me, sweetheart,' he said. 'Go on, shout!'

Maruja remained silent, and at that moment he knew she would be his. She began to whimper softly, and collapsed on to the bed, sitting with her head down. The young *xarnego* sat beside her and slipped his arm round her, gently kissing her eyelids with real emotion until he had dried her scalding tears. Finally yielding to his embrace, she lay back on the bed and pulled away the sheet.

Her tanned, trembling knees emerged in the gloom, covered in a thin coating of sweat and astonishment; she watched as his fine, rebellious head leaned urgently towards her, delving into the shadows, until his forehead was pressed against a skin burning not from the stupid sun of privileged beaches, but from desire. For him on the other hand, to slide his lips up and down her young, tanned body, memorising it with his eyes shut, meant also to have the taste of salt in his mouth, meant discovering the impenetrable secret of an unknown sun, a collection of dazzling, luminous images in the album of life.

And all the world's beaches, fancy girls' hats, gauzy fabrics in blue, green, red, rough sandals on tanned feet with painted toenails, multi-coloured parasols, breasts quivering beneath flimsy striped T-shirts and silk blouses, dazzling smiles, bare backs, golden, tranquil, wet and firm thighs, hands, the backs of heads, adorable waists, hips dripping money, all the marvellous beaches of the coast shimmering as they dozed in the sun, a gentle music – where is it coming from? Slender necks, clear, noble brows, blond hair and wonderfully harmonious gestures, painted mouths, ending in delicious clouds like strawberries, and tanned, long, slow and solemn thighs with sun-kissed glints like golden lizards – can you hear that music? Where is it coming from? See the canoes' silvery wake, the yacht's white sail, the mysterious sailing boat, the foaming waves, look at the wonderful breasts of the foreign girl, that song, that photo, the scent from the pines, the embraces, the leisurely kisses with the sweet taste of lipstick, sunset walks along the gravel in the park, velvet nights, dissolving in the sun . . .

On top of the girl, elbows firmly planted by her shoulders, he dictated the rhythm of their bodies; he could feel her small hands gliding over his back, moulding his thrusts, together with that other shapeless caress that was infinitely more tangible, far more present, the caress of the entire Villa that rose above their bodies, above the darkness and the ceiling itself; the whole weight of the other rooms, the noble, antique furniture, the carpeted staircases, the living rooms filled with shadows, the lamps, the voices. He entered her the way one enters society: enraptured, solemn, glittering and splendidly invested by a ceremonial fantasy, the lost marvel of his wretched adolescence.

He also realised something important in our latitudes: the girl wasn't inexperienced, and this produced a momentary confusion in his feverish, delirious mind. For one brief moment it was as if he was lost. It never amounted to a feeling, but was nothing more than a sensation, a sudden recoil of the blood, an emptiness in the mind; but that was all, and it quickly vanished.

It wasn't until the sky began to lighten in the window, until the grey pre-dawn clarity began to pick out the objects in the room, not until the skylark began to sing, that he realised his incredible, enormous blunder. It was only when, stretched out beside the sleeping girl, still daydreaming and with a vague happy smile playing on his lips, the first light of day slowly revealed in all their grotesque nakedness the black satin uniforms on the hangers, the white aprons and caps: it was only then he understood the reality and slowly accepted the disillusionment.

He was in a maid's room.

He was only dimly conscious of the long, fevered hours gathered within the bedroom's sad four walls, which once had nurtured a wild, desolate dream similar to his own. His first impulse was to slap her.

He sat up in a rush and stayed upright in the bed, bewildered, eyes wide open. Apart from the insulting, brutal meaning lent it by this early light, there was nothing special about the room: it was small and unappealing, with a very high ceiling, the only furniture a wardrobe with twin mirrors, a bedside table, two chairs and a clothes stand. On the bedside table was an alarm clock, a packet of Virginia cigarettes, a cheap romantic novel and a framed photograph in which Maruja was standing next to a Renault Floride parked outside the main entrance to the Villa in her black satin uniform and starched collar, alongside a young blonde woman, hand raised to protect her eyes from the sun: her face was in shadow and was hard to make out. Maruja's face by contrast was perfectly lit, but had been caught as she was turning back towards the car's open door, as if at the last moment she had thought the photograph would be better with it closed.

With a sweep of his hand, the Murcian dashed the photo to the floor. Just as people drowning are said to see fond images from the film of their lives flash in front of their eyes, as he flopped back on to the bed, and before his hand could instinctively slap the maid awake, the Interloper glimpsed perhaps the most deeply ingrained image from his childhood: gliding across time, under a twinkling starry sky, he was once again embracing a little girl clad in silk pyjamas.

Maruja remained curled up in bed, eyes tightly closed. She didn't moan once when he began to slap her: for a while she covered her face with her arms, but then desisted – motionless, submissive, ignoring the blows. Her muscles completely relaxed beneath her dark skin; it was as if she were about to respond with another shudder of pleasure that the Interloper had not anticipated. As a result, his shocked hand paused a few centimetres from her hot, naked body, which now turned towards him. It was as though being awakened by slaps was not in itself any surprise, as if she had long since become accustomed to the idea. The Interloper jumped out of bed and went over to the window. Leaning his elbows on the sill, he stood peering into the distance, beyond the shadows still floating in the pine wood. A vague, sad smile played on his lips.

'So she's a skivvy!' he muttered to himself. 'A miserable, fucking skivvy! What a joke!'

Maruja didn't dare move. Her cheeks and forearms were stinging. Huddled at one end of the bed, she slowly stretched out her hand to the floor to pick up the sheet and cover herself, but froze once more when she heard him exclaim: 'Shit! That's really funny!' Her hand flew back to its place over her heart, her knees drawn up in front of her. Her alarmed eyes followed every move the Interloper made.

'Who does this Villa belong to?' he asked, turning back to her. 'Didn't you hear me?'

Maruja said nothing. She was glancing stealthily and tearfully at him, sleepy glances full of a special understanding that implied something deep-seated and sordid, something he knew only too well and immediately recognised: the acceptance of poverty; that soft fraternal look pleading for unity in misfortune, for mutual consolation between people struggling with the same unhappiness, the same wretchedness, the same state of abandonment; that impulse of solidarity common to everyone united in misfortune by identical shared destinies (as in prison or a brothel), a feeling of renunciation and resignation that had terrified the Interloper from an early age, and which he had spent his whole life fighting.

'Answer me, you dormouse. Who owns the Villa?'

He was still leaning on the windowsill, looking over his shoulder at her. She could sense the power of his body: he was standing there relaxed, back slightly bent, and the pale early-morning light slid gently down from his shoulders, disappearing at his dark, narrow waist.

She lowered her eyes.

'Why do you want to know?'

'That's none of your damn business. Tell me, who lives here?'

'A family. The owners of the Villa.'

'Your employers?'

'Yes . . .'

'What's their name?'

'Serrat.'

The Interloper shook his head. The contempt on his face gave way to a scornful smile.

'What a wonderful job you have,' he said. 'And what do your employers do here, apart from going swimming and scratching their balls all day?'

'Nothing . . . they're on their summer holidays.'

'Are they very rich?'

'Yes . . . I think so.'

'"Yes, I think so!" You don't even know what world you're living in, you've become so dumb! Are there lots of them?'

'What's that?' Maruja was talking in a whisper. 'No. The head of the family only comes at weekends.'

'Well, there were lots of people here last night.'

'Friends of their daughter...'

'I can't hear you!'

'Friends of the daughter.'

Maruja closed her eyes again. He peered curiously at her for some time: the same strange mix of dreams that had brought him here now led him to consider the girl's situation with an irony shot through with pity. He came back over to the bed.

'You think you're very smart, don't you, doll?'

She shook her head almost imperceptibly, on the verge of tears again. She was biting her lower lip, and her eyes were gleaming in the semi-darkness like two glowing embers.

'Ricardo...' she whispered.

'My name isn't Ricardo! We're going to get a lot of things clear, starting with you!'

He kneeled on the bed. Maruja straightened up and sat on the far side, back turned towards him. She ran her fingers through her hair.

'I have to get dressed now,' she said faintly. 'I have to prepare breakfast.'

'Stay where you are. It's early.'

'She always gets up very early in the morning...'

'Don't turn your back on me when I'm talking to you!' he roared. He sensed the shiver that ran down her back and jolted her upright. Her hand still in her hair, she changed position and sat sideways on to him, her face in profile, eyes lowered.

'That's better. So she gets up early? And who is she?'

'Señorita Teresa.'

'Who?' He sat there pensively, and then remembered: 'That blonde girl at the party, the one you said was your friend?'

'Yes.'

The Interloper slowly lowered himself on to his back, amused. 'Teresa,' he muttered, his eyes fixed on the ceiling. From his expression it appeared he was convinced not of having got the wrong girl, but simply the wrong room.

When Maruja tried to stand up, he leaned across the bed and seized her by the arm, forcing her to stay seated.

'So now tell me, dormouse, spit it out. Why did you do this to me?'

'What have I done? I haven't done anything.'

'You know what I'm talking about. You lied to me like a slut.'

'That's not true. It was your fault – I told you not to come. I don't know what you imagine about me, but I never tried to deceive you. I thought that . . .'

'What?'

'I thought you liked me a little . . . that you loved me a little. On Saint John's Eve you told me all those pretty things, and tonight as well . . .'

'You're off your head! Do you think I'm an idiot? What on earth were you doing at that party?'

'Please, let go. You're hurting me.'

'What was a skivvy like you doing among all those posh people? Answer me!'

'I'm in too much of a hurry now,' she said, struggling to get up. 'Please!'

He forced her to turn towards him, and after struggling to open her arms wide, was about to slap her face with the back of his hand. But Maruja clung to him, weeping. The Interloper muttered an obscenity: suspecting he was the only imbecile in the room, he felt a strong urge to punch himself. There was a lengthy silence, interrupted only by Maruja's sobs, her face still buried in his chest. He wished he was a hundred kilometres away, but something prevented him from freeing himself. Then all of a sudden, wounding his eardrums with its furious metallic buzzing, the alarm clock on the bedside table went off. It seemed to him as though everything was starting to shake; it felt as if that damn creature was ringing inside his head.

'Just my cursed luck!'

'If you truly loved me, Ricardo . . .' she began, but he wrenched himself free and collapsed once more on to the bed.

'Go to hell, do you hear me? And my name isn't Ricardo, it's Manolo!'

The alarm clock was still ringing, dancing about on the bedside table like an insect in its death throes. Its sound gradually grew fainter and fainter. Recovering her composure, Maruja switched it off with one hand and then stood up, head bowed, using her forearm to dry the tears coursing down her cheeks.

'I have to get dressed. Tecla will be up by now . . .'

'Who on earth is Tecla? Another skivvy? What kind of name is that?'

'She's the cook.'

'Get out of here as quick as you can – I don't even want to see you.'

Naked, she stepped lightly and timidly to the window and half closed it. The Interloper couldn't help being impressed when he saw her body in motion: it had the calm softness of a married woman's, a pliant elasticity, the soft areas quivering slightly, detached from the aggressive forward thrust of the hips and the lazy but agile flexing of her knees. For a few seconds there was a delicate balance between the only slightly bent knee, the bowed shape of the advanced leg, and the trembling movement of the more sensitive parts of her body. The enchantment came from a certain restraint, an economy of gesture that no doubt had less to do with shyness or modesty than with the polite manners of the well-off and the healthy diet her employers enjoyed that occasionally, in some obscure way, impressionable maids manage to make their own. The vixen has a way about her, that's why she fooled me, the Interloper said to himself. The charm was completed by weak, slightly bony shoulders embellished by the full hips and breasts the size of lemons that pointed not forwards but out to the sides, swaying jelly-like now as they followed the graceful rhythm of her footsteps.

After half closing the window, Maruja picked up the framed photograph he had thrown on the floor and carefully wiped it with the palm of her hand.

'Is that photo yours?' he asked.

'Yes.'

'Why do you keep it? That's so stupid. Who is that with you?'

'The *señorita*. It was when they bought her the car . . . She gave me the photo.'

'Tremendous! You're a sentimental *bleda*, a sad case.'

When Maruja left the photo on the bedside table, he picked it up. 'Let's see . . .' he said, trying to sound casual. He wanted to compare the woman in it with the blonde girl at the party, but her face was completely in the shadow of the hand shielding it, so that all he could make out was the colour and shape of her loose, thick hair. Maruja went over to the wardrobe and began to get dressed.

'Manolo,' she said. 'Why do you always speak so roughly?'

'I speak the way I want to, get it?'

He left the photograph on the table and lay back on the crumpled sheets, gazing up at the ceiling. All at once he realised how good it was to be there . . .

'So you're still angry?' she murmured after a while, not looking at him. He didn't reply, so she turned and asked:

'What are you going to do? It's very late.'

'Why don't you shut your mouth, girl?'

Maruja smiled timidly at him. He closed his eyes, hands clasped behind his head. Shortly afterwards, he heard the patter of bare feet coming closer, then felt a soft, warm weight on his chest. The sweet fragrance from the girl's skin engulfed him. He heard her voice as if in a dream: 'Manolo, my love, you can't stay here...'

He opened his eyes and looked straight into hers, black and shining, smiling a few centimetres from his face. He could also see the slight red mark a blow of his had left on one of her cheekbones. You animal, he told himself. You absolute animal.

'Don't talk nonsense. But tell me, who was the first?'

'What's that?'

'Come on, don't be such a prude. Who was the first?'

Maruja buried her face in his neck.

'You promise not to laugh?' she asked. 'Promise me you won't laugh if I tell you. A boyfriend of mine... a lad from the Canary Islands doing his national service in Barcelona. I never saw him again.'

'Did you love him?'

'At first, yes.'

The Interloper burst out laughing.

'Of course, it had to be a conscript. You really are dumb, aren't you? Don't you know that all of them are bastards who only want to fuck with dummies like you?'

'Don't swear.'

'Where are you from?'

'Me? From Granada. But I've lived in Catalonia since I was a child.'

'What about your parents?'

'My father lives in Reus. He's the housekeeper on one of Señor Serrat's estates. That's where I was brought up, and where I met the *señorita*, because she used to come and spend summers there. They don't go to the farm in August any more, because they have more money ... My mother died when I was fifteen, and the *señora* brought me to Barcelona to help in the house.'

She also told him about her grandmother and a brother who had also just been called up, both of them in Reus. The Interloper was still caressing her, but just as he was about to roll on top of her again, she struggled free and leapt to her feet ...

'No, it's late ... You'd better go.'

'Of course I will. What else do you think I'll do? Get you out of my sight as quickly as possible, that's what.'

He jumped from the bed, threw on his clothes and went over to the window. When Maruja saw him straddling it, she ran to him.

'Wait! You're leaving just like that? When will I see you again?'

She was holding a small carved wooden casket in her right hand and had just put on a pair of earrings she must have wanted to surprise him with. But by then he had already jumped down from the window and was in the middle of the flower bed, looking towards the sea with a slightly anxious expression, tucking the tails of his shirt into his trousers. Still only half dressed, Maruja eyed him sadly. Behind him, a dense nocturnal silence still reigned in the pine wood, broken only by the murmur of waves on the beach. There was no breeze, and there was still no sign of sunrise. He pushed the hair back from his forehead. As he turned towards the maid, his face was tense, but he wasn't looking directly at her: his eyes seemed to be registering some deep earth tremor or long-lost distant voices that the waves brought back to him, hanging there, vibrating, in the cool early-morning air. All at once he fixed his eyes on Maruja, and a smile lit up his face.

'Is that jewellery? Where did you get them? Did your mistress give them to you ...?'

'These earrings? No. I bought them a week ago. Pretty, aren't they? Tell me, when will I see you?'

The Interloper couldn't take his eyes off the little box in her hand.

'Very soon. So long, dormouse,' he called out, turning and strolling off towards the pine wood.

The motorbike was where he had left it. He rode it out on to the main road and travelled at breakneck speed back to Barcelona. Throughout the journey a single thought obsessed him: over and again, he saw Maruja standing at the window, holding up the tiny casket where she kept her cheap jewels.

By the time he reached the city, the sun was already lending a rosy glow to the summit of El Carmelo. Just at that moment, in her house on Calle Mühlberg, Lola was getting out of bed to go to work, irritable and depressed, seriously annoyed with herself for the umpteenth time . . . She crossed paths with the Interloper on one of the bends on the main road as she was walking down to Plaza Sanllehy. He looked distant, lost in thought, his black hair rippling in the wind like the wings of some big, ill-omened bird. Streamlined by his self-absorption and the crazy speed he had been travelling at, the Murcian's profile stood out in the crisp early light like a ship's prow. All Lola could catch sight of as she was enveloped by the motorbike's deafening roar was the stark profile of a bird of prey soaring over the handlebars, fixed for a fleeting moment in the blink of her astounded eye.

For the first time as he was rushing towards the top of El Carmelo, the Interloper began to think of stealing the jewels from the seaside Villa. He didn't see Lola until he sped past her; his rear-view mirror caught a glimpse of her back for a moment, distorting it in its cold, concave universe, making it smaller and smaller until it shrank to nothing.

At dawn from the top of Monte Carmelo you can occasionally glimpse a distant, unknown city rise out of a mist: strips of fog and lingering nocturnal shadows still float above it like the ghostly sprinkling of dust that veils our eyes when we awaken from dreams. It is only a while later – as if a big, solemn curtain was being drawn back in the sky – that a harsh light begins to spread, bouncing off the surface of the Mediterranean and striking the hillside full on, crashing into window panes and the tin roofs of the shacks. The sea breeze cannot reach this far; it fades out long before, drowned and dissolved by the dirty smog rising above the jumble of buildings in the port and old city, amid the smoke from the factory chimneys, but if it could, if the distance were shorter – or so the Interloper thought wistfully, sitting on the grass in Parque Güell beside the motorbike he had just stolen – it would reach the highest flat roofs in La Salud, beyond the tennis courts and the Cottolengo del Padre Alegre, climb the main road to El Carmelo without following its snaking route (just as the local people do with their shortcuts), sweep across Parque Güell and carry on up Montaña Pelada until finally, after losing its salty tang and the force that must have arisen far out in the Mediterranean, a force that swept it for days and nights across the foaming waves, it ends up in the silence and senile, poverty-stricken docility of the Valle de Hebrón.

    The Murcian felt very lonely and very sad.

Sleep and tiredness were starting to overpower him; he had seen the light from the streetlamps on the eastern slope of El Carmelo gradually dim, folding in on itself as dawn approached. The damp from the grass that had clung overnight to his pink shirt and jeans had evaporated. He thought that in the end a day at the beach would be best: it's good down in those pine woods – maybe Lola isn't such a gossip as I imagine; my God, though, what a load of old women in this neighbourhood. She must still be asleep, she was probably happy last night cooking for me, I can see her counting the hours . . . But I bet she's a girl who only allows petting. He told himself that Bernardo, although he was already trapped, in that respect at least still wore the trousers: the lad had learned something from him as well as how to break into cars and steal motorbikes. Despite everything, he was a good kid, a true friend – his chimpanzee mate, ugly as sin. When it came down to it, it was best the Cardinal didn't want to do the deal right now, or even keep the bike at his place: Bernardo didn't deserve that job.

In his mind's eye, the Interloper could still see Bernardo the night before, sitting next to him on a bench on the Ramblas, clutching his knees, waiting for the signal that meant a command to steal. Was this the last job they would do together? When he didn't feel like working, Bernardo would say he was bored of robbing from cars and that, anyway, the Cardinal didn't pay like he used to, but the Murcian knew the real reason for his increasingly stubborn refusals was something else entirely: it was Rosa, that stupid affair with Rosa that Bernardo insisted on calling love but which he, with his own special way of categorising passion, refused to see it as. He sensed that Bernardo was one of those soft-hearted individuals that are irremediably predestined to experience only a spurious love with a spurious woman, and that even in an atmosphere of boisterous family joys, in the end they would be nothing more than a spurious family experiencing spurious joys. Recalling the previous evening's conversation, he tried to pinpoint the meagre hope beating timidly beneath Sans's refusal, that nauseating little shop assistant's nuptial dream, a dream gradually and insidiously robbing him of the only true friend he had left. It must have been past midnight, the two of them were opposite the Dancing Colón on the Ramblas, and the Murcian was impatiently observing the youngsters in a motley array of shiny leathers who were parking their motorbikes on the pavement or the central promenade on both sides of the bench where he and Bernardo were sitting. The monotonous succession of gleaming metalwork, the ridiculous equivalence these young men out on the town had established between their outfits and their speedy machines, was something that usually painted a look of infinite pity and scorn on the Interloper's lips, convinced as he was that he knew how pointless and ephemeral human passions are. Some of them were with their empty-headed girlfriends; when they got off their bikes and looked at one another, the couples rapidly shared a sense of smug self-satisfaction. Little by little, the line of motorbikes grew, in a spectacular display that must be a natural extension of the same vaguely erotic sensation that their brilliant dynamic shape gave their swaying riders.

'Look at those sad cases,' the Murcian had said. 'What do you reckon to that car we saw in Plaza del Pino?'

'No,' Bernardo answered hastily. 'I told you it's impossible. Besides, what have you brought to work with? We didn't bring a torch, a screwdriver or anything . . .'

'I've got my flick knife.'

'That's not the point. It's no. We agreed I'd only lend you a hand with the bikes, and on condition we took the girls to the beach tomorrow morning.'

'I don't need you for that, I can manage on my own.'

'But I want one as well, I need it.' He fell silent for a while, then added: 'Manolo, just think how good Lola is, and forget about that car.'

'You'll never have a cent,' the Interloper muttered.

From that moment on, the depression he was feeling only deepened. He wrung his hands; his eyes, so intensely black it was as if they had been dipped in ink, were fixed on two US marines dragging two girls from the Cosmos into the Colón. Soon though, he blinked drowsily, and buried his head in his chest, clicking his tongue: he was so sick and tired of the lack of ambition and desire he saw around him; the way everybody simply accepted their lot stifled him like a shroud. When Sans spoke again, it was almost plaintively.

'I'm not like you – I think of other things as well. I mean, I think about Rosa – in the past few days she's all I can think of.'

'You're an idiot. You think you're in love. Ha! Ha!'

'I have to change my way of life, I'm fed up with it.'

'You'll never amount to anything, kid.'

Later, the number of people on the Ramblas thinned out. Some came to a standstill in the middle of the promenade, wondering what to do next: they had lost the eagerness that had driven them from one place to another, compelled by God knows what need to congregate, their remaining strength spent arguing over taxis. The Murcian and Sans waited a while longer. They had been following closely – but without showing any special interest or urgency, as if their eyes were accidentally drawn in that direction while their minds were a blank, and they were simply sitting there – the rapid movements of a youngster who looked like a provincial in the city for a Saturday night spree, hesitating before clumsily parking his motorbike under a tree and then running towards a group of friends getting out of a taxi a little way beyond the Colón. His companions were all dressed to the nines, and slapped each other on the back before walking off towards the Cosmos. I bet, thought the Interloper, seeing them smoking cigars and displaying a certain digestive heaviness, they've been eating in a Barceloneta restaurant and are now here looking to pick up girls. Kiddo, that fuck is going to cost you dear, he said to himself as his eyes rested on the one who had just parked his motorbike.

The Interloper had a pair of black leather gloves in his belt, and now slowly put them on. 'Okay,' he said. 'You first.'

'I'll wait a while,' replied Sans.

'There's no point waiting, this is the moment.'

'Better safe than sorry,' Sans insisted, turning to look at him. 'If it wasn't for me, you'd have been nabbed I don't know how many times.'

'Shut it, Bernardo, you're getting on my nerves tonight.'

'All right . . .'

'Speak when I tell you to, and don't forget who's in charge here.'

'Fine, but don't say I didn't warn you.'

'Come on, what the devil are you waiting for?'

He almost had to push Sans. It's not that he's scared, the Interloper thought to himself as he saw Bernardo walk off. He's never been scared of anything. But how that slut has changed him! She's got him round her little finger!

He remained seated on the bench, but now his eyes had come to life and swivelled around to detect every movement around him. He saw Sans heading slowly towards the motorbike, hands in pockets and walking bowlegged like an amusing, harmless, lovable monkey. The Interloper felt a wave of tenderness towards him: he was momentarily distracted and let his guard down (something he was usually careful to avoid) in a way that could have cost them dear. By the time he recovered, Sans was astride the motorbike and was about to make a huge mistake. He looked completely calm, and didn't hear the Murcian's warning whistle, or see him spring up from the bench. Imbecile! What are you thinking? Another whistle, but it was too late: Bernardo had got the wrong machine – they were both Ossas, parked alongside each other, lovingly cared for, polished until they shone – and the owner, a scrawny, well-dressed youngster, had just left his bike, but at the last moment had turned his head to look back at it with the devoted, moist-eyed expression he must have had when saying goodbye to his girlfriend (and doubtless, given the times we live in, driven by obscure sexual urges that may possibly have found more satisfaction in the motorbike than in the girlfriend) at the precise instant when Bernardo, unaware of his error, was settling on the seat. A look of surprise on his face, the stranger shouted at Sans, who froze. From where he was, the Interloper couldn't hear what they were saying: Bernardo dismounted, spread his arms in an apologetic gesture, and began to laugh; he managed to convince the dolled-up reveller he had simply confused the bikes, before climbing on board the other one. The youngster walked off towards the Venezuela night club. Breathing a sigh of relief, Manolo sat back down on the bench.

But Sans, doubtless to satisfy his wounded professional pride, or simply because he had regained a taste for danger, got off the other bike as soon as the youngster vanished, clambered on to 'his' bike again, snapped the chain and kick-started it nonchalantly – even from a distance, the Murcian could make out his ape-like grin – before speeding off. Sans dropped down from the promenade into the gutter, feet brushing the ground, crouching like a cat as he steered the bike skilfully up the Ramblas, its engine clattering infernally, and disappeared up beyond Plaza del Teatro.

Alert as ever to omens and symbols, victim yet again of one

of those associations of ideas that are a curse for volatile minds like his, the Interloper interpreted Sans's spectacular escape as the swan song for a stage in his life that it would probably be best to declare over and done with. His frustrated encounter with that fabulous girl at the party already more than filled the world of his dreams; recalling it seemed to prevent any others from taking shape. He realised that, like all the rest of the gang, Bernardo too would soon abandon him. None of them lasted more than six months, and they didn't have much ambition; they lost heart, stupidly got their girlfriends pregnant, got married, looked for a job, preferring to rot in workshops or factories. Bernardo talked of getting used to it, but getting used to what? Working all hours like a peasant? Leading a slut dressed in white up the aisle? Allowing your blood to be sucked all your life? The Interloper didn't ask for much to begin with: give me a pair of blue eyes I can see myself reflected in and I'll conquer the world, he could have said, but then his spirits sank once more as he thought of the Mercedes in Plaza del Pino and all he had seen inside it, everything he had missed out on. And the idea of the next day wasn't exactly appealing: the beach, the boring beach and that heavenly Lola with her stupendous backside who according to Sans was ripe for the picking.

He looked up: four drunken Yanks were arguing with a skinny waif behind a row of parked cars outside the Sanlúcar. Just then (looking without seeing), he became aware of the suspicious immobility of the stranger who had come to a halt a couple of metres to his left and was also keeping an eye on the motor-bikes. He noted something instantly familiar about the gleam in his eye, like that of a dozing cat, and the slight slackening of the jaw that precedes imminent action. The Interloper stood up brusquely, looked the man in the eye as he walked past, and headed straight for the bike. He sat astride it, still staring at the stranger, unblocked the steering (employing a simple but effective technique that consisted in pulling the handlebar sharply to one side: there was a click and the lock snapped open cleanly), put his foot on the pedal and set off blithely, without thinking of anything but the other man, who simply watched him, a slight smile playing on his lips, judging his movements with an expert eye. It was not exactly the look of a rival who has seen himself beaten to the punch – competition was getting tough – but simply that of a colleague studying somebody else's work in a calm, amused and critical spirit. In fact, he went even further: for a moment his eyes darted from side to side to see what was going on around them as if he wanted to cover the Interloper's escape. Feeling especially low that night, the Murcian had a sudden desire to give him a hug. He wheeled the motorbike in a tight semicircle, his feet still dragging along the ground to get his balance, and it was only when he looked up that he caught the warning signal in the stranger's feline gaze as he blinked, turned on his heel and walked away. The old one-armed nightwatchman had seen them, and was coming up, in no great hurry but with an interrogatory expression on his face, a question on the tip of his tongue. Just as he thought he could hear him shouting, the Interloper got the message and sped off, leaving the old fellow standing there. A close shave, he thought to himself, deciding at the last moment to cross the central promenade and go down the opposite side past the second-hand bookstalls, so that instead of going up the Ramblas as Bernardo had done, he headed off at top speed towards Puerta de la Paz and then along Paseo de Colón towards the Ciudadela.

Despite his fears, he didn't hear any whistle, and no one pursued him. He rode up Paseo de San Juan, General Mola, General Sanjurjo, Calle Cerdeña, Plaza Sanllehy and the main road up to El Carmelo. At the Cottolengo turning he slowed down, then glided gently to the left off the main road before coming to a halt outside the side entrance to Parque Güell. He didn't dismount, but pointed the bike's headlight into the park. As the beam pierced the nocturnal shadows he could make out the trunks of pine tree, grass and, at the far end of the beam, a shiny black ball that bounced off into the darkness: a cat. No sign of Sans, although this was where they had agreed to meet. He must have gone for something to eat, thought Manolo. He sat there for some time, unsure what to do, then kick-started the bike again and set off up the hill at a steady speed. On the bends the headlight shone over the dark right-hand edge, where the city lights were visible in the distance; the Montjuich illuminations, which from up here in summer looked like an explosion of symmetrical flashes rending the night sky, were already turned off. To his left, grass and rocks, the lower slopes of Monte Carmelo. Reaching the summit, he accelerated at the final curve until he arrived at Calle Gran Vista, where he braked and dismounted. The shops and houses facing Parque Güell were closed, inhospitably blank in the coagulated light from the six streetlamps along the only row of house fronts: the areas of darkness lent the street a depth it did not really possess. Not a soul was to be seen, and the silence was absolute, and yet to the young *xarnego* the air was full of disturbing presences, a familiar human beat, deceptive hopes. At this time of night, Monte Carmelo is like a giant dormant septic boil, steeped in its own invisible, festering fluid, its daily stabbing pains, its diffuse sensual aura.

He went down the slope lined by small whitewashed houses seemingly perched in mid-air, this peculiar layout forced on them by the steep hill, giving rise to an intricate network of small side streets with flights of steps, hidden corners and low ramps. He bounced his way down, his route barely lit by dirty streetlights, turned right and left several times along streets that seemed almost toy-like, feeling the same sense of childish joy that had marked his first forays into the neighbourhood. Although it was no longer the sunlit labyrinth where once upon a time everything had seemed possible, it still bore traces of what he had brought years earlier from his home village in the south: a sense of self-reliance created by the precariousness of the surroundings, the same transient nature he had always noted about things here, the same air of poverty that enveloped them. Further down the hill he walked round the wall of a neglected garden and came to a halt outside a small wooden door that had once enchanted him. It stood out from the others due to its age and the intricate carved designs on it, all but washed away by the rain, but above all thanks to the improbable door knocker in the shape of a tiny, delicate, moulded hand – a woman's hand, he always thought – holding a ball. The only one like it in the entire neighbourhood, the door belonged to a dilapidated two-storey tower, facing waste ground reverberating with the chirping of crickets. The Interloper knocked three times, then stood back to see if the light on the upper floor came on. It was still pitch dark, and the stars seemed to be shining with greater intensity. He heard voices inside, and the sound of a piece of furniture being knocked against.

'Who is it?' asked a croaky voice.

'It's me, Cardinal, open up.'

After a while, the door edged open, and a head of completely white, tousled hair poked out. Despite being unkempt, the long, silky hair allowed a glimpse of the noble, sculpted shape of the man's skull, and his face, although puffy from sleep, had regular, soft and pleasant features, with a slightly beaky nose and blue-veined cleanly shaven cheeks. The tanned forehead contrasted agreeably with the white hair. Why is he called the Cardinal? the Interloper wondered yet again.

'What is it?' asked the man. 'What do you want at this time of night?'

'I don't have much time. I've got the bike, and can give it you right now. It's a brand-new Ossa. What do you say?'

Narrowing his eyes beneath long lashes, the Cardinal peered at him. A light was shining in the house behind his head, so that when he moved, his gleaming white hair looked as if it was crowned by a leaping flame.

'Come closer.'

The Interloper didn't move. He was still out of breath from his descent and remained a few steps away, swallowed by shadows. Manolo had a lot of respect for the Cardinal, whom he considered the most intelligent man in the neighbourhood, the only one who knew how to read other people.

'Didn't you hear me? Come closer.' Manolo obeyed, almost immediately recoiling from the smell of talcum powder and brandy.

'Where's Bernardo?'

'No idea...'

'Have you spoken to your brother?'

'The workshop's shut. I've just got here.'

'You know I don't want to deal with you two. I only do business with your brother. So be off to bed with you.'

He made to shut the door, but the Interloper put one hand on it, casually closing his fingers around the knocker.

'Wait, Cardinal. Everyone says you're someone we can trust. Why won't you help me?'

'What the devil has that got to do with it...?' A friendly smile suddenly lit up his pink, suspiciously youthful-looking face. 'You're very smart, kid, I always knew you'd go far. But you must listen to me.'

It wasn't entirely clear what the Cardinal meant: maybe there was a suggestion of ambivalent emotional impulses – something eagerly commented on in the lewdest manner by the neighbours – but to the Murcian, admiring as he did in the Cardinal precisely his superior sense of decency and discretion, this was nothing more than an additional layer of mystery and majesty to add to the many this lofty man already possessed.

'I always listen to you, Cardinal. What annoys me is having to deal with my brother. I can't take the bike home, there's nowhere to put it, and I'm broke. Please don't leave me in the lurch. Keep it and pay me whatever you think fit . . .'

'But what's preventing you from leaving it at your place?'

He stepped forward, and the Interloper could feel his alcoholic breath on his face. Why did they call him the Cardinal?

'My brother's stubborn as a mule,' muttered the youngster. 'He says he doesn't want any more bikes until further notice . . . Does that sound fair to you, Cardinal?'

'He's right. I advised him we should let a few days go by.' The Cardinal paused, looking the young man in the eye, then lowered his head and stepped back to close the door. 'Put it in the workshop and strip it.' His habitual cheery but distant expression was back. 'I'll see what I can do, but remember: if you want to do things on your own, learn to carry them through right to the end. I don't know what's wrong with you, but lately you're messing everything up.' The Interloper looked down at the ground. 'Be careful, Manolo, the motorbikes aren't there for going on outings with girls; the summer is a dangerous time.' He gave him an affectionate tap. 'Well, don't give up . . . Hortensia asks after you all the time. She's not well – won't you come and visit her? We can have a coffee and chat. But for now be off with you, there's a good lad . . .'

He closed the door very slowly.

'Good night,' murmured the Murcian.

Or rather, good morning: a milky whiteness was beginning to spread across the sky above El Carmelo. As he climbed back up to Calle Gran Vista, Manolo weighed up whether it would be better to go home or to wait for Sans at the agreed spot. Deciding on the latter, he climbed on the bike and rode off up the road, preoccupied by vague, disturbing feelings of remorse: the Cardinal had the strange knack of pricking his conscience. And the promise he had made to Sans to take the girls to the beach, the conviction he was getting caught in a trap, became increasingly acute as the new day dawned.

Not a single light now shone on the slopes of Monte Carmelo. A great guy, the Cardinal, thought the Interloper. He glanced at the bike lying on the grass next to him. Bernardo must have gone to fetch the girls. The rising sun struck motes of dust in the air among the park's vegetation; Sunday had finally arrived. He dozed off.

Sans came down the hill at breakneck speed on his Ossa, almost tipping over on the bends. As he entered the park he slowed down, left the engine ticking over and pushed his way along between the trees, a half-eaten apple in his mouth. He collapsed on the ground next to his friend.

'I was hungry,' he said. 'The girls will be here in a while. I gave them a fright!' He laughed, pointing to a stone. 'Look, I threw one as big as that at Rosa's window ... Have you been here all this time?'

'Are they bringing food?'

'Of course. They prepared it last night. Well, how did you get on?'

The Interloper said nothing. He was lying back on the grass, arms folded over his eyes. After a while he roared:

'Damn it all! But when we get back from the blasted beach, I'm going to lock the bikes in the workshop, and we won't take them out until they go straight to the Cardinal – got it?'

'Whatever you say. Don't worry, nothing will happen on a

trip to the beach . . .' He was silent for a while. 'Listen, are you falling asleep?'

The only sound in response was of birdsong. The Murcian turned from side to side as if in bed, breathing heavily, until finally settling on his back once more, arms folded over his face. Then, in a flat, drowsy voice he confessed to Sans that, in spite of the agreement they had, he had tried to get rid of the motorbike, but the Cardinal had failed him. He didn't explicitly apologise, limiting himself to telling Sans what had happened in an impersonal, weary tone of voice, as if talking in his sleep and through someone else's mouth about a matter he had absolutely no interest in. He said only a few words, but couldn't help the pauses being freighted with meaning: Sans could comprehend and be thankful for his friend's display of trust. He punched his shoulder affectionately. 'Bastard,' he said.

The Interloper made no reply. Before he fell asleep again, he could be heard saying in a strangely accented Catalan steeped in melancholy: '*Tots som uns fills de puta.*' We are all sons of bitches.

Unconsciously over the years the Interloper has made a kind of mechanical selection of memories, obeying the same obscure criterion as someone who each January makes a selection of the names of friends written in an old address book before copying them into a new one: he has kept only the most faithful, the best loved.

Manolo Reyes – since that is his real name – was the second son of a beautiful woman who for years scrubbed the floors of the Marquis of Salvatierra's palace in Ronda, and who conceived and gave birth to him when already a widow. Manolo's earliest childhood was spent between a shack in the Las Peñas district of Ronda and the luxurious rooms in the marquis's palace, where he stood for hours clinging to his mother's skirts without moving, his imagination wandering over the gleaming tiles she was scrubbing.

A strange story did the rounds, according to which, shortly after being widowed, his mother had relations with a young, melancholy Englishman who for several months was the marquis's guest. The boy was born on the date predicted by the wagging tongues. Manolo always challenged the supposed authenticity of this story, and made such great efforts to refute it that he even astonished his own mother: he fought savagely with his playmates when they laughed at him, calling him 'the English boy', and flung himself on adults and swore at them if they made any sly comment. Actually, this precocious anger came not so much from a wish to defend his mother's honour as from a strange, instinctive and deep-seated need to see justice done according to the dictates of his own view of himself. As a boy, he fought this idea because it threatened, or at least cast doubt on, the existence of yet another version that kindled his fantasy a lot more, and which meant for him the possibility of far nobler origins: that he was in fact the son of the Marquis of Salvatierra himself. And so as he grew up, all the facts relating to his birth – being the child of someone who could not reveal himself because of his social position in Ronda, having been conceived at a time when his mother was practically living in the marquis's palace and, most importantly of all for him, the coincidence that he was born in a bed in that same palace (which in fact was due to his premature birth, virtually on those very tiles the beautiful widow scrubbed, which meant she had to be attended to in the palace) – crystallised in his mind in such a way that from childhood on he created his own original notion of himself.

To some extent this was akin to one of those lies that, due to the confused moral nature of the world we live in, can pass perfectly for the truth when, thanks to the power of the imagination, they replace even greater lies. Manolo Reyes was either the marquis's son, or was, like God, his own son; but he couldn't be anything else, certainly not English.

When, in order to help his mother with a little cash, he became a luggage porter at the Ronda railway station and occasional tourist guide, taking great pains over his appearance and manners, his colleagues began to dub him 'the Marquis'. Questionable or otherwise, this nickname won general approval. Nobody was ever aware that he himself had created it, or of the clever manner in which he spread it. Manolo did not in any way consider this as his first professional achievement – since the nature of that profession was still unclear on the horizon of his dreams – but at least he could for the first time savour his power. However, it did not take him long to discover that all these timid beginnings brought no immediate benefit, and that he would have to wait.

These were in reality his only childhood playthings, ones never broken or cast aside. He grew up good-looking and spirited, with a rare disposition for both lies and tenderness. His mother forced him to go to night school, where he learned to read and write. He had an older half-brother who worked in the cotton fields and some years later migrated to Barcelona. Of his mother he remembered above all her damp hands. They were always wet, red and soft (for as long as he could recall, his idea of being a servant and being dependent was represented by this wrinkled, viscous pair of hands that dressed and undressed him: they were not exactly lifeless or uncaring, but nonetheless lacked warmth and joy). He loved his mother a great deal until she got together with a man, and suffered knowing that he was unable to save her from poverty. His daily battle with hunger left an animal glint in his eye, and a way of tilting his head that only fools thought signified submission. He soon discovered the most pressing and useful truth about poverty: that it's not possible to free yourself from it without risking your life. And so from early on, lies were as essential to him as food and the air he breathed. He had the ugly habit of spitting a lot; and yet, if you studied him closely, you could see in his way of doing so (his eyes suddenly fixed on some point on the horizon, combined with a complete lack of interest in the spittle and where it might land, an intimate, secret impatience in his expression) that firm, unalterable determination born of pent-up rage that often freezes the gestures of peasants on the brink of emigrating, or those of provincial youths who have already decided that someday they'll run away to the big city.

The day that, whistling and with his hands in his pockets, he approached the Moreau family's *roulotte* to offer his services as a guide and at the same time warn them that if they stayed on the outskirts of Ronda they should beware of tinkers and tramps, Manolo Reyes was still the Marquis of Salvatierra's son. A week later he no longer was that, or more precisely, he was no longer interested in being that; by then, however demeaning the change might seem compared to being a marquis, Manolo Reyes was in his mind a student in Paris, the guest and future son-in-law of the Moreaus. A *charmant petit andalou*, as *madame* would say. He was eleven at the time, his half-brother was about to be married in Barcelona; his mother had received a letter and a photograph of Monte Carmelo. Her elder son had triumphed. 'I'm getting married to a girl from Malaga who has a father with a bicycle business just where the cross is on the picture I'm sending you, Mother,' said the letter Manolo read out to her, without paying it much attention, because his mind was constantly on the French tourists who had arrived in their *roulotte*.

The Moreau family immediately came under the spell of Ronda and the boy. The River Tagus and Puente Nuevo bridge, Manolo's friendly attitude and black eyes, the bullring and its ecclesiastical atmosphere, and the Casa del Rey Moro, kept them in the town for a week. Manolo spent all day with them, accompanying the family everywhere and amusing them with tales of his mostly invented experiences as a guide. Every morning he went to meet them at the *roulotte*, posted their letters for them, bought food, took their clothes to the laundry, etcetera. One day when they invited him for lunch in the caravan he told them the story of his birth, taking great care to leave in emotive suspense the possibility of his true origin. It was then (he would remember it for ever: he was glancing at their daughter, sitting on the grass sunbathing, her dress pulled up to her knees, and it was an unsettled afternoon, windy, with strips of white cloud racing across the sky to hide behind the hills) that Madame Moreau offered him a cup of Nescafé and for the first time asked if he would like to go with them to Paris to study and make a life for himself. He looked down and made no reply. Another day, when she saw some ragged children playing in the street, Madame Moreau suddenly became sad and asked him the same question: a question that in reality was not posed in expectation of any answer (that didn't really interest her) but which in a confused, hard-to-pinpoint manner, expressed her own selfishness like a nervous reflex. But this time *le petit andalou* responded in a choked voice: 'I'll think about it.' Of course, *madame* didn't even hear him.

At night, unseen by them, he would spend long hours sitting on a rock some way from the *roulotte*, head in hands, staring at the light that sometimes shone in the caravan's tiny window. He was equally fascinated by their car: in the moonlight, the thick layer of dried mud covering its sides took on the wearily joyous aspect of venerable wrinkles or glorious scars, souvenirs of distant roads, unexplored highways, luminous beaches and vast cities, all the marvellous places Manolo had never been.

On the eve of the Moreaus' departure, a great deal of wine

was consumed, and *madame*, suddenly excited by who knows what vast array of emotional entanglements with life, began to embrace Manolo and smother him in kisses. In addition, she decided, with the agreement of her husband – who could hardly get his views heard (although hardly less than usual, as he was a tall, taciturn man of few words with a loud bass voice) – that she was going to take the boy to Paris. To the sound of laughter and much clinking of glasses, Madame Moreau made her daughter and the boy seal their eternal friendship with a kiss. A sense of fun hung in the air, one that was quite hazy and hard to define but doubtless typical of tourists saying goodbye as they are about to return home, those tiny orgasms of the heart that simply conceal a lack of seriousness and counterfeit affection, but against which the inexperienced young lad was as yet defenceless.

Manolo had learned in childhood a very simple but effective technique, usually born of winning reluctant permission from his mother for his first adventures out in the street, which consisted in quickly changing the topic of conversation once permission had been granted. That evening, choosing to leave suspended in the air (before the Moreaus could change their mind) the question of his trip to Paris, Manolo began to talk instead about his elder brother, who was married and lived in Barcelona and owned a prosperous business. Then all at once he stood up, thanked them, said goodbye until the next day, and left.

He had been sitting for half an hour on a rock behind some bushes when he saw the Moreaus' daughter come out of the *roulotte*. Her parents were asleep. The light from their little window had gone out some time ago, and silence reigned. The young French girl was wearing a pair of silk pyjamas that gave off silvery glints in the moonlight. There was a clearing in the wood in front of her, which she began slowly to cross, as if sleepwalking, heading straight for the bushes where Manolo was hiding. As he looked on, enchanted, the young girl advanced, enveloped in that astral glow where her outline was blurred due to the glimmers of light it created on the silk, her real image transformed into a pure chimera or evocation of herself; indifferent, weightless, utterly oblivious to the tender, despairing dream that, like a luminous coating of dust, her bare feet raised with each step. Manolo watched her approach as if she really was coming to meet him, searching for him without knowing it, writing his name in the dust. It was as though this encounter had been decided on since the dawn of time, as if the brightly lit clearing were nothing more than the final stage in a long journey that had always, unbeknown to her, been leading her here – lost to the world, her parents, her beautiful, prosperous country – and to her own destiny. She did not appear to know she was alone, or even that solitude could exist; in the boy's eyes she was full of life, the bringer of light. But suddenly, only a few metres from him, the girl unexpectedly veered off to the right and headed through the wood to a spot filled with thyme bushes (which the refined Madame Moreau, foreseeing the urgency of certain necessities, had chosen as the most appropriate). The boy finally understood.

He rose to his feet, disappointment etched on his face, but reacted rapidly before she could carry out what doubtless she had come out to do. He approached and politely wished her good evening; he told her he had returned to make sure everything was all right, and unexpectedly asked her (purely in order to provoke the reply he wanted to hear) why she had left the *roulotte* at such a dangerous time of night. Startled, but with a laugh, the girl replied that naturally it was to get some fresh air. Manolo offered to accompany her for a few minutes, then took her by the hand and strolled along with her. He tried to make her understand he had decided to go to Paris with them the next day, and asked what she thought of her parents' promise. Would they remember it in the morning, and take him with them? He talked at great length, then suddenly stopped, lost in thought, arms folded. She looked at him with amusement, trying to grasp what he was saying, nodding her head. Her face was one of the prettiest Manolo had ever seen: fair-skinned, warm, with clear blue eyes. He turned to her and took hold of both her hands. He pressed his forehead against hers; she lowered her eyes and blushed. So then, somewhat awkwardly, Manolo put his arms round her and kissed her on the cheek. Contact with the soft fabric of her pyjamas produced a strange sensation inside him, one of the most marvellous he had ever experienced, a sensation perfectly in keeping with the tenderness of the kiss, or possibly indeed establishing and fixing it, as though the emotion entered through his fingertips like an electric current transmitted by the silk. The girl stood still for a few moments, cheeks burning, head to one side and chest heaving, then broke free and ran back to the *roulotte*. Manolo remained standing there, arms dangling by his sides, still feeling the smoothness of the silk on his fingertips.

That night he couldn't sleep: he was planning the details of his departure from Ronda.

The next day when he arrived where the French family had been, there was no sign of the *roulotte*. He searched in vain for them all over Ronda. They left as they had come: the same confused restlessness, the same superficial impetuosity and narrow-minded enthusiasm that had brought them there had borne them away for ever. The Moreaus belonged to that class of tourists who use the dreams of locals as a bridge to attain a myth; a bridge they pull down behind them when they no longer need it.

At nightfall, completely exhausted, Manolo returned home and threw himself on his bed. The Moreaus were nothing more than phantoms, but that frustrated journey to a far-off country, that artificial moonlight gleaming on the girl's pyjamas, that illusory rendezvous with the future, the emotion, the crazy dream of migrating, the touch of the silk and the stabbing pain of disillusion remained with him – and now in Parque Güell, just as back then, he awoke from his deep sleep at the sound of familiar, friendly voices, ones striving as ever to convince him of the dangers of straying from the path they all took. This time, however, it wasn't the plaintive voice, the still-beautiful face of his mother leaning over him in a corner of the light coming in through the shack's window, as she said, 'Wake up, son. Look, here's your new father' (he barely had time to get a foreshortened view of the gypsy's neatly combed, brilliantined hair and haughty profile), because he was already planning to flee to Barcelona on a goods train and seek refuge in his brother's home. This time it was the face of a girl smiling as the sun began to beat down on Parque Güell, but which despite her smile already foretold the little it had to offer: a tedious Sunday petting session, if that. It was Lola, and behind her Rosa and Sans, weighed down with beach bags and food. Bernardo was brushing off the grass stuck to his trousers; the motorbikes were beside him.

'Hi there, lazybones,' said Lola, one hand in the neckline of her summer dress as she bent over him as if trying to drink his features. 'We're off to the beach. What are you doing sleeping . . .'

Perhaps because Manolo's eyes still reflected the cruel disappointment of the memories that had resurfaced, or perhaps because he was at an age when sleep, rather than sinking its claws into the face and ruining it, somehow renders it more beautiful, in the same way that a drinking spree can sweeten the features in youthful relaxation, Lola caught something in his gaze that must have frightened her and so when he asked her to help him up, she didn't hold out her hand. Too bad, he said to himself. Once he was on his feet, he shouted something in Catalan that none of the others could understand. He glanced sceptically at Lola's hips.

'Okay,' he muttered. 'For fuck's sake, let's get to the beach.'

They made love to the murmur of waves.

'It's almost daybreak, Manolo. You have to leave.'

'Not yet.'

'I'm scared,' she would insist each time. 'What we're doing is too risky, my love, it's crazy ... There are people in the house.'

'Listen, sweetheart,' he would answer cheerfully, pulling her towards him, his eyes fixed on the ceiling, or up beyond the ceiling. 'Here we all play the game, or we throw away the cards ...'

Like certain croupiers at gambling tables, the Interloper's fingers contained a secret nostalgia: nothing he touched belonged to him except, possibly, the girl. As the nights went by and he made love to her slowly, thoughtfully, with a knife grinder's skill and dedication, he learned to distinguish on her skin foreign grazes and marks of kindness, the tranquil fragrance of other rooms, other atmospheres, things that flourished beyond the four walls of a maid's room. Sometimes, especially if that night she had served dinner in the garden, she brought a eucalyptus flower or mint leaf in her mouth (a habit she had acquired in the country), and then her kisses had a sweet aroma that in some strange way led the Murcian to feel part of the daily round of leisure, bathing, reading and siestas that the exquisite shadow of someone, a woman, presided over benevolently high up in the Villa. He really came to believe that the only risk he was running was being found out by the owners of the house; for now, Maruja was happy to do whatever he asked, and didn't seem to want to demand anything in exchange, apart from some small, immediate emotional recompense apparently without any future consequence. The Interloper, though, sensed that one's strength is sapped by any emotional exchange, and that women are aware of this. He sensed that just as there are rules that still apply at the decorous Spanish gaming tables, so their strict moral equivalent always implies responsibilities and the payment of debts, and that it is best to keep this in mind. It often happens that skill in love-making, the simple expression of a rebellious nature, the furtive intimacy in a pair of sheets shared excessively with someone merely out of a sense of nostalgia, a flattering idea we have of ourselves, or an absence, have sooner or later to be paid for in self-esteem, solitude, or the loss of willpower as it gradually becomes diluted by a feeling of compassion and gratitude that the aura of a supposed manly prestige had previously prevented from surfacing:

'I love you, I love you, I need you . . .'

And so, as the night-time visits to the bed of the obliging little maid in that huge Villa by the sea multiplied, the young *xarnego* began despite himself to feel an irrepressible tenderness towards Maruja and her fragile happiness, as well as a dangerous tendency to respect her situation, or rather to feel sorry for it – dangerous because of everything about it that they shared, everything inherited from a specific destiny that was the very thing the Interloper absolutely refused to accept. It would perhaps be too much to say that he was falling in love: in those days he fell in love with symbols, not women. And yet it was no doubt something like it – a certain natural inclination to become part of a web of erotic and emotional reference points that his repressed outsider's good nature was drawn to, even if that inevitably meant abandoning nobler, more decisive spiritual endeavours. The animal solidarity in mutual misfortune and poverty exuded by her body, her despairing embraces, her kisses or simply her meek way of curling up beside him or being close to him, a solidarity Manolo had already noted uneasily on Saint John's Eve, the loneliness and sense of abandonment, that urgent plea for love that is asking for far more than love or pleasure, those eyes like a lost bird's staring at him from the hollow of her pillow, from a primeval world that knows only gratitude, a slavish dependency of the flesh, her meek eyes (her poor red-rimmed, sickly-looking eyes, almost without eyelashes – how had he not from the outset recognised her true nature in them? How had he not guessed they were the same feverish eyes spying on him from among the bushes on the night of the party?), immersed always in a curious mixture of submission and common sense, constantly inviting him, mute and loving, to renounce all ambition beyond being happy in the here and now. Eyes that occasionally succeeded in undermining his willpower not only during those wild summer nights but also those of the following winter, even though by then he had to some extent succeeded in wriggling free of her, increasingly conscious of the subtle shift taking place in their love-making, and had begun to let her see him less often, to disappear for weeks on end.

The powerful call of the species, the all-embracing buzz of common sense and sanity emitted by a woman reduced to silence, is somehow linked to the fundamental concern every female experiences regarding the future of her man. Against all expectation, this ancestral urge suddenly spoke with the voice of the maid and frightened the young delinquent: the brutal revelation of his misdemeanours, his motorbike thefts, not only failed to deal her a heavy blow, but in fact reaffirmed the redemptive power she had already begun to acquire in their love-making.

LAST EVENINGS WITH TERESA

So winter arrived, and back in the city and the monotonous daily routine in the Serrat family home, far from the Villa and its somnolent echoes, the fear of completely losing Manolo drove Maruja to repeatedly go in search of him in his neighbourhood. He never wanted to say where he lived, but she soon learned where to find him: in the Bar Delicias, close to the stove, playing cards with three old-age pensioners – with whom his youthful aspect fitted in shockingly well – completely absorbed, forgetting or disdaining who knows what other pleasures for the wisdom of cards and old men, offering with them the solemn worship of silence and the studied calm of gestures and looks, a rite for which the young man from the south of Spain was particularly suited, especially in the winter months. The reasons for this were to be found not only in his daily confrontation with the cold, the lack of work, and wretchedness that abounded in the city's poorer districts, but also because his rare taste for adventure, partly frustrated by the winter, could be mitigated by hieratic forms of expression. With playing cards in his hands, or in a seat in the stalls of a cold local cinema, hibernating like a transplanted flower, he was able to conjure up events from sunnier, more auspicious days; holding the cards as he considered what to play, he could imagine he was seeing the uniforms, the aprons and caps hanging on the clothes hanger in the pink glow of dawn at the Villa on the coast.

On her free afternoons on Thursdays and Sundays, Maruja would take a bus that dropped her in Plaza Sanllehy, then walk up the main road to El Carmelo, passing Parque Güell on the way. Before the last bend she would take a shortcut through fields of burnt stubble and up a rubbish-filled embankment that children slid down as if on a sledge, reaching the top out of breath, cheeks burning and tears in her eyes from the wind. The people in El Carmelo grew accustomed to seeing this timid figure beneath a blue umbrella, wrapped in an unfashionable short checked coat and sporting a maroon hairband. Her aimless strolling, her patient walking up and down whenever she couldn't find Manolo, soon became familiar to them. Before entering the Bar Delicias, she would tidy her hair and straighten a skirt that was too short for her and, once inside, would stand quietly by the door, at a safe distance from the card table, motionless, embarrassed, desperately pressing her knees together, deliciously obscene and enchantingly vulgar in her loitering – so obviously wanting to belong to someone, standing there just as she had on the night of the party, waiting for him at the bottom of the garden while he dealt with the posh *señoritos* – until Manolo became aware of her presence. Sometimes it would be raining outside, and through the steamed-up windows of the bar blurry, hunched figures could be seen struggling against the wind. Inside, the Interloper was seeking refuge: silent, taciturn, dishevelled, withdrawn and defeated by the winter like a snake hidden in the undergrowth waiting for bright sunny days, although still with a golden sheen on its skin and, like the rusty shells of ruined cars that had once been shiny, magnificent machines, enveloped in the halo of past splendour and the thousand phantoms of bygone adventures. He always played one final hand, if only to make Maruja wait long enough for him to win respect from the old men, whose sly chortles he pretended not to notice; and yet he never received her coldly or made her stand there for long. On the other hand, he never showed a great deal of enthusiasm; he simply acknowledged she was there, got up, took her hand and led her out. He accepted these meetings with a curiously resigned deference, similar to those people who, rightly or wrongly, believe at all times they are the creators of their own destiny and are therefore willing to accept some awkward consequences with a heightened sense of responsibility, as if such encounters were the proof of their mysterious pact with the hidden laws of life.

Because, in addition, by now he was on his own: Bernardo Sans had married Rosa earlier that winter, and was about to have a child (the final, lethal death ray) and the Murcian's scattered band of thieves had finally fallen apart completely. Maruja only knew what little he told her about his relationship with the Cardinal and with his family. Of his home, Manolo once told her, 'When it rains the electricity goes off,' and that was all. Her questions on this score enraged him, and he more than once threatened to leave her if she insisted. He seemed determined to make out he was an orphan.

'Manolo, have you never thought about . . .?' she would begin to say.

'No, I'm not thinking of changing my life! Come on, let's go for a walk.'

Discovering El Carmelo was for Maruja a hopeful confirmation of principles: the same impoverished, resigned fabric her love was made of seemed to have been used to create this neglected neighbourhood, isolating it and confining it to the outskirts of the city, reducing all its dreams to a single one: that of surviving. They walked along the paths on the west side, through the pines and fir trees of El Guinardó park. They climbed the hill and from the summit stopped to watch the children flying their kites, or looked down on Valle de Hebrón, Horta, the Tididabo, Turó de la Peira and Torre Baró, grey in the distance and with the winter mists. They walked in silence or chatting (it was here she first mentioned getting married) and almost always ended up entwined behind some bushes. Occasionally the cold or rain forced them into a small, densely packed local cinema or a crowded Sunday dance as odorous and stifling as being shut in a wardrobe. Throughout that winter, Maruja struggled to neutralise and swaddle with her own body the golden flow of incurable nostalgia, that purring of a jealous cat on the prowl that emanated from deep within Manolo.

Nothing of note happened that winter, apart from what for the young Interloper was a serious professional setback (losing Bernardo Sans, his last ally) and a few fleeting glimpses of Teresa Serrat in the city.

'Look, the *señorita*,' Maruja would say, pointing at her: a rapid sighting from the tram (she was at the university entrance in a duffle coat and tartan scarf with books under her arm, smoking and talking with a group of students), or one day from the pavement on Vía Augusta when he accompanied the maid back to her house (Teresa and her car gliding slowly close to the gutter outside a bar, hooting to attract someone's attention), or from the balcony in a city-centre cinema (accompanied by a young, athletic-looking black man as she walked down the carpeted slope of the stalls). On another occasion, Maruja showed him a photo of her in the magazine *¡Hola!*, seated in the midst of a handful of young men in tuxedos and young women dressed in white; the coming-out party of one of her friends, the maid told him, adding something the Murcian couldn't comprehend: Teresa was furious at having appeared in the photograph, and didn't want anyone to see it or to mention the party. She was so angry she had torn up the magazine. 'But I bought another copy,' said Maruja.

The first actual meeting with Teresa Serrat took place at the garden gate of her home in San Gervasio. It happened about ten o'clock one Thursday night, and her odd behaviour disturbed the *xarnego* to such an extent he was tormented yet again by his inability to understand, the mental confusion he often felt when he heard rich people express themselves. For the first few minutes Teresa Serrat remained at some distance from them, enveloped in the garden's long shadows, apparently sheltering from any admiring gaze that her alluring figure might attract. She stood there, body tilted slightly backwards, as though determined not to expose her face to any light she might imagine, which meant the Interloper could make out almost nothing of her beautiful eyes. Possibly it was this rather than the blatant rich girl's tone of voice she adopted to call the maid that made Manolo particularly rude to her. He had also just spent a stormy evening with Maruja: he had once again refused to make their relationship official, and she had burst into tears. Whenever that happened, his uneasy conscience obliged him to see her home. He had already said goodbye and was walking away – Maruja still staring after him, tears in her eyes, hand on the gate, unsure whether to go in – when he heard Teresa's voice calling to her.

'Maruja! Maruja! What are you doing there? It's very late! Mama will be ... furious.'

They heard her rapid footsteps on the gravel, and then saw her running towards them. She came to a sudden halt under a tree a few metres from the gate, arms folded across her chest. A dazzlingly white raincoat was thrown carelessly around her shoulders, over a dress with a flared skirt that gave off coppery glints. When she stopped, her slender agitated figure, shivering daintily in the cold, was silhouetted against the light from the porch lamp behind her and the lit-up ground-floor windows. Her whole person gave off a feeling of warmth, no doubt acquired in some elegant, crowded drawing room. Her legs had something tremulously musical about them, their youthful excitement hinting at a party or a pleasant surprise, which made him think of those wild young women he occasionally saw in Hollywood movies, emerging hot and breathless from a family gathering to get some fresh night air in the garden, and to tell their fathers in an emotional scene how happy they were, how wonderful life was. Teresa looked slightly unkempt, in a way that demonstrated her solid, comfortable existence – the raincoat belt about to slip out, its buckle brushing the ground, a red silk scarf dangling from one pocket, her blond hair falling over her face as she pushed her foot nervously back into a shoe that had come off as she ran – the charming inattention to detail that in beings pampered by nature and good fortune is a sure sign of not having to worry about money, of confidence in one's own beauty, and of an intense, passionate and promising inner life, yet another of her charms.

But what made her come to a halt so abruptly and above all softened the sharp tone of her voice was not just that one of her shoes had come off, but because she had discovered the unexpected presence of Maruja's boyfriend. Teresa lowered her voice to call Maruja's attention to how late it was and, in a gentle reproach, remind her they had dinner guests and that her mama was concerned. Mumbling an apology, Maruja was about to enter the garden when the Interloper, hands in pockets, tough-looking and a proud smirk on his face, turned towards the two women and told her to wait. After coming slowly back to the gate, he stopped and with a bizarre sweep of the hand wrapped his scarf more tightly around his neck before looking up at Teresa. He asked what was going on, why she was in such a devil of a hurry – was the house on fire? And then made his first blunder: he said that if they were so concerned they should get the cook to serve dinner. His conviction that he was being slighted, tinged with a manly pride that made this sound even more ridiculous, and the seriousness with which he said it, made Teresa laugh: a clear, affectionate, spontaneous laugh in no way intended to make fun of him. It was more an expression of solidarity, and even he could see that she was right.

Confused, the Interloper averted his eyes from Teresa and muttered to Maruja:

'I'd like to know what that idiot is laughing about.'

The astonishing thing was that the blonde girl not only did not reply in the haughty, offended manner he was expecting – and hoping for – but that, even as she murmured an almost inaudible apology, she bowed her head (her hair, as silky as honey, parted in two at the nape of her neck) and stared down at the tips of her shoes like a schoolgirl caught out in some prank. This amused Manolo, but only partially: he wasn't stupid enough to believe he had managed to impress this *señorita* just because he had been tough with her; he glanced inquisitively at Maruja. As a result, he didn't notice an imperceptible smile appear at the corners of Teresa Serrat's mouth: little more than a twitch, a hint of enjoyment that was hard to explain.

Fixing her poor, sick, red-rimmed eyes reproachfully on him, Maruja said:

'I'm coming right away, *señorita*.'

'Just a moment,' he protested, taking her by the arm. 'This is your day off, isn't it?'

'Come on, I'm dying of cold,' Teresa began in a changed voice, one that sounded suddenly vulnerable, as if she needed something from them. She continued standing there, her slightly trembling legs pressed together, fists clenched. Manolo took advantage to sneak a few looks in her direction, staring first at the ground as though he wasn't interested in the slightest. He discovered she still had that deliciously tobacco-coloured skin and those wonderful blue eyes that had once delivered such a blow to his heart. Despite the darkness, he could also make out the shape of her mouth, a nebulous pink, the slight swelling of her top lip – the Cupid's bow deliciously raised, as if the proud snub nose were pulling it upwards – that gave her whole face a pampered air, a bored innocence, a mixture of aristocratic ill-humour and childish stubbornness.

With a smile, Teresa concluded:

'We've got some really tiresome guests, and Mama is a little indisposed. A bore. We have to go to the chemist, Maruja . . .'

Just as in her blue gaze, given a drowsy look by a particular languor about the movement of her smooth, pure eyelids, endowing her with a strangely statuesque quality (as she spoke, her eyes were fixed on the woollen scarf Manolo had wound untidily round his neck), so too in her words, as she almost jokily excused herself for having to take Maruja away, there was what appeared to be an attempt to convey something more, to establish complicity with him, a kind of connection with a hidden power that could condemn her, and which she was sure the Murcian was also aware of, a link whose secret was known only to the two of them, and which excluded poor Maruja – or rather, went mercifully over her head. It was something that would take him some time to comprehend, and which for the moment, thanks to one of those quirks of the female character, was concentrated on his woollen scarf (a scarf which, contrary to this rich young university student's assumption, had not been lovingly knitted by his mother's humble, hard-working hands, but by chance was a thoughtful, sly gift from the Cardinal).

This encounter would of itself have been unimportant, were it not that it contained the seed of what would happen months later. The Interloper's mind was elsewhere; as he listened to that soft drawling voice with its slightly nasal twang, in which the pronounced Catalan accent showed itself not as an inability to pronounce words more carefully, but more as a clear assertion of character, Manolo, completely oblivious to those hidden realities, only grasped that knowing how to lose one's temper with the servants is truly a difficult, important skill. It also seemed to him that this beautiful blonde was curiously self-deprecating in the necessary exercise of her position as Maruja's mistress.

'... in short, the dinner party is a nuisance, but what can you do?' said Teresa, her eyes still fixed on Manolo's scarf.

'I see,' he said drily, in a tone that his instinct, somewhat perplexed but still sharp, told him was the most appropriate. 'I won't be a minute. I just have to tell her something important. Something personal.'

Of course he had nothing personal to say to Maruja; nothing of any sort in fact. He simply slipped his arm around her shoulder and led her to one side, still watching Teresa out of the corner of his eye. Her head bowed, Teresa was shifting on her heels and seemed ready to leave. He was struck once more by her submissive attitude, but even though a few seconds later she was to say something even more bizarre, he thought that in the end, damn it, maybe he really had made an impression on her.

But Teresa Serrat had turned and, looking him in the eye, pronounced the enigmatic words that would rob the Murcian of sleep for days afterwards:

'Don't take me for a stuck-up and spoiled brat,' she began, before adding in an oddly strangled tone: 'We're all on your side.'

With that, she turned on her heel and ran back up the garden, the red silk scarf floating in the air and the buckle of her coat belt clinking on the gravel path. The sound of her footsteps had already faded, but the Interloper was still transfixed by a confusion that, in spite of everything, seemed to him to be full of good omens. He wanted to give Maruja an enquiring look, but she had already broken free and, standing on tiptoe, gave him a quick kiss on the cheek and hastened inside the gate.

In the days following this encounter, Manolo asked Maruja several times what her mistress's words could mean, but got no clear answer.

'I don't know. The *señorita* is very odd . . .' she told him one evening as they were coming out of the Roxy cinema. She said this off-handedly, her attention focused on the traffic in Plaza Lesseps. 'She's become strange – she wasn't like this before.'

'What have you told her about us?'

'Me? Nothing.'

'You must have told her something, and she grew curious.'

'Not a thing. That we're going out together. And as she's such a good person, perhaps she meant that . . . well, that she's happy for us.'

'Don't talk rubbish! You're such a booby, you'll always be taken in . . . What I want is to be respected. Don't you know that these stuck-up girls don't even have any respect for God?'

'Teresa is very good to me.'

Manolo looked pityingly at his companion and pulled her to him. As usual, her words had an alarming undertone, a tenderness that appeared wounded or threatened by loneliness, the consequence of that combination of frustrated youth and a faded quality that occasionally appeared in her eyes, her smile, her voice. It was the constant fear that the only qualities she possessed would not prevail or be taken seriously: her gratitude, a gratitude for heaven knows what, and a natural disposition not to believe in the evil of this world, something typical of those who, accustomed to the benign treatment received during years of service, lack any real sense of evil, just like some well-meaning priests.

They never again mentioned the incident that had taken place at the gate to the Serrat mansion. It was only much later, by which time unfortunately it was too late to prove to Maruja that nobody had ever repaid her for her sense of gratitude (the obscure cause of her death, like her discreet passage through life, being in fact nothing more than an exaggerated expression of this gratitude), that Manolo came to understand just how misguided Teresa's words had been.

In October 1956 there were disturbances and demonstrations by students at the University of Barcelona. Thanks to a conversation with Maruja, Manolo heard of the leading role played in these events by Teresa Serrat and a close friend of hers, Luis Trías de Giralt, an economics student.

'We may not be able to meet for a few days,' Maruja announced one Sunday as they were sitting in the small square inside Parque Güell. Manolo was dozing on this warm, sunny morning; some old people were enjoying the sun on other benches and children were playing football. 'Do you know that the other day, when there were those demonstrations, the *señorita* came home at an ungodly hour, with her dress torn? Apparently the police had questioned her about what the students were up to – it seems she was one of the first to cause trouble. You should have seen how her mother reacted! Teresa said they might expel her from university, and that it was all the same to her! Her father is furious. He wants to send her to the seaside for a few days with his wife and me: he says it's the wisest thing to do. It's obvious the *señorita* is very caught up in this mess.'

The Murcian, who had spent a busy night breaking into a car in Plaza Real, laid his head on Maruja's lap and yawned. At first he wasn't particularly interested in this abstruse story, and just the image of Teresa played behind his drooping eyelids, as hazy as light on a rainy day, but lacking any real significance. To him, the students were like spoiled pets who with their antics merely proved how idiotic and ungrateful they were. Even though he sensed there might be a political aspect to the street protests they organised, he never saw them as any more meaningful, and naturally no more important, than the traditional uproar they created with the little dressmakers on their patron Saint Lucia's day. And yet once again Maruja commented on how strange Teresa had become since she began going to university and was seeing that student friend of hers. She drew such a disingenuous, picturesque image of her *señorita*, one so exaggerated – at least, that's how it seemed to him, as he listened to her half asleep – saying with a vehemence she herself wouldn't have been able to explain, that Teresa, if he only knew, really liked going to bars with her friends to find out what real life was like, to talk with workers, drunkards and even with those sort of women, you know – trollops. 'Because that's the way she is, very extreme and very revolutionary – gosh, you should hear her sometimes at home, the *señorita* doesn't mince her words, I'm telling you . . .!'

She also told him that Teresa often went out with weird, existentialist boys – a word the maid used almost reverentially – strange individuals, bearded students, and said they spent all the time telephoning each other, arranging to meet and lending one another books. Sometimes Teresa shut herself up in her room with a group of girlfriends and stayed there the whole evening, and when she, Maruja, brought them coffee or drinks she always found the air thick with cigarette smoke, and they would all be sitting on cushions on the floor, amid piles of gramophone records, heatedly discussing politics, Spain and other strange things.

As Maruja spoke, she again showed signs of that quiver of admiration and respect that so depressed Manolo, and he preferred not to make any comment that might encourage Maruja's confused and doubtless fanciful tales. Besides, on this particular morning the urge to sleep almost stifled the interest that the mere name of Teresa usually aroused in him. However, possibly due to an instinctive reaction to the numbed heaviness preceding sleep, an image began to take shape in his mind: that of this strange young woman, the light glinting on her golden locks as she talked to some rough-looking strangers in a low dive, a glass of red wine in her hand. Apart no doubt from expressing a rich girl's caprice (that of occasionally rubbing shoulders with the 'lower classes'), on this occasion it gave Manolo the feeling that there was something positively salacious and lewd about it, and that this made her vulnerable in some way he could use to his advantage, although he didn't as yet know how. In his mind's eye, he saw her standing there holding the wine glass, earnest, receptive, real, and the image stayed in his brain with that bittersweet flavour of a first not properly consummated sexual experience. It was as vivid as those memories of events that stick in the mind not for what they were but for what they could have been, and which over the years often demand we revisit and analyse them to discover where or at what moment we went wrong – just like the night he embraced the little girl in the silk pyjamas glinting in the moonlight, the night that could have changed the course of his life for ever.

Around that time, a period so intense at the University of Barcelona, so pregnant with sublime, heroic decisions (which, however, would not yet alter the shameful course of history even at the sacrifice of the best of our youth, as Teresa Serrat herself confessed one day to her comrade-in-arms), there occurred another incident which meant that the Interloper's recently created image of a different Teresa, still strange and distant but now vulnerable in some way or other, came to the fore once again and took on a deeper significance. It happened towards the end of May, when Manolo visited the working-class area of Pueblo Seco on an urgent errand for the Cardinal (to hand over a heavy suitcase full of stainless-steel cutlery worth fifteen thousand pesetas) together with Maruja, who had the afternoon off and was keen to accompany him.

Night was falling. They were walking close to a long factory wall down a deserted, muddy and foul-smelling street when Maruja suddenly cried out in surprise: she had recognised Teresa's Floride parked outside a low gateway. This led her to comment once more on the strange friendships her *señorita* had; Manolo said nothing. As they approached the car, the sound of machinery grew louder and louder, like an enormous beating pulse behind the endless wall, the muffled sounds of a factory. Manolo slowed down and told Maruja to be quiet. As they walked past the doorway without stopping, he turned his head and peered inside: Teresa Serrat was there in the shadows, leaning against the wall in a limp embrace with a young man. The stranger, who had his back to them, had long, shoulder-length hair, and was wearing a red roll-neck jersey; he was kissing her clumsily with that lack of enthusiasm that betrays inexperience. He seemed to be struggling, not with her, but with himself or his own shadow. Teresa was passively allowing him to kiss her. That was all: a fleeting glimpse Manolo had seen copied by others dozens of times at night in his own neighbourhood, the details of which had never interested him. But here, in what looked like an entrance to offices, the noise from the factory was deafening, and it seemed inconceivable that a girl like Teresa would permit herself to be embraced in such circumstances. Her gleaming sports car parked outside in a puddle full of dyes and chemicals was an almost equally unbelievable sight.

The image was as brief, unsettling and confused as an apparition: all that stood out in the semi-darkness were Teresa's tanned knees entwined around the stranger's legs with a fervour the lad didn't seem to appreciate to judge by his awkward embrace, the way her hands were moving up and down his back, while her face, eyes closed, emerged from the shadows over his shoulder. When they had gone past the entrance, Manolo asked his companion if she knew who the boy was. Maruja, who had suddenly clung to his arm, expressing her surprise with a nervous, almost conspiratorial laugh, replied that she had hardly had time to see him properly, but that from the back view he looked like one of those odd fellows the *señorita* occasionally went out with. What was she doing there? Well, it seemed obvious.... Why on such a disgusting street in a neighbourhood like Pueblo Seco, somewhere so distant from her own, in such a run-down doorway and with such a lowlife? There was no easy answer. A coincidence.

'Has your *señorita* had lots of boys?'

'You mean boyfriends?'

'Well, no, not what you might call proper boyfriends, never.'

They carried on walking for a while. With the infernal noise of the factory still reverberating in his head, Manolo's mind was wandering, the image of Teresa looking so passive and submissive still imprinted on his eyes. All at once there came, perhaps for the first time since he had been living in the city, something he saw as a glimmer of comprehension. It was nothing more than a rapid succession of chance circumstances that even he could see were strung together only by a thread, a despondent intuition that nevertheless was from then on to shape his view of Teresa Serrat and her world. The way he stubbornly clung to this bitter notion, to an idea he found hard to accept, the effort he had to make to come to a moral judgement about a woman of Teresa's status, also showed how far the Murcian still was from being ready to take up arms. In other words: he resisted the idea that a *señorita* like Teresa might be shameless – that is, what might be called a loose woman. And not because he was unaware of the shamelessness of this world – he had had more than sufficient proof of that since childhood – but because his concept of social classes had for too long been linked to a scale of values. At any rate, we must allow him the momentary benefit of that conviction, debatable but praiseworthy for the effort implied, and be fair towards him, admitting that, with or without the casual aid of this event one spring evening, he would have, by going over the idea again and again, come to see the light. Precisely because his growing interest in the beautiful, phantom-like university student (as yet, Teresa Serrat had only a sporadic impact on his life) lacked the superficial, mechanical calculations of the dowry hunter, the Murcian genuinely had to struggle to accept the idea that Teresa Serrat was quite simply a flirt, someone who liked to fall into the arms of neighbourhood lowlifes (of course, this is not at all how he saw himself), driven by nothing more than sexual desire.

At the same time as he felt a vague disappointment, the Interloper's head was filled with a jumble of strange possibilities. First and foremost, his instinct told him it was important to keep what he had just seen to himself, with the obscure aim of some day reaping possible gain from it.

'Listen,' he said to Maruja, 'don't ever get it into your head to tell your *señorita* we saw her. Not even as a joke, if you're confident enough to do that. She could get angry . . .'

In this way, even though the characteristic traits he had spotted in Teresa Serrat had not as yet acquired the solid reality he was later to come into contact with, the Interloper was beginning, against all expectation, to show signs of the intelligence that would take him far.

Part Two

The winter went by, filled with vague omens, and when summer came the Serrat family again transferred to their Villa near Blanes, taking their household staff with them. Manolo renewed his reckless night-time visits to the maid's room. He always travelled on a motorbike stolen as he left the city and abandoned on a street somewhere when he was back in Barcelona. He arrived at the Villa exuding an air of risk and adventure he seemed unaware of: his slanting black eyes and jet-black hair were charged with electricity, while the way he looked and moved were imbued with a sense of loss. Of the danger and youthful splendour of these nights of love there eventually remained nothing more than the arrogant, ambitious dream that had been behind them in the first place. He didn't rush to the coast like the wind, driven merely by his desire to again possess the pretty young servant. It wasn't only the intrepid bed-hopper who climbed through the window of the imposing Villa, skulking like a thief in the shadows; some nights he was simply afraid of sleeping at home.

Possibly also it was that, as every year with the arrival of summer, the Interloper possessed a particularly keen sense of the vast collective neurosis for happiness, the gilded prestige of money pouring through the most exclusive areas of this Mediterranean coast like liquid honey, a dream that floats under the blazing sun like a seed of the real life, and which on some seemingly endless hot nights flows through the veins like alcohol. What he was searching for in Maruja's arms was everything she brought with her when she came down from the Villa's brightly lit terrace or the big rooms already sunk in nocturnal silence, once her work was done and the guests had left or were asleep. Stretched out naked on her bed, he absorbed something indescribable exuding from her body, just as one can grasp a sense of the vastness of the air by stroking a bird's wings. The tangy taste of salt he discovered on her skin conveyed traces of a day on the beach, invisible presences, gentle desires born of leisure, as well as fragments of meaningless words, relaxed bodies and a dispassionate tenderness, none of which expressed any regret (how lucky the rich are) for all we cannot achieve in this life, all that is never going to happen.

Sometimes, lying on the bed in the darkness, he had to wait hours for Maruja to arrive. Above his head floated a murmur of voices and laughter, leading him to think they were having a party; he could hear the barking of dogs that he imagined as big, beautiful, majestic. On other occasions he heard the noise of children, whom he never caught sight of. Maruja told him about those mischievous little ones she had to look after: they were the sons and daughters of her mistress's sister, who came to the Villa for a fortnight every summer.

'They're a real handful,' Maruja would say, 'and at night nobody can get them to go to bed, but they're so lovely, so blond! Can't you hear them running off when they escape me? Their room is right above this one.'

Manolo did in fact often hear their tiny feet rushing back and forth, their yelling and tireless high spirits, and when silence fell (the signal that Maruja would soon be down, if there were no guests that day) he would think about those children asleep in their big beds, tucked up, secure in the knowledge they were protected now and in the future. Sometimes he fell asleep at the same time as them, as if he too were exhausted by the hustle and bustle of holidays. Hours later he would wake with a start in a foul temper, angry with himself and wondering what on earth he was doing in a maid's room. This happened especially after he had been going through some of the imaginary stickers in his favourite personal album, where the rich university student played an increasingly important role. Fire! A terrible, devastating fire is ravaging the Villa on all sides; he leaps out of bed and rushes through the smoke and up the stairs (which collapse behind him), sprints and rescues the blonde, blue-eyed girl from the flames (unconscious at the foot of her bed, wearing a pair of gleaming silk pyjamas that he has quickly to remove as they are already alight), and carries her in his arms to her parents. Or, as on another night, when he is hiding his motorbike in the pine woods and sees her walking alone on the beach, followed by a huge German shepherd dog, looking dreamy, sad, bored, her blond hair ruffled by the sea breeze – suddenly the earth begins to tremble, the pine trees are toppled, enormous cracks appear in the sand: an earthquake! 'Quickly, *señorita*, launch the launch' (he wasn't interested in getting the dialogue right, but took care over the details of the images): three months drifting on the open seas, the two of them, with no food, at death's door, and her in his arms . . .

Of course he always ended up kissing her, but these were not erotic dreams, or at least possessing the girl was not their main point. They were dreams from childhood, in which heroism and a secret melancholy triumphed over everything else, at least at the outset. The erotic element invariably appeared towards the end, when he had already rescued the damsel in distress, when he had given more than enough proof of his uprightness, bravery and intelligence, as he was carrying her to restore her safe and sound to her parents, before the admiring, astonished gaze of a crowd of onlookers. Because at this point he felt a pressing need to stop time and the action, to prolong this moment for as long as he could: it was like walking on ground that rolled backwards beneath his feet, because he knew instinctively he wouldn't survive the outcome, that he was irredeemably condemned to slip back into the shadows. It was only then that, as a consolation or possibly revenge for having to be parted from her, he would kiss her tenderly on the lips. What sweet, almost nuptial innocence there was in these adventures that he had relived every night as a young boy, curled up in his hard bed in the Ronda shack! They always included a blue-eyed girl (for a long while it was the Moreaus' daughter) who was about to fall headlong from Puente Nuevo. Following the inevitable handover to the grateful parents, Manolo would quickly return to the dream's starting point: once again the girl cried out for help, dangling from a bush above the River Tagus, swinging perilously above the ravine. He would push his way through the crowd, defy the abyss, sweep the young French girl into his arms, take her to her parents – but before returning her to them, he preferred to return to the start all over again, until at last he fell asleep. The following night, as soon as his head hit the pillow, he would set out the characters and the scenery (deep ravines, devastating flames, furious waves, earthquakes, wars) and off he would go once more.

He still cherished the most intimate secret of this strange childhood game: the promised encounter. Stretched out on Maruja's bed, he often told himself, to justify his momentary failure to act: I'm here because the skivvy has an arse and tits to die for, that's all. Or again: when it comes down to it, what I'm waiting for is the chance to make off with the jewels for once and fucking all.

But the very fact of possessing Maruja ideally, the essentially sublimated nature of his kisses and embraces, his moving, simple adolescent relationship with desire, tended to undermine the calculated musings of his tough adult self.

'I love you, I love you, sweetheart, I really do . . .'

In the end it was by chance that he was shaken out of his inertia, and in an unforeseen way. One night in early July, after he had left the motorbike among the pines (a splendid crimson Moto Guzzi he would have loved to keep) and climbed in through Maruja's window, he was surprised by how silent the Villa was. It was already past midnight, but Maruja hadn't come down yet. He collapsed on to the bed and as usual picked up the photograph from the bedside table (Teresa's face hidden by the shadow of her hand, Maruja's as ever reflecting her concern over something trivial), staring at it for a long while. It seemed to him that over time something had changed; he noticed that the image of Teresa Serrat gave off that soulless, domesticated and porous impression of bodies already known and possessed, and this made him feel strangely depressed. All of a sudden, he heard the rumble of a car reaching the Villa, a braking sound and doors slamming. Then voices: he thought he could hear Maruja's and Teresa's in between that of a man, and finally footsteps heading towards the Villa's main entrance.

Shortly afterwards, the bedroom door opened and Maruja appeared. She wasn't wearing her maid's uniform, and the mask of fatigue usually covering her face at that time of night was missing. She had on a pair of blue slacks, a loose, light jersey that was too long for her, and a pair of very odd sandals. Manolo stared at her in surprise. She ran to the bed and flung herself in his arms, completely forgetting the precautions she normally took – lowering the window, switching the light off and locking the door.

'I was afraid you weren't coming today,' she said, kissing him. She lay down on the bed beside him. Her eyes were moist and sparkling, she was perspiring, her cheeks flushed; the whole of her body gave off a feverish heat. Her ill-looking, deep-set eyes (in which forever lurked the shadow of imminent disaster), normally completely dull by this time of night, seemed to be blazing beneath her half-closed lids.

'What's wrong?' he asked. 'Are you ill ...? Why are you dressed like that?'

'I've had such fun this evening. They took me in the motor-boat...'

'Who?'

'Teresa. And Señorito Luis, a friend of hers who's more or less her boyfriend. It was wonderful. Teresa gave me these trousers and sandals. Do you like them?'

Manolo laid a hand on her forehead.

'You're burning up, little one.'

'I just feel very tired, very sleepy ... But let me tell you about it ...'

Her drooping eyelids softened the gleam in her eyes. Stretched out shrunken and feverish beside him, mouth parched, her chest heaving, she told him that Teresa and her friend had invited her for a spin in the motorboat, and then all three had gone by car to Blanes, to a lovely place where there was dancing. She found it hard to express herself, obviously struggling with a mental confusion that only grew as the night wore on, and which at first Manolo thought was due to tiredness and the effects of the sun. Besides – or possibly precisely because of this – that night Maruja was more beautiful than ever.

'I didn't dance,' she said. 'They were kissing and cuddling, the *señorita* today was ...! But don't think I was bored. On the contrary. There were foreigners there. Teresa was talking to me in French ... it was hilarious!'

'Where are they now – didn't they come with you?'

'Out walking on the beach, or in the pine wood ... I don't know, I told you, today the *señorita* is in such a mood ...'

Manolo listened to her, astonished and amused.

'Come here,' he said.

Maruja started to laugh, then suddenly turned serious and raised her hand to her head. She shivered, cuddled up to him, wrapped her legs round his waist and murmured: 'Kiss me.' As he did so, he noticed her brow was burning, and her teeth were chattering. She pushed him away to take off her slacks. Manolo got up from the bed and went to look out of the window.

'Do you know tonight they've left us alone here?' Maruja said.

Quickly calculating the importance of this news, he turned round. Maruja was immobile, the jersey over her head but her arms still in the sleeves, lying flat as if she were asleep. In a weak voice she added that her employers had been invited to a party in Barcelona and wouldn't be back until the next day, that Señorita Teresa and the student were out walking, and that to judge by the way they had been looking at each other all evening, they would be on a romantic stroll for a quite a while. The old cook was asleep, and so were the housekeepers, which meant she and Manolo were practically on their own.

'Come with me,' he said, heading for the door. 'Come upstairs with me. I want to see everything.'

'Wait,' said Maruja. She sat up, leaning on an elbow, staring at him with anxious eyes. 'Before that, come over here ...'

'What's wrong?'

'Oh, Manolo!'

He approached the bed.

'Are you scared?'

'It's not that ... But you ... Why do you always think the same thing?'

'The same thing? What do you mean, little one?'

'You know what I mean. I know what you're planning. I've known for some time . . .'

'I'm not planning anything. Quick, put something on and come with me . . . What are you waiting for?'

'I'd really like to talk to you, Manolo!'

'Don't be silly.'

'Please . . .'

'The people up there are asleep, they won't see us. I just want a look round. Don't worry – we'll be back here in no time.'

Maruja switched off the bedside lamp and stretched out again. It wasn't exactly meant to attract him, but more of an excuse.

'It can't go on like this, Manolo. It can't go on.'

'What the devil has got into you now? What can't go on like this?'

'Everything: us, this . . . You have to understand, it's impossible.'

The Murcian sat down beside her.

'Don't you love me any more, Maruja?'

'You know I do, more than anything in the world.'

'Well, then?'

'Oh, Manolo! We have to get married.'

He tried to calm her.

'There's no need to cry.'

'Who's crying? We have to get married, and that's that. This can't go on . . .'

'Listen, are you pregnant?'

'No, but I'm telling you this has to stop.'

'All right,' he said. 'We can talk later, I promise. Yes, we can plan things. But now put something on and let's get out of here . . . Good girl, that's what I like to see. And dry your eyes, cry baby.' He kissed her on the cheek. 'Come on, hurry up. I just want to see how those damned masters of yours live, sweetheart.'

'Don't swear.'

Muttering to herself, Maruja put on the first thing that came to hand – Manolo's pink shirt – and followed him. They emerged into a darkened passageway; she told him to be quiet, took his hand and pulled him on. Barefoot, they walked down the corridor, turned right and came to the entrance hall. The moonlight gave the room a greenish glow, as if they were in an aquarium. The distant murmur of the sea wafted in through the big, barred ground-floor windows. Maruja didn't want to switch on the lights, but Manolo convinced her she shouldn't worry.

For the *xarnego* this was above all a sentimental journey. He did not even want to see the Villa's left wing with the servants' rooms, kitchen, garage, the boat shed and an annexe for the housekeepers (a childless couple from Blanes). The right side contained the living room, dining room and the library with a parquet floor and French windows that opened on to the pine wood and the sea. The dining room was at the rear, linked to the garden by a terrace lined with big, irregular tiles, and yellowing, dried-out grass growing in the cracks. A broad carpeted staircase led to the first- and second-floor bedrooms with balconies that gave on to the cliff and jetty. The interior of the immense Villa did not correspond at all to the idea the Murcian had formed of it, but he was still impressed: from the outside, the building with its two slender towers looked like a fairytale castle, but inside it had a more relaxed monastic style with shining white vaulted ceilings, whitewashed arches and walls – all very geometrical and aseptic in a way that had none of the gravity and magic of its exterior. Only the heaviest, most solid pieces of furniture – old console tables, beds from Olot, panelled doors, framed antique maps on the walls, Mallorcan chairs, and especially a pair of armchairs in the library with lion's claws at the end of the armrests and feet – seemed to retain some mysterious connection with the Interloper's idea of luxury.

It didn't take him long to realise he was mistaken: the parquet floor smelled of wax and creaked deliciously underfoot (parquet flooring and its gleaming musicality had always been for him an incontrovertible token of wealth), while the atmosphere in this part of the house had a discreet life of its own. An ingratiating presence hung in the air, like an attentive servant always at hand but never visible; even Maruja, who had wearily sat on the living-room couch and was idly leafing through a magazine, seemed to fit perfectly into these surroundings, in his pink shirt that came down past her hips and left her thighs bare.

When he entered the spacious living room, Manolo had automatically, almost imperceptibly, slowed down: he had the impression he had been here before. Standing there in the midst of these big luminous spaces, smooth surfaces, and furniture that did not get in the way and apparently had no wish to grow old, he sensed the accumulation of time floating there as if inside a bell jar, the complete opposite to his house and neighbourhood, where objects were handled every day and soon became worn and old. This impression had more to do with a past lived he had no idea when or where – as if in his mother's womb in the Salvatierra palace in Ronda, he had walked hundreds of times through luxurious rooms such as these.

He strolled in a leisurely way round Maruja, hands behind his back, first once, and then again and again. At some point as he passed behind her, he stroked her hair and the back of her neck; in here it was possible to think of tomorrow, to love the future and to love one's neighbour as oneself, and although he could sense the tedium in the room (something in the still air suggested the empty hours, an embalmed leisure), it was a dignified, respectable and fruitful tedium. After a while, however, the nostalgia imprinted on his gaze and gestures turned to spite. Sitting on the couch, he grasped Maruja by the shoulders and fixed his black eyes on her.

'Where is your mistress's bedroom?'

Maruja instantly guessed his intentions, and tried to stand up.

'No . . . don't even think about it.'

'Oh, come on – don't start,' he said. 'I just want to see what there is.'

There was nothing to see, she said in a voice close to tears, there were no jewels or money, or anything that might interest him. 'Please, please, forget it, it's a mad idea, these things always end badly. Don't you see they would only blame me, they would regard me as responsible, and sooner or later they would worm the truth out of me . . .'

'Listen . . .'

'Please, I don't want to hear, I don't want to!'

She began to tremble, and the tears began to fall; she was on the verge of becoming hysterical. Her nerves had been tugging at her, and now something snapped. She started to yell, and Manolo gripped her again. Although he was well aware of the main reason for her outburst – she always grew furious whenever he mentioned the jewels – he began seriously to think there might be something else. After that everything happened very quickly: what at first seemed like a simple bout of weeping soon degenerated into an attack of nerves. Frightened somebody might hear her sobs, Manolo forced her up off the couch and dragged her back to her room. He laid her down on the bed, then returned to the main living room to switch off the lights.

Coming back into the maid's room, he found she had drifted off into an uneasy doze, from which she gradually emerged, her eyes still bathed in tears. He asked her if she felt ill, but she said no, it was just a headache.

'Wait,' he said, going over to the bedside table. 'Do you have any aspirin?'

'In my bag in the wardrobe.'

Manolo went to the kitchen for a glass of water. When he returned and held it out to her, for a moment Maruja looked him in the eye imploringly, as if she wanted to say something, but then no doubt thought better of it, and said nothing. He caressed and cuddled her to try to convince her she shouldn't be scared, that everything would be all right.

'Nothing will happen, silly – these people don't even know what they've got, they won't even notice . . .'

Her only reaction was to start sobbing again, clasping the sides of her head. Manolo grew increasingly irritated, but could get nothing more than garbled nonsense from her. He lay down beside her and deployed all his unfailing charm on her. It was useless. An hour went by.

'You don't love me,' she said, in between sobs. 'You've never loved me!'

He waited for her to calm down and then, when he couldn't stand it any more, slapped her gently a couple of times. Shaking like a leaf, she clung to him, body bathed in sweat. She had stopped crying.

'Don't hit me,' she said, 'come here.'

With clumsy, trembling hands, as limply as if obeying a mechanism operated from afar by someone else, she slowly took off his shirt and lay still, breathing heavily. They had not switched on the bedside lamp: moonlight filtered in through the window and shone milky white on the crumpled sheet at the foot of the bed. Maruja's body and eyes gleamed in the semi-darkness. All of a sudden she looked extraordinarily beautiful to Manolo. Her skin was burning like an ember. He kissed her, whispering fresh words of love in her ear and caressing her with a tenderness that even he realised went far beyond what he had anticipated, and threatened yet again to demolish his plans. Moments later he gave a start: it was as if there was something in her kisses that was struggling to express itself, and an indescribable, almost metallic taste of alarm on her lips; the shadow of imminent misfortune that had never ceased to veil her sick-looking eyes suddenly surfaced and tore her from his arms like a hurricane, without even giving him time to comprehend what was going on. He had gently eased himself between her legs when Maruja's arms fell from his neck and dropped on to the bed like heavy logs. He could feel the strength ebbing away through all the pores of her body. 'My head, Manolo, my head,' she murmured, still fixing her horribly dilated pupils on him, consumed by a premonition of what was about to happen. A terrible shudder shook her whole body – he had raised her head off the pillow a little, as if he could sense the outcome and perhaps wished, in a useless reflex action, to prevent her from hitting it on something – a muscular convulsion. She cried out, and lost consciousness.

Maruja lay in his arms with her head flung backwards like a disjointed rag doll. Panicking, Manolo tapped her on the cheeks to try to bring her round.

'Maruja . . .! Maruja, answer me! What's wrong, talk to me, I'm here . . .!'

He stood up with her in his arms. His first idea was for her to get some cool night air. He took several steps but, not knowing what to do, laid her back down on the bed. He went out into the passageway to call for help, but was afraid of causing a scandal, and told himself perhaps it was no more than a fainting fit that would pass. When he re-entered her room, he thought Maruja must be dead: she was lying spreadeagled on the bed, her head twisted horribly to one side, legs dangling down by the bedside table. He tapped her cheeks again.

'Mari ... Marujita ... Wake up!'

He considered giving her some water or, better still, something stronger, but by now he was in a complete panic. He felt guilty, guilty from the first moment, the first day he had entered this bedroom. Without fully realising what he was doing, he hurriedly got dressed. Before jumping down from the window, he glanced at Maruja one last time. Then he ran towards the pine wood. He couldn't remember where he had left the motorbike; it took him some time to locate it. Looking back, he saw the Villa bathed in moonlight and rubbed his face several times: the idea that Maruja was dead had by now become a certainty. You're in trouble, kid, he told himself. He finally found the bike, jumped on, and kick-started it.

He was at the rear of the Villa on the track leading to the main road. He had to kick the pedal three times: his hand on the clutch was so clumsy and trembling, he kept stalling the engine. The splendid Moto Guzzi sneezed and belched for a few seconds, then fell silent. You're a louse, kid, he said to himself. At the third attempt there was a deafening roar and the motorbike sped off, jolting him backwards like a dummy. He quickly righted himself on the seat and raced along the bumpy track, still terrified.

During the holiday season, any motorbike ride along the coast was a wild career: crouched catlike on the roaring machine, hair and shirt-tails streaming in the wind, staring resolutely at the road in front of him and showing complete contempt for the pleasurable sights swirling and vanishing around him, the Interloper ate up kilometre after kilometre, enveloped in an aura of aggression combined with remorse – a wish to make amends, of caresses begun but never satisfied. He suicidally overtook cars and buses laden with tourists, sped through celebrations in villages and squares, leaving behind him bustling terraces, lighted villas, hotels and camp sites. Thighs gripping the petrol tank, he governed and directed a tremor in the metal and in the blood, controlled the blind power of the engine with slight adjustments of waist and knees, vaguely imagining he was keeping his own impulses and impatience in check, as though the machine, his muscles and the dust covering them were a single substance that had no choice but to launch itself endlessly through the night. He had no idea where he was heading. Often in the shadows at the far end of his headlight beam he thought he saw maids' uniforms hanging from a rail in Maruja's room. Despite these phantom images his speed created, he was acutely aware of the movement and colour all around him. It was as if two films were being simultaneously projected on either side of the bike, two strips of photographic stills he could see out of the corner of his eye: the fleeting, chaotic stream of pleasures that tourism generated at night on the coast, sights he both celebrated and loathed.

Indifferent foreign tourists and kind-hearted local lovers were enjoying themselves, but as he raced madly along, the Interloper could see only night pouring its grey, uncaring tenderness over them, distilling its ancient sap of silence. He watched as the rancorous blue-tinged moon rose above the green glow of the treetops, saw it glinting over the sea, now a moribund silver pond, how its light spread slowly over beaches, chalets, hotels, over gardens, terraces, the parasols and hammocks still pointing towards an invisible sun with what remained of their day-time spirit.

A gentle music that gets under the skin like a sun-tanned body shivering in a breeze – a music that seems to come out of nowhere, everyone's favourite song – spreads along the shore every night, together with what looks like an invasion of red termites streaming from hotels and guest houses, their shoulders raw, their hearts tropical, to fill discotheques, dance halls and terraces. Despite the speed he is travelling at, the Interloper is able to distinguish the locals. He recognises them by their obscurely offended but dignified gaze as they cross the street, hands in pockets, looking disparagingly over their shoulder at him as his motorbike threatens to run them down (their suddenly terrified eyes undermining their supposed dignity, their lamentable attempt to believe they are still the owners of the ground they tread on), then spinning round like dolls on a turntable before being swallowed by darkness. But above all there are tourists: these are the rich ones you can see, he thinks, those who can sometimes even be touched, whom we can at least say that they exist; those who still permit (though not without annoyance) all the enthralled natives arriving in their droves at the weekend by train or motorbike to gawp like wretched mongrels at their noble bronzed bodies, their enviable good fortune. The phantom biker could see these compatriots of his, dressed up in their Sunday best for a Sunday that will never arrive, crowding around terraces and dance floors, ogling Swedish girls with fiery golden locks and big, fragrant mouths – yellow eyes gleaming in the dark, eyes that in the early hours begin to acquire, like a centuries-old veneer, the anonymous agony of offices and workshops. Whether astonished or oozing respect, their gaze is like that of children excluded by their own playmates from a game, stuck in a corner, overlooked for some incomprehensible reason, hanging around just in case they might be invited to join in. Theirs is an ancestral, pitiful longing, but one at any rate infinitely worthier than the desire simply to get rich (as he was to hear Teresa say on one occasion), reduced as it is to an opportunity for immediate, surreptitious love, a dance obtained without paying or a roll in the sand behind a fishing boat.

His speed blurred outlines into a series of flickering images: middle-aged, placid Nordic couples with fresh faces and blond children as beautiful as flowers; flocks of delightful pink-faced old ladies arriving in coaches with their wonderful striped hats; willowy Swedish girls and angular, warm French ones straight out of the pages of magazines ('*Cet été vous changerez d'amour,*' says the horoscope in *Elle*); mongrel English girls who go dancing in shawls and ample, rustling dresses as if they were at a formal reception, and who end up allowing themselves to be slobbered over by fishermen and off-duty waiters; and so on. All these people are visible, they are beautiful; contact with them sometimes creates a feeling of resentment, but it doesn't last.

But there are others who are even wealthier, those who barely let themselves be seen, the truly inaccessible ones. It might seem as if they didn't exist, were it not that occasionally they have been spotted in public. On their rare visits to town, they smile absent-mindedly at the milling couples: it's obvious they're accustomed to being happy, that their passions lie elsewhere. Their charm and their silence suggest distant, pleasure-filled worlds; their bodies appear to have acquired a sprinkling of gold dust as they come nonchalantly to sit a while with us on the terraces, always with that cold, serene clannish air glittering on their brow, marking them out and accompanying them wherever they go, shielding them from the crowd's curiosity, from being forgotten and from scorn. Among them, certain older men particularly impress the tempestuous biker. Such people are neither tourists nor locals: they live in holiday villas, which also remain almost unseen, surrounded by gardens and pine woods, swathed in silence and the leafy murmur of leisure. They look at us without seeing us, their eyes putrid with money, their powerful minds marked with old scars of cut-throat deals. Like retired gangsters, they lounge beside specially designed swimming pools barely visible through tall hedges, next to tennis courts where young girls who could be their daughters (though you never know) are playing. From a distance it's impossible to tell if they live there or are guests, or whether they really are as young as they appear.

Among them were Teresa Serrat and her friend Luis Trías de Giralt, who had been invited to spend the weekend at her family Villa. Even though tonight she had allowed herself to be seen in Blanes with her friend and her maid, Teresa rarely left her domains, and when she did it was very rarely to go into town rather than to Barcelona itself. But thanks in part to a favourable coincidence (her parents were away), the young university student had been spotted in Blanes, drawn there by her friend and by certain impulses she was at this very moment busily and bitterly analysing.

Outside, piercing the silence of the night, the motorbike's first desperate explosion filled the air, a prelude to its headlong flight. The echo rose clearly above the swish of the waves and came in through the open window of Teresa's bedroom. She was lying on her bed, staring into the semi-darkness, thinking things over. She slowly turned her head on the pillow with an expression of melancholy remorse. On hearing the second explosion of the bike engine as it still refused to start, Teresa Serrat got out of bed and sauntered across to the adjacent terrace. Her nubile movements were only in appearance languid: each casual flexing of her knees, thighs tensed, her lithe hips swinging slightly in advance of her shoulders, displayed a strange violence, a consciously aggrieved or resentful air. As she walked barefoot she did up her blouse with limp hands, folded over like broken flower stems. Her yellow shorts had become stuck to her groin; she pulled the hems down nervously with thumb and forefinger, as if touching something infectious. She closed her eyes, a disdainful smile playing on her pale lips: it was not her own body she was so aware of, but the exasperating presence she could still feel of someone else's. As she reached the French windows, a gust of wind stirred her hair, baring her long, shapely neck. For a few seconds, enveloped by the moonlight streaming into the bedroom like a wave of white foam, her figure was immobilised as though caught by a sudden camera flash.

If it is true that a woman's pedigree can be judged by her neck, then Teresa Serrat was a wonderful example of her class. From her mother she had inherited a beautiful, slender neck, a shapely mouth made for kisses, and sufficient vivacity for this to give her an enchanting, almost mythical sense of gestures. Consider, for example, the way she tilts her tousled head, straining to catch the rumours of the night. She has the soul of a butterfly-fish; her destiny is to live in a perfect combination of light and the blue transparent waters of the tropics. And yet Teresa feels nostalgia for a violent, shadowy sea replete with superb, dangerous creatures; a longing for wretched slums where her comrades are fighting a surreptitious, heroic fight. She sighs like a bored, pampered cat longing for roofs and moonlight. Her provocative, adorable bare feet – all of her, and all the attributes of her beauty, from the blue gleam of her eyes and her somewhat childlike hips to the old gold of her hair, the honey and silk of the nape of her neck, and her languid, adolescent back – they all reveal the heritage of a maternal line exquisitely fed even during hard times, and whether the progressive student regards it as fair or not, they evidence the class privilege that since childhood has been proclaimed by her graceful roe-deer neck and the shape of her mouth. Because it was there, in the pink, dry and slightly swollen lips – especially the top one, whose Cupid's bow (as the Murcian had once observed) was drawn towards the nose in a charming curl of disdain – it was there that the origin and secret of her slightly childish look, spoiled yet at the same time challenging, that, spreading like a summer fog over the hostile fullness of her sun-drenched limbs, defined the young woman's ambiguous nature, a mixture of candour and insolence, of pink childlike languor and tanned adult rebelliousness.

Enveloped in the pale astral light, Teresa rested her elbows on the balustrade. By her on the terrace were folded parasols, tubs of plants with enormous, burnished leaves, a pedestal table and two hammocks. Forgotten on a wicker chair, a small transistor radio was pouring out a tender fashionable pop song:

> *... the moon confessed to me*
> *she had never loved before,*
> *that she had always been alone,*
> *dreaming on the shore ...*

From where she stood, Teresa could see the jetty, and to her right, above the bushes, the metal fence of the tennis court. On the far side of the Villa, somewhere close to the pine wood, the motorbike engine was still refusing to start, and its painful wheezing and coughing sounded like an alarm call in the middle of the night. She heard footsteps in the bedroom behind her.

'Now what does he want, what is he after?'

There was another explosion, a sustained one this time, and she realised the bike had set off towards the road at precisely the moment – one she would have liked at all costs to avoid – that Luis Trías de Giralt stepped on to the terrace. The illustrious student leader had just come from the bathroom, wiping his wet face and hair with his forearm. Leaning on the door jamb of one of the French windows, he gave a sad smile, his eyes fixed on Teresa's back. He was wearing a baggy white jersey and tan linen trousers.

'Oh, so this is where you are,' he said dully. 'That water is so hot ...' He listened closely to the throb of the motorbike as it faded in the distance, and added: 'Can you hear it? Our friend the *xarnego* has been at it again ...'

Teresa still had her back to him. He's more of a man than you are, she thought. Instinctively, she clenched her thighs, fully aware for the first time of the insult to her body. Feeling indignant, she thought bitterly that there are many ways to be an imbecile, and that Luis Trías de Giralt (who would have thought it?) was one of those imbeciles who show it by trying as hard as they can not to be one. Turning towards him, she thrust her elbows behind her so that now she was leaning with her back against the balustrade. She didn't appear to see her friend: her misty eyes were directed elsewhere, their gaze lost in the night far above his head. He was rubbing his knee, a painful look on his face.

'He's charming,' said Teresa. 'He reminds me of lots of friends I've forgotten.'

She was oblivious to the ambiguity of her words, her scornful, offended gaze still fixed on the depths of the night.

'Who? The maid's boyfriend?' asked Luis. After a pause, he added: 'Look, we can talk about what happened between us calmly . . .'

'There's nothing to talk about.'

He rubbed his knee again. In a surprisingly authoritarian voice, he said he had just banged himself hard on the edge of the bath tub, and would be on his way as soon as it stopped hurting.

For the first time, Teresa focused on him. He may even have had a shower, the idiot . . . Yes, who would have thought it, but behind the facade of a student leader, of a passionate visionary of the future, there was nothing more than a soft, disgustingly limp and inexpert manhood. Those veteran orator's hands had trembled with an uneasy bourgeois conscience as they closed round her strawberry nipples. And those shining, apostolic eyes of his, always raised to the heavens as they contemplated future visions, had strayed ashamedly, pathetically, over her body. And yet his voice still boasted that refusal to be amazed typical of wise old men crowned with glory and experience, and appeared determined not to accept anything, to dismiss as unimportant what had happened that night between the two of them. Teresa suspected that his voice, even at those historic moments when it had fearlessly uttered his famous slogans, had never expressed anything but total and complete ignorance of anything and everything.

'When are your parents coming back?' asked Luis.

'Tomorrow, I've told you a thousand times . . . Or maybe tonight. That would be best.'

'Tere, you know there's a logical explanation, and I'll explain it to you,' he declaimed, calmly and coolly. 'You're no prude, and...'

'Yes, of course. But please, don't wheel out your dialectic for such a wretched business. Please, please just stay silent.'

At that time, Luis Trías de Giralt's prestige in the university was sky-high. He had twice been in jail, and was always accompanied by the melancholy ghost of being tortured (sometimes he could even be seen in close conversation with that ghost, wrapped in expressive silence). It was said of him in the lecture theatres that he was one of the important ones – strange praise that, if it meant anything, was nothing more than that. A year earlier, Teresa Serrat had felt impelled to collaborate with him in endless cultural and extra-cultural activities: Luis Trías de Giralt was said to have 'political connections'. An outstanding economics student, he was the grandson of a Mediterranean pirate, and the son of an extremely smart trader who made millions importing rags in the early fifties. Luis was tall and good-looking, but his features were slack, deceitful, essentially those of a politician. He had a pink face, with thin, curly hair, and a luminous but weak gaze: he looked simple-minded, like a distorted version of a Capetian monarch with jowls (a certain cocky young fellow from Barcelona's Barrio Chino with whom he had a strange on-and-off friendship was in the habit of calling him 'Isabelita', which he found rather embarrassing, and as inexplicable as his weakness for the lad). He had the slightly bemused air of a timid seminarian on holiday, his head bobbing from theological vertigo, the transcendental weight of ideas, or from a simple weakness in his neck, as if it were oddly dislocated.

Teresa averted her eyes. She wanted him to leave once and for all.

'It's late,' she said.

The sound of the motorbike had faded into the distance a long while ago. Simple, joyous, common boyfriends of vulgar maids, the world is yours! If Luis came up to me now and held me tight, she thought, very tight, perhaps not everything would be lost . . .

The two of them were standing motionless a couple of metres from one another. Luis didn't dare come any closer. He lit a cigarette, almost braying: 'Would you like one? They're really good . . .' (pathetic – you know they're dreadful). 'They're authentic Russian . . .' (worse still, this is no moment to boast of your proverbial solidarity). 'Jacinto brought me some packets from the last Festival de la Jeunesse in . . .' (that's enough – be quiet, won't you?). He began puffing on it nervously, almost secretively, waving his hands at the smoke hanging dense and heavy above him under the only lamp lit on the terrace. Studying him, Teresa confirmed the impression that had only recently occurred to her: she was dealing with an impostor. The legendary student leader seemed determined to live day-to-day life only half-heartedly, as if it implied activities unworthy of his exalted position: dancing, swimming, making love and even, as he was now demonstrating, smoking. He took in the smoke without swallowing, and left it trailing out of his mouth, spreading over his lips like repugnant foam. Teresa recalled that she had always questioned the moral integrity of people who, when they have a cigarette, don't inhale the smoke.

'It would be best if you leave, Luis,' she said, lowering her gaze. She would have liked to add, 'After what happened, we're only linked by things that are above and beyond our feelings and our personal interests,' but given the vulgarity of the situation, this sounded too solemn. It was a neat response, though, and she would have loved to utter it, and so stored it in the back of her mind. A rational being, she was also now perfectly aware that she found it impossible for him to be close to her. In view of the arousal that had tantalised them for so long and had led to this current painful situation, who would have thought that they had spent such a marvellous evening? And yet she had to admit that for some time now their relationship had been suffering under an odd, unbearable weight, an electric current that threatened to paralyse them at any moment: their feelings and desires were being mutually and constantly revised, scrutinised, analysed and valued according to a concept of life that, unfortunately and however hard they strove to deny it with visionary talk, was not yet in place and therefore bore absolutely no relation to the reality of their class (you have to accept that, Luis, my bourgeois leftie friend). As time wore on, they discovered that the bond between them was exactly the opposite of what their progressive ideals seemed to advocate: a horribly conjugal relationship cemented so quickly it had not even given them time to overcome certain sexual inhibitions, a hangover from their conventional education, so that any gesture or word, any insignificant look or action (such as, for example, smoking one of those awful Russian cigarettes) that still bore the symbolic mark of what had brought them together became endowed with an annoying, redundant meaning that grew before their eyes into a monster with a life of its own, with independent movements and meaning that undermined those emotional links that they, based on a sacred sense of solidarity, had sought to elevate to the level of passion.

Turning her back on him, Teresa listened closely to the silence of the night, still trying to make out the echo of the Murcian's motorbike. From a shimmering distance and happier skies, the song on the transistor radio was also lamenting:

> *... She told me that the night*
> *kept hidden in her shadows*
> *the echo of other kisses ...*

Luis Trías interpreted this as a clear sign that he was dismissed, and decided the moment had come to leave. It was only years later that he realised he could have tried again and would probably have been successful if he had only had the courage to take her in his arms. For some reason, overcome by his secret sadness and his inability to put things right, he suddenly saw in the night sky the mocking, mouse-like face of his friend from the Barrio Chino, smiling at him against a background of crimson wallpaper.

'Okay, Tere, I'm going,' he said. 'Your parents might come back tonight... and yes, what can I say, I think we both had too much to drink. These things happen, and besides, it's not unusual... it's a well-known phenomenon. The next time...' (There won't be a next time, as you well know.) 'Shall we see you tomorrow in Lloret... or in Barcelona?'

Lloret was where Luis was spending the summer with his family, and Teresa would sometimes take the car and return his visit, on the way dropping in on some other student friends who holidayed there. On other occasions, she and Luis agreed to meet in Barcelona. But now...

'Goodbye.'

A few minutes later, alone at last, Teresa heard Luis's Seat 600 setting off from the Villa's front entrance. She closed her eyes and buried her face in her hands to suppress a wave of something she could not define ('your weeping, Teresita, your *femme-enfant* weeping-laughing,' Luis had written about once from prison) that rose from her chest and was burning hot: she was just becoming aware, in horrified fashion, that in reality she had been expecting him to stay and try again.

'Go on then, you stupid pig!' she shouted inside her head, running into her bedroom and flinging herself on to the bed.

She couldn't sleep. It was no easy task to begin analysing what had happened, to accept her share of guilt. As ever, she tried to find the most objective explanation possible that would safeguard ideological convictions that went far beyond her and Luis and their petty disasters. Recalling everything they had done that day, it seemed to her that the terrible seed that had been sown and ended up demolishing everything had its origin late in the afternoon, at the moment when she was casting off the motorboat from the jetty. Luis had been talking about Maruja, about how pretty and reticent (as he described it) she had become ever since she had a boyfriend. That was when, without exchanging so much as a word on the subject, they agreed to invite the maid to go with them.

'I was just going to suggest it,' said Luis, jumping on to the boat. 'It's a great idea.'

'She gets terribly bored, poor thing,' said Teresa. 'She'll be so pleased. I'll go and get her.'

'I'll wait for you. Hurry up!'

They were both delighted at having taken this decision. Ever since that morning when they were left on their own after learning Teresa's parents would be away for the night, their silences had become strangely heavy. In fact, they were inviting Maruja as a necessary nervous displacement; they needed to communicate through a third person, and there was nobody better suited to this than her. She allowed them to transmit their desire to each other thanks to a special essence they saw emanating from her: the essence of her nights of love-making with the Murcian, their intimate relations, which they had known about since Teresa discovered them the previous summer, and which they secretly envied and admired.

Teresa returned to the jetty shortly afterwards, saying Maruja would be down shortly; she was just finishing cleaning Luis's bedroom in case he decided to stay the night. Teresa added that she had given Maruja a pair of slacks and some sandals that were no longer fashionable but still as good as new. She said the maid looked lovely in them, perfectly charming. That was when – and as she recalled it now, Teresa understood it was no coincidence – she and Luis had exchanged a first kiss. They were on the boat, waiting for Maruja. The sky was completely clear and although it was late afternoon, the weather was still hot and bright. A weak red sun shone directly on to the steps cut in the rock down to the jetty where Maruja would appear. Both of them had a clear view of her silly fall – one of the sandals got caught and she tripped. If this had happened anywhere less dangerous – on the wooden planks of the jetty, for example – it would have made her laugh. She had been jumping almost despairingly down the steps – doubtless concerned she had kept them waiting too long – and was waving at them in a very vulgar way ('Yoo-hoo, yoo-hoo!') when all of a sudden her legs and bare feet (the flimsy sandals were the first to fly off) flapped in mid-air as if she were stamping, and they clearly heard the crack of her head against the bottom step. Crying out, they leapt off the boat and ran towards her. Maruja lay flat on the ground (alarmingly immobile for a few seconds) until Luis reached her, when she rapidly got to her feet. She laughed with embarrassment, rubbing her head ('How silly of me, *señorita*'). Poor thing, Teresa thought as she searched the steps for the sandals Maruja was so pleased with.

'It's the sandals that made you fall,' said Teresa. 'You're not accustomed to them. If I'd realised you'd have problems, I wouldn't have given you them.'

'They're so pretty . . . I'll soon get used to them.'

'Have you really not hurt yourself?' Luis asked anxiously.

'No, no.'

'You could have killed yourself, child,' said Teresa.

'It was nothing. Just a bump. The thing is, I was running because it took me so long to make the beds, and . . .'

Teresa recalled the scene. Perhaps, now I think of it, it would have been better to send her back, she thought. First, because I'm sure she must have really hurt herself – she tried hard to hide it, poor girl, but it was a tremendous thump – and secondly because later maybe everything would have turned out differently for Luis and me. We didn't know that then, of course; at that moment we thought we needed her company, and besides, we didn't want to give up on the pleasure of offering her a bit of fun... Or perhaps it wasn't that exactly? I don't know...

For her part, Maruja insisted (I remember that well, very well) that it was nothing and they should set off. So the three of them sailed along the coast for almost an hour, bathed in a small, deserted cove and ate fresh fruit she (obliging child) had been thoughtful enough to bring along. As they ate, stretched out on the sand, Teresa and Luis were practically all over the maid, asking her about Manolo, taking an interest in how their relationship was going and offering her wise, vaguely contraceptive advice (which was of no use at all to her) with a kind of paternal concern mixed with erotic complicity. Their questions sought, almost demanded, the confirmation of a magical idea they had of the furtive love between a maid and a worker. Maruja lied; she found herself obliged to do so to please them, and said nothing about the terrible dark moods and no less terrible behaviour of her beloved Manolo, while Teresa and Luis were all over each other, fondling right in front of her with a strange, blind insistence, as though the same imaginative arousal was forcing them to do so, almost against their will, even though they didn't really enjoy it. Their intention seemed to be more a way of affirming their own identity, to prove they were still there, rather than explicitly sexual.

When they returned to the Villa, they decided to have supper in Blanes, and then go on to dance somewhere. Maruja was astonished, not at the *señorita*'s generosity, which she had already demonstrated on many occasions, but because she knew Teresa didn't like Blanes – she thought it was a town full of uncouth holidaymakers – and above all because the impatient way the couple had been looking at one another during their excursion had led her to believe they would get rid of her as soon as they disembarked.

Blanes was very lively. Holding hands or with their arms round each other's waist, Teresa and Luis walked along the streets and terraces thronged with tourists, giving a perfect lesson of how to belong to the select band of chosen natives: they didn't paw one another at all. After a quick meal at a bar counter – Maruja was embarrassed because she was still tripping all the time over her sandals, which kept coming off – they went for a *Cuba libre* at a bar where there was music (that was where Luis drank his first two neat gins) and they danced. Maruja didn't get up from her seat, and although several young men asked her to dance, she never accepted. (Now I think of it, I don't know whether she refused out of a silly faithfulness to her boyfriend, or because she felt unsure on those sandals. Naturally the excuse she gave, 'I've got a bit of a headache, so thanks, but I'm not dancing,' was a lie . . .) She referred to Manolo only once, regretting he couldn't be with her. Luis and Teresa promised that one day all four of them would go out together. As the evening progressed, the awareness that this was the night destined for them since the dawn of time had gradually imposed itself: the way they looked at each other, their embraces and, above all, the way they drank. For a long while they danced closely entwined in front of Maruja, staring into each other's eyes. Once they realised she was not only terribly bored but that her eyes were closing (it must have been that she was sleepy; 'Wow, that Murcian must be a brute,' Luis had joked. 'He may be a worker with all the class consciousness you like, Tere, although that remains to be seen, but he could control himself a bit and let the girl get some rest some nights'), they decided to visit other spots they thought would be more enjoyable and familiar for Maruja, and for them – small, sophisticated taverns and cellars where they could drink wine and chat to strangers. But even though she seemed contented, Maruja was unable to shake off her drowsiness. She seemed not quite there, staring into space and oblivious to them and their kissing and cuddling. She no longer acted as the touchstone for their happiness, and so they decided to return to the Villa.

On the journey back, they sang (how ridiculous it now seems to Teresa, as she recalls it) popular songs from the French Resistance ('*Ah, compagnon . . . !*') that they had learned from an Yves Montand record of Teresa's. They got out of the car at the main entrance, said goodbye to Maruja, who thanked them, half asleep but happy, then went for a walk along the beach. When they were on their own, something very bizarre happened: all of a sudden Luis's burning desire to communicate evaporated, replaced by a kind of serious, intimate lucidity, a coldness that threatened to overpower them both for the rest of the night.

(Why on earth did it occur to me just at that moment to talk about Paco Lloveras and Ramón Guinovart, the last two Spanish exiles in Paris?) They commented on a book of poems by Nâzim Hikmet that was being passed round at the university, which Teresa had promised to lend Luis. On the moonlit shore she could see the serious, alluring profile of the prestigious jailed student leader, and was reminded of Hikmet:

> *Tu es sorti de la prison*
> *Et tout de suite*
> *Tu as rendu ta femme enceinte . . .*

> You came out of prison
> And immediately
> You made your wife pregnant . . .

So powerful in the midst of the sweet sensation of knuckles brushing against hips, waiting, hoping for a reaction from him (*Tu la prends par le bras / Et le soir tu te promènes dans le quartier.* You take her by the arm / And in the evening you walk with her around the neighbourhood . . .) that never came. Luis was still immersed in a silence so familiar to his close friends: that must have been what torture was like. This led her to say, in a voice that sounded surprisingly unlike her, 'Don't think of it any more,' which led to an awkward pause. Possibly to try to save the situation, Luis suddenly began to behave oddly, demonstrating a ridiculous, childish mischievousness that irritated her. He took advantage of things like a schoolboy.

'Look, look, there's a light on in the Villa,' he said, coming up behind her and rubbing himself against her as he pointed to the lighted windows in the house. 'Look, can you see? Can you see? Who can it be? Burglars, do you think?'

'Who do you think it is. It must be Maruja, who had some chores to finish . . . And stop fooling around, will you, you're being silly.'

And as they were walking through the pine wood: 'Look, look, you've got an insect on your knee . . .!' he said, surreptitiously fondling her.

The fact is, he was really annoying. This wasn't what she had been expecting. What had gone wrong? They were deep in a hole filled with impressive exiles, headed by Nâzim Hikmet. The intellectual alibi didn't last long: all at once Teresa flung her arms round his neck and forced him to give her a proper kiss. The venerable phantoms of Paco Lloveras and friends evaporated, and Paris along with them. Then, when he was wildly aroused, Teresa said it would be best to go back to the Villa and have a drink while they talked. That was a mistake. Looking back now, she thought this sudden decision was the origin of her part of the blame for what had happened subsequently, her contribution to that night's failure and shame. It was true that if Luis had protested, insisting on continuing to kiss her there (in fact, not then but earlier, what he should have done was force her to lie down in the sand with him rather than going on walking and walking), she would have offered only token resistance, with objections such as 'Not here, it's very damp', that would have implied an implicit acceptance long before they reached the bed, and perhaps the dreaded cloud of insecurity surrounding them would have been dissipated. But Luis didn't say a word, and walked several paces in front of Teresa, wrapped in a laboured silence that only made things worse.

'Look, your burglars have switched the lights off,' she said with a laugh, trying to restore at least some humour to the occasion.

Luis quickened his step, kicking the clumps of bushes.

Teresa carried a bottle of gin, two glasses and some ice out on to the terrace. They flopped into hammocks, listening to music on the radio. They were so disconsolate that they (both of them this time) made yet another blunder: they began talking politics and student activism. At first they weren't even aware of it; everything was still an extension of that nervous contagion that had led them to invite Maruja to join them and to give her the sandals, then go for dinner in Blanes, dance and walk along the beach. And now, in one of the mysteries of that generation of university heroes, the discussion of serious matters gradually absorbed them, in spite of themselves, in an extraordinary, inevitable way. Only for them to discover they had fallen into yet another trap.

'Yes, Tere sweetheart, I agree,' Luis said irritably, 'that the current position of socialism with regard to capitalism has changed all over the world, but it's a qualitative change, not a quantitative one, do you see? Besides, why do you want to talk about that now?'

'Who, me? Come on, I just want you to know I understand that perfectly, Mister Know-It-All, which is why in October I was one of the first to go out into the streets ... Pass me the bottle, would you ... I understand, and that's why I've personally made more visits to your father's factory than all the rest of you put together, although not much has come of it, and that's why I've called for more contacts, more unity. And that's why I'm here talking to you about it right now ... Of course, I know there are calls from outside for a policy of peaceful resistance, without that implying in any sense a retreat from the ultimate objective ...' (Where on earth did I read that?) 'But we also have to take the circumstances into account ... Hey, don't drink any more, you're emptying the bottle all on your own; afterwards you won't know where to put your hands ...' (she was referring to him not being able to drive, but the student hero smiled what by now was only a feeble smile at what he took to be an enticing implication). 'What was I saying? Oh yes ... all right, let's leave it.'

Now it was his turn to insist.

'I never talk politics casually, Tere. Not simply to pass the time ... But let me tell you one thing ... the repercussions of the general crisis of capitalism is something we in the upper classes aren't always able to perceive, due to a fatal lack of perspective, but within five years it will be obvious. Things are only just starting.'

'Crisis?' she said, astonished. 'Where did you get that from? There's no such crisis. The lack of initiative and immobility of the bourgeois opposition, always supposing that such a thing exists, because I only know of three or four lost souls, of whom you are one ...'

'Thanks so much, darling.'

'... doesn't mean there's a crisis. Take Papa, for instance. You know very well he would only join the opposition if he were to see his income diminish. But instead of that, it's increasing, and will do so for years to come!'

'What are you saying? You're so mixed up! It makes me despair, Tere, the way you mix everything up! Tell me, what do you know about the opposition parties? And are you really denying that the gravity of the economic situation isn't real?'

'Real for whom? Not for Papa. Can't you see you're confusing the general standard of living with the purchasing power of a privileged class, and ...'

More than on any other occasion, all this sounded like phrases they had read somewhere, constructed with metal and cement into lifeless blocks that had the frozen rigidity of reports to study groups. Dead as a doornail. They were vaguely aware that nothing they were saying bore the slightest relation to reality (why, why exactly did it have to be tonight?), and this was what most piqued them, not the fact that they disagreed; this and the awareness that they were becoming increasingly distant from one another. And the worst of it was that they were (a truly bad choice) sitting opposite each other rather than together, and now, sunk in their hammocks like two feeble consumptives, enveloped by the shadows of the night, they couldn't even pat each other on the shoulder, pretending to be upset; they could barely see one another and didn't have the strength to move. Teresa tossed her head and sighed. Each minute of silence contained an explosive charge: they couldn't avoid these pauses being more meaningful than any words. Teresa thought that only she perhaps realised how awkward the situation was. (Can it be he doesn't like me enough? Maybe I've said something silly like a little bourgeois girl, one of those remarks he can't bear?)

As he rocked to and fro in his white jersey, lying flat in his hammock, Luis seemed to emerge and then disappear in the darkness. And yet he could see Teresa's crossed knees against the yellow background of her shorts: they were like two polished apples, darker even than the night.

'Listen,' he said. 'You know very well that when I talk about these things I'm not being in any way sentimental. Not even an intellectual. As I told Modolell and Jordá the other day, my advantage is I don't have any kind of artistic aspiration.'

'I don't understand a word of what you're saying, Luis.'

'I don't want to stop being a realist. You talk about organising study groups, having more contacts with the lower classes' (he didn't mean to say that, but there it is; 'I hope you don't misinterpret me'). 'Well, I don't think that. I've said hundreds of times that the university needs people ready to go out into the streets every day, not to meet up to study the sacred texts, which always ends up in Byzantine debates about blasted sex . . .' (he didn't mean to say that either) 'and listening to records about French partisans. No, my dear Tere, sweetheart . . . The students are starting to open their eyes at last. We no longer go out into the streets to kick up a fuss for its own sake – now we're there for a reason, in the name of something. Isn't that enough for you?'

'I wasn't talking about that. And anyway, you can see where that's got you; everything has gone back to how it was. I think . . .'

'It's not the way it was. We're organised now, and for the first time we know what we want.'

'Not precisely, though. I think we need to study, study and study. Especially us girls.'

'That's where you're wrong.'

As he said this, Luis's eyes narrowed: Teresa had just pushed her hand into the top of her blouse. She noticed how he was looking at her and suddenly thought that perhaps if she got up and asked him to help her do it up, if he decided to ... (One, two ... the seconds went by.)

'I thought I saw your good-looking *xarnego*'s bike among the pine trees,' Luis said unexpectedly.

Teresa was silent for a while. She stopped fiddling with her blouse, but still feeling cold, pulled up the collar, and sighed.

'He's not mine,' she said. 'And as for good-looking, it has to be said that yes, he is that.'

'Ha!' exclaimed the university hero. 'Caught you! I've caught you! You're crazy about him, just like Maruja. Only sadly for you, you're at a great disadvantage because you are a respectable *señorita*.'

'Yes, my boy, my destiny is to suffer,' Teresa muttered sarcastically.

'You ought to know,' he said, adopting a professorial tone, 'that it's absurd to talk of destiny without relating it to the social status of the world in which you live.'

'Don't talk such nonsense, Luis, please.' She too fell back in her hammock; it was as if the night had swallowed her. 'I've only seen him once, this winter, when he accompanied Maruja home one night, and I've told you what a wonderful impression he made on me then. But joking apart, what Maruja said about him is interesting, don't you think?'

'Maruja didn't say a single word about her boyfriend that made sense.'

'Please don't make fun of her. I mean, the poor girl has only a very vague idea about all this. She did get mixed up when she tried to explain, but I understood at once that he knows how things are, perhaps better than we do, in his own way. At least, the contacts he has are with the workers, and are good ones ...'

'I don't believe it.'

'Why not?'

'I don't know, but I don't believe it. Let's see, just because he works in the Maritima y Terrestre steel factory?'

'I don't know where he works – Maruja couldn't tell me, you know she never remembers names. But you should have seen him that night. His foul temper is hard to forget, and so is the way he looks at you. He's one of those who knows where he stands. He had that ... that class pride, if you follow me? Something neither you nor I could ever possess.'

'Bah,' said Luis. 'He'll be with Felipe or an anarchist, although that remains to be seen. I know them, they're very theatrical. They're very willing, but they're not clear-headed and they lack method. You can check it: try talking to him some day, and you'll soon see his mental confusion. The thing is you like him because he's got balls, which, dammit all, I think is great, but just admit it.'

'Luis, you're becoming really unbearable.'

Now roused, the hero straightened up and climbed back on his pedestal.

'Okay, don't listen to me,' he said in that unctuous political voice of his. 'You know that our lack of unity worries me a lot. Seriously, I admire all of them, and I understand they're doing what they can. It was just my little joke.'

Teresa sat up in the same position as before, legs crossed and a sandal dangling from one foot, her misty eyes fixed on her friend. An awkward silence ensued. They could hear the seconds dripping like drops of water from a leaky tap. Changing the subject, they were still able half-heartedly to exchange opinions about the books they were reading: Teresa was enthusiastic about a Juan Goytisolo novel, *Duel in Paradise* ('I'll lend it to you, remind me later ... it's on my bedside table'), while Luis spoke about *I Ask for Words and Peace*, by Blas de Otero. Teresa poured herself another gin. Luis started going on about the sexual problems of

Spanish youth (another blunder, a very serious one this time). He was leaning forward, accompanying his words with sweeping gestures, head sunk on his chest as if he had the weight of the stars upon him. They began to argue again. Their eyes seemed to be calling to one another, but their mouths were determined to talk, and to talk only of things they knew at second hand. Perhaps it was the alcohol, but Teresa had the impression they were somehow impersonating other people, who had taken them over. She understood they would never emerge from this dead end unless one of them did something quickly. It would have been enough, for example, for him to clasp her hand as he passed her the bottle of gin, or for it to occur to him to put the sandal back on her foot: anything that implied physical closeness. But since he didn't seem willing to take the first step, she decided to do so, regretting that she had perhaps been a bit harsh on him. Like all heroes he was timid and needed help in this kind of battle. She rose to her feet and with a smile took the bottle from Luis's hands.

'I'm not going to let you get drunk, do you hear?' she said, taking advantage of her proximity to ruffle his hair once, twice, three times, and pressing her body against his left shoulder. At the same time, noticing anxiously the dissonance between what she was saying and what her hand was doing, like music out of sync with a dancer's movements, she said, to mitigate her forwardness: 'You have to admit, Luis, that in this country it's all still to do. And you can't make everything change overnight. Not even by sacrificing the best of our youth will we make the course of . . .'

When it seemed to her he was about to get up from the hammock, she turned on her heel and went to her bedroom to leave the bottle of gin there. Her legs began to tremble when she heard his footsteps behind her. Turning round as if in surprise, she discovered herself in his arms.

Even though now as she sat alone in the Villa all that seemed grotesque, mainly due to the strange impression Luis Trías de Giralt had created of being a man-god, it had been a long, arduous journey (and a mistaken one, as she had just bitterly proved) to get where she now found herself. Teresa Serrat was, it should be said, without any trace of malice, one of those brave, outspoken female university students who back then decided that a girl who at twenty knows nothing about a boy will never know anything. And the merit of this has to be recognised when it comes to being faithful and committed to an idea, to youthful generosity and emotional openness, something that was bound to be abused given the state of our country and how inconsistent all of us are regarding our own beliefs. However, if someone, even someone whose mental acuity greatly impressed Teresa – such as, for example, Luis himself, who until tonight had cast his spell over her – if someone had explained that her solidarity with a particular ideology, everything she did both inside and outside the university to organise and lead demonstrations, and above all her leading role in the famous October events, was in fact nothing more than the convoluted expression of a deep-seated, repressed desire to find herself in the arms of her hero on a night like this and become a woman of her time, she would naturally never have believed them, and not even understood what they were saying. But that's what it was: an unconscious, laborious preparation to rid herself of a complex once and for all, a procedure which she was in the habit of saying that, when it came down to it, you had to undergo with the same calm stoicism as one would surgery for appendicitis: because it's a useless, troublesome organ that only creates complications. And although one should not forget the part played by a certain natural disposition (Maruja had defined it in a vulgar but very expressive way: 'The *señorita* is very up for it today'), it should be said in honour of the innocence and beleaguered chastity of our young female students that the intellectual imperatives dominated the physical ones.

This was why – out of pure camaraderie, she was to say later, in a delicious, almost perfect synthesis – Teresa Serrat was allowing herself to be led to the sacrifice, weak and slightly perplexed, to find that her hero was also trembling. Perhaps to lessen the solemnity of the moment, as he led her to bed, arm around her waist, Luis, with the remnants of a bourgeois education they could never curse enough, gave a big yawn in a poor attempt to show how relaxed he was. She was still saying something about an imprisoned student (who would have thought that the poor fellow would serve the noble cause of tomorrow even in this bedroom?) in a miserably fake voice . . . Nothing. They soon became aware of the absence of any ritual, of the need for some kind of sacred fire, and understood the reason behind certain apparently empty ceremonies . . . Anyway, none of that would have helped, because from their first embraces when they were still standing there fully dressed, she sensed that she was going to share her bed to no avail. She did not desire anyone in particular, not Luis or anybody else, simply a depersonalised, faceless being, a sweet, unknown weight she had dreamed of, all the better of course if it were someone who militated in their common cause, but someone almost a stranger, simply a thrusting body, breathless in the dark, words of love, a caress of her hair, nothing more, she didn't ask for anything more. As far as the act itself was concerned, she had a hazy, painless awareness of it, as if in a dream, without fully living it in reality: a true appendicitis operation. Paradoxically, her dream was like that of the spinster princess who in times of war waits, secretly expectant, for her palace to be stormed by faceless soldiers from the invading army. But the fact was that her bed had none of the functional, anaesthetised welcome of the operating theatre, nor the permissible vulnerability of some palaces, with the result that she found herself lying on her side, still dressed and completely lucid, next to an elusive but all too real person, someone who apparently wasn't even going to have time to take off his clothes. Luis Trías de Giralt, the dreamed-of conqueror, the chosen surgeon, was now sweaty, trembling, frightened, Maruja frightened, terribly clumsy and stiff, Manolo stiff – Lord, who would have thought it! – and suddenly deliquescent.

Now, unable to sleep, Teresa was trying unsuccessfully to forget the experience: it was like having someone vomit or die as they clung to her. She had scarcely had time to unbutton her blouse. Nor did she have time to feel his weight: stretched out grasping her shoulders with his hands, like a bird's claws, his damp face buried in her neck as if afraid of a punishment from the heavens, he gave a sudden shudder, his hands clenched horribly on her arms ('*Què fa aquest ximple, però què fa aquest ximple!*' What is this idiot doing, what is this idiot doing!), and shrank, whimpered like a rabbit and was gone.

That was all. Intact, bemused, humiliated, dying of shame, Teresa turned her back on him (never again, never again) and after a while, when she could have heard a fly buzz, she realised he was no longer beside her. It was only then that she took in the voice that had miserably announced, 'I'm going to the bathroom,' and heard running water. When he comes back, he'll start talking about Freud, she thought. Much later – she had no idea either how long it had been – she heard Maruja's boyfriend's motorbike, and was filled with a strange reminder of when she was ten, a sudden, sweet drowsy sensation that led her to tenderly breathe in the warm smell of her pillow, at the same time as her whole body shook with an infinite sadness. As she lay here, curled up in a ball, a feeling of being lonely and helpless made her tuck her head into her chest like a wounded animal. She knew the window was open, that beautiful stars were shining in the sky, that the waves would be lulling her to no avail all night, and that down there, somewhere in the pine wood, a young man with jet-black hair and sardonic eyes still glinting from the frenzy of other kisses had just departed on his motorbike. How false, what unbearable lies were all these nights of hers on the coast, holidaying like a consumptive young maiden in this boring castle of the Villa!

Realising she would never get to sleep, Teresa got up again, put on her bathrobe and left the bedroom. She crossed the first-floor hallway, switched on the lights and started down the staircase. She would have liked to talk to someone – Maruja, for example. It was curious what she was thinking: on the ground floor of this same house, in that small, sordid maid's room, two human beings, two healthy children of the healthy working class, had once more been happy, had loved each other directly, without tormenting themselves with preliminaries or tortuous arguments, without *arrière-pensées* or any other nonsense. How did they manage it? Were they in love? Perhaps. They made love and planned for the future, that was all. The perfect combination. And Teresa knew this wasn't the first time; she had been aware of it since the previous summer. It had been one night when she went down to the kitchen for something or other and saw the strip of light under Maruja's door. She heard voices, and couldn't resist the temptation to peep through the keyhole. What she saw was so beautiful she would never forget it: Maruja was lying on the bed, eyes closed and with a sweet smile on her lips, while the lad, bare-chested and tousle-haired as he sat on the edge of the bed, leaned down to kiss her.

Teresa did not remember she had been unable to sleep that night either, or the details of the strange conversation she had with Maruja the following day, perhaps their last on the beach. They were about to return to Barcelona for the start of the university term, and the weather was no longer so good. The days dawned cloudy and windy, and she was the only one who went down to the beach together with the children, her cousins, whom Maruja was as usual looking after. Around mid-morning, she followed the maid and children into the pine wood, wearing the same bathrobe she had on now. Teresa was carrying a Simone de Beauvoir book Luis had lent her, and which she found fascinating from the opening line ('We know that today's bourgeois is frightened'). She was walking along with the book open, the accusatory phrases leaping up at her in the sun's glare, aware of a delicious tickling sensation in the back of her mind. Familiar voices could be heard in the wood: she knew her uncle Javier, who had arrived from Madrid a couple of days earlier to fetch his wife and children, was with her father and the housekeeper. At his wife's insistence, Señor Serrat had at last reluctantly agreed to go and take a look at the fence destroyed by 'those Sunday louts who come to have their disgusting meals on our property and to go at it like dogs in heat', as Señora Serrat had put it.

Maruja was walking a few metres in front of Teresa with Aunt Isabel's children, who as soon as they reached the wood started to run, without the maid (who didn't realise anybody was watching her) doing anything to control them apart from shouting their names half-heartedly and mumbled something – a bored, irritated refrain apparently directed more at herself than at them. Sometimes when she took them for a swim on her own, Maruja went barefoot, and wore a very short, flowery sleeveless beach robe that Teresa thought looked ghastly. That day, though, Teresa closed the book, smiled sympathetically, and studied the maid closely. In the slow, plodding way Maruja walked she thought she could discern unmistakable signs that persist in the body after a night of love: the maid's head was slightly thrown back on her soft neck, and her chubby, dark arms hung inert by her sides, still bearing traces of the previous night's passionate embraces. Unconsciously, Teresa's eyes remained fixed for a long while on the backs of Maruja's knees as they moved indolently, transmitting the haughty voluptuousness of a married woman. The autumn breeze moulded the loose robe to Maruja's body: in front, the skirt chafed magnificently against her thighs; behind her, it streamed out like flames. For one brief moment, Teresa foresaw the blazing future, the strange, uncertain fate of this young woman walking a few metres in front of her. What can she be thinking? she wondered. She used to tell me everything ... She doesn't confide in me any more. Teresa decided the first thing she should do was to ask her if that lad she received in her room was her fiancé. No, that's stupid. What does it matter if he is or not? She didn't know where to begin. She trailed after her just as she had when they were little girls.

In her mind's eye, she once again saw Maruja's cheerful, dark-skinned face bending over the still waters of the pool. Her eyes were half closed and dreamy, as if she could read her destiny as a grown woman on the sunlit surface of the water, and covered her small, naked breasts with her hand: the image of Maruja as a child bathing in that irrigation pond one summer in the forties somehow brought Teresa's bemused childhood to a close, paving the way for the disturbing marvels of adolescence. She would never forget it, or the words the girl uttered at that moment ('I'll also live in Barcelona some day, like you, Teresa'), because since that afternoon when they had bathed together she became aware (as if suddenly someone had switched a light on by her ear) of the electric buzz life transmits: an awareness of self. That had been six years earlier, when Teresa used to go with her mother to spend the summer at their estate near Reus (they didn't yet own this Villa or live in San Gervasio, but close to Paseo de San Juan, in the Gracia neighbourhood) and the two girls were close friends. Maruja's parents were the caretakers, living in a house alongside the main building with their children and a grandmother who was always busy with her flowers, and looked after the little house as if it were a grand palace. They were Andalusians who had migrated from a village near Granada and were already working there when Teresa's father bought the property, intending to turn it into one of the first poultry farms in Catalonia. Teresa loved those vacations, and was won over from the outset by the warmth of the caretaker family (the opposite of what she felt for the administrator – a *catalán futú*, according to Maruja's grandmother – a man of few words who always arrived on a motorbike as shiny as an insult whose tyres Teresa always wanted to burst, as if practising for the phantom course in rebelliousness and sabotage she was now following at university with her friend Luis Trías). The two friends played together and were in the habit of telling each other all their secrets and desires. Maruja's brother, who was three years older, worked in the fields with his father, and she had little to do with him.

In those days Maruja was a happy, half-wild little girl who made fun of the boys when the two of them went shopping in the village, telling Teresa about the extraordinary things she got up to with them in secret after school. The *señorita* was astonished and impressed. Maruja was a year older than her, a difference that back then – over four summers, from when Teresa was eleven to fourteen – was much more marked when it came to what they regarded as astonishing. Teresa was impressed by Maruja's lively nature and even her looks, which made her seem two years older than her: she was still a pink-faced, frail little girl, with delicate, big blue eyes that, faced with the countryside and her mischievous friend's experience, could only express curiosity and timidity. She admired the caretakers' daughter because, with her cheerful flashing eyes that looked everywhere fearlessly, her dark skin and delightfully uninhibited gestures, her thick black hair that her mother combed every day carefully, religiously (her daughter's mop of hair was apparently the only thing that mattered – to the disgruntlement of Señora Serrat, who saw a certain lack of care for their farmhouse – to that tall, solemn, silent and surprisingly majestic Andalusian woman, who was already incubating the illness that was to carry her off three years later), she was for Teresa the image of life itself.

Later, after her mother died, Señora Serrat decided to take Maruja to Barcelona to help with the housework, and this made Teresa very happy. But in the city, Maruja's new position and the treatment she received as a servant soon snapped the invisible link that had once united them. Teresa's university studies and the passage of time helped widen the divide that money had already secretly opened up between them, in spite of the promises that one afternoon life had whispered in their ears as they bathed in the pond, proudly showing one another their budding breasts. There was nothing to unite them any more. Maruja didn't even seem to notice the change, and it was left to Teresa, with her clearer, more educated mind – above all from sharing the new ideas that had penetrated the university lecture classes – to deeply regret it. She loved Maruja like a sister, offered her advice, gave her dresses, told her how she should comb her hair, wear clothes, and behave in different situations. A few months earlier, she had insisted on introducing her to her closest friends ('This is Maruja, we used to play together when we were little girls') at a party organised in their house. Maruja not only served drinks as usual, with Teresa's help, but towards the end also joined in the celebrations in her own way, alongside her *señorita*, in a dress that was too tight for her and with a slightly silly smile on her face. Fortunately she was asked to dance often enough for her feelings not to be hurt: partly because she was undeniably attractive (she let her partners press up against her when none of the other girls did, and hardly said a word) and also because in reality there was as yet no social ill-feeling among that bunch of infant *señoritos*. But that did not prevent Maruja (unaware that she was there to embody another of Teresa's romantic myths, another gilded legend of a misguided progressive attitude: comradeship through solidarity, beyond class barriers) from having a dreadful time. In addition, her *señorita*'s closeness to her appeared odd to many of her friends, at least at first. Even Luis Trías de Giralt, who took everything in his stride, and whose meditative gaze (he had just come out of prison) heralded important, urgent events, was led that day to ask: 'Who is that gorgeous creature?' And when he was told it was the Serrats' maid, could scarcely believe it. For a moment he was afraid that perhaps Teresa and the proletariat had launched the revolution without him.

But this generous attempt by Teresa to try to integrate Maruja into her world, at least into some private gatherings – she could not for the moment do anything beyond that – came to an end a few months later due to an incident during the celebrations on Saint John's Eve, which she went to accompanied by Luis and Maruja, and where (as she heard later, because, tired of all the idle chatter, she had gone for a spin with her friend Nené and Luis) Maruja, who in theory was only there to help serve, had been seen at the bottom of the garden kissing a gatecrasher who hadn't been thrown out, as the son of the house later explained, all of a sudden displaying the courage that the Murcian's black look had dampened earlier, because they thought he was one of Teresa's weird friends. Once the incident had been cleared up with Maruja, who said she didn't know that cheeky intruder and had not heard from him again, Teresa laughed in the face of the son of the house, and took the opportunity to yet again mock his petit-bourgeois fears and to point out the obvious cracks in the defensive posture of his disgusting class ... On that occasion, Luis had checked her rhetorical impulses and taken the girls home. Teresa told Maruja that not only was she free to do as she pleased, but that in her opinion she had done the right thing in allowing herself to be kissed by a stranger in front of all those stuck-up friends of hers.

'They need to be taught what life is all about,' she insisted. 'You were brilliant, Maruja, I can see you're learning ...'

Sitting beside her in the car, Maruja said nothing. Teresa was oddly stirred: she could see her friend's burning cheeks, how the lipstick had been rubbed off her swollen-looking lips, her mouth enviably possessed, and at that very moment, contradicting all her enthusiasm, a voice inside her whispered that she had never been so distant from Maruja as she was now. The only person there who was freely living a progressive existence was this timid, uneducated child. This was such a clear, simple truth that Teresa felt indescribably sad when it hit her. Maruja had never been persuaded by her progressive ideas, but had always made her own way, quietly and as she saw fit, without needing to embrace any kind of theory; it was obvious she was already well ahead of Teresa, at least as far as amorous experiences were concerned. Who knew whether she had already rid herself of that accursed virginity, thought Teresa.

And now, as was demonstrated once and for all by what she had discovered the previous evening spying through the keyhole, Teresa realised that her suspicions had been well founded. She felt a sincere affection for Maruja, and was pleased that somebody loved her, and yet at the same time she was surprised and disorientated. All of this continued to be a source of covert excitement and envy. Being with Maruja, Teresa felt just the same as she had when they were little girls.

Teresa speeded up until she was alongside Maruja, and linked arms. 'Hey there, sly boots,' she said. Startled at first, Maruja burst out laughing. 'Yes, they're little devils,' added Teresa, referring to the children. 'But you've not long left: they're leaving tomorrow.' Maruja laughed again. She said that when it came down to it, she would miss them: she had enjoyed being with them, and they had made her feel less lonely.

'You're right,' said Teresa. 'I'm also getting bored with these endless summer holidays ... But I'm bored in Barcelona as well. Do you know something? I can't wait for term to start.'

Arm in arm, concentrating in an exaggerated way (they suddenly didn't know what to say next) on where to put their feet, the two of them walked through the wood just behind the children. From a distance came the sound of men's voices.

'Aren't you getting undressed?' asked Teresa, removing her bathrobe.

'I'm not going in today.'

Maruja was setting out the spades and buckets for the children, who immediately rushed off to the edge of the sea. The sun was occasionally disappearing behind clouds, and there was a cool breeze blowing. Teresa stretched out on her towel with the open book ('We have begun to ask ourselves the terrible question: can it be possible that our civilization is not *the civilization*?' wrote Sartre's companion, quoting Jacques Soustelle), then left it lying on her stomach for a moment as she turned to look at Maruja.

'Maruja, there's something I'd like to ask you ...'

Making sure her cousins were far enough away, and possibly due to an unconscious reflex of the urgent desire she had to communicate with the maid, Teresa did what she had often done when she was on her own, here on the beach or on the terrace of the Villa: she pulled down the straps of her bathing costume to expose her breasts to the sun's caress. Maruja, who had been watching the children running about on the beach, suddenly stared at her *señorita*'s pink breasts. Her face remained blank: her thoughts were elsewhere. Then, when she realised what she was doing, she smiled faintly and looked directly at Teresa, who also smiled.

'Mmm . . . it feels good,' said Teresa, opening her book once more. 'Do you remember when we were little girls and used to bathe in the pond at the farm in the summer?'

Maruja absent-mindedly scooped up a handful of sand.

'Yes . . . Did you want to ask me something?'

('Whether he is a proletarian or an intellectual, man is radically cut off from reality,' wrote de Beauvoir, 'his consciousness is passively subjected to ideas, images, and affective states that leave their mark by chance. At times these states are produced by the purely mechanical play of external factors. At other times, they are fabricated by the subject himself, beset by deliriums of imagination.') Teresa made up her mind. Briefly, without displaying any emotion, she told Maruja what she had discovered the previous night. She didn't want to hurt the girl's feelings, or allow her to see the embarrassment felt by a novice when confronted by behaviour which deep down she approved of. All she did was confess her disappointment and surprise at the fact (which she described as suicidal) that she and her boyfriend used the Villa for their encounters.

'Maruja, don't you see they're going to catch you just when you least expect it? What if instead of me being the one who came down to the kitchen last night it had been Mama or Aunt Isabel? Just imagine the row there would have been. Who is he, by the way?'

Maruja started to sob. She hadn't understood that she wasn't being criticised for what she had done, but for doing it in her room at the Villa. She stammered a whole list of excuses on behalf of herself and Manolo; at first this confused Teresa, but subsequently, as she interpreted them according to a peculiar idea she had of young working-class people who give their all in life (she had decided that the maid's boyfriend must be a worker), she was left not only surprised but enchanted.

'We're going to get married, *señorita* . . .' said Maruja.

Teresa smiled, sat up and slid over to her friend to give her a warm hug.

'I'm not talking about that, Mari. Why are you crying? Are you in love?'

Maruja nodded. 'You . . . you won't say anything, will you? You won't give me away?'

'I won't say a word,' Teresa promised. 'How long have you been seeing each other in your room?'

'A few weeks. We'll get married . . . please, Teresa, don't say anything. I'll ask him not to come here any more . . . He is what he is, but he's very good really. He's like you, sometimes he's so . . . so revolutionary, he gets angry at the slightest excuse . . . But the bad thing is that . . . sometimes I think he has to hide, and that's the only reason he comes to see me.'

'What do you mean?'

'Oh, *señorita*, I'm not sure I should say anything. I don't dare. Promise you won't tell anyone.'

('The woman who bleeds and gives birth will have a deeper "instinct" of the things of life than the biologist. The peasant has a more accurate intuition of the earth than a licensed agronomist,' de Beauvoir had explained to Teresa.)

'Come on, child, don't be silly – aren't we friends any more? Why should your fiancé want to hide, and who from?'

Teresa was almost certain she knew, but wanted confirmation. She pretended not to be interested, with the book open in front of her, but in fact she was busy reading between the lines, listening closely to the words spoken by Marujita de Beauvoir, the enviable companion of Manolo Sartre or Jean-Paul Interloper, whichever you preferred.

'Well . . .?'

'It's such a shameful thing,' Maruja was saying. 'If one day he finds out I've told you, he'll be furious. And besides, there's nothing to be done about it, more's the pity . . .'

'Whoa, my child, calm down; it's not like you're talking to Mama. Come on, tell me, perhaps I can help . . .'

Maruja swallowed hard, looked a couple of times at the *señorita*, and twice shook her head. Teresa, who was holding the book in one hand and pressing the swimming costume against her chest with the other, sighed and lay back once more, visibly upset by her friend's lack of trust. 'As you wish, child.' ('In practice, the bourgeoisie is committed to the class struggle,' de Beauvoir whispered in her ear.)

'It's ridiculous,' she exclaimed, without looking at Maruja. 'Do you know what I think? That you also have lots of silly prejudices, Mari.'

She pulled her swimsuit down again. By now the sun was hot. She became aware of a gentle warm sensation in her breasts and, reacting nervously, cupped them in the palm of her hands. She did this hastily, as if to defend herself, although she wasn't really thinking about it: she had no idea that in fact the feeling of sensual arousal she had longed for was now enveloping her and her ideas; she vaguely sensed that, by prowling round the Villa and her own idle life, this anonymous worker somehow symbolised the evolution of society. Her nipples, like early lilac-coloured grapes, slipped through her fingers. And all at once she was sure: she didn't know if it was the brusque irruption of the worker into her mind, or the sun's rays that sent a shiver right through her, but something forced her to sit up; perhaps it was what Maruja finally, screwing up her courage, was confessing about her Manolo. But the maid fell silent almost as soon as she started to speak: she didn't have the courage to pronounce the terrible word (thief) that would have explained everything, and the memory of the planned robbery of Señora Serrat's jewels, even though it was still only a vague idea, drew a sob from her that definitively confirmed Teresa's heroic imagination.

'I knew that's what it was,' said Teresa, as though talking to herself. 'I don't know why, but I was sure of it. How did you meet him?'

'At the par— At a meeting of friends.' (I'm not going to tell her he's the one who was at the garden party. She might think he gate-crashed to steal something there.) 'Yes, in a private house.'

'He's a worker, isn't he? I was sure of it.' Teresa wasn't in the least bit interested in hearing Maruja's reply: there was now a slight hint of dismay in her voice, a sense of loss, just as when they were children and she asked her friend for the details of her passionate escapades with the boys. For some reason, perhaps because she was suddenly aware of the superhuman presence of the young workman, Teresa rapidly pulled up the straps on her costume. 'Does he often take you to these meetings?'

'No, he doesn't ... Oh, Teresa, I tell him, I beg him not to do it, because it's very dangerous, and that the best thing would be for us to get married and live a quiet life, but he ...'

'Where does he work?'

Surprised by the turn the questions were taking, Maruja was about to reply that unfortunately he didn't work anywhere, but Teresa interrupted her:

'And another thing: do you help him?'

Maruja flushed with pure, saintly indignation.

'Me! God forbid ...! He's crazy, completely ungrateful, he only remembers me when it suits him ... I'm fed up with him, so fed up with him!'

'All right, calm down,' Teresa said pensively. 'And don't talk like that. There are things you can't understand, Mari.'

'Me . . .? What can I do, the Lord help me? I love him, I love him . . . and you don't know the worst, *señorita*, the crazy idea he has right now!'

She was about to tell Teresa about the jewels, but the *señorita* didn't seem to be listening, or rather was listening to her and looking at her in a very special way. The expression on her face was that of a music lover: thanks to the illusory enthusiasm of her imagination, Teresa was staring at the maid without seeing her, and wasn't really paying attention to her explanations, but rather to a tune she could hear between her words. With a smile, she put her arm round Maruja's heaving back, and said: 'Everything will be all right, child, don't worry.' She stared dreamily at the sea, already thinking about how she would tell Luis. Here's a surprise: the country isn't in such bad shape as some people believe, life isn't as monotonous as we think in this bittersweet almond that is our summer vacation, our upper-class bad faith. Things are being done, people are at work, plotting things . . . She sighed.

Maruja had no idea what to do (she would later recall a curious coincidence: one of the books she had found on the *señorita*'s bed when she was cleaning her room was called *What is to be Done?*) and so decided to lie back on the sand and dry her tears. At that moment, the eldest boy came up behind them with his plastic bucket full of water and poured it over Teresa.

'José Miguel, you idiot!' shrieked Teresa. 'Don't come near me or I'll give you what for! Look what you've done!'

Teresa was soaked, as were her bathrobe, towel, cigarettes, the Simone de Beauvoir book, her blond hair and sun-kissed breasts. She was furious. Her cousin stood motionless in front of her, laughing with the empty bucket in his hands. Teresa did up the bathing costume straps once and for all, while Maruja gestured to the boy.

'Come here, José Miguel.' When he approached her, she wiped his nose with a handkerchief, pulled his trunks up over his little stomach, and sent him on his way with an affectionate pat on the backside. 'Keep an eye on your sister. Don't let her get too close to the water. Or better still, go and fetch her, and all of you come back here. We can play forfeits.'

As she was drying herself, Teresa looked sadly at her friend, silently turned the towel over and lay back down on it. Maruja collapsed on to her back on the sand. Her head was only a few centimetres from Teresa's, and every now and then she would glance out of the corner of her eye at the *señorita*'s adorable profile and her wet blond locks as she stared up into the sky. What can she be thinking? Doesn't she want to know anything more about Manolo? Of course, thought Maruja. Nobody could help her.

'Have a smoke,' said Teresa, offering her the cigarettes. Their heads came together above the match's violet flame as they leaned over to protect it from the breeze. For a few seconds it was as if they were reading the same book or sharing the same idle curiosity. 'Where does he live?'

'Who? Manolo?'

'Yes.'

'In Monte Carmelo.'

'Monte Carmelo . . .? Oh yes, I remember.'

She smiled, as if something funny had just occurred to her, and was about to carry on speaking when she heard the voices of her father and Uncle Javier behind her. To judge by the way they were laughing, they weren't talking any more about the damage to the fence caused by loutish Sunday couples trespassing on private property. Maruja stood up before they reached them and went off to join the children. Teresa understood she was leaving so that they didn't see she had been crying.

All this was merely the result of confused, disparate emotions. Maruja regretted her confession to the *señorita*, and from then on, whenever Teresa asked about her fiancé, she gave only vague answers. She noticed that the way Teresa treated her seemed more flexible, more sensitive somehow, than was warranted by her role in the household. She frequently caught Teresa observing her with a fixed stare as she was carrying out her daily chores (laying the table, for example, or answering the telephone), as if searching for heaven knows what secret meaning to her actions. As soon as the *señorita* realised Maruja had noticed, the stare would turn into an affectionate smile or a wink that implied complicity. What was going through that blond head at those moments remained a mystery to the maid. When, during the winter months in Barcelona, Teresa by chance was able to see the good-looking Murcian from up close and even exchange a few words with him through the garden railing, the extravagant idea she had formed of the young worker that day on the beach became fixed in her mind like dogma. Prior to that, she had sensed the happy possibility gliding over her like the rays of the sun on her bare breasts: a dreamed-of caress. But once she had met him, she was utterly convinced of it. Luis Trías refused to believe her when she told him about her marvellous discovery in great detail (embroidering her version with exciting hints of a supposed active workers' militancy that would have astonished poor Maruja). In order to make sure, the prestigious student leader, who when it was a question of people's identity adopted a grave air of responsibility straight out of the Central Committee (something that tremendously impressed Teresa), attempted to ask the maid more questions. On that occasion Maruja gave definite proof, if not of her intelligence, at least of an instinct for self-preservation that was characteristic – as Teresa saw it – of the disciplined members of secret societies: she pretended she couldn't follow the political import of his questions. Her fiancé must have forbidden her to talk to anyone about her activities, as a security measure. What more proof did Luis need?

This and similar reflections about Maruja's good fortune – so different to hers that night, which had been such a disaster – were filling Teresa Serrat's mind as she walked down the staircase in the Villa, still hesitating about whether or not to wake Maruja for a chat. She crossed the hallway, switched on the living-room lights, stretched out on the couch and picked up a copy of *Elle*. Soon, though, she threw the magazine on to the floor, stood up again, her eyes moist as she recalled something (never again, never), went into the kitchen (there was no light from under Maruja's door), poured herself a glass of fruit juice from the refrigerator, was on the verge of tears – the silence in the house was preying on her nerves – straightened up, walked back along the passageway (still no light under the door), entered the living room and, glass in one hand and the copy of *Elle* in the other, lay back on the couch, her raised knees swaying nervously from side to side. The murmur of the waves was barely audible. Beyond the barred window, on the sea's horizon, a first pink glow was spreading. The bathrobe fell open as her knees moved regularly to and fro. Lying on her back, Teresa tried to submerge her wounded femininity in the bright, welcoming world of *Elle*, with its silk dresses and models with perfect skin. Unconsciously, the soft sway of her burning thighs began to follow the rhythm of the waves. It would soon be day. Just when she had managed to take an interest in what she was reading (the horoscope) something caught her attention: the chafing of her own skin. She stopped moving her legs. Her blue eyes were veiled as if by a layer of frost. It was there, hunched on the couch, head bowed on her chest and hair obscuring her face, that the bitter tears at the death of a beautiful myth began to drip on to the glossy pages of *Elle*, whose horoscope did in fact predict: '*Cet été vous changerez d'amour.*'

Oriol Serrat entered the Balmes clinic, said a friendly hello to the doorman, climbed the stairs with unexpected agility for a fifty-year-old and walked down the stuccoed first-floor corridor until he came to the door of Room 21. Stopping for a moment to wipe the sweat from his brow with a handkerchief, then, hand on his side as if he had a kidney pain, opened the door and went in: '*Ja estic emprenyat.*' I don't have much time. It was eleven in the morning.

Bathed in the milky light filtering through the Venetian blinds, his wife and daughter were sitting in the small room adjacent to the one where Maruja lay prostrate. They were talking to one another in an undertone.

'How is she?' he asked.

'The same,' said Señora Serrat, taking handkerchiefs and some clothes out of a bag. 'All she does is call for someone called Manolo . . . Have you had breakfast?'

'Who is that?'

'You can imagine. Have you had breakfast?'

'Yes, woman.'

'He's her fiancé, Mama,' cut in Teresa, slumped in a leather armchair. 'Her fiancé, I've told you. And we ought to tell him.'

'That's all very well, but as far as I know, Maruja doesn't have a boyfriend, and never has.'

'You don't know anything, Mama.'

'Fine, do as you like. I'm not bothered about that. The person we need to tell, and as soon as possible, is her father.'

As she said this, she glanced at her husband, as though expecting him to agree with her suggestion. But Señor Serrat ignored her and headed towards Maruja's room, his shoes squeaking on the pale-green tiled floor. He opened the door a little and peered in. Maruja's head poked out from the sheets: her eyes were closed, her lips half open and her chin raised, as if she was about to drink from an invisible fountain. Her pallid forehead was bathed in sweat. In a chair close to the window sat a young nurse reading a magazine. She lifted her head to look in the direction of the door. Señor Serrat acknowledged her with a slight smile, before closing the door again. Good, the nurse was there and the maid was being monitored and looked after, so everything was going perfectly, as he had been expecting. A private expression of reproach and annoyance flitted across his face, not directed at anyone except possibly himself. He turned to look at his wife and daughter, who were still talking in hushed tones, then walked back across the room to an armchair. Stuffed in his blue summer suit, his face was flushed and he was breathing heavily through the nose. He walked with the palms of his hands turned backwards, moving them not with his usual freedom but with a discreet restraint, as if afraid to stir the clinic's uncontaminated air. His arm movements had a certain mechanical rigidity to them reminiscent of a recently oiled, smooth-running machine. Oriol Serrat was tall, thickset, with hair going white at the temples and a grey-speckled thin moustache. His long, dark-skinned face with its heavy jowls and stubborn or severe-looking chin (an unintentional severity created partly by the habitual use of a pipe, which had deformed his jaw so that it looked as if he were just about to spit or curse) still displayed the remnants of the kind of virile beauty fashionable in the thirties, a kind of poor

Catalan version of Warner Baxter. The vague look of a junior officer occasionally flitted across his features, so that aesthetically at least he looked like a member of that distinguished clique of meticulous, anonymous and identical middle-aged men who apparently wished to proclaim for ever their youthful support for the victorious Nationalists thanks to a carefully groomed and curiously trimmed military moustache. But beyond any ironic comment inspired by this humdrum attractiveness, Oriol Serrat stood out thanks to his small, pointed mouth that always mimicked that sly look possessed by ruminants and some Catalan businessmen – a truly curious, speculative little mouth with a life of its own, ready to pout sceptically at the least sign of what he considered a futile display of intelligence (for example, talking about politics). Before sitting down he glanced across at his wife, hand still on his painful side. His wife knew this gesture well: it almost always preceded a bad-tempered outburst.

'Marta,' he said, dropping into the armchair, 'may I remind you that your sister is arriving from Madrid this afternoon and that you ought to be in Blanes to receive her . . . There's nothing more we can do here, and this is going to be a long-drawn-out business. I think it's absurd for you to spend hours sitting here doing nothing, when you know full well . . .'

'Oriol . . .'

'. . . that we've already done everything we should. There's a nurse with her day and night. What more do you want? Go back to the Villa. I'll be there tomorrow or the day after, once I've sorted out a few things. It's enough for you to come and visit her from time to time . . .'

'Oriol, please, lower your voice,' Señora Serrat begged her husband. Looking at him, she paused long enough for it to become obvious she thought silence was good for Maruja. 'We'll do what's best, but in a calm manner.' She turned to her daughter.

'Teresa, what do you want to do . . . ? Just look, the poor girl is at her wits' end.'

Overcome with tiredness, Teresa was dropping off to sleep.

'I'm staying,' she murmured.

'Another one being silly,' her father grunted. 'You should go home and get some sleep.'

'I'm fine, Papa.'

'She hasn't slept for three nights, and her nerves are ragged,' said her mother, trying in vain to lay her hand on her daughter's forehead.

'Oh Mama, let me alone – I'm fine!'

Her blue eyes, sad-looking beneath her fine, smooth eyelids, glanced around the room. Maruja had been brought to the clinic three days earlier in a grave condition that had not improved, and Teresa had spent those nights, as well as a previous one her parents knew nothing about, almost without sleep. Since early that morning when, dozing on the couch in the Villa's living room (the copy of *Elle* having slipped from her grasp hours before), she was awakened by the cook's screams, she had been unwilling to leave her friend's side. It was the old cook Tecla who had found Maruja unconscious on her bed when she went to wake her up, surprised at how late she was. With her help and that of the housekeeper, who kept on talking about a cold shock response or sunstroke, Teresa, anxious and filled with a vague feeling of remorse, had immediately wrapped Maruja in a blanket, put her in her car and taken her to the dispensary in Blanes. From there the maid was transferred by ambulance to a private clinic in Barcelona, where Señor Serrat, alerted by a telephone call from his daughter, had made sure everything was ready for her, and was waiting with his wife and Doctor Saladich, the clinic director who was a close friend of the family. Teresa followed the ambulance in her car. Doctor Saladich wanted to know what

Maruja had done the day before, and Teresa told him of her fall on the steps down to the jetty.

'But she didn't hurt herself,' she said. 'At least that's what we thought then. She spent all afternoon with me, and in the evening we drove into Blanes. She was very sleepy, and went to bed early . . . What time do you think she lost consciousness?'

'Perhaps while she was asleep, or this morning when she got up; it's hard to tell,' said the surgeon, adding that it could sometimes take days between an accident and losing consciousness. An operation was not necessary, simply complete rest. 'We can't operate,' he added, 'because the symptoms aren't clear. There is no bruising, apart from extensive small hemorrhagic suffusions' (small wounds that didn't justify surgery, he clarified, glancing at the distraught Señora Serrat, who was in a dreadful state). It was very serious, but all one could do was wait.

Maruja had not recovered consciousness, only occasionally whispering a few incomprehensible words. Teresa spent that night and the following one in an armchair alongside her friend's bed. From time to time Maruja groaned feebly in her drowsy state and called out the name of Manolo. Just once she had opened her eyes and stared at Teresa, but seemed to be looking straight through her. From that moment on, she appeared to have lapsed into a much deeper, alarming lethargy. Doctor Saladich made sure a nurse was always with her.

'Did you see?' Señora Serrat said to her husband when she recognised the nurse on the day shift. 'It's that girl Saladich introduced us to last summer at the hotel in Palma . . .' Her husband cut her short tetchily, saying she was mistaken.

For the first two days, Teresa's mother had stayed at the clinic until midnight, trying to convince her daughter to get some rest. 'Maruja and I will leave here together,' Teresa responded, 'or me on my own, if we are unlucky. Until then, I'm not moving.' At about four in the morning on the third night, Teresa was sure Maruja was about to die. Feeling terribly alone, she began to cry in the nurse's arms. 'Maruja, Mari . . .' she sobbed. She could still see her waving from the top of the steps above the jetty, then her legs flailing and those stupid sandals flying through the air, and when she recalled Luis Trías, her ridiculous argument with him and their unfulfilled embrace, the tears flowed so hard she even moved the nurse, a flighty girl from Mallorca with an aquiline nose, bright red mouth and ample hips who coincidentally had just had her appendix removed (entirely successfully) by Doctor Saladich himself. The nurse took her in her arms ('*No plori, confiem en es doctor . . .*' Don't cry – we must trust the doctor . . .) and advised her to go home, but Teresa was determined to stay. She would study Maruja's suffering face, her forehead bathed in sweat, her lips moving occasionally, always mouthing the same word: Manolo. At nine o'clock Teresa went out for a coffee; when she returned she found her father with her mother, who seemed not to be paying much attention to what her husband was saying.

'There's nothing more to be said, Marta. You take the car, I don't need it.'

He knew that after putting up token resistance, his wife would accept, but he didn't want an argument. He looked at her. Wearing a cotton dress with big African appliqué motifs in red and blue, and holding a beach bag of the same material, she was sitting upright in her armchair, legs together and her back to the Venetian blinds. The indirect, floating light showed her off to good effect. She was much better preserved than her husband: at forty-five, her muscle tone was still remarkably firm, without any apparent sign of sagging. Whenever he saw her running along the beach followed by her dogs, nephews and nieces, her skin burnished by water and sun, a surprised Señor Serrat was obliged to admire the secret power of her body, while being reminded that life is not always harmonious: he was a terribly jealous man. And yet, although he had no real idea why, every time he looked at his wife's legs, he was reassured. Marta Serrat had firm, slightly heavy legs, but her ankles were shapeless, red and sunburnt, something she always refused to acknowledge. She also had a delicate oval face that looked slightly English thanks to her prominent chin, freckles and watery eyes, not to mention her hair that appeared so youthful she could wear it in almost exactly the same way as her daughter. This meant she kept the air of a distinguished young girl that Señor Serrat had so admired in his youth (a difficult, wayward youth, it had to be said, a fact that was little known to his friends of today) and which still gave him secret qualms. But when it came down to it, his wife had truly Catalan legs: strong, familiar, comfortable, reassuring legs that spoke of their owner's mental stability and unshakeable loyalty (apart possibly from some small adventures) to the comforts of home and obedience to her husband, legs which in the end embodied submission and even financial complicity, the symbols of a robust common sense, a solid Catalan virtue. Her legs declared: 'Whatever you wish, Oriol.'

Brought up in a musty world of weighty encyclopedias and learned tomes (her father, from an illustrious family fallen on hard times, taught French at the Instituto de Palma de Mallorca before the Civil War), Marta Serrat was in the habit of occasionally condoning surprising things – for example, her daughter's rebelliousness at the university on behalf of culture – but always let her husband decide everything.

'Saladich will keep us informed by telephone,' he was now saying, 'and besides, you can drop in from time to time. Teresa can do as she pleases.'

'I'm staying here, Papa.'

'But where will you eat?' her mother wanted to know. 'Vicenta is coming with me – I need her. Poor Tecla couldn't manage on her own there, especially not now Isabel is arriving with your cousins . . .'

As well as Maruja and the cook, the family had another servant, an elderly woman from Valencia who stayed in Barcelona until August to look after Señor Serrat, who because of work could only spend weekends at the Villa.

'I need Vicenta here,' he protested.

'It's only for a few days,' said his wife. 'You can eat in a restaurant.'

Señor Serrat had heard enough. He rose to his feet. 'It's not a matter of a few days, Marta. You heard Saladich: the girl could be like this for a week or for six months . . .'

All at once they heard a stifled sob from near the window. Teresa had leapt up and had her back to them. Her honeyed shoulders, left bare in her pink dress, were trembling in the stripes of light filtering through the Venetian blinds.

'Teresa, my child,' exclaimed her mother, going over to her. 'There, there, don't cry . . .'

'How can you talk like that when she's just next door!' the blonde, politically aware student said accusingly.

Her mother took her by the shoulders and made her sit down next to her. She looked at her husband as if to say: 'See what you've done?' But what she actually said was: 'Well, we'll have our hands full with this girl's tragedy, that's for sure.'

'Has Saladich been in yet?' bellowed her husband, peering at his watch.

'Half an hour ago. Please, I'm asking you to tell your daughter she has to go home and get some rest . . .'

Señor Serrat was less concerned about his daughter's tears than the fact that for the past three days he had been arriving half an hour late everywhere.

'And what did he say?'

Passing a handkerchief to Teresa, his wife sighed.

'What do you expect? The same as yesterday. That we have to wait, that there's nothing to be done. My God, I don't understand how this girl can have given herself such a blow . . .! She must have had something wrong in the head already.'

'Calm down, Marta.'

'I tell you, we need to speak to Lucas.'

'I don't think that's necessary for now. We're doing everything we can. We lose nothing by waiting a while, and if we can spare that poor man some heartbreak . . .'

That poor man Lucas was Maruja's father, out at the Reus farm. Puffing and panting from the heat, Señor Serrat headed for the door. 'Well, anyway,' he added, 'I'll see if I can make a quick trip to Reus. Now I'm going to find Saladich. I'll be back to take you home.' He went out, closing the door carefully behind him.

Teresa had stood up once more and was standing facing the blinds, her back to her mother and her arms folded.

'Are you still thinking of going to El Carmelo?' her mother asked.

Irritated, Teresa closed her eyes. At first, her mother had not been against informing Maruja's fiancé; she was even glad that the maid was engaged, and that there was somebody else to share this misfortune. But when she learned where Manolo lived, her attitude changed dramatically.

'Monte Carmelo! I'm responsible for Maruja to her father,' she said. 'You should have warned me about her relationship with that individual.'

'He's her fiancé, Mama.'

'Her fiancé! He's one of those shameless louts who take advantage of maids like her. I'm sure that's what he is. Besides, he lives in El Carmelo. Please, daughter, forget about it. You never know what could happen in a place like that . . .'

To Señora Serrat, Monte Carmelo was somewhere akin to the Congo, a distant, sub-human country with its own very different laws. Another world. Occasionally through the rose-tinted lens of her current existence, she was assailed by distant red flashes: an old anti-aircraft gun firing from the top of El Carmelo, shaking the window panes in the entire neighbourhood (during the Civil War they lived in Gracia, where people baptised the thundering gun 'Grandpa'). She also recalled, from the early post-war years, the rowdy gangs of filthy youngsters who every so often swarmed down from El Carmelo, Guinardó and Casa Baró to spread like thick lava over the peaceful upper districts of the city, with their ball-bearing trolleys, their exploding carbide tins and stone-throwing battles: real hordes. The children of war refugees, urchins armed with catapults and leather slings, they smashed streetlamps and hung from the back of trams. All this was in Señora Serrat's mind as she said to her daughter:

'You won't remember now, but when you were a little girl, a brute from El Carmelo very nearly killed you . . .'

Teresa gave an odd smile: for a split second she again breathed in the dampness of that dark recess in her home, close to Paseo de San Juan, remembering the heavy breathing, the strong smell of acetone given off by the boy's clothes, and his filthy hand grabbing her plaits, forcing her to turn her head slowly and repeat several times that strange word ('Say Zapastra, rich kid, say it!' 'Zapastra.').

'Of course I remember, Mama. Zapastra!'

'At least let Luis go with you.'

'I've told you, I don't need anyone to chaperone me.'

Smiling, she turned round and went to sit with her mother. She put an arm round her shoulders. All that had happened a long time ago, when things were bad for everyone and she was still a fearful little girl. Now everything was different, there were no hooligans in Monte Carmelo, she said, kissing her mother's cheek, a kiss intending to convey that she would do exactly as she pleased anyway. She would go to El Carmelo alone. She stared at her mother with sparkling, stubborn eyes, indicating that this was more than a spoiled child's whim. Eight months earlier, when Teresa had problems with the police and was on the point of being expelled from university, her mother had found herself confronted by the same expression. And just as she had then, she now said, somewhat anxiously: 'You're the same as your poor grandfather, daughter.' And just as on that occasion, she was wrong again.

When her husband came to collect her, she rose to her feet.

'I hope,' she said to Teresa, 'that you don't do anything rash, and that you come back to Blanes as soon as possible. Put these clothes in the wardrobe.' She opened the door to Maruja's room and glanced at her bed. 'See you soon,' she said to the nurse, then shut the door once more. 'And keep me up to date with everything. Call me tomorrow. Bye, and behave.'

Teresa went into Maruja's room and put the clothes in the wardrobe.

The nurse smiled at her. 'She doesn't need any of that.'

'My mother's idea,' said Teresa. She went over to the bedhead. Maruja still lay there without moving, her eyes stubbornly closed, eyebrows knitted, in the grip of who knew what obsession or vision. He has to see her, he must see her, Teresa told herself. Every time she gazed at that pallid mask, she caught a glimpse of a terrifying emptiness: the waxy eyelids, the pain-wracked brow clouded by some inner voice or vision. In her pursed, ashen lips, Teresa vainly sought, beyond indications of lost virginity, of love and death, other signs that would set the maid apart for having at the very least brushed against some as yet unacknowledged truths, penetrated into unknown regions of the future, that would explain why this strange, needy child was always ahead of her, lived more urgently, more passionately and intensely than she did . . .

'Listen,' she said all of a sudden, looking at the nurse. 'Can a friend come to visit her?'

The Mallorcan nurse spoke in a professional tone, like the soporific cooing of a dove.

'The doctor doesn't want more than two people in the room.' Then after a short pause: 'Of course, if it's only for a moment . . . who is it?'

'Her fiancé.'

The nurse lowered her eyes. The white stockings made her shapely legs look fat.

She was driving the Floride slowly up to the top of El Carmelo, improvising an amusing, hazy, incognito personality (blond hair hidden beneath her red headscarf, blue eyes shielded by her sunglasses). In the bend round the side entrance to Parque Güell, by the Cottolengo, on the esplanade where children play football, she was able with complete impunity to contemplate the strange statuesque group of what no doubt had once been a military band – two old drums and a battered bugle sounding an endless, monotonous reveille in the midst of the rocky landscape – standing to attention as if they were blind or like all those men who finally had something to do, a reason for living. They were skinny, shaven-headed youngsters in baggy trousers held up by plastic belts, faded army shirts, standing tall as they obeyed distant orders with a pathetic martial air. It was no more than an instant, a signal, a glint of the sun on the bugle's burnished metal, a rare trembling in the drums' neurotic sadness, but it was enough for Teresa to make a jubilant, hazy promise to herself: from now on . . . She carried on to the top of El Carmelo and it was only when she braked (coincidentally very close to the bicycle workshop) and saw half-naked urchins playing and a few busybodies approaching the car that she realised that, for a start, she should have left it at the bottom of the hill and walked up, so as not to attract attention. The midday sun was beating down, the air completely still, and the sound of the bugle and drums seemed to be coming from all sides.

The beautiful, almost unreal combination of girl and car produced a shimmering mirage that faded like a siesta dream; not only the youngsters, who by now were crowding round her, but some of the women neighbours watched from their doorways as Teresa got out of her car in her pretty pink dress with its thin shoulder straps and her high-heeled white shoes. Momentarily disoriented, she recovered and asked one of the boys: 'Hey, little one, do you know someone by the name of Manolo?'

The answer came from the bakery doorway: two broad smiles or grimaces melting in the heat, two fat but still young women shielding their eyes from the sun with their hands. 'Here, lady, in the workshop . . .' one of them called out, glaring at the girl's bare shoulders. But the boy was pointing to the end of the street, next to the chapel. 'No, he's by the fountain.'

Teresa thanked him and set off, preceded by a group of children spontaneously accompanying her, to the sound of drums and a bugle. As she passed the Bar Delicias she heard indecent catcalls that did not manage to drown out a plaintive note from the band, and saw two young men in polo shirts, arms around each other's shoulders, supporting one another as they followed her with their eyes. Further on, by the fountain, Teresa saw another group of children who almost completely obscured the coppery gleam of a bare wet back leaning into the stream of water. The heads all turned as one: Teresa came on slowly, untying the headscarf (she had no intention of taking off her sunglasses) so that the gold of her flowing locks shone. The youngsters thronged around her with short, rapid steps, arms waving happily, their small heads almost brushing up against the elegant swirl of her pink skirt, like pilot fish guiding or protecting her. When she came to a halt a couple of metres from the fountain, a tiny special envoy detached himself from the group and pointed: 'That's Manolo.'

The Murcian still had the back of his hand under the gushing water, his bare torso twisting and turning (in her mind's eye she suddenly recalled the night when she saw him bending over Maruja to kiss her) and the kids began to tug at him. He looked asleep or drugged. He didn't hear Teresa's greeting, but did catch her timid question ('You remember me, don't you?') and turned his head to look at her. Maruja is dead, he thought, and carried on splashing water over his body, before finally straightening up. 'Yes, hello there.' The water streamed from his skin; his body shone in the sun like dark, dusty silk. He snorted as he shook his head, his powerful neck tense, his hair soaking. He groped for the polo shirt a boy was holding for him; his dark abdomen, muscled like a tortoise shell, was heaving like a frightened animal's: he was panicking.

'Fancy seeing you here.'

'I've brought bad news . . .' she said. 'About Maruja.'

'Who?'

'Maruja, your fiancée . . .'

Manolo was staring down at the ground with half-closed eyes. He tilted his head and rubbed his neck. The polo shirt was still in his hand; he didn't seem to want to put it on. Did he prefer to wait until he was dry, or was he acting out one of those brightly coloured images he had been collecting since childhood? That was probably it. Not for nothing were all the children staring at him expectantly: they instinctively sensed the air of adventure surrounding the Interloper, even when they saw him wandering round the neighbourhood, alone and bored. Down below, the drums and bugle were playing the call to arms.

'I don't have a fiancée,' he said all of a sudden. 'And I don't know any Maruja.'

For a moment, Teresa was stunned. Then she smiled and said: 'I understand.'

The Murcian seemed to be lost in thought, staring at the

ground, hands on hips. He looked up at her. Those sunglasses. He had always hated talking to people who hid their eyes behind dark glasses. Three horrible, despairing days without knowing whether he had left Maruja dead or alive, and now he had to guess the answer through those damned dark glasses. 'Hey, kids, off you go, get out of here!' he shouted, but they took little notice.

'I understand,' Teresa repeated. 'But there's nothing to be afraid of.' And in the same patronising voice as she had once said to him, 'We're all on your side,' she now added: 'No need to worry, I know everything.'

Turning his back on her, Manolo stroked the curly hair of the boy closest to him: he was still panicking. What was this blonde girl after? What did she know?

'She's very ill,' said Teresa. 'She slipped on the jetty, hit her head and has been unconscious for several days. She calls for you . . .'

The Murcian had begun putting on his polo shirt (it was black, with very short sleeves and a wind rose printed on the chest). He was holding it over his head, searching for the armholes; the sides of his body and the underside of his arms were a pale-brown, almost luminous colour. 'Where did she fall?' he asked, his panic subsiding. But Teresa suddenly seemed dejected and was talking about something else.

'. . . my fault, of course, entirely mine. Because if I hadn't given her those sandals, if I hadn't made her hurry up . . . She's so obliging, you know what she's like . . .'

'Where is she? At the Villa?'

'No, here, in a clinic. My, what a disaster. I thought we had to tell you, that you'd want to see her . . .'

'Of course.'

'Shall we go now?'

The kids fell back as he took a few steps towards the road,

pushing past Teresa and coming to a halt. He still didn't understand a thing, not a thing ... He saw her sports car parked fifty metres away, surrounded by onlookers (free from Rosa for a while, with time to drink a vermouth in the Bar Delicias, Bernardo, by now completely under her thumb, was one of those there, admiring the car's dazzling lines with his ape-like curiosity). A little further off, in the workshop doorway, his brother was about to close up.

'Now?' he mused. 'Do we have time?'

'If you like,' said Teresa, coming alongside him. 'Afterwards I can bring you back.'

'You don't mind?'

'Oh no, not at all. I have the whole day to myself.' There was something very intimate about the way she said this, which did not escape Manolo. She went on: 'In fact it could be said I'm alone in Barcelona. It's the first time that's happened to me during the holidays.' To compensate for who knows what emotional trouble, she quickly added: 'Bah, in the past I would have been delighted, but now I'm not so sure ... It's all the same to me. Besides, I can't stop thinking about Maruja.'

The car upholstery gave off a sweet smell of polish. Poor Bernardo was simply dumbfounded as he stood aside to let Manolo through: he circled round the Floride at a safe distance, like an old, rheumy wolf around a flock he knows he can no longer catch. The Interloper made a mess of closing the car door (as he feared he would) in a way that, contrary to what he feared, Teresa found charming. 'Leave it, don't worry,' she said, leaning over him (her fragrant shoulder brushed his chin) to open it again. 'Like this, look? Pull hard,' she said, tugging the door shut. The car set off, the children running after it until it reached the first turning, where they came to a halt to watch it slowly zigzagging down the hill.

By the time they reached Parque Güell, Teresa had told him all about Maruja's fall at the jetty and how she was found unconscious the next morning, fifteen hours after the accident. She decided to keep for later the fact that she knew that he, Manolo, had been with Maruja that night. As he listened, he stared straight ahead of him, his face solemn, arms folded across the wind rose on his polo shirt. It all sounded quite complicated. Closing his eyes, he again saw Maruja coming drowsily into her bedroom, eyes feverish, wearily dragging her feet. So she was already injured, she had already hit her head when he slapped her in bed: he wasn't to blame! What he didn't understand was how Teresa and her friend could invite a maid to go with them on their motorboat, and why they hadn't told her to go back to the Villa after she fell. One thing was clear: for some reason, perhaps out of carelessness, they had really messed Maruja up. 'You're a fool, they'll always cheat you,' he recalled telling her more than once. He felt sorry for her, but at the same time he was relieved, because that night when he abandoned her on her bed, he had thought she was dead. Teresa meanwhile was driving her car gently; there was a deliciously mythical dimension to the way her hands moved on the steering wheel as she drove with all the ceremony the moment called for: her companion, and the fine panorama of the city stretched out at her feet. She felt a secret satisfaction at the squeal of the tyres at every bend, every gear change; without realising it, she gradually picked up speed. Manolo was concentrating on the road and Teresa's profile. Seeing her from the side like this, he began to turn once more to his precious sticker collection of blue-tinted adventures: an accident, Teresa badly wounded, the car on fire, he saves her . . .

'You're very quiet,' she said. 'I suppose you're affected by what Maruja's going through.'

'Yes.'

They drove past the esplanade where the ragged band was still playing in the sun.

'Look, how wonderful!' Teresa exclaimed. 'I love your neighbourhood. Why are they playing? Who are they?'

The Interloper glanced at her out of the corner of his eye.

'Meningitis sufferers. The children of syphilis, hunger and things like that. They're from the Cottolengo over there.'

'Ah.'

'How did you know where I live?'

'From Maruja. I've known for quite some time. I know a lot about you two ... Why did you say just now that she wasn't your fiancée?'

'Because it's the truth ... things aren't always the way they seem. I'm not engaged to anyone, and never have been. I don't know what she's told you, but we're only ... friends.'

Teresa took advantage of a flat, straight stretch of road to look across at him and change up into third gear. 'I understand,' she said, and accelerated. The car lurched forward, throwing Manolo back in his seat. Oh boy, a modern girl, with a different culture, he thought. But what he said was:

'Only friends. It happens a lot with the youth of today.'

'Don't pretend, please,' said Teresa. 'As I told you, I know everything.'

The Murcian decided to change the subject.

'So Maruja is seriously ill?'

'I couldn't say, she's unconscious. But I think she's suffering a lot ...'

That must have been true, because when Manolo entered her room (the nurse left, saying she had several telephone calls to make) and saw Maruja lying there looking so pale, he was affected much more than he had expected. A thin rubber tube was protruding from one nostril, stuck to her forehead with a plaster, then clipped on the pillow. She seemed not just dead, but mistreated, abused and then forgotten, as if she had been lying there for years. What strange illness was this? What had he done to her? It was obvious she was suffering – all you had to do was look at her knitted brow – but long before she had to endure this pain and abandonment, long before becoming a sad, not very bright young woman, even before she became aware that she would never be anything or anybody, it seemed as if something terrible had happened to her, something obscure and nameless. Stretched out in the bed, enveloped in silence, defenceless and frail, and perspiring with a pale, cold sweat, it was as if she was no longer connected to anyone, not even to that tremulous future she had dreamed of for the two of them, not to hope nor to love, not even to him, nothing that would stay with her in any way. Was his hand when he slapped her also responsible for leaving her prostrate like this?

To his surprise, he found himself sitting in a chair stroking one of Maruja's hands. He felt a burning sensation in his chest, then noticed a pink, perfumed blotch moving stealthily behind him: Teresa's skirt. He sat silently for a long while, and when Teresa asked in a whisper, 'Why don't you try calling her?' he closed his eyes. For a split second that damp, tousled little head appeared to him sunk in another pillow, and he heard a murmur of waves, the breathlessness of entwined bodies.

'Marujita, little one . . . what have they done to you?'

It was then he felt Teresa's hand on his shoulder. Afraid that tenderness or compassion could play a trick on him, he put all his strength, suppressed for three days out of fear and remorse, into an indignant outburst. Teresa, who was standing behind him, her back up against the door, saw him stand up and confront her violently. 'What's wrong?' she asked. In his face she saw the grim determination that precedes a street brawl: before gripping her arm in his strong hand, he wiped the palm on the faded leg of his jeans (a *trinxeraire* wouldn't have done it any better, she had time to think, harking back to a hazy childhood summer when a Civil War refugee's son cornered her under the stairs, slapped and hurt her until she managed to escape) and the wind rose on his chest expanded as he took a deep breath. As he did so, Teresa noticed the warm perspiration on his skin, a smell of bitter almonds that mingled with her own perfume and penetrated everything. His face was only a few centimetres from hers, but she could not make out his features properly; she could only hear him shouting as he shook her arm:

'Why didn't you tell me before? Tell me why. And why didn't you take her to the doctor straight away, why on earth did you want her in your boat? Answer me!'

Teresa looked at him in alarm. 'Please, you're hurting me . . .' She groped for the door handle behind her back. 'Please don't shout, let's get out of here . . .' But she wasn't able to move: all she could do was try to restrain his rage. She was simultaneously terrified and fascinated at the sight of his face, where his white teeth and furious eyes glittered, a lock of jet-black hair dangling down, his ridiculous swear words and curses. He was closer still, and she suddenly discovered her own hand on the wind rose of his polo shirt, not pushing or trying to stop his chest pushing against her, but simply resting there, as if contented. 'Calm down, I beg you. Maruja is very sick . . .'

From that moment on, she no longer heard the outpouring of insults: 'Why the fuck are you always between the legs of your friends in a doorway? Come on, tell me!' She had to get him out of the room. By squeezing up against him, Teresa managed to open the door slightly, but when she turned her body to escape, she lost her balance and for a moment the two of them were stuck in the doorway, unable to take a step forward or back, enveloped in that blue almond haze.

'Let me go, are you crazy?'

The door creaked. Teresa struggled as if in a nightmare, terrified by his frantic voice, scorched by the incredible accusations he was making, driven not by any supposed love of Maruja (she was aware of that, even in the growing heat of their struggle) but more by indignation and fury. How did he know – what contacts could he have to know about her encounters with an employee at Luis Trías's factory, and above all, her moments of negligence and irresponsibility? Respect, fear, the impressive moral authority she suddenly noted in him were a fresh revelation. Her arm hurt and her eyes began to fill with sweet tears, sweeter than she could have ever imagined.

Exhausted, all her strength gone, she leaned her head on the Murcian's chest, when all at once the anteroom door was flung open and the nurse appeared. Her face betrayed no hint of surprise (in an undertone, as if talking to herself, she was saying: '*Que fa aquest al-lot? Es doctor no vol escàndol . . .*' What are these two doing? The doctor wouldn't want a scandal . . .) as she approached them. The first thing she did was move them away from the door to close it. They separated abruptly from one another. The three of them stood in the anteroom while the nurse attended to Teresa. 'It's nothing,' she murmured.

Manolo began to pace up and down like a caged animal, peering all round him as if looking for something to smash. He punched the walls and furniture, cursing God and the devil under his breath, while the nurse chased after him. The situation would probably have ended in the most grotesque and humiliating manner for him (how to round off these fireworks, apart from offering excuses and feeling ridiculous) were it not for – thanks to one of those happy accidents with which fate occasionally rewards those endowed with imagination and audacity – the unforeseen intervention of love and blood, that all-powerful, ever-present mixture. In his fury, when he punched the Venetian blinds with his fist, muttering, 'Maruja, Marujilla ...' as if in agony, the Interloper cut himself badly between the knuckles. Blood flowed freely.

The nurse reacted prosaically but practically. 'Bring alcohol and gauze, they're in her room,' she told Teresa, taking hold of Manolo's hand. Fascinated, Teresa obeyed like a shot. The cut was in a place where it would be hard to heal. Slumped in an armchair, defeated by the circumstances, dignified, pallid and absent, the Murcian let the nurse clean and bandage his hand.

The Mallorcan nurse had only to look into the boyfriend's eyes to understand what had happened. And since she had her own ideas and explanations concerning poor lovers who rebel against pain and death, she chided the lad.

'Silly boy. See what you've done? I understand what you're going through, but you won't get anywhere by becoming desperate and creating a scene.' As well as dismissing the spectacle (she had no artistic imagination, was simply sensitive and a music lover, like her friends the doctors, and besides, had never found herself confronted by a smell of bitter almonds), she was about to make a second blunder as she looked at Teresa: 'Still less by blaming someone who doesn't deserve it. Calamities happen in the strangest of ways. Your fiancée fell all by herself, and nobody at that moment could have anticipated the consequences ... you're being really silly. If this happens again, I'll tell the doctor and I won't allow you to come and see her. Don't you realise she's very sick? You've given yourself a deep cut, and for what?' After finishing bandaging his hand, she walked back towards Maruja's room. Before opening the door she turned round: 'Is that clear? Let's see if you can behave ...'

'I'm sorry. I didn't mean to do it.'

'It was nothing,' said Teresa, voice trembling. 'Nerves ...'

The nurse winked at her to show she understood perfectly. Who doesn't know what love is? Then she went into Maruja's room.

Teresa tidied her dress and hair. Manolo was still sitting, despondent, in the armchair, head in hands.

'I'm sorry,' he murmured. 'I didn't mean to shout at you. It was all my fault. Did I hurt you?'

'No . . .'

'Yes, I did hurt you. I'm sorry.'

Teresa sat down opposite him and took out a packet of cigarettes. 'Don't worry about me.' Her hands were trembling. 'Want one?'

The Interloper offered her a light, and she leaned over to take it. They heard the metallic clank of a trolley in the corridor: it was lunch time. 'Fine, dammit, fine,' he muttered, rising to his feet.

Teresa looked at his bandaged hand.

'Does it hurt?'

'No. Let's go.'

He strode out, Teresa following him. His shoulders were slumped forlornly as they walked down the stairs. Out in the street, when Teresa (who didn't take her eyes off him, as though expecting to see him collapse at any moment from grief) pushed past him to open the car door, he came to a halt on the pavement.

'Are you feeling bad?' she asked.

'You get in first.'

'I know this isn't the moment,' said Teresa, 'and besides, we don't really know one another, but there's something I want to talk to you about. Shall I take you up to El Carmelo?' She switched on the ignition and looked at him. 'It's about Maruja and you.' Manolo sat beside her, and this time managed to close the car door firmly the first time. He was about to say something, but she got in first: 'No, I don't mean your encounters at the Villa . . .' (taken aback, he looked askance at her) 'I know all about that, I found out a long while ago, but don't worry – no one else at home knows. No, I mean the other thing . . .'

'What other thing?'

'You know.'

The Murcian didn't know, but he had a good nose for danger.

'Another day,' he suggested. 'If you don't mind, we can talk about that some other day.'

The car sped off with a jolt.

'Maruja told me a lot about you,' said Teresa, changing up to second gear. 'But don't be mad at her . . .'

'Don't you worry, she also talked about you. We know the kind of student you are, demonstrating and all that . . . Can't you go any faster? I'm in a hurry.'

'I want you to know what I was doing at that factory in Pueblo Seco. You're wrong if you think I was there to enjoy myself . . .'

'I couldn't care less. You can explain some other time.'

He looked down at her tanned knees.

'Will you come to see Maruja tomorrow?' she asked.

'I don't know.' Then, after a silence: 'Do you go every day?'

'Of course.'

As they started up the main road to El Carmelo, Teresa looked at his bandaged hand once more, and asked again:

'Does it hurt?'

This time the Interloper could not contain himself:

'Yes, it's starting to.'

Maruja's condition had stabilised. Her face was deathly pale, but she was breathing steadily. She was fed soup and puréed meat every three hours. She slept and slept; sometimes an uncomfortable expression appeared on her face, as if a twinge of pain was coursing through her. The Serrat family's visits gradually became routine, mechanical and resigned. They were desperate to see Maruja recover, but that was all they could do for her. Only Teresa went to the clinic every day, generally early in the afternoon. Aggressively and disturbingly elegant in her pirate's attire (black blouse and trousers, a red scarf around her head), she prowled the corridors shielded by her sunglasses, a book under her arm and an expression of serene determination on her face. Her youthful beauty was suffused with sadness, adding to its gravity, and for the first time leading her to experience the hot summer in the city with a new, strange awareness of her body's strength and audacity akin to how some people live their youth: as if it will never end. She didn't care that she had been obliged to interrupt her holidays on the coast. Her father, who alternated his commitments in Barcelona with weekends at the Villa, appeared on some mornings at the clinic, always in a hurry, more to talk to Doctor Saladich than to visit their maid. He only saw Teresa at mealtimes. In the first week, Señora Serrat visited Maruja twice, on one occasion with her sister Isabel. Marta was concerned not only by the state of the patient, but also of her daughter: sleepy, dark shadows under her eyes, dressed whimsically ('Stubborn girl, you finally got your way and bought those dreadful trousers'), and wanted to take her to Blanes.

'Don't insist, Mama. I've no intention of moving from here until Maruja is well again.'

The maid's impetuous, grief-stricken fiancé came to the clinic every day at around five. Silent and dignified, he brought with him private bitterness and an air of general condemnation. When she saw him enter, Teresa would close the book she was reading so as not to miss anything of a spectacle she saw as more significant day by day. The Murcian would approach Maruja's bed with the utmost respect and stand immobile at the head, looking dejected. At that moment, his wounded hand (whose showy, excessive bandage, the glorification of a heroic view of life, appeared to be changed every day by someone), hanging inert like a loving offering next to Maruja's pillow, was so close to the patient's wan face it seemed to be showing solidarity with it. The dark skin of his arm contrasted with the foamy white of the bandage wrapped round and round almost up to his elbow. Apart from that, the Murcian's dark, shuttered face, and the way he stood stock-still staring (for four or five minutes) at Maruja, revealed nothing apart from the nobility of his features. After that he would slowly withdraw from the bed and, thumbs hooked in his back trouser pockets, would enquire how Maruja was getting on. He spoke briefly, addressing all his questions to the nurse, glancing only seldom at Teresa. After this he would say goodbye and leave. For several days he behaved in exactly the same way. Teresa Serrat continued to ask herself to what extent he still held her responsible for what had happened.

One afternoon, Manolo arrived before Teresa. He came in without looking at anyone, muttering a gruff 'Afternoon' (there were people in the anteroom; he could vaguely make out the elegant silhouette of a woman, who fell silent when she saw him enter) and went to stand by the bed. After a while he noticed footsteps behind him, and heard the voice of the nurse informing someone about how Maruja had been vomiting, usually in the morning, when they changed her position in bed. Then he heard her say, 'He's her fiancé,' in a low voice. He became aware of a soft, perfumed presence beside him, and the clinking of bracelets. A prolonged silence ensued; he did not move or say anything, simply continuing to stare at Maruja's face (he thought vaguely that with every passing day it looked more like a mask) at the same time as from his left-hand side he received the agreeable impression of female eyes taking an interest in his profile; probably those of the unknown woman. Teresa's mother, he thought. When he turned his head, whoever it was had disappeared, and the nurse was sitting by the window. At that moment, Teresa entered.

'Hello,' she greeted him. 'Mama was just asking me about you.'

'I already informed her,' said the nurse.

At this, Manolo turned to look at her in a strangely mistrustful manner, as though to make plain his astonishment at the fact that nurses can speak. Then he headed for the door. Teresa accompanied him out of the room to ask if he was still angry with her.

'Me? Why should I be?' he answered, resting his bandaged arm on the door close to her blond head. As he did so, she once again caught the smell of bitter almonds.

'I don't know . . . you look as if you are,' said Teresa. 'I want you to know that nobody is to blame for what happened to Maruja, least of all me. And I'd like to talk to you about that, because you've got some explaining to do as well. I can give you a ride home if you like.'

Manolo seemed taken aback.

'Thanks. The fact is . . . I'm not going home. Another day.'

Then, after thinking it over for a few seconds, he added coldly: 'Today I've got something important to do.'

A week after surprising Teresa with a bloody baptism, the distressed fiancé now gave her another one by unexpectedly turning up in a new, perfectly tailored, magnificent pearl-grey suit, and his arm in a sling. Impeccably dressed and respectful as he stood next to Maruja in his devoted, almost religious, attitude, Teresa could not take her eyes off him. How appealing the new outline of his shoulders was, what mystery in the straight back that gave him a domineering, unexpected elegance. And the sling? Had the wound become infected? Teresa immediately recognised the chocolate-coloured silk scarf wrapped round his bandaged hand: it was one she had given Maruja some time ago. Without knowing why, this troubled her. There was a new, strange relationship between the admirably impassive nature of the Murcian's body and the brand-new suit covering it, as if these two elements – until this moment mutually unaware of one another – had just sealed an alarming pact that heralded danger. The adventure was about to begin.

'What happened?' she asked, pointing to the arm in its sling.

'Dina has stepped out for a moment . . .'

'Who is Dina?'

'The nurse. She'll be back soon. Why don't you show her your hand?'

'It's nothing,' he said. 'It's more comfortable like this.'

He stayed for a while sitting next to Teresa, absent-mindedly leafing through some magazines. But even though today he was wishing and hoping she would offer to take him home in her car, she didn't even come to the door with him. She must have a commitment, he thought.

The next day was different. They left the clinic together, and since it was early and he had nothing to do ('I have a day off,' he told her), he suggested they stop for a drink on the way back. She didn't seem particularly interested, but didn't say no either. She wanted to try a bar on Monte Carmelo, which surprised Manolo.

'There's nothing special there,' he said. 'But I know somewhere nearby, and on our way.'

He had remembered the Tibet, at the foot of El Carmelo. A sophisticated spot: a fake rustic hut, with varnished wooden logs, a thatched roof and bottle lights, on the roof terrace of a 1930s villa converted into a guest house and restaurant. There was soft music from the loudspeaker; it was a calm, isolated place that delighted Teresa. They stood on a terrace that looked out over the road, beyond which they could see kitchen gardens and carob trees, a pond that glinted like a mirror in the sun and an old farmhouse long since swallowed up by the city. After dark they would be able to see the sky lighting up over Parque Güell, behind the Tres Cruces mountain. Teresa stood for a long while enjoying the view, elbows on the rail, next to Manolo.

'I like your neighbourhood.'

'Can you see those tennis courts down there, among the trees?' he said, pointing to them. 'That's La Salud tennis club. I worked there as a boy, picking up the balls, like Manuel Santana ... I bet you've never been here before.'

'You'd be wrong,' she said, looking up at El Carmelo. 'All this is in a way familiar to me. I haven't always lived in San Gervasio. As a girl we lived in Plaza Joanich, in Gracia. That was after the war; I remember I used to escape to play in the street. There were some horrible boys, but I wasn't scared.' She burst out laughing. 'Mama was terrified by how reckless I was – she still is, because she reckons I haven't changed. That was where one day under the stairs at home a boy from El Carmelo tugged at my plaits. He kept me prisoner behind the door for quite a while, until I said a password, the secret formula.' She looked at Manolo, an amused smile on her face. 'Who knows, maybe that boy was you.'

'No,' he said, laughing. 'I didn't live in Barcelona back then.'

'Where are you from?'

'From Malaga. Listen, are your parents Catalan?'

'My father is. My mother is half Mallorcan, but she grew up here.'

'Shall we sit down? Come on, what do you want to drink?'

'I don't know, a *Cuba libre*. Tell me about Maruja, about the two of you. You work in a factory, don't you?'

They sat opposite one another. Manolo looked taken aback.

'Me, in a factory? They'd have to kill me first. Who told you that nonsense?'

He was smiling, but didn't seem to like the idea. Teresa was disconcerted.

'Maruja.'

'I'll never understand that girl. I work in my brother's business. Buying and selling cars. The bad times are behind us.'

It was obvious he was lying, and Teresa Serrat thought she knew why. Is he being over-cautious? she thought. How ridiculous. I've not given him any reason to mistrust me – quite the opposite. She had decided not to get involved in all that, but to respect Maruja's boyfriend's secret. She had something else in mind.

'Do you remember,' she began, leaning back in her chair and putting on her sunglasses, 'that the first day we went to the clinic together and in the car when we were leaving I told you I wanted to talk to you about something important . . . ? Well, I've changed my mind. I can see you don't like me interfering in your affairs.'

'That's right,' he said, sniffing danger.

'But there's something you should know, something connected to what you said when you wanted to throttle me in the anteroom ...' She burst out laughing again, and he followed suit. 'You were criticising me for my behaviour with that lad who works in the factory in Pueblo Seco owned by Luis Trías's father. How did you know about that?'

'Aha, it's a mystery,' he said, smiling.

'Well, I'm not that surprised, given all the contacts you must have ... But you don't know the whole story, or you wouldn't have shouted at me like that. I want to clear it up: I don't like misunderstandings. Basically, I couldn't care less whatever you've been told about me and that lad and our encounters. But let me warn you, there are lots of people out there who have such old-fashioned ideas although they pretend to be progressive, Manolo. I go out with whomever I please and don't have to justify myself to anyone.'

'I didn't ask you anything. This *Cuba libre* is good.'

'Anyway,' added Teresa, bowing her head, 'I've decided that's over and done with. I don't want to have anything to do with those cretins at the faculty ... or with anyone else. There are more important things to be done.' Saying this, she gave him a serious look steeped in solidarity, and raised the glass to her lips. 'Don't you think so?'

'Well, that depends.'

'Recently I've had one of those experiences you never forget.' Teresa's eyes were barely visible behind the dark glasses, and all of a sudden her lips began to quiver.

'My, oh my,' he said, for something to say.

'If I told you ...'

'Go on, then.'

'I prefer not to talk about it.'

She sipped her drink, while Manolo looked at her without saying a word. She took out a packet of Chesterfields and they both smoked. Teresa added that just thinking about it sickened her, and that it would be years before she would let anyone touch her again. 'But that's a personal decision on my part, which doesn't alter the facts,' she said resolutely. 'What I wanted to say was: that boy you seem so interested in, the one I was with in the entrance to the factory offices, was presented to me by Luis Trías. His name is Rafa, and he's a good sort...'

From then on, Manolo gave her his full attention, trying hard to comprehend the strange mixture of conflicting emotions her words evoked. It seemed a very complicated affair. She said she had resolved to tell him all this not because she was ashamed about it, but so that he wouldn't think (as others had done) that she was friendly with Rafa just to canoodle with him. He was the person in charge, or something similar, of the firm's Cultural Section; he looked after the library and directed a theatre group. The poor lad didn't know much, but was very willing, and in some ways was worth more than many students from good families that she knew.

'Me and a girlfriend of mine,' Teresa went on, 'advised him to try to put on something or other by Brecht. Do you know Brecht?'

'Carry on, carry on,' said Manolo.

Teresa insisted the lad was really interested in the idea, although it wasn't easy to put into practice. She lent him books and magazines, and they often met to talk about it. One day it occurred to her they could organise study groups after the rehearsals. For example, if they couldn't put on Brecht, they could at least read him.

'I don't know if you're aware what happens with Brecht here...' she started to say.

'Carry on, carry on', Manolo insisted.

'Unfortunately,' she sighed, 'it all came to nothing, partly because of Luis Trías, who soon lost interest... But that's another story. It was a good idea of mine, although perhaps a little premature. You can't imagine how I was criticised, but I still think that staging Brecht in the university is unimportant, whereas if it's done in a workers' centre . . .'

'Yes, but what happened with that Rafa of yours?' Manolo wanted to know.

'Nothing. We saw each other for a couple of weeks. I told you he was very pleasant and friendly. But tongues began to wag; and that's what I wanted to say: the only important thing in all that was what we were trying to do, even if it was unsuccessful, and all the rest, what went on between Rafa and me, meant nothing. That's what I don't understand: it wasn't as if we were threatening the future of the revolution,' Teresa exclaimed indignantly. 'All that dogmatism is absurd, don't you think?'

Manolo thought it over. He stubbed his cigarette out in the ashtray.

'What I say is that people shouldn't mix obligation with devotion. There's a time for everything. Because let's see, what did you want from Rafa – to lend him books or to kiss him?'

Teresa paused for a moment, then burst out laughing.

'How silly! Is what I do or don't do so interesting? Because it seems even you get to hear of it!' She closed her eyes a moment, but the smile remained on her lips. 'It could be there's a detailed report about me and my lovers. That would be hilarious! And forgive me for insisting, but I'm really intrigued: how did you know about it?'

It was his turn to give a slight smile. Go for it, kid, he told himself, and reached across the table to slowly remove her sunglasses. He stared her in the eye and said:

'Everything gets known in this life. I was closer to you than you think. You look better without them.'

'I'm talking seriously, Manolo.'

'So am I. But that's in the past, let's forget about it.'

'Well, the other day in the clinic you behaved like a real political commissar. Look, I've still got the mark on my arm. And it was because of that, wasn't it? Go on, admit it.'

For want of anything better, the Murcian chose to smile. Teresa stared at him, thrust her face forward and said:

'Why do you always play dumb? Don't worry, comrade. I won't ask you anything that might compromise you. If you like, we can talk about something else. Your family, your friends . . .'

Laughing as she leaned back in her seat once more, she raised her arms and stretched voluptuously. This is the joyful, lively Teresa, the real one, the one who's so easy to love! thinks the Interloper, and tries to please her by talking about his neighbourhood. He somehow senses in her rapt attention not only fascination with the city's margins, but also a clash of cultures he can't as yet identify. In her deep-blue eyes staring at him dreamily and trustingly he sees the pure, suspended twilight. What strange suspicions and hopes, what feelings and emotions are floating in the warm, encircling liquid blue of her gaze? Sometimes she listens to him like a diligent, studious schoolgirl, elbows on the table and chin in hands; at others it seems her mind's pink languor is elsewhere, chasing a fleeting evocation that immediately vanishes, even though she is still gazing at him with that serene, pure expression of hers. Her pensive, slightly exaggerated attitude contrasts with the simplicity of what the Murcian is describing, and the involuntary incoherence he occasionally lapses into. Teresa isn't really searching for the meaning of his words, but for what is drifting beneath or around them, a background current or subtle weave of ideas and emotions that she herself is unwittingly prompting with her questions. She is searching for a harmony that will gradually expand in the air between them, in the increasingly small space separating them, and will end up enveloping their heads like a small, invisible cloud. She asks lots of questions, but they are purely emotional ones: they're not pursuing the truth, but rather an ideal climate for that truth; they express not so much a desire to know as a deeply felt desire for confirmation. Teresa Serrat already knows; that is, she has made up her mind and come to her own verdict about the life of a young man like him on the margins of a city. So, some opinions she utters enthusiastically ('Well, anyway, the life of a Communist Party member must be fabulous, even entertaining in your neighbourhood, on summer nights with your comrades, the debates in the café . . .') are so wide of the mark they lead to an instant, vigorous rejection by the Murcian ('What party and what summer nights? In my neighbourhood there's nothing but boredom and poverty'). But this denial only slid off her contented smile; it didn't encourage her to change her ideas, or reconsider her scale of values in the slightest. Her clear, enthusiastic gaze went on insisting: 'Yes, what a wonderful neighbourhood.'

This blinkered vision was very useful to Manolo at those moments when, despite his noble efforts to satisfy the nostalgia for life in the margins behind Teresa's questions, he evoked the real, sordid truth of his neighbourhood and home, and his ancestral rancour came to the surface. Tired of lying, his voice threatened to disperse the cloud laden with emotional undertones that enveloped them. However, none of this prevented them both really enjoying themselves: every so often their knees touched under the table, and this simple contact made the world seem suddenly infinitely more real, exciting and coherent than the one Teresa's vehement assertions were desperate to evoke. Little by little, they settled into a comfortable silence, and soon two hours had gone by without them realising it. By now Teresa was drinking gin on the rocks. The Murcian had recovered his supreme self-confidence; nothing suggested there might be a return to the always slippery subject of the supposed conspiracy when a chance incident occurred, the black fate constantly hounding him (this time in the guise of a boiling hot cup of coffee balanced in a waiter's shaky hand), and raised yet again the question of the bizarre personality Teresa Serrat seemed determined to impose on him, while finally making plain the political nature of her cultural conflict. As the waiter, an old man plagued by aches and pains who was always muttering angrily to himself, but whom Teresa liked, was passing by Manolo, he stumbled and spilled the cup of coffee over the Murcian's brand-new suit. The liquid scalded his neck, and he jumped out of his chair.

'Animal! Why don't you watch where you're going?'

'Agh, agh . . . I'm going to fall,' moaned the old man.

And it was true: he was still toppling, and if Manolo hadn't grabbed him by the jacket collar, he would have hit his head on the table edge.

'Shit, grandpa, it's no joke!' shouted Manolo. 'Look what you've done to my suit, you son of a bitch!'

He continued to curse the old man in no uncertain terms. By now the Interloper was in full spate and couldn't hold his tongue; he even forgot about Teresa, and it was only once he had finished the lengthy litany of insults (as the poor man limped off grumbling and rubbing his knee, after spraying the lad's jacket with soda water) and looked over at her that he noticed her reproachful expression.

'What?' he asked, slightly flustered, rubbing his lapel with a handkerchief. 'Wasn't I right? If his hands shake, they should make him retire. That's what I say. Look what the clown has done to me. And by the way,' he said, lying openly, 'it's not because of my suit, but the thing in itself . . .'

Teresa was looking down, swirling the contents of her glass, and contemplating him as though she was bitterly disappointed by his attitude.

'Well,' said the Murcian, even though he suspected it was already too late, 'what's done is done.'

'That man works,' said the progressive student.

'Fine,' replied the motorbike thief. 'We all work.'

'Exactly, Manolo. It wouldn't have surprised me in someone else, but it does in you.'

'Why?'

'Just then you were behaving like a *señorito*.'

Annoyed, Manolo went on rubbing the lapel with his handkerchief. He didn't look at Teresa.

'So maybe I am a *señorito*. Especially when I'm mistreated, when someone scalds me . . . It could be I'm really fed up.'

'I imagine you're not serious.' Teresa's voice became stern. 'You're not going to tell me you've never formed certain principles. You can't be that cynical. All right, so it was the old man's fault, but there are lots of ways of doing things, and . . .'

Manolo thrust his face across the table, glowering at her. Two almost invisible wrinkles appeared at the top of his dark brow, suggesting a twisted mental strength, a power he perhaps did not really possess: one of the advantages of beauty. Their heads were so close that Teresa could also appreciate the bitter perfection of his mouth, and the strange harshness at its corners. Manolo interrupted her:

'Just a moment. Let's see. I only know one way to do things: that's to do them well. And that old fool stained my suit and burned me; I'm sorry, but sometimes you women are too sentimental. I know he's a poor fellow, on his last legs because he's always worked so hard, but aren't we allowed to complain?'

'As a matter of fact, no,' she said, and finally from those strawberry lips, that adorable pink bubble where the conspiracy was always bound to founder, came a slogan that was a revelation to him: 'Not when you have class consciousness, Manolo.'

A shudder ran through the young man from El Carmelo. Does she say that because I've been so badly dressed before today? was his first thought, and then: so that's what this is all about! Where's this going to end, Manolito? But say nothing and carry on playing dumb.

Teresa was still talking, and her eager voice, dripping with solidarity, merged with the soft music from the loudspeaker:

'... and that's where we need to start: the way we treat one another. Those are the things that really matter, and not that someone lets themselves be kissed in a doorway. But everything still has to be done in this country, everything is topsy-turvy, even in the opposition, as María Eulalia says...'

'Who?'

'A friend from the faculty.'

Manolo, feeling defenceless and vulnerable when it came to Teresa's favourite topic, decided the time had come to fall back on the hidden powers he was reputed to represent.

'Let's not say any more about that, shall we? It's dangerous.' The music from the loudspeaker, redolent with vagues promises, led him to stretch his hand out towards hers. Pensive, Teresa ran her finger along the folds of the tablecloth, and said nothing. 'Look, if we're to be friends, Teresa, you have to do me a favour: let's not mention that matter for now. Later on, if I can, I'll tell you a few things about me... For now, don't ask me anything, don't remind me of anything, okay?'

She glanced at him for a second, then lowered her eyes once more. 'I understand,' she murmured. Her submission made her beautiful. (Being obedient is good for all women, he thought, but above all for the snobbish ones.) She added: 'You're right. Don't listen to me.'

Manolo smiled affectionately and squeezed her hand.

'Take it easy. You're very impulsive, Teresa.'

'I'm nervous; I don't know what's wrong with me these days. So many things have happened all at once, all I do is think and think and think . . .'

'You study too much.'

'I don't study at all.'

'How old are you?'

'Almost nineteen. And now don't ask me if I have a boyfriend, I couldn't bear it.' Smiling, she added: 'I think I'll order another gin, to see if it livens me up. By the way, you look very elegant today. Why's that? Blue jeans and sports shirts suit you better.'

'We have to ring the changes, don't we? But if you say so . . . Once, in Marbella without meaning to, I took the hand of a German girl at the beach, in the water . . .'

'You've been on the Costa del Sol?' she interrupted him.

'For a season. The German girl . . .'

'Working? What were you doing?'

'Off and on. Anyway, that German girl stole a pink shirt of mine.'

'She stole a pink shirt of yours?'

'Yes, I swear,' he said, laughing. 'On the beach. A faded shirt. She said she liked it. She gave me twenty bucks for it. It wasn't worth it.'

'The German girl or the shirt?'

'The shirt, of course.'

They both laughed. Teresa lounged back in her chair, stared at him for a while, and then said brazenly in an ironic tone:

'I can tell that one of these days I'm going to do something really silly. I know more than one girl at the faculty who would have done so already . . . Have you never heard that we university students are loose women?' A strange joy was coursing through her veins; what was happening to her seemed odd, because she hadn't drunk a lot – but she was starting to realise that no doubt it was one thing to drink with Luis Trías, and something else entirely with a worker like Manolo. 'What? You've never heard that? Well, now you know ...' She burst out laughing, and changed her tone. 'Okay, don't blush, I'm only joking.'

How little you know me, he thought. Blush, my arse. But what he said was:

'Are you trying to impress me, showing you're an intellectual?' Despite his confusion, he had hit the target. Teresa gave a forced smile, and he added: 'I don't know if you're very ... that way. I reckon that, like all women, only when it suits you. What I do know is you're all very clever. Look at silly Maruja on the other hand. She couldn't wait to tell you everything. Silly, and without a penny.'

'Please don't talk about Maruja like that. We're good friends. But you're wrong: she hardly dared talk about you two, I almost had to force it out of her. I knew you two slept in her room ... Did I ever say anything? In my place, anybody else would have raised the roof, admit it ... But I have my beliefs, and I try to stick by them.' She sighed, looking down at her neckline. She let her hair fall over her face, then shook her head violently to sweep it away. 'You can't deny that what happened last October was crazy.'

'Yes, it wasn't bad,' he admitted, struggling to remember what she was talking about. He wanted to change the subject once more. 'This *Cuba libre* is good. Want another one?'

'Tell me the truth, Manolo: did you love her?'

'Maruja? She's still alive, isn't she ...? Yes, we have loved one another, in our own way. We've always wanted to do everything as we see fit.'

'She's very much in love with you. You know that, don't you?'

'There's no need to exaggerate. The thing is, she's such a good person, poor thing. What went on between us was all about bed. Well, I don't need to explain things to you, you're a woman.'

'Don't be afraid of spelling it out.'

'Look, I'm very frank. I like doing what I have to when I have to, but don't think that means it's all I look for in a woman ... On the contrary. I've met lots of sluts, and I've never enjoyed wasting time on them.' A note of urgency crept into his voice when, without knowing it, he paraphrased Fray Luis de Léon: 'But an intelligent girl, who isn't afraid of life, and is distinguished and cultured, is a treasure. If you fall in love with her, you'll be rich all your life. This is a holy truth.'

He saw his reflection in Teresa's eyes. Night was falling, and in the distance behind her, the city lights were starting to glitter. Teresa lowered her head and picked up her sunglasses. Without quite knowing why, he said:

'You should lend me a book, Teresa.'

'A book?'

'Yes, a book.'

'What for?'

'Why do you think? To read it.'

'Oh, of course, whenever you like.' She didn't seem very interested, and glanced down at her watch. 'It's late. Shall we go? You're near your place, so I'll leave you here. Do you mind?'

'If there's nothing else for it ...'

When they said goodbye at the car, they seemed ill at ease (a lethargic shake of the hands, an expressive silence), with an air of frustration and disappointment, but one directed at themselves, like after a young people's party when you feel you made a mistake not only with your hair but with the topics of conversation.

'Life is so boring, isn't it?' she said, settling in the driver's seat. 'In this heat, I really miss the beach ...' As the car sped off, Teresa turned her head to look at him, and Manolo eagerly waved his bandaged hand.

The mystery behind the heroic bandaging went by the name of Hortensia, better known in the neighbourhood as the Syringe. She was also responsible for the smell of bitter almonds, medicinal sweets that came from the pharmacy where she worked and fell out of the pockets of her white coat.

'Is this all right, Manolo?'

'Give it a few more turns. I don't want it to get infected, then we'd really be in trouble, kid.'

Every afternoon after lunch, Manolo went to her house for her to change the dressing. The Syringe was the Cardinal's niece; a serious fifteen-year-old. Pale, silent and reserved, with light-blue, almost translucent eyes and ash-blond hair, she hardly spoke, and when she did it was in fits and starts. She observed everything suspiciously, as if she were short-sighted, and always went around on her own. According to the Cardinal, she had inherited her clumsy, dazed character from her mother. But her cindery eyes, and hair that nowadays was as dull and dry as a thistle, had once been shiny, and apparently, as her uncle said, it was true that some things you never lose, because lately Manolo would gaze at her face without knowing what attracted him in it, until one day as she was bandaging his arm he suddenly realised how much she resembled (and in what a strange, disturbing way) Teresa Serrat. And what he found curious was that, having known Hortensia for many years, this had not occurred to him the other way round – that is, it would have been logical for Teresa to remind him of the Cardinal's niece. Why could that have been?

Hortensia was nine when the Murcian began to frequent the Cardinal's house. He would play in the garden with her, take her for a walk in Parque Güell and let her ride on the rental bikes. This activity – which he threw himself into body and soul, without the slightest qualm about becoming a babysitter, just as he had none later when he stole a record player and his first motorbike if it meant he won the Cardinal's affection and trust – delighted the little girl, except for the times when Manolo, trying too hard in his efforts to win over the old man (whose susceptible eyes had already on several occasions been troubled by the boy's elastic stride), used her in strange games in front of her uncle that left Hortensia in tears. Was she able to sense, even back then, the urgent need he had to spread his wings – could she read his future betrayals in his face? For example: in the summer they were in the habit of bathing in the big washing tank (now dry and full of stones and charred rags) at the bottom of the garden. Hortensia loved having Manolo empty buckets of water over her; they would splash around and pretend to fight, and her little friend was very funny when he allowed himself to be 'drowned'. But her uncle soon acquired the habit of watching these innocent games of splashing and bronzed limbs; from the ramshackle arbour, seated in the rickety orange wicker armchair in his threadbare dressing gown, hands clasped round the ivory pommel of his cane, the Cardinal would observe them silently through a luminous mist with his nostalgic former dancer's eyes. Always respectful and correct, he would study almost imperceptible signs – the suddenly feline grace of a limb, the glistening reflection under an armpit, the fleeting throb of a back muscle – with the lofty dignity of a ballet master looking for future glory among his pupils.

And Manolo, who was usually very gentle with the girl, would start to treat her roughly, just as she herself would do with an old doll in front of her uncle when she wanted a new one. She found herself pushed, cornered. 'Look, Cardinal, look!' she would hear the boy shout, and see him jump from the wall over her head into the water. His agile, bronzed body seemed to hang in the air for a few seconds, shining in the sun like the effigy on a medal, as he plunged in before suddenly erupting from the water to hug her so hard he hurt her, trying to tickle or nibble at her, though it upset her, as they rolled about out of breath, creating a thousand shapes and attitudes, awkwardly but without any improper intent on his part.

Thanks to his boundless enthusiasm – unthinkingly getting Hortensia to swallow water, and making her cry – Manolo innocently conjured up an entire lost world, as a young girl might do, flirting too openly, for someone whose life was ebbing away only a few metres from him. Behind long eyelashes, the Cardinal sought to dismiss a distant, adolescent dream: the rushing waters of the Río de la Plata, with shiny tongues of sunlight licking youthful skin, the joyful shouts from another summer buried in time. Now all he could hear was the fading beat of his old, forlorn heart: the Cardinal, the great lord who was to give the Murcian the key to the city and the future.

'Hold your hand out. Like this. Does it hurt?'

'No, no . . .'

It must have been back in her childhood that the resentful frost appeared in Hortensia's eyes, and the sadness in her hair. She had lived with her uncle ever since she was born, in the ancient tower that stood slightly apart from the rest of El Carmelo, hidden on a flank of the hill. Nobody seemed to know much about either of them. Was she really the daughter of the Cardinal's sister who died in hospital giving birth to her in the spring of 1943, or was it that, as others claimed, her mother had run away with a young Galician who was the Cardinal's closest friend, abandoning the little girl to his care? In El Carmelo, where rumour floated from the waist down like gas ('caught with his trousers down' was a favourite expression for many years), all kinds of gossip did the rounds, some of which reached Manolo's ears. 'Think bad of someone and you can't go wrong,' he had been told in the Bar Delicias, so often a den of malicious tongues. Manolo was fifteen at the time, and liked to play the innocent in front of the Cardinal.

'Is it true you've lived in Buenos Aires?' he asked on one occasion.

'Yes,' the old man replied with a smile.

'And that you played the piano for Carlos Gardel?'

The Cardinal's noble head wobbled slightly, as if a shiver had run down his spine: 'Possibly, possibly.' (It goes without saying that the bit about Gardel was the youth's personal addition to the legend, according to which the Galician had been an antiques dealer and a pianist in Argentina.)

'And that you had a lot of money and lived the high life? Is that true as well, Cardinal?'

'It's not a lie, son,' answered the old fox with his decorous prelate's voice.

In the past, Manolo had really liked hearing him talk: the red and black silk of long-severed friendly links, an indefinable tenderness towards friends half buried in the memory of time, half known and half understood, a longing, a vague sense of sorrow not only for what one has done in this world, but more for everything one hasn't done and will perhaps never succeed in doing. Such suggestions always fluttered around the old man's words like a small caged bird. Occasionally there was something almost solemn about his tone of voice and demeanour, which could be haughty and humble at one and the same time. Perhaps that was why he was known as the Cardinal.

But all that was in the past now. In El Carmelo things had gone badly for the old man; hard times came that at night were more or less bearable, but not in the daytime. Sometimes at first light he could be seen on the neighbourhood streets heading home, almost unrecognisable because he looked so defeated, so sad and decrepit as he walked along, leaning on his cane. This must also have been partly why Hortensia's eyes were left cloudy and colourless, veiled by the stupor produced by those always unknown but always so similar faces that came to the tower with something for sale, making a noise, laughing – she could hear the sound of the motorbikes from her bed – youthful, nondescript faces, fleeting nocturnal angels who burst into her room, smiling at her, and who the next morning, while her uncle was still asleep, would leave with a strongly animal chill in their bones, after drinking a rapid reheated coffee in the kitchen. Was that when her eyes and hair were ruined?

At the age of twelve, in jerseys and ruinous boots, her body suddenly shot up in a strange, decisive way. She attended a school run by nuns on Calle Escorial, where she was kept all day and fed for a peseta. When she got home at nightfall, she would discover new stolen goods and stumble in on increasingly secretive conversations. Her uncle would send her into the garden, where she would shrug her shoulders and walk along the overgrown red-brick paths among the small wild flowers she loathed and whose names she didn't know. She would smile and talk to herself (about what, who with?): all the sadness of the neglected garden, the entire neighbourhood, all the sadness of the uselessly sunny hill, vainly standing out against the joyous blue sky, all the sorrow of everyday life in the margins accumulated in the extinguished ashes of her eyes.

One day she saw Manolo approaching their gate carrying a huge record player. She didn't want to let him in.

'Aren't we friends any more, Hortensia?' he asked.

'I don't have friends.'

Manolo quickly invented a story: he had bought her the record player as a gift so they could dance and have fun together for the rest of their lives. This was another of his ruses: Manolo was using her yet again for his own ends; and, thinking it over now, that day was the last time he could remember seeing any light shining in her eyes. She opened the gate for him, took him to her uncle, and then heard Manolo say: 'This is for you, Cardinal, do you like it?' She wouldn't speak to the Murcian for a month.

A long time later, in winter when he spent entire afternoons in the Bar Delicias playing cards next to the stove with the old men, he would see her come in occasionally and order a coffee with milk at the counter. She would stand there, drinking it very slowly, staring at the card table with half-closed, empty eyes, peering at him over the top of her cup (he was always scared she would end up dropping it and smashing it on the floor, as she often did at home), until finally she came over and told him: 'Hurry up, my uncle wants to see you.' When they were out in the street, she would add, 'It's not true,' and run off. At other times, when it was true, she would simply follow a metre or so behind him, repeating over and over: 'Manolo, when are you going to take me for a ride on your motorbike?' To speed along with him, wrap her arms round his waist, press her cheek against his back and see his tie flapping in front of her eyes, hair streaming in the wind . . . 'Tomorrow,' he always said, but he hadn't ever kept that promise either.

'Tell me if it's too tight.'

'No, no, it's fine.'

Manolo never thought she was ugly, but nor did it occur to

him she might be pretty, or in what way. Now that he had met Teresa, he knew: Hortensia was like a sketch, an unfinished and clumsy first draft of Teresa. All he had to do was look at her with his eyes screwed up: what he could see, enveloped in a milky light, was like an out-of-focus photograph of the beautiful student, a delicious indistinct feline face and with the same long blond locks (yes, just like Teresa in that framed photograph on Maruja's bedside table, standing by her car), the blurred, almost phantasmal outline of that other luminous, joyous person flourishing in one of Barcelona's residential areas, but which here in El Carmelo had for some reason not had the time or the means to bloom. A debased version of Teresa, a hybrid imitation, one that was faded or possibly ruined. As Manolo sat beside her now, it was like being next to an aromatic medicinal plant. He didn't like her sweets, but a deep-rooted sense of guilt left over from the days of their games in the water tank, a kindly feeling that he ought to make amends, obliged him to take them whenever she bandaged his hand, leaning over him as she concentrated on her task. She had a delightfully prominent brow, and there was something doll-like about the strange dryness of her hair that made it look artificial, hanging loose in what could have been a golden mane. Her forehead was covered with a silken fuzz, and although at certain moments, when the light struck her face, her eyes could look blue, it was always an impure pearly colour that quickly faded.

'Would you like some sweets?'

'Okay.'

She had almost finished. They were sitting on the sofa in the dining room, with the school bag she used as a medical case next to them. Hortensia looked up at him for a moment: just like Teresa, her delicate nostrils had a strange, eager emotional life of their own, and like her, the childish solemnity of her high cheekbones stood out. Behind Hortensia, sunlight flooded in through the window. In the garden beyond stood two eucalyptus trees, an orange tree that produced small, hard yellow fruit, and a cherry tree that flowered in February. Manolo had always really liked the Cardinal's tower: it was big, with high ceilings, and silent. Some dark and poorly ventilated rooms were seldom used; crates left open at random still retained the confusing aroma of velvet-lined boxes, that arcane smell of wealth he remembered from the Salvatierra palace in Ronda. Hortensia's bedroom upstairs was wall-papered; there was a time when the house had been filled with mirrors, old speckled ones covered in a cloudy film, as well as thick curtains, musty carpets, all kinds of curious heavy old ornaments and pieces of furniture (which had gradually been disappearing). Apparently the Cardinal had once been a furniture expert. Manolo never discovered where he kept whatever he didn't manage to sell, but suspected it could be a back room upstairs next to Hortensia's that was kept locked. He kept a radio in almost every room, as well as an electric shaver, a refrigerator and a record player. But nowadays, doubtless due to him having sold a lot of things and having others on offer (there were parcelled-up goods and open suitcases in many corners), the house had a cold, transient feel to it, as if prefiguring a removal that would leave it completely empty.

'You take them,' he heard Hortensia say, her head lowered again. 'In the top pocket.'

This pocket was to one side of her breast, and whenever Manolo tried to fish out a sweet (he didn't want one, but it was impossible to refuse), his first and middle fingers always brushed against the small hard cherry of her nipple. Little devil! thought Manolo uneasily. The delicate, laborious bandage and the sweets were perhaps the timid, silent token of some secret emotion: the feeling that the Syringe was plotting something became particularly intense when he felt her ashen gaze clamped on his throat.

Seated at the table, the Cardinal was drinking brandy from a purple balloon glass. Manolo noticed that the food in front of him (an enormous steak with fried potatoes) had hardly been touched. All he does these days is tipple, he thought. The Cardinal was wearing a shabby scarlet dressing gown, with open lilac lapels that revealed a thick mass of grey chest hair. As he savoured the brandy, the Cardinal's melancholy eyes didn't waver from the two youthful heads leaning so close together they were almost touching, the evening sun making their hair blaze.

'Hortensia,' he said. 'That's enough. I need to talk to Manolo.' He watched as the youth raised his bandaged hand: pierced by the sun's rays, the fingers were a glowing crimson. 'Don't you hear me, child? I know this show-off, there's nothing wrong with his hand.' He laughed gently, as if to himself. 'And you're silly, just silly, and you know why . . .'

She clicked her tongue with annoyance, but didn't look up from her work. Through her paper-thin eyelids Manolo could see her disdain for the old man. She tied the bandage, snipped off the end with a pair of scissors and lifted Manolo's hand level with her eyes.

'Is that okay? Do you like it?'

'Oh, that's fine, thank you.' He got up lethargically, clutching his wrist as if it was hurting. The Syringe packed up her things and went to sit at the far end of the room. Manolo approached the Cardinal, wary of a receiving a reproach.

'Sit here, Manolo,' the old man invited him. 'Here, opposite me so I can see you. There's something going on with you. Did you eat at home today? Yesterday your sister-in-law was telling me she hardly ever sees you, except for when you eat or sleep. That's not good.'

'The fact is, she doesn't notice. I go to bed very late, and get up early.'

'Is that so? So what do you do, where do you go every evening, who do you go out with . . .? You're very thin.'

Manolo could see that, beneath his aquiline nose, the smile on the Cardinal's thick, kindly lips was still friendly and comforting, and yet how the rest of his face had changed in a short space of time, becoming strangely puffy and scraped in appearance. Solitude had buffeted his cheeks, giving them the sad look of raw meat.

'I was in your brother's workshop,' the old man went on. 'He says he barely sees hide or hair of you. He's worried . . . But sit down. Do you want something to eat?'

Manolo sat down grudgingly at the table, propping himself on his elbow. 'No, thanks,' he said.

A red-flecked lampshade hung over the pale-yellow oilcloth. The Cardinal's head was bowed as if deep in thought. Manolo saw the Syringe put a disc on the record player on the low table in her corner, and soon the crooning voice of a bolero singer could be heard. 'Take that off,' her uncle ordered. 'You have the whole evening to listen to music.' Hortensia reluctantly obeyed, and went out into the kitchen. Almost at once they heard a plate smashing on the floor. The Cardinal didn't so much as blink.

'You'll have a coffee,' he decided, lifting his head. 'Hortensia, coffee for Manolo!'

'Coming up . . .!'

The Cardinal looked across at Manolo.

'We've been very elegant recently, haven't we?' He often used the plural when speaking to Manolo; it was one of the few liberties he took with him. Startled, the youngster examined himself, and the old man added: 'I mean the suit we wore for the first time the other day. Your poor sister-in-law told me.'

'Ah. It's at the laundry.'

'I see,' said the Cardinal. 'Things are going well for us, apparently.'

'Getting by.' The Murcian pushed back his hair. 'Just getting by, Cardinal. That's what I wanted to talk to you about. I need a loan.'

'What plans do we have?'

'Plans? I don't have any.'

'Come on, come on, you can tell Uncle Fidel. What's the problem? Do we have extra expenses this summer? You look so thin . . . Why aren't you working? Don't people ride motorbikes any more? You look well, but I could swear you're thinner and that you've grown. Are tourists coming in armour-plated cars this year? Or maybe it's much simpler, maybe we've fallen in love.'

'Stop talking nonsense,' Manolo protested. A white shape was approaching him slowly from behind, dragging a chair. Hortensia's arm, with her sleeve rolled up, passed over his shoulder and put a cup of coffee on the dining table. Once again he was engulfed in the aroma of bitter almonds. 'I've been wanting to talk to you for days. I've been thinking. Everything is different now; I'll tell you about it, but first I urgently need you to lend me some money, three thousand or so.'

'Are you thinking of leaving us?'

'No, it's not that. I said I'll tell you.'

'There's no need, I can see you have a plan. Why didn't you say so before, you mule?'

'I haven't decided anything yet. It doesn't matter to you for a while – I mean, you don't need me, you've got other irons in the fire' (he knew this was no longer true) 'and you have all the others – Paco, Fermin Pas, the Hermanas sisters.' (This wasn't true either: Paco no longer wanted anything to do with the old man, and the others, including Bernardo, had not been seen for some time.) 'They're still working for you, aren't they?'

'Don't play the innocent. Things aren't going well at all, and it's partly your fault. The trick you played on Paco was the start of it. You can't be so disloyal with your friends, my boy – I've told you so a thousand times. But let's leave that. Why don't you want to carry on working?'

'It's not a good idea. I'm too visible, I'm scared . . .'

'Scared, you? Don't make me laugh. I bet the thing is you've got a girlfriend.' The Cardinal was thinking of that timid girl who the previous winter used to appear on Thursdays in El Carmelo in her ridiculous checked coat and umbrella. He was thinking that the others could have become scared, or were taking their goods elsewhere, or had been nabbed, or had decided he was too old and doddery . . . Whatever the case, Manolo said nothing, and all of a sudden seemed at a loss. Perhaps from often having to make a getaway pursued by nightwatchmen, the painful sensation of going up a blind alley was very vivid in his mind. And now he received another shock: the Syringe, who had sat down without a word beside him with the cup of coffee, was wrapping her icy gaze round him, staring at his profile. The Cardinal poured more brandy into his glass and added:

'By the way, weren't you the one who was laughing at Bernardo?'

'Bernardo got married.'

'At least he's got that excuse. But you're the one who must be crazy. What do you intend to live on? Your sister-in-law doesn't have money to spare. And your brother is fed up to the back teeth with you, like before. Do you expect them to keep you for free? Are you aiming to turn into a crook?'

'No way,' said Manolo, on his high horse.

'So what do you intend to do?' Raising the glass to his lips, the Cardinal drained the contents. He was sweating profusely.

Manolo studied his tearful, drowsy eyes. 'Tell me, what are you thinking of doing?'

'I don't know yet. It could be that ...' (was that really the Syringe's knee pressing against his under the table?) 'I might look for a job. Yes, a good job. I've made friends, I'm contacting people ... Well, it's too soon to tell, but I want to be ready.'

'You don't say.'

'I'll repay you to the last cent, or better still, bring you a bike when I can, to settle the debt. But now I need a holiday, to test out the ground. And something towards my initial costs. That's what I wanted to talk to you about, Cardinal. What do you reckon?'

'I don't reckon anything, mousey.' The drunker he got, the stranger the terms the Cardinal used became, but by now his niece and the Murcian were used to it. 'I don't understand you, that's all. Tell me about your girl ...'

'There is no girl,' the Interloper cut him short. 'No slut is going to make me change.' (From this moment on, and all the time she was sitting there, the damp ashes of Hortensia's eyes had a suctioning effect, like a greedy insect's. At the same time, the thought that he was heading up a blind alley continued to grow in his mind.) 'I swear this is serious, Cardinal. Lend me a thousand at least ... And don't make me waste more time.'

'I'd like to know,' the old man said, 'how you manage to live without working. I bet you survive thanks to bag-snatching now and then, even if that only gets you enough for cigarettes, the movies and ice cream for your demoiselle. The high life, baby rabbit! And of course you don't want to know about motorbikes; they're only for taking her to the beach ...'

'She has a car, if you must know,' Manolo let slip (beside him, Hortensia's gaze wavered for a moment, then immediately recovered its terse immobility and its strange greyness). 'But that doesn't matter. That's not the point. I don't have a cent. At least a thousand . . . I've helped you earn loads, you can't refuse me this favour.'

Disheartened, he peered into the bottom of his coffee cup, then realised the Syringe was trying to attract his attention, banging his leg with her knee. He looked at her: a slight smile, a slow lowering of her eyelids appeared to want to convey something. But by now he had had enough. He rose to his feet. The Cardinal was muttering, as if to himself: 'Yes, snatching a bag every now and then, that's what you lot have always liked. Savages.' Manolo knew the old man had never approved of this practice (snatching a woman's handbag without getting off the motorbike, then speeding away) because, according to him, it was very risky. In fact, as Manolo knew, it was because the Cardinal had no control over what was stolen, and often couldn't sell it. However that might be, Manolo himself had not snatched anything since he met Maruja.

All at once, the Cardinal stood up and rushed out of the room. Manolo followed him. Clad in his dressing gown and shuffling along in his slippers, the old man began charging through the ground-floor rooms, and then the first-floor bedrooms. The Murcian was accustomed to this kind of roaming. In the past, they had been inspired by a sudden, obscure need to see that everything was in order, a kind of inspection (the Cardinal would take the opportunity to put back any misplaced objects, to dust a little, check something wasn't there, and so on), but nowadays they were increasingly rapid and superficial, carried out at a frantic pace, with strides so impressive and majestic that the youngster was almost forced to run after him if he wished to be heard.

'Are you listening, Cardinal?'

'No. Tell me who your friends are, and I'll tell you who you are,' the Galician quoted as he sped along the passageways, the edges of his scarlet dressing gown flying behind him. 'What world do you live in, butterfly? There's nothing like staying at home, Manolo. You never lose anything by staying at home.'

'I know how to look after myself. Listen . . .'

'Tell me. Tell me.'

'Are you angry with me? If you are, say so. Can you really not lend me the money? Or don't you want to?'

The Cardinal made no reply. After a while he concluded his inspection and returned to the dining room, still followed by Manolo. Sitting at the table, he filled his glass once more. He fixed his glittering eyes first on the youth, who had also sat down, and then on his niece. His hand, which was groping on the table for the top to the bottle, knocked a glass of water over.

Manolo stood up. 'I'm off,' he said, going over to the glass door of the veranda and looking out at the garden. This definitely isn't my day, he said to himself.

At that moment, Hortensia took out a handkerchief and blew her nose loudly. Her uncle glanced at her, his dignity ruffled.

'Don't blow your nose at table – it's bad manners.'

His look no doubt was meant to instil respect, but Hortensia, staring back at him over the handkerchief with her spiteful little eyes, blew her nose again, even louder this time. Biting his tongue, the Cardinal tapped her hands with his fingertips as if she was having a toddler tantrum, until she dropped the handkerchief. She smiled and went on staring at him with that shrivelled insect's look of hers. 'Shameless hussy,' said her uncle, scarlet with rage. Endowed with an absurd middle-class idea of politeness, this trait of the Cardinal's often came to the fore at table, especially at table, where, with the decorum worthy of a waiter (a trade he had plied in his youth), he proudly demonstrated an exaggerated love of good manners. He had never properly learned them, but for him they were reduced to two or three elementary principles (wash your hands before meals, do not sing or read while you are eating, and sit on the left of older people) which he tried hard but unsuccessfully to impose on his niece. His greatest obsession was blowing one's nose at table without turning the head. Hortensia calmly picked up the handkerchief, stuffed it down the front of her dress and, humming to herself, got up to leave the table. From that moment on, the Cardinal rapidly became incoherent. 'She was so polite as a little girl,' he mumbled.

'Well, then,' said Manolo as he passed by him. 'Will you do me this favour or not?'

'First let's think it over. I can survive a period without working, but you can't.'

'Don't be such an old grouch,' said Manolo, patting his shoulder. 'You can't do this to me.'

'It's for your own good,' the old man said sweetly. 'The thing is, it's a pity...'

'Do you know something, Cardinal? You're rotten through and through.'

The old man's voice was at first a whine, and then a whisper:

'Yes, it's a pity. Every year when summer comes, it's sad but you always do the same: you go off chasing some bit of skirt or other and being made a fool of in your new suit. In the past it never lasted very long, but now things are more serious, you ungrateful wretch: you're not a kid any more, Manolo. Look, I'm old and know about life. You're going to be taken in and laughed at, and you've never been tough enough to defend yourself...' With that the Cardinal fell silent, as if his mouth had been suddenly gagged. Feeling strangely uneasy (but this was more because of Hortensia, who had remained standing in the dining-room doorway), Manolo decided yet again to leave and try another day, but by this time the Cardinal had already launched into one of those one-sided dialogues he dreaded.

'Can you really not stay any longer?'

'I'll be back.'

'Then have something to eat, my boy. One day you're going to collapse from being so weak.'

'It's not that, Cardinal ... Look, I'll make do with three hundred.'

'Why? Do you have something important to do this evening?'

'I can make do with that, damn it!'

'You're so thin ...'

As he spoke, head bowed and eyes fixed on the tablecloth, the Cardinal was carefully pushing away everything in front of him: the glasses, his brandy balloon, the cutlery and bottles. He smoothed the oilcloth as if he wanted to perform some extremely delicate task on the space he had cleared. Hortensia and Manolo watched what he was doing closely, afraid he might break something, but he didn't. When all the colour had drained from his face and it was no more than a pallid mask, he repeated weakly, 'What world do you live in, butterfly?' before slumping face down on to the table. His white hair lay like a flame across his brow, and two stiff brilliantined tufts stuck up from his ears like two green-tinted bird's wings. He lay there with his head on his forearm.

Manolo rushed over to him, with Hortensia close behind. Holding him under the arms, the two of them lifted the Cardinal from his chair. Manolo noticed that she dealt with her uncle expertly, as if accustomed to emergencies like this; the Cardinal's attacks had probably tripled in recent months. He wanted to lay the old man on his bed, but Hortensia said sharply: 'Outside, in the garden, come on.'

They sat him in a wicker armchair in the old arbour that had lost its creeper and was now nothing more than a skeletal, worm-eaten trellis that let the sun through. There were mouldy cushions and empty bottles on the floor, and next to the chair was a wobbly bedside table with an array of medicine bottles and tablets on it. Motionless, as correct as ever, the Cardinal lay speared diagonally by the rays of the sun that filtered through the once blue trellis. Standing next to Manolo as she plumped up a cushion, the Syringe stared at him with her glazed eyes. She seemed quite calm.

'Can you pass me that bottle?' she asked, pointing to the bedside table. 'I'll go and get a glass of water,' she added, and disappeared inside the house.

Manolo picked up the bottle and tried to open it, but the top was stuck. With a big sigh, the Cardinal moved his head and muttered something. His favourite corner smelled of dust, damp and rancid clothing; as he struggled with the bottle top and looked at the old man, Manolo dimly reflected how quickly, in little more than a year, time had wreaked its havoc on the whole house, what was left of the garden, the furniture, the Cardinal's noble features and Hortensia's eyes. Damned misery!

Looking for something to open the bottle with, Manolo rummaged in the drawer of the bedside table and saw, peeping out from under an old passport and a stack of letters tied up with a pink ribbon, a bundle of two-thousand-peseta notes.

'Not that one,' said Hortensia's voice behind his back, taking the bottle from Manolo and passing him another one. 'This bottle. Take a banknote. Just one.'

'What's that?'

'Take one of the notes, if you want. He won't notice.'

The Murcian didn't hesitate. The note disappeared into his pocket, and he slammed the drawer shut. He didn't know what to say: he was almost tongue-tied. He couldn't distinguish anything special in Hortensia's eyes as she poured the tablets into her hand, but suddenly sensed he had fallen into a trap, just as he had sometimes felt in Maruja's arms. The Cardinal brusquely opened his eyes, stared mischievously, then closed them once more.

'I think he's better already,' Manolo said.

'Yes, it's nothing.'

'Okay, bye then.' He turned on his heel. 'Be seeing you.'

Hortensia, who was pushing the tablets into her uncle's mouth and bringing a glass of water to his lips, turned for a moment to look at him. Before going back inside the house, Manolo said:

'When he wakes up, give him lots of coffee.'

He walked through the dining room and started down the long, dark passageway. As he reached the front door, Hortensia caught up with him and opened it before he could. The Interloper was taken aback: he hadn't expected this. She stood there very still, pressed against the edge of the open door, clasping it in both hands, unconsciously possessive. The second button on her white coat was undone, and the weight of the sweets in the top left pocket pulled the lapel open, momentarily revealing the blue-tinged shadow, the dark fishtail between her breasts. Manolo leaned towards her slightly to whisper cheerfully:

'Syringe, sweetheart, I won't forget what you just did for me.'

Hortensia didn't even blink. Once Manolo had left, she pushed the door to, without completely closing it: one dull eye followed him as walked off in the sun. She was the one who wasn't going to forget it.

The first steps were haphazard and confused, no more than a hesitant coming together of hips during their short evening strolls.

Everything began one hot evening in that month of July when they decided to leave the clinic earlier than usual. Maruja's hospital room had for them become a kind of sanctuary for love in ruins (with an undisputed high priestess: the Mallorcan nurse Dina), a place that called for silence, random memories and overpowering respect for the patient's critical condition. No reaction, no improvement, no sign of life to disrupt that lethargy and silence (Maruja's endless silence – how strange, what a glimpse of the future as they sat with her: what can be done for you, poor dear friend, what more can we do for you?), leaving them inhibited by a hazy feeling of remorse. Until now Teresa and Manolo had spent most of the time seated in the armchairs in the anteroom, talking about Maruja or flicking through magazines, with long pauses (occasionally disrupted by the flash of a furtive glance), and it was only at dusk that they felt free to leave. Manolo always behaved in a reasonable, reserved manner, allowing Teresa to decide everything; the fiery sun of resolve and audacity was not yet shining in all its glory in the Murcian's sky. More often than not it was the nurse Dina, with that mysterious smile of hers behind which dark romantic blooms withered in the bud, who plunged their enchanted bodies into the warm green bath of an indescribable tropical paradise:

'You young people! If I were you, on holiday and with a car, instead of coming here, getting hot and doing nothing – because, don't pretend, you both know there's nothing you can do for her; if it was me, rather than waste time here I'd be off to Sitges.'

Merely from the way she pronounced the word Sitges (a click of the tongue, a nacreous iridescence, and the word dissolving in her mouth like fresh seafood), they were bound to admit she was right. What could they do on stifling evenings like this in a city that seemed blighted and asleep?

At first, Teresa would take him back to El Carmelo, and they stopped off at some bar or other to have a drink. After that they drifted down the Ramblas and the Barrio Chino. Teresa steered them to the left, naturally heading for Calle Escudillers and its crowded, heterogeneous bars. Their great adventure was not yet under way, but their blood was already stirred by a succession of brief amorous incidents, subtle emotions felt by one or other that oscillated between them at chance moments, such as when standing at the crowded bar in a tavern. It turned out that Teresa knew quite a few of them, and loved going quickly from one to another, as if to check they were still there, recalling her past in the company of student friends, places with the same depressing flamenco fauna, the same good wine (foul, in fact, thought Manolo, but said nothing), the same prostitutes and female lottery sellers, standing so close their hips unintentionally brushed against each other, and feeling protected by the false impunity of the commotion all around them. There was no way for Manolo to be aware of it, but the same emotion Teresa had felt that winter's night at the gate to her house in San Gervasio when she saw his coarse woollen scarf came flooding back whenever their fingers or hips touched, or when they chatted to a tram driver, a street vendor or a supposed old militiaman or Republican. To her, this was something more than the simple agitation caused, for example, by his strong hand clutching her arm as they ran across a street between cars, even if she didn't lend it any importance: after all, she was a modern female university student, from the 1956 intake, dialectical and objective, expert at grasping reality.

But as yet, reality was no more than a foetus curled up in the damsel's sweet womb, mysteriously conceived by cultural antecedents of notorious, frightening ideological force. Teresa, generously and unconsciously pregnant with light and feelings of fraternal solidarity, was now looking to her new friend for some progressive moral gratification, and for the moment confused this with desire. But any tender ballad, any record heard in a bar was enough for the Murcian's velvet gaze (he contemplated her with heaven knows what contrasting sort of solidarity) to offer her a brief glimpse of the existence of a higher, more immediate and urgent reality, that indescribable tropical paradise that Dina the priestess had suggested to them. No doubt these were fleeting moments, the illusions of a repressed, dissatisfied young *bourgeoise* (as she told herself, very given as she was to self-criticism), selfish impulses of the flesh that now, faced with a real militant, seemed to her unworthy and ridiculous. As a result, due to the ambivalent attraction the Interloper exercised over her (three levels of seduction: the conspiracy, love and danger), there still existed an emotional imbalance that tinted these first evenings a comical pink. Once, for example, this happened in a local cinema she had insisted they go to. Marlon Brando was nodding sagely and seductively (learn from that, kid!) with his legendary bare chest and Emiliano Zapata's black moustaches, sitting up in bed with his young bride on their wedding night, while Teresa slid down until her head was resting on the seat back, radiantly carefree, revealing a great deal of tanned thigh. Childlike, relaxed and happy as she studied the hermetic beauty of the film star's jaw and brow, she also noted out of the corner of her eye the uneasy glances Manolo was shooting at her. The scene in the film (a moving portrayal of the popular hero, the illiterate revolutionary who, conscious of his responsibility to the people, on his wedding night asks his beautiful bride to give him lessons in grammar rather than in pleasure) was so moving that Teresa, believing the Murcian was experiencing the same satisfaction as her, kept turning to him and smiling, biting her lip, becoming pensive, approving heaven knows what with her eyes, until finally, when she leaned towards him to praise the class consciousness of the Mexican peasants, she became aware of the red-hot current given off by his yearning skin, and something about the adoring looks he was giving her, openly admiring her legs, neck and hair, so disconcerted her that she said nothing, but turned her attention back to the screen. At that moment she felt something stirring under her head, leaving it in mid-air, and realised that all this time she had been resting not on the back of the seat as she had thought but on his strong, patient and discreet arm. Even with good movies, one can lose all sense of reality.

The worst, most ludicrous of these one-sided adventures took place one night during a breakneck, almost suicidal race Teresa undertook in the Floride when they were returning to the city along the main road from Castelldefels. They had simply gone out for a drive at the end of the day, but Teresa had wanted to go on further, and by the time they were coming back it was pitch dark. Teresa was wearing a striped, collarless blouse and a red silk scarf that streamed in the wind with her hair. The car radio was playing a lively cha-cha-cha. The Murcian had never experienced the thrill of speeding in a sports car, and was looking alternately at the beam of the headlights on the asphalt, the speedometer (the needle had passed the one hundred and twenty mark) and Teresa's beguiling profile. He had one hand pressed hard against the windscreen; his other arm was round the back of her seat.

'Do you like going fast?' she shouted. He nodded uncertainly. He could feel his stiff black hair whipping against his temples, and the fury of the wind on his face, adhering to his skin like a hot mask, while somewhere inside him a soft buzzing gradually grew louder until it completely filled him. They were going faster all the time and the buzzing became increasingly sharp and high-pitched, rising from stomach to chest and then flooding all his senses, finally dissolving into a silent, stellar plenitude, a childish sensation of moonlight and weightlessness floating in the air. But Manolo didn't trust these instinctive emotions (he vaguely recalled the Cardinal once telling him about slot machines in the United States that when you put in a coin, a plastic hand swung out and slapped you in the face: it must be a joke) and suspected everything had conspired to bemuse him: the moon, the stars, the dark blue night were all showering him with deceitful promises. His habitual sense of ease with Teresa had not foreseen this treacherous attack, this intoxication of the senses, and for the first time in his life he felt fragile, small, vulnerable and somehow dirty, conquered in advance by the beautiful combined force (automobile, cha-cha-charming rich girl) hurtling him at dizzying speed through the night. He did not know what it was: Teresa's adorable profile, her mouth half open and blond hair fluttering in the wind with the red scarf (a brilliant flame in the darkness) or the burning touch of her thighs, but the fact was that all of a sudden a soft delight, a sweet emptiness in his bones (slow down, you lunatic, slow down!), an excitement he had never felt before, as well as a piercing sensation, brought about the second, definitive change to his senses. His ears were suddenly blocked as he entered some ethereal region and gently tilted his head back (stop, sweetheart, stop!) and peered up at the firmament, the cha-cha-cha music enveloping him as he floated, shuddered, and thought he was going to dissolve there and then ... At that very instant Teresa braked sharply by the side of the road and she laid her exhausted head on the steering wheel and let out a deep sigh.

'Phew...! That's a relief,' she said. 'We were lucky, they're not following us.'

'What ...? What's that?' the Murcian stammered, still descending from regions bordering on madness, so distractedly that his hand strayed like a drunken moth towards her fragrant knees and alighted there, all energy spent.

'What are you doing?' asked Teresa. She was smiling, but looked anxious. 'Were you scared? It was the traffic cops: when I saw them, I was worried they would stop me. Best to steer clear of the filth ... I was thinking of you, above all ... Are you all right?'

The moth flew off: the flower had closed up and Teresa, pleased with herself, magnificently unaware of the way she shone even brighter than the stars, drove off again and headed straight for the city, oblivious to the doubly sweet weight she was now carrying.

After that, the welcoming circle slowly spread. First there were short strolls around the clinic (Paseo de la Bonanova, gardens with palm trees and pines, houses with slate-lined conical turrets, railings and endless pavements filled with chatty servants and rushed, determined-looking priests), a pious local pilgrimage that widened around Maruja like ripples in a pond. Later on, thanks to the Floride and the lethargy of those summer evenings, which by now contained the seed of precocious ashes (the circle collapsed with the first nocturnal September winds), in successive evenings they covered the entire city and its outskirts, from fashionable bars and cafés in the centre to unsuspected taverns, stalls and poor-looking terraces on its outer limits. The car was a constant presence (a reassuring promise of return), as were moments of ice cream, soft drinks and watermelon slices eaten spontaneously in the shade of an awning by the roadside (a tempting promise, Teresa's milky-white teeth sinking into the scarlet pulp) with flies buzzing round them, and cheeky children who came and went (Teresa gaily sliding down an embankment with ragged little imps: a tear in her blue jeans), to finally end up in the reddish gloom of romantic clubs, sunk in leather sofas, lulled by sophisticated music for rich, educated couples.

Teresa apparently loved to read, and at first in all their outings she stubbornly insisted (as if she fought against breaking the cultural ties that still kept her anchored in her peaceful cove) on taking some book or other with her which, if it didn't fall victim to its owner's pre-amorous carelessness (Teresa asking for his hand so that she could jump barefoot on the breakwater in the port, then slipping on one of the big concrete blocks, and the book falling into the water), ended up forgotten and yawning behind the seats in the Floride, turning yellow in the sun. She swam happily in her blue tropical waters, planning visits that never took place ('One evening I want to go to Somorrostro beach, but on my own'), with the Interloper displaying his most captivating characteristic, that of putting himself in someone else's shoes ('I won't allow you to go alone'). And naturally, once the risk involved in this odd nostalgia for out-of-the-way places had been brought up, they never went there. They skilfully combined red wine and suburban or marine surroundings (Teresa Moreau nibbling at prawns among the blue-striped jerseys young fishermen were wearing), gin and tonics with music by Bach and soft leather sofas and a discreet atmosphere (Teresa de Beauvoir flicking through books in the Cristal City Bar-Librería), stifling cinemas where they showed repeats ('When is censorship going to end in this country so we can see *The Battleship Potemkin?*'), or working-class neighbourhoods for the Fiesta Mayor celebrations, as well as casual encounters with lost tourists (Teresa speaking in French to the tanned, young, half-naked couple who pulled up alongside her Floride: '*Regarde ce garçon-là, oh comme il est beau!*'). And the tangy breeze down in the port, the summer hustle and bustle of the Ramblas, beer and squid in Plaza Real, lazy strolls round Parque Güell, blazing sunsets seen from Monte Carmelo, the car parked on the road as they bade each other goodbye.

Every day, this was the moment when the Murcian peered into his friend's Teresa's transparent blue eyes for the signal. In vain as yet. Because things didn't always end well: they had many arguments. Teresa talked endlessly and in what the Interloper felt was a very complicated manner. Above all, she enjoyed talking about love as if she was speaking about a dead relative for whom she had a great deal of affection. One night, as she was dropping Manolo in El Carmelo, she suddenly asked him:

'Would you be willing to die for a great love?'

'Yes.'

She burst out laughing.

'I knew it! How silly!'

'I don't see why,' he said, eyes blazing. 'Don't you believe in love?'

'It's not a question of believing. I put more trust in desire. It's a more valuable, less sullied emotion. Of course, only if it's mutual and doesn't involve any kind of moral responsibility.'

'You're asking too much.'

'Not me, the times we live in.'

'I don't get you.'

'It's very simple, my boy,' Teresa said with a sigh. 'This is a transitional period, don't you agree? I mean regarding moral values, which are at a low ebb . . .' Arms folded on the steering wheel, staring up at the night sky above Monte Carmelo, she launched into her theory about why love was in crisis at present.

Listening to her with a faint, tolerant smile – or more exactly, drinking in the sound of her voice, the pleasure of hearing her – Manolo said nothing, and then tried unsuccessfully to bring her back to reality with a childish ruse: quickly flicking the car headlights on and off. He moved closer to her as she continued to pontificate, pushing back a lock of hair that had fallen over her eyes, and leaned over her face . . . and then, incomprehensibly to her (by now she had fallen silent, anxiously awaiting what from his closeness she imagined was going to be the passionate response that would bring her theory crashing to the ground), Manolo froze and withdrew, leaving her perplexed as he got out of the car.

'You think you're an intellectual, a well-read woman, don't you?' he said, slamming the car door. 'See you tomorrow, then.'

With that he strode off down the road to the Bar Delicias, hands in pockets and whistling.

The purpose behind his unexpected reactions was not merely a basic assertion of power: they might well upset his refined companion, which made them risky, but the fact was he couldn't see any other way of defending himself, of bridging the cultural abyss between them. Best to take drastic measures. By persisting and perfecting this simple strategy, the Murcian hoped gradually to discourage the complex university student who liked nothing better than to indulge in Byzantine discussions and leave him instead with the happy, bewitching eighteen-year-old who loved to spend her evenings with him and found any excuse to enjoy herself. This tactic of refusal and withdrawal was equally successful with regard to the occasional displays of exhibitionism or *señoritismo* that Teresa, despite her passionately progressive ideas, could occasionally not avoid; unforeseen, wild moments typical of a modern, free and presumably deflowered young woman (how she loved to rest her arm on Manolo's shoulder and press herself against him in public, openly displaying a sexual intimacy she was as yet far from deigning to give in to) that drove Manolo crazy.

Yet none of their arguments lasted more than twenty-four hours, and often it was Manolo himself who ended them by calling to say he was sorry. Whenever he did so, Teresa would insist it was entirely her fault, accusing herself of being a snob. This led the Murcian to wonder if he wasn't being too cautious in his approach. One evening, when they were sitting in the anteroom in the clinic, the door opened and Señor Serrat appeared.

To see Teresa so flustered (when the door opened she was very close to her friend, her head leaning over him as they read the cinema listings in a newspaper) was a novelty for Manolo. Looking serious all of a sudden, he stood up and held out his hand, trying in vain to read something in the Catalan industrialist's eyes. With a snort, and barely breaking stride, Señor Serrat grunted some sort of greeting and shook his hand, before immediately entering Maruja's room. He was in a hurry: he had come, among other things, to tell Teresa that he was off to the coast for the weekend and that she should give instructions to the gardener who would go to their house the next morning, because you know we can't rely on Vicenta, she never remembers anything. Teresa followed him into Maruja's room. Manolo stayed in the other one, but could hear Señor Serrat speaking through the half-open door: '*Nena, qui és aquest noi?*' Daughter, who is this fellow?

Then something in Teresa's voice, as well as the falsely cold and indifferent tone she adopted, something in the pause before she answered her father's question, revealed to Manolo the hidden emotional motives born of a particular nostalgia that she stubbornly confused with some ridiculous political intrigue. 'I hardly know him, Papa. He says he's Maruja's fiancé and comes to see her every day,' was her devious, off-hand reply. As Manolo tiptoed towards the door, she went on: 'I feel sorry for him, poor lad' (another grunt from Señor Serrat).

Manolo thought: so this was how, according to Teresa, their relationship was to be seen from the outside. He was nothing more than the supposed fiancé of the sick maid, who during his daily visits to the clinic meets the *señorita*, who kindly takes him home in her car. Fine. Nothing special: all this is no more than an unimportant episode in a summer that won't last for ever; they're both on holiday and practically without any family supervision, on their own and accidentally united by Maruja's misfortune, but his background is so vastly different to hers nothing will come of it. 'I feel sorry for him, poor lad.' It's natural enough, he thought, there's no reason for her to mention our jaunts in the car. And yet, due to the mixture of truth and lies hidden behind Teresa's words (she wasn't exactly lying, but wasn't telling the whole truth either), Manolo realised he was being over-cautious and that he could and should act more quickly and decisively. Which is what he did.

Entering Maruja's room, he saw: Dina bending over the bedside table to connect a saline solution for her patient. Her preparations were being watched by Señor Serrat, who was standing beside her. On the other side of the bed Teresa, hands behind her back, was still replying with an innocent air to the absent-minded questions her father was asking about what she did after visiting Maruja. Teresa appeared to be excessively keen to demonstrate she had barely noticed the young Murcian. He approached the bed slowly (none of them looked at him, but they fell silent), stood quietly next to Teresa and carelessly laid his hand on the drip stand at the bedhead, so that his fingers were almost touching Teresa's shoulder. That evening she was wearing a simple light-green sleeveless dress that had no belt but a zip all the way down past her waist. Casually, while like the others he was watching what the nurse was doing, Manolo moved his hand, as if fidgeting, up and down the metal pole very close to Teresa's back. Then, as he was sliding his hand down the bar, he suddenly closed his thumb and forefinger like a bird's beak around the pull at the top of the zip, and in a flash had tugged it all the way down. The dress material peeled back like a skin, releasing a golden glow: he caught a glimpse of a smooth, gently rounded back that was slender, almost childlike, its suntan uninterrupted by any white stripe (he already knew that she was one of those daring young student women who rarely wore a bra), deliriously concave as she leaned forward, tapering at the youthful waist, then swelling once more with renewed impetus under the pink gleam of the nylon material covering her buttocks. It was all so rapid and unanticipated that Teresa was left speechless, her mouth wide open; the front of the dress was secured at the shoulder, which completely thwarted the other half of the Murcian's crazy fantasy (that is: for the deceitful, capricious young woman to be seen by her father and the nurse with her little breasts in full view).

Señor Serrat, who at that moment was saying something about local and general amnesia, raised his eyes to his daughter but, not noticing anything unusual about her (except that she was hugging herself as if she were cold), turned his attention back to what Dina was doing. Teresa's cheeks turned scarlet. She glanced furiously at Manolo as she tried surreptitiously to pull the zip up, then edged her way back to the door and left the room.

When he joined her, she rebuked him (astonished, but not really upset) and wanted to know why he had done something so foolish in front of her father. 'If I didn't, you'd still be telling him lies about you and me,' he said, taking her by the arm as though he wanted to explain more fully but not there, and forced her to leave the clinic.

That night Manolo invited her for a drink in Jamboree. Teresa was delighted to show herself with the Murcian in the cellar on Plaza Real. Gliding along like fish in an aquarium, several illustrious student leaders were to be seen, Luis Trías among them, plotting and up to no good in semi-clandestinity, surrounded by a green-tinged aura of exile and Paris. A strange, primitive Spanish jazz band that played on bone instruments (a donkey's jawbone producing sound and philosophy, according to the handbill), their music not taken seriously by anyone (apart from an attentive couple wearing glasses, both of them short-sighted arts students, who recognised Teresa and wanted her and her companion to share their table), which at least meant people could dance without profaning what was a true cathedral of jazz. In the semi-darkness, dancing cheek to cheek with her new friend to the puzzled gaze of the students (who, as she whispered in Manolo's ear, she despised for being so old-fashioned and reactionary), for the first time Teresa allowed him to brush her temples and forehead with his lips.

The next day when they left the clinic, Manolo suggested they went to the beach. It was early afternoon and very hot. More sure of himself by now, the Murcian saw this as a positive step, even if the sword of Damocles was hanging only a few centimetres above his head: he was about to run out of money, and couldn't see how to get his hands on any without risk. The decision to go for a swim was spontaneous, and since neither of them had a swimsuit, Teresa suggested they should pass by her house.

'We can find a pair of Father's trunks for you.'

She didn't want him to wait outside in the car, but invited him in.

'I have to get changed,' she told him as they were crossing the garden. 'Just a minute. Do you mind?'

'No, no.'

Manolo followed her up the gravel path, in the shade of leafy trees. (Suddenly it was a winter's night, and he was wearing his leather jacket and his woollen scarf and Señorita Teresa was running on her thin high-heeled shoes, her snow-white raincoat round her shoulders, the belt buckle dragging on the ground, and the red silk scarf dangling from her pocket . . .) Teresa opened the front door with her key and showed him into a spacious, sunny living room.

'Make yourself comfortable,' she said, slipping off her shoes. 'And pour yourself a drink, if you like, there's everything over there. I won't be a minute. Don't look at the paintings, they're horrible.'

She disappeared down the entrance hall, shoes in one hand and unzipping her dress with the other. As she climbed the stairs, she called out: 'Vicenta, it's me.'

Manolo strolled round the living room. The paintings on the walls were Swiss landscapes, and didn't seem that horrible to him. There was also the portrait of a lady gazing at him smugly from a blue, pleasure-filled distance; her slender pink neck emerged from a mass of lilac chiffon that swathed her shoulders. That must be the mother. How beautiful, with such a sweet expression. The house was completely silent; a silence unlike any other. To Manolo the silence in rich people's houses was like a powerful sleeping force, similar to stilled fans or the vague background murmur of central heating. Over the hearth hung a big painting of hunting dogs. That wasn't so bad either: they must be good company in winter when you sat by the fire after an exhausting day doing business . . .

The Interloper sat on the sofa in front of the fireplace and crossed his legs slowly and contentedly. All at once to his left he heard paws scrabbling towards him: a small fox terrier with curly fur, its head tilted to one side, was staring with a sad expression at this strange visitor, its suspicious eyes barely visible behind a curtain of hair. Manolo studied him for a while in a friendly way, then held out his hand to stroke it, but the dog lifted its head and withdrew, taking a couple of turns round the sofa. Its suspicious air only grew when, rejecting a second friendly gesture, it sat on its haunches and turned its head in the direction of the door, hoping to see someone from the house appear, visibly unconvinced or, rather, filled with serious doubts as to who this intruder might be. Manolo now saw it was a female. The terrier's comical head, like a crazy but highly intelligent young girl, was still disdainfully turned to one side and only occasionally did she deign to look at the suspect stranger, as if to avoid any reproach even before it was made.

'Come here, sweetie, come on . . .' Manolo murmured.

The little dog approached him slowly without looking at him, carefully sniffed at the trouser leg of his jeans, his trainers, the dark-skinned hand wanting to stroke her, and then, head lowered – as if this examination had only served to increase her doubts – turned on her heel and took up her watchful position once more. Manolo leaned his head wearily on the back of the sofa and gazed once more at the bright paintings on the walls and the tranquil intimacy of the hearth with a vaguely dissatisfied, obsessive yet agreeable sense of curiosity. He felt like having a smoke.

The feeling of security he felt here, surrounded by this comfortable sense of order and silence, contrasted with the growing awkwardness and difficulty he had been experiencing in recent days in his usual surroundings: in his own house, even in the Bar Delicias, or with the Cardinal and his niece (he recalled his last visit there, and how he had stolen the money). It was as if, casually and carelessly, he had lost some of his influence and power over them; he had a feeling that everything was going too fast, of having forgotten something in his haste, of having made a mistake that at the moment of arrival (arriving where?) they were bound to remind him of and call him to account. Perhaps that was why, as a warning, at that very moment the Hermanas sisters appeared, up to mischief. The afternoon was full of surprises.

He had to accept it calmly as one of fate's little sarcasms. He had finally calmed the little fox terrier and had his back to the open window that gave on to the garden; he was standing next to the piano (he couldn't decide whether to press some of the keys) and so failed to spot under the trees, at the far side of the double row of geraniums, two figures who were crossing the garden towards the house. They were two young girls in Technicolor (chocolate-dark arms and legs, violet lips, blue eyeliner extending to their temples like tiny face masks) with high bouffant hairstyles glittering in the sun, in thin, gaudy summer dresses as tight as second skins. Their round faces had that over-intense suntanned look that betrayed the use of too much oil and too many hours sunbathing on the roof, ruining their complexion. Their rapid, nervous trot up the path showed an urgent determination that wasn't reflected in the indifferent, even bored expressions on their moonlike faces. The shorter one was carrying an enormous basket with coloured designs on it, and had her hands on her hips as if she was worried some undergarment or other might fall down because of the haste they were in. Manolo heard the door bell ring. No one went to answer it. He didn't see the two girls arrive: had he done so, he would have guessed immediately why they had come and could have intercepted them in the garden. Fortunately, however, the elderly servant was slow in reaching the door, which meant the Murcian had time to rush into the entrance hall just as she came lumbering up, heavy hips swaying beneath the grey uniform. As Vicenta went by, she gave him a perfunctory smile and opened the door. At first Manolo was blinded by the flood of light from outside; by now he was at the living-room door, half turning back (he was about to re-enter the room, having finally decided he would play a few notes on the piano), but when he recognised the two sisters he froze. It couldn't be, this had to be a joke in bad taste, the black fate that endlessly hounded poor people; it was no simple coincidence, more like a caution, a warning that pursued him from his own neighbourhood.

In fact, he shouldn't have been so surprised, because he was well aware that the Hermanas sisters preferred to operate in residential areas during the holidays in order to find servants on their own. Manolo had not seen them since the previous winter; he knew they no longer had anything to do with the Cardinal, but that they continued with their speciality, a swindle known as 'the underwear trick'.

He also knew how dangerous this unforeseen and untimely visit was for him (an encounter with real intrigue, something Teresa didn't even suspect). It threatened to bring everything crashing to the ground. If this light-fingered pair recognise me in front of Teresa, I'm done for, he panicked.

At that very moment, beach bag on her shoulder and wearing white trousers and sandals, she appeared in the entrance hall. 'Who is it, Vicenta?' The little dog ran towards her wagging its tail. 'Stay, Dixi.' Out on the porch, the two sisters (how outrageous their dresses are, it's so obvious what they're up to, thought an alarmed Manolo), put on their most innocent expressions, despite obviously being taken aback at seeing Manolo. For a moment it was an embarrassing situation: the servant was waiting for the visitors to speak; they themselves exchanged worried glances with Manolo, as did he with Teresa. She in turn sensed subtle vibrations that suggested some kind of link between the worker and the two girls, and came to a swift, generous mental deduction that for the moment went no further than: they're either whores or factory workers, or both. Manolo himself imagined that the Hermanas wouldn't dare do anything and would quickly make an excuse and leave. But he was horrified to see they had no intention of turning back, because one of them (the specialist in their patter) was about to launch into her story about the elastic in her companion's knickers snapping in the street, so that ... Before she could do so, he leapt towards the door, saying to Teresa:

'Don't worry – it's for me.'

The Hermanas sisters' jaws dropped when they saw the Murcian confronting them. One of them stammered:

'You ...'

'It's for me, I'll deal with it,' Manolo repeated, this time to Vicenta, almost knocking her over in his rush. The servant stood back from the door, looking at her mistress with a resigned expression. Manolo grabbed both sisters by the arm and dragged them out as far as he could into the garden. All three of them spoke at once:

'For Christ's sake ...!'

'Manolillo, what a surprise!'

'Get out of here!'

'Hey, hang on!' the other sister protested. 'You must be joking! Let go of me, handsome. Is this your house, then? What are you doing here?'

'Shut up if you don't want me to break your arm,' said Manolo. 'Start walking and don't look back. Try someone else with your game, sweetheart. That's it, start laughing. What were you thinking? Today of all days! Didn't you see the car out in the street, you idiots? Meaning someone was in?'

'What's wrong? If we found the owner in, we'd leave empty-handed. But how could we imagine ...' began the one with the faulty garment. 'Let go of me, you're hurting. What are you doing here? What right do you have to order us around?'

'I don't have time to explain. Out you go.'

'Don't push, okay? And explain . . .'

'Yes, that's right,' said the other sister. 'Can we know what you're doing here, if we can know?' Perhaps attempting to rectify the repetition, she added, only making things worse: 'Listen, what a surprise seeing you, it's been so long since we saw you . . .'

Manolo led them to the gate.

'I'm leaving right away. Wait till the Cardinal hears about this.'

The taller one broke free and confronted him:

'Hey, listen, don't threaten us! Who cares about the Cardinal? We don't have anything to do with that dirty old man . . .'

'I don't want to argue. Get out, there are people here.'

'Are you still with him? I didn't think you were so innocent, my boy. That Cardinal is a piece of work! The day you're least expecting it, he'll land you in trouble, Manolo – you mark my words! Let go of me, will you?'

'Don't shout, you clown.'

'And don't you insult me, pretty boy.'

By now they had reached the garden gate. Manolo realised he couldn't just get rid of them.

'Okay, I'll explain. Another day . . . How are you anyway? And Paco? Do you still get together with him? What about Xoni . . .?'

'Better than you, you good-for-nothing. As for Paco, you'll see when he gets his hands on you. We're still waiting for you to pay us what you owe, you bastard!'

'Sshhh! I don't owe you anything.'

'That's what you say! Was it you or the Cardinal?'

'It was him, sister,' said the other one. 'Can't you tell by his face?'

'All right, now be off with you . . .'

'As I was saying,' the other one insisted, 'the Cardinal is a bloodsucker. Can't you see it?'

'All right, that'll do.'

'The thing is,' said the smaller sister, patting his shoulder, 'now we have another dealer: Rafael. Do you know him? His wife has just had twins born together on the same day. But do you mind telling us what you're doing here, if you don't mind?' The younger of the Hermanas always came out with extraordinary things, because her tongue was much quicker than her brain, but today Manolo wasn't in the mood to enjoy them. 'Or do you mind?'

'Yes, I do mind. Now please go. I'll tell you all about it some other day ...'

Teresa was watching them from the living-room window, the beach bag on her shoulder, combing her hair while she waited. 'Stay, Dixi,' she again ordered the dog, who was rubbing herself against her legs. She couldn't hear them, but could see Manolo growing angry, gesticulating and pushing the girls out into the street. They laughed out loud as they said goodbye, giving him kisses on the cheek (it was incredible: all of a sudden the taller one tried to kiss him on the mouth! Teresa saw her trying anxiously and shamelessly to force him into it, ruffling his hair and wrapping those dark, plump arms of hers round his neck, even though he resisted and kept on pushing her out of the garden), before they finally left.

'What did those two want?' she asked when Manolo came back inside the house. Still combing her hair, she adopted a tried-and-tested expression and tone of voice, and said jokingly, pointing her finger at him: 'Let's see, young man. Answer me: do you know those two ladies?'

Pensive, Manolo turned his back on her and went over to an armchair.

'Was it you they were looking for?' Teresa insisted. 'It's curious ... All of you are subversives, reds under the beds: we know all about you. Come on, don't lie: how did they know you were here?'

The Murcian jerked his head sharply in her direction. He didn't allow himself a moment's hesitation:

'Please, I'd be grateful if you didn't ask me anything!' His voice softened. 'I left word at home that if ever there was anything urgent, they would find me either at the clinic or here ... I'm sorry for taking the liberty.'

Embarrassed, she looked at him, then lowered her eyes.

'Don't worry about me. I understand. I was only joking.'

'Well, then, don't,' he said cuttingly, although with an aching soul. He had to admit Teresina was a wonderful person. 'And forgive me, I've no right to shout at you, but things are much more serious than you can imagine. There's no need for you to get mixed up in all this.'

Teresa put away the comb in her bag and came slowly over to him. She saw how he slumped in the armchair, head in hands with a weary, worried look on his face, as if overburdened by something. How to escape, seeing those strong, dark hands, those features both gentle and harsh at one and the same time, how to escape the hint of a more just future? At that time Teresa was so convinced there was a political conspiracy behind everything that it was enough for her to imagine a slight tremor of fear in those hands and that jet-black hair for her to happily become part of the supposed circle of danger:

'Is there something wrong, Manolo?' She was standing very still next to him, legs together in her elastic white trousers. Still running his fingers through his hair, the Murcian lifted his eyes to the level of her hips, closed them again, and said:

'Nothing. Let's go.' He stood up. 'Let's go to the beach, please. I need to have some fun.'

In the car on their journey to Castelldefels, Teresa felt the urgent need to pass judgement on the two girls, for the sake of the plotters' safety.

'One of you needs to convince them not to use so much make-up. They look like tarts.' After which she added: 'I've found a pair of trunks. I hope they fit.'

'I'm sure they will. And now, step on it as fast as you can . . .! Overtake them all!'

Teresa Simmons running in a bikini across the beaches of his dreams, or lying on the sand, stretching beneath a deep-blue sky, droplets of water on her waist and arms aloft (a golden glow in her underarms, shimmering like reflections on water under a bridge), then swimming impeccably, her joyous, slender-hipped body emerging from the foamy waves and finally heading up from the water's edge towards him like a living, resonant bronze statue, her small abdomen heaving, her whole body covered in glistening droplets. Jean Serrat smiling, waving an arm in greeting to him, to the shady Murcian, this elastic, cat-like, crouching bundle of aspirations, desires, shameful urges and agonising fears (I'll lose her, this can't be, she's not for me, I'll lose her before I have time to be a Catalan like you, you sons of bitches!), sprawling now on a big colourful beach towel that wasn't his, wearing swimming trunks that weren't his, nor were the sunglasses or the cigarettes he was smoking, all of this as if he was a lodger in someone else's house. (What are you doing here, kid, what are you hoping for from this fleeting, capricious friendship stuck between two seasons of the year; is it just the whim of a rich, pampered young woman, and then 'so long, it's been good to know you'?) Just to see her like this, walking slowly, half naked and sure of herself, against a background of palm trees and unexplored jungle – wasn't this summer the blue lagoon on the lost island? – was reward enough, and she was his, his for the moment rather than her parents', or her future husband's, more his than any of the lovers who might adore and possess her in the future. His private collection of glossy images opened in his hand like a rustling fan: the two of them lost on the golden tropical isle, alone, beautiful, free; happy survivors of a ghastly nuclear war (in which of course and in fact we have all died, dear reader – this couldn't last), they build a cabin like a nest, run along the endless beach, eat coconuts, dive for pearls and coral, contemplate fiery emerald sunsets, sleep together on a bed strewn with flowers, caress one another and learn to make love free from metaphysical possessive anxieties while putrid life carries on elsewhere, far away from this fluidity of tanned limbs (Teresa was still walking slowly across the sand towards him) that now lag slightly behind his imaginary world, her bare midriff not seeming to move in the hazy atmosphere, a painful promise that begins at her shoulders, curls round her hips and sways down her legs before plunging free at last, spilling out like light at her feet, at each footstep. Breathless, soaking wet, she is approaching with her luminous smile, a coconut held between waist and arm, bringing with her something of the cold green marine depths, then bends her beautiful knees and sits slowly next to him, dropping the coconut. Her body seemed completely accustomed to running and lying on beaches, as if she had grown up on them, strangely gifted by nature to always live here, in the sun ...

'Aren't you going in again?' she asked.

Teresa had dropped the beach ball. She squatted down, her head lowered as she searched in her bag for her sunglasses. Her hair covered half her face, and there was an animal grace about her wet hips, her back curving above her narrow waist. What torture in her sunken, childlike abdomen beneath her bikini top, a favourite target for the Murcian's roving eyes.

'Where on earth did I put my glasses?' she asked. 'Have you seen them?'

'No,' he lied cheerily: he had buried them in the sand. 'Come on, lie down and forget about your glasses. I have to talk to you about something, to ask a favour.'

'A favour?'

'Yes . . .'

Lying there, chin on his forearm, he was studying Teresa's movements closely, lost in thought. His straight black hair slanted across his forehead. There were few people on the beach (the busiest part was down by the pine trees); only a few, and all indistinct in the distance through the hazy air. The two of them were on their own at one end, near the edge of some marshes that stretched to the horizon. Behind them, on a flat field of stubble next to the main road, the white Floride was sleeping in the sun like a pedigree dog. Teresa had brought a book, which she had been reading until now. It was at that moment, watching her reading, on her back on the sand as peacefully as if she was at home, her head resting on the ball, her crossed knees swaying gently from side to side, that Manolo felt like a wretched sneak thief. An idea that would soon become an obsession flashed through his mind. What if we wiped the slate clean? This is our opportunity, Teresa (and with Teresa, her father): I could find a proper job, a good situation, maybe one of those that last a lifetime, with a chance to . . .

'A favour?' Teresa repeated. 'What kind of favour?'

Manolo pensively traced circles in the sand.

'Not now,' he said. 'It's too soon. We're on holiday. I'll tell you later on. For now I only want you to know it's important to me. Are you very close to your father?'

'Yes, of course. Well, this is strange.' She was talking about the missing pair of glasses. She poured the contents of her bag on to the sand. 'Didn't you have them?'

'No, bwana.'

Teresa dug in the sand around her. After a while, seeing how thoughtful he looked:

'What are you thinking about?'

'What do you expect? About you.'

'You don't say! You really are a strange one. There's something I'd like to know.' She smiled mysteriously, her smile half hidden behind the curtain of hair as she crawled around in the sand. In previous conversations she had already shown an exaggerated, insatiable curiosity about her friend's past, but not his emotional experiences (apart from his affair with Maruja), all of which remained a mystery. 'I suppose someone like you ... Have you had many adventures with those ... companions of yours? Don't tell me if you don't want to, of course.'

'The two you saw today? In all honesty, I hardly know them. Why do you ask?'

'Oh, no reason. I'm just a gossip.'

'Besides, outside work, I don't like them.'

'Well, it seemed as if they ... Look, there's a plane!'

'Were you spying on me? I hardly ever see them, but they're like sisters to me. You know, I've wanted a sister since I was little.'

Teresa laughed. 'It's good you are so innocent,' she said, staring up at the plane, which came flying low towards them above the crest of the waves.

'Would you like me to be your sister?' she asked. 'Hey, would you like me to be your sister? I've always been on my own, I'd also have loved to have a brother like you. As handsome and dreamy as you.'

What did she say? Manolo stretched out, caught a leaflet in mid-air, and as he dropped his hand, grabbed hold of one of Teresa's feet. She carried on looking up into the sky, shielding her eyes with her hand and watching the machine disappear into the distance. Be careful, you idiot, Manolo told himself, you're being stupid: Teresa is an intelligent girl who will tell you to stop.

'No,' he said, releasing her foot. 'I wouldn't want you as a sister. You're too good for that.'

The sand all around them was littered with leaflets. Teresa read one, then threw it away.

'Too good in what way?'

'You're made for something else.'

'For what, might I ask?' And then: 'Dammit, where did I put my glasses?' She was still searching on her knees, turning round and round.

'I hope you've lost them. For love, you're made for love, Teresa.'

'Don't go all romantic on me, will you?'

'I'll go whatever I like, if the *señorita* has no objection.'

'You were wearing them a while ago, I saw you with them on. Where did you put them?'

'Look, a canoe . . .'

'And, going back to those girls . . .'

'What do you want to know? The older one is married and . . . separated. She's had a hard time. She has a great little boy, you'd like seeing him, he's as golden as the sun, like you.'

'And the other one?'

'Just look at that canoe. It's an old man paddling it, you should see him. Not many people come this far, do they? Come on, lie down and forget about your glasses.'

'I need them to read.'

'It's not polite to read in company. The thing is, the *señorita* is a spoiled brat, and deserves a good spanking. I'd make you run, you'd see . . .'

'Talking of running,' she said, 'have you ever run with a policeman's truncheon centimetres from your head? You've missed something . . .'

LAST EVENINGS WITH TERESA

Still happily caught up in that circle of danger, in the huge network of clandestine contacts she imagined as somehow emanating from the Murcian's skin (by the way, how good my father's old, faded pair of maroon trunks look on him), she began telling him about some of the risks involved in the student struggle.

'Another student was running in front of me,' she said, finally giving up in her search for the glasses and falling back on to the empty half of the towel, 'but we got separated on Calle Pelayo. The biggest danger in these demonstrations, which I have to admit are great fun, is to lose contact when the police block you off. It's the opposite to your situation, where it's best always to be cut off from one another . . . So I returned to the main part of the demonstration, which had managed to regroup, but then the mounted police charged again and I suddenly found myself on the ground. Look, I've still got the mark on my knee. Somebody picked me up, a really young cop. I remember he had very light-green eyes, from the countryside of course. He seemed more scared than I was, but he pushed me gently towards the police van. I turned on him, punched and kicked him – I still don't know why he didn't hit me with the truncheon. Anyway, I managed to break free, but there was no escape because it was chaos, there were at least a hundred of us students on that corner, all piled on top of one another, elbows and legs flailing in all directions, we only wanted to get away . . . Look, have you got enough room? Do you want to . . .? Wait, pull the towel towards you, that's right, now you've got more than enough, come closer, will you? Do you want a cigarette?'

'Yes, fine.'

'As I was saying . . . It should interest you, it's an aspect of the struggle you don't know about. You light up first . . . Well, all we could think of was . . .'

Manolo held out the match.

'Here.'

The fragrance of her golden hair was further torture to him. As he cupped his hands, he deliberately let the flame die out, simply to be able to smell again the lingering traces, that indescribable aroma of an adolescence lost who knew where. He brushed his lips against her smooth forehead above the match's pink flame; she pulled away and her blue eyes took on a strangely serious look, but only held his gaze for a second.

'Well, that's how things stood, so I shouted it was best to take cover in the university, but I suppose no one heard me. It was the only way out, and to a certain extent we'd already achieved our objective. But people were getting in the way rather than helping, because there's no point hiding it, a lot of them were looking on without lifting a finger, as if they were in the front row. Some of them were even smiling as though it was a joke, the bast— In the end, I was caught properly, my dress was ripped, and I didn't see Luis or the others until I was taken to police headquarters. We were interrogated . . . It was grotesque, what can I say, just imagine . . .'

Eyes wide open, she was staring up into the sky, lost in one of those idealistic crises that years later, beset by monotonous conjugal rows, she would miss so dreadfully. The sunlight brandished tiny glittering swords in her blond locks. Manolo observed her profile against a misty background of sand and sea. While he listened to her, he nodded his head occasionally without saying a word, fleeting illusions flashing through his mind (Teresa beneath the hooves of a police horse, dress in tatters, Teresa shouting at the head of a student demonstration, and then being interrogated by the police in a dark little room with a gloomy light, then rescued by her father from headquarters). He drew closer to her, unsure whether it was to breathe in the smell of her hair more deeply, or to uncover some intimate, secret desire she was hiding behind her endless tale (didn't it remind him, in its own way, of Lola's verbal diarrhoea?). And yet he knew that this desire, whatever it might be, could grow calmly and happily deep inside her or in her adolescent breast because, sooner or later, it would be fulfilled. Except that he would probably not be on hand to see it.

'And weren't you ever afraid?' he asked. 'You're a brave girl.'

'Manolo, is your passport up to date?'

'Why do you ask?'

'It's best to be prepared. You know: if you had to get away quickly, to cross the frontier. You wouldn't be the first.'

'What ideas you have, little one. I'd die.'

'What's that?'

'I'd die if I had to leave here.'

'I don't understand . . .'

Her mind still on his hypothetical flight, Teresa turned to him on the towel. She cupped her hands under her cheek like a little girl going to sleep, and looked closely at her friend: 'What do you mean by that?' Her twinkling eyes met with an unexpectedly wistful look in his. The weak evening sun played on grains of sand stuck to his smooth shoulder, creating iridescent glints. Seeing him so close up (she was squinting slightly), Teresa thought back to the moment when they had walked down to the sea after stripping off in the car. She had been a couple of metres behind him, judging whether the old pair of trunks fitted, taking in his slender back, the strong outline of his shoulders, and thinking absent-mindedly: that endearing little creature has trembled in those arms, night after night, while I was reading de Beauvoir about them, all alone in my room . . . It was as if in his muscular dark back, in his way of walking, she caught a glimpse of certain crazy dreams.

He pushed back her hair and she lowered her eyes. His hand (the wounded one, of course) moved down, pressing lightly on the back of her head. Teresa's thin neck beat in his fingers like a frightened bird.

'You're very pretty, and I'd hate to have to escape all of a sudden, for whatever reason, and have to leave you. None of that political crap could make me forget you . . .' (Wrong, you're setting about it the wrong way, you idiot, he told himself.) He drew closer to her, brushing against her warm, half-open lips.

'Please, what are you doing . . .' murmured Teresa. She seemed to be thinking things over intensely, entirely self-absorbed: she was on the point of surrendering.

'I knew this would happen,' Teresa added in a whisper. 'I knew it . . . Life is disgusting.'

'Don't say that, child.'

'Even if you kiss me, don't imagine I'll go to bed with you. I'm very frank, Manolo, you don't know me yet. I had an experience I've no intention of repeating.'

'Who's talking of repeating it? You have nothing to fear with me,' came his reply.

'Never again, do you understand?' insisted Teresa, her eyes still closed.

'Look, if all of a sudden I had to leave, would you miss me?'

'If something happened to you, you mean?'

'Yes.'

'Yes, I would.'

'Why?'

'Because . . . I don't know.' She sighed. 'All this is so odd, isn't it? You and me here so close, and yet a month ago we didn't even know each other . . . This is such a strange summer. If, at home, if my friends knew I'm going out with you . . .' She giggled nervously. 'But it's true, why am I so afraid to admit it? I'd be very upset if anything happened to you.'

'You'd soon forget me.'

'Possibly. I'm not sure.'

'You're very young, still almost a girl. You would forget me, and marry some cretin or other . . .'

'It's possible I would forget you; life has so many twists and turns. But I'll never marry a cretin, however much money he has.'

'I bet you will.'

'How little you know me!'

'It's only normal.' He was stroking her hair, the soft line of her shoulders, the nape of her neck. 'It's so easy to love you, so simple. The simplest thing in the world. You're beautiful, intelligent . . .'

'What are you talking about?'

'Just that, the fact that you're made for people to worship you.' (Bad, very bad, you loser, what's wrong with you?) 'You're an angel.'

Their bodies touched. Teresa was still looking down.

'Please . . . we mustn't forget that Maruja . . .'

The air was shimmering above the sand, as though a cloud of vapour was draped over their bodies. Teresa looked at him; the Interloper could see himself reflected in the pale circle of her transparent, innocent eyes. Stirred by the breeze, the advertising leaflets (*Get in with the in-crowd in K. swimwear!*) swept round the Murcian's dazed head. Teresa suddenly leapt to her feet as if she had just woken up.

'Are you coming in?'

'In a while . . .'

'Lazybones!'

She ran off to the sea. It happened when she came back: it had seemed to him almost inhumanly cruel that the promise of her body in movement was so inaccessible, the nonchalant flexing of her waist, the fleeting, delirious verve of her buttocks, the strange display of tenderness and abandonment in her slightly thick ankles, the soft spring of her knees. He realised he was making poor use of the time offered him, and the advantages of being so close, and even though, perhaps, if something happened to her when she was swimming, if she fainted, he would carry her out of the water, and lay her down, wet and expiring, on the sand... Of course, though, that wasn't how things were: he was leaning on his elbow toying with her sunglasses (he had dug them up again), keeping a close eye on Teresa as she emerged from the sea. He saw her pause for a moment at the water's edge, bend over and shake her blond hair, then run her fingers through the bewitching strands. Her skin gleamed like bronze in the sun. Manolo put on the sunglasses and collapsed on to his back on the towel. He saw Teresa coming straight towards him, stepping slowly and lightly on the sand, not looking to right or left, in an azure night, and something replaced the vapour rising from the burning sand, something like patches of mist in a forest; and in that prodigious blue or green twilight (were the lenses of the sunglasses tinted green?) he saw her coming towards him as if she was continuing a walk that began one distant day he had never forgotten: the same unreal steps the Moreau family's daughter had taken that night on the outskirts of Ronda as she crossed the moonlit clearing. It was as though, ever since then, this friendship born against the nebulous, longing backdrop of a dream had been advancing towards him, and was still doing so now in Teresa's slow, measured footsteps. This time she didn't carry on past, but sat down next to him.

'Aren't you going to kiss me?' he heard her ask timidly (in fact, what she said was, 'Aren't you going to miss me?' adding, 'So you hid my glasses, did you?') and sat there, droplets of light falling from her hair on to his shoulders, only a few centimetres from his mouth, her thighs pressed together as if she could sense the invisible threat, as if almost consciously preparing to defend herself. But above her, high in the sky above her virginal head, the flaming sun of desire and possession (a combination that made the Murcian's world go round) was finally shining in all its violence, so that Manolo took her by the shoulders and pushed her down, not roughly but with authority, seeing his reflection in her eyes as deep as the sea, and murmuring something she couldn't follow (it seemed like one of those obscure curses dictated by virile urgency, the voice of sex itself forcing its way through her bourgeois squeamishness and narrow-mindedness), preoccupied as she was with the way his head was looming over her, almost completely blocking out the sun. She could still move her head from left and right (as happened one day with her ideas, when eventually she had time to reconsider them) and yet she didn't do so, but let him give her a lingering kiss on her salty lips. The pleasurable surprise she felt as his mouth pressed eagerly against hers (which she could not help but follow in its daring explorations) was matched by the weight of his ebony stomach against hers. Her cheeks flushed; feeling sudden life stirring in her embrace, she lifted her hands and took hold of Manolo's head, grasping his hair with a desperate tenderness: her first kisses, just like her first steps in student revolt at university, were dreadfully uncoordinated.

She left all the initiative to him, taking no precautions and unconcerned about being seen by other bathers in the distance. She allowed his roaming hands to slide underneath the wet bikini top, and, by shifting slightly – pretending to move from an uncomfortable position that in fact didn't bother her – also allowed him to wriggle on top of her. But that was all; she would surrender for a while that blond cloud floating round her mouth, would even accept a few risky caresses (all the girls do that) – but that was all; she was not going to let him take her for one of those dizzy little bourgeois girls who allow themselves to be possessed so easily, oblivious to other (urgent) realities far more important than any youthful fling. And yet, a few moments later, already confused about what really was urgent, she couldn't help but stealthily open her legs a little wider.

Fortunately, just then two portly men arrived, wearing ugly black trunks that sagged over pale, spotty buttocks. They sat a few metres away from the couple, openly staring at them. Teresa gently pushed Manolo off; he peered round to discover the reason for this interruption. His gaze must have possessed some secret power, because Teresa saw the two peeping toms quickly stretch out on the sand, draw up their knees and stare at a few clouds drifting across the sky.

Teresa closed her eyes. She didn't resist as Manolo returned to her still hot lips with renewed passion. He seemed so powerful and self-assured, so much in control, that she felt a wave of warmth inviting her to yield, and yet his unruly hands continued to disturb her. By now he had secured her waist by slipping an arm underneath her body, and pulled her towards him until she was resting on his shoulder, and then began to rummage under the bikini elastic as in a bag of apples. The top half had slipped, and Teresa's breasts, like the solemn faces of children pressed up against a window, were nuzzling the Murcian's broad chest while, amid an explosion of dazzling lights, she was still vowing to herself that she would not surrender. Just then, as if somehow he had read her mind, the Interloper let go of her . . .

'Those men are looking at us,' said Teresa, in a futile, belated attempt to wrest back the initiative. But Manolo was the one who had resolved not to take things any further, and that disconcerted her. Without further explanation, their hands alighted simultaneously on the packet of cigarettes, and they both burst out laughing. After that, feeling calmer (and above all happy, happy, happy), Teresa allowed him to make a fuss of her, like a kind and tender lover. Kneeling beside her, Manolo slipped a cigarette between her lips, lit it for her, brushed the sand from her back, tidied their things, sat up, shook the towel and spread it again so she could sit comfortably.

They smoked and gazed at the sea for a while without speaking, tight up against one another, and when night began to fall, they decided to leave. On this occasion, the paunchy, melancholy voyeurs were left disappointed.

... the fragrance of the garden that night, the couples dancing, the music and fireworks on Saint John's Eve. I was very scared. It was during a pause after I'd prepared and handed round another tray of canapés (I knew there wouldn't be enough). I said to myself: come on, let's sit by the pool for a while to watch them dance, we'll be next to the *señorita* who's alone now, she's always the prettiest at any party, always the most interesting, the most envied, but also the one most criticised, and then all of a sudden I could feel his eyes on me and I saw him approaching, glass in hand, calm and determined. He didn't have to stop once or change direction; it was as if the couples on the dance floor instinctively made room for a presence that had always been there and didn't need to announce itself. He was so sure of himself he didn't appear to notice anything around him, who would have thought he would be so bold. My heart skipped a beat when I saw he was heading for Teresa, but when he reached us ... I thought it was impossible, impossible to go and dance with all those other people – it wasn't possible, my love, do you understand? Our place was in the garden's darkest corner ... He lays his head on my stomach and stares at the pine wood and the beach bathed in moonlight beyond the open window, and talks and talks until he falls asleep, whispering with his beautiful wolf's mouth and that sweet trill in his voice, a tremor, a sort of amazement and abandon that the back of his head transmits to my innards, talking endlessly about that other coastline and how and why he came to the city a few years ago, only to end up so stupidly in the arms of a dormouse, in a mousetrap, I think he said, but I don't really remember. I remember more his silences, the things he never talked about, his mysterious friends and the bold girls from his neighbourhood that are there asleep in his eyes, the violent everyday clashes with the street, with delinquents, and with his own family too. Because he pretended none of that existed: he never spoke about his family, he even refused to say their names, his half-brother, his sister-in-law, his nephews and nieces. They're nothing more than shadows behind him, faceless beings, hazy characters in a story who he has always been determined to dismiss. And yet he must have a home and somewhere there must be a woman's hands working hard for him, washing and ironing those nice, warm-coloured shirts of his, and putting a plate of food on the table for him every day... And that house of his in El Carmelo, how near and yet how far it is: when it rains the electricity goes off. That's the only thing he's deigned to say bad-temperedly whenever his Maruja asked him, and she could only think of a sad naked light bulb suddenly flickering off in a dining room while the rain pours down outside, beating down on the uralite roofs and corrugated iron of the shacks. That is how dark and all-consuming such a poor existence must be, how unbearable family life must be for a young man like him. Because love is the only treasure the poor have; he will never learn to love those who love him. I know that; we are what we are, *señorita*. I may be ignorant and not understand much about men, but the little I do know, learned in bed and with them, is that his beautiful shark's teeth belong to me, and he couldn't fool me that night at the party: only a loner like him could confuse wealth with a pretty face and kiss so despairingly, as if he wanted to swallow the whole world. It was hard to believe he had parents or brothers and sisters, a family he loved that was waiting for him somewhere, because at first it was impossible to imagine his house, his room, his bed, the mirror he looks into and combs his hair in front of every morning. He really didn't seem to need anyone to care for him, no woman; he seemed to rely completely on himself, and his constant roaming round the city also made it seem he had no home, even more so when I saw him riding a motorbike or playing cards with the old men. All this is written on his face while he sleeps, when his voice has fallen silent, his head on my shoulder, and the illusion of his first steps towards her is still floating in the air. There he is, walking on his own along the streets of Marbella, a beach bag slung over his shoulder, just after his escape from Ronda. He comes to a halt, peers at shop windows, listens to music on terraces, to the language of the tourists. He goes down to the beach and dips his toes in the water, watches, eyes narrowed, as a canoe dances on the waves ... and then his gaunt, dark face, tense from wave upon wave of surprises and decisions, emerges once more against the background of a building site, a tumult of iron and bricks crashing around him, and in a cloud of dust he confronts a pair of cold eyes beneath the mean brim of a foreman's hat. We want work, brother, we need work. A year as a labourer: the dark, calloused hands destined for me, with knuckles as beautiful as mahogany, carrying buckets of water and bricks and sand in a wheelbarrow, obeying orders and shouts that swoop from the scaffolding like birds driven crazy by a merciless sun, and at night his hands lie like rusty hooks on the bed of a room shared with a fellow worker, a native of Mijas who keeps his savings from the summer in the lining of his jacket. His body lengthens and grows stronger, and those hands that every day dress and undress him, that on Saturday nights spend the money they have earned during the week strolling up and down past the terraces filled with tourists, still reeking of cement and plaster, those hands are the same ones that on the beach one radiant Sunday fasten desperately under the water on another hand, pretending to mistake the other person. Because that was how it all began. His eyes swiftly apologise, with a winning smile: he is fifteen but looks eighteen, and the hard work and sun have moulded a torso that a pair of green eyes are now devouring. I can see her now: a small, slightly plump woman with a nice waist and beautifully tanned skin. This lady is a good catch: there is curiosity, fear and somehow infinite patience in the gentle curve of her mouth; a tenderness fatally dependent on summers about her soft, mature, sun-tanned stomach. Is she Swedish, German? How many days has he been bathing on this beach at the same time, close to her, spying on her, stretched out on the sand like a lizard? No doubt (yes, no doubt) the pink shirt with pockets he was wearing that day was the excuse: she took a fancy to the shirt when she saw it on him as she left, and wanted to buy it because it was so faded by the sun it looked beautiful and original, a whim on her part like the very cheap blue-and-white striped T-shirts the *señorita* discovered one summer in a shop in Blanes, which became so fashionable among her friends ... As for what follows, yours truly isn't sure if he told her the story or she simply dreamed it (wait, my love, don't go yet, don't leave me, it's still a long time until dawn), but yours truly will ignore and would like to forget the crazy daily labours, the avid red mouths of the night and the drowsy faces smothered in creams that at dawn, sleepy and grateful, turn towards him as though down a dark tunnel; because the new day, just as years later when he woke up here beside me, was still telling him that real life is elsewhere. So he quits the job he is on and does nothing throughout the month of September apart from spending his savings perched on bar stools. The mature, sad German woman goes back to her own country,

LAST EVENINGS WITH TERESA

autumn arrives and the prospect of another winter carting sand and bricks becomes unbearable. He slowly works his way up the coast (Torremolinos, a kitchen assistant in a restaurant, then a waiter) until he arrives at Malaga (a fortnight working at a petrol station), his head gradually filling with the sound of a train whistle until finally he decides to head for Barcelona, to his brother's house . . . At this point she no longer follows the story, sits up a little in bed, props herself up on the pillow, and leans over the powerful naked body exuding sleep. 'Are you asleep, Manolo?' The moon has long since set, but she is still awake – turned towards you, she never tires of looking at you. A past of silence and shadows: either because you're ashamed of talking about it or because you're overcome by sleep, you never speak of the person who brought you here, or how you met her – no doubt in the same petrol station where he worked. Nor has he ever commented about the trip or the things he saw – all he says is that you learn about life when you hitchhike, and with three hundred pesetas in his pocket, the beach bag slung over his shoulder and a nice pair of sandals that once belonged to an Englishman (another story he didn't want to tell me), in mid-October of the year 1952, he steps out of a car with a foreign number plate in Plaza de España. Barcelona grey in the rain, wisps of mist at the end of its avenues, a subterranean rumble beneath the asphalt – you'd love to be twenty already, wouldn't you? She only knows the final scene of this headlong race, a kiss the traveller evokes wistfully: a head appears at the window of the foreign car that brought him, a beautiful, slender head with very short red hair; he stands there, waving his hand as the car disappears on its way to France. He approaches a policeman and asks about Monte Carmelo and then strolls round the city, the bag still on his shoulder, and eventually cannot resist boarding a tram. He must be smiling, pushed up against the window by the crowd of passengers, staring at everything with marvelling eyes: he still can't distinguish a thing among all these people; it's still a long while before he loses his innocence, before he learns to shoulder his way through these elegant, confident couples – advancing towards me, the poor lad doesn't know who I am, he doesn't know I've just put down the tray of canapés, that I saw him come in, but if he asks me to dance, I'll say yes even if they kick us out, even if they all point at us. It's probably better they don't see us, my love; let's head for the dark, the darkest corner . . .

'I'm in.'

He was always particularly attracted to the magical moment of bluffing when the stakes were raised, defying luck. Perhaps it was because of his capacity for imaginative concentration on the pack of cards, his seriousness, his patience and imperturbable silence, that the old *manilla* addicts had welcomed him to their table in the Bar Delicias from an early age. For a long while, Manolo had played with them for enjoyment, not to win money: he flattered the old men, affirming that *manilla* was the noblest of card games. But in recent days, he preferred the noisy table of the single men in their thirties who bet (sometimes as much as a peseta a round) on games of *ramiro, julepe* or *cuarenta y dos*, and completely abandoned the old men. All of a sudden, everything had changed: behind him there was always a group of onlookers studying his hand, commenting on him as if they saw his five cards flashing with far greater possibilities than those of all the other players. On many nights he left the table with winnings. He shuffled and dealt precisely and rapidly, but disdainfully, as if to be done with the cards as quickly as possible and escape. The patient dealing, the leisurely, austere way of playing that had been so surprising in a young lad, the sense of slow ceremony learned from the warmth of the old men and of the stove, all the difficult, ambiguous science of waiting that came from the wrinkled, coffee and nicotine-stained fingers as they shuffled their cards, softened a rolled-up cigarette, brushed the ash from their lapels or picked up from the green baize table a trick won with effort and not thanks to a slice of luck (the old men frowned on betting games) – Manolo had left all that behind; now he had no time to lose. From their tranquil, silent table, the old card players watched him with a partly nostalgic curiosity: they dimly imagined that the Murcian's distancing was yet more proof of how out of step age made them. Yet it was far simpler: he needed money to go out with Teresa, and with them he had no chance of winning any.

Apart from this, the Interloper was seen only rarely in the neighbourhood; he always seemed to be in a hurry, as if he had urgent business to settle. It was as if he had overlooked something in his haste, as if he didn't live there any more. Above all, the disturbed silence elsewhere – that subterranean rumble – that he had first begun to perceive a few days earlier in Teresa's living room, had remained with him ever since. He particularly noticed it one day when he arrived at the clinic just in time to see Teresa rapidly crossing her legs as she sat in the armchair. This came as a double shock to him (for some reason, it brought home to him not only that Teresa was rich, but also that he didn't have a cent that day), which made him think in a confused fashion that when they cross their legs in front of you, girls from good families do it very elegantly but at the same time with an air of refusing something: around this childish gesture floated the shadow of a no-less-childish decision, one that was decidedly negative.

'It's over and done with. I'm going to Blanes,' Teresa said without looking at him, opening the magazine and tugging her skirt down (something she never usually did when he was present). Manolo wasn't particularly surprised by either her decision or her attitude. For some time now, the earth had begun to shift beneath his feet: the problems constantly arising from his lack of funds (he was no longer willing to carry on stealing: any slip-up would mean losing everything) concerned him a great deal. A lucky night gambling at cards won him three or four days' respite, but after that it was back to square one. At three o'clock that same afternoon, as he was going to pay for a coffee in the Bar Delicias, he discovered he only had five pesetas left. Looking round, he saw a man in his thirties, with thick black eyebrows and brilliantined hair (he worked as a domestic-appliance salesman – according to him, a job with a great future – and was known in the neighbourhood as the King of the Boogie) staring at him from the far end of the bar, a glass of brandy in front of him.

'How are things, Jesus?'

Two employees from the metro were also studying him from a marble table near the door, swatting away the flies and fanning themselves with their peaked caps. Manolo went over to the man. 'Can you come outside a moment? I need to talk to you . . .'

He led him out into the sunshine, where Jesus sat slowly on a chair on the terrace, also crossing his legs, as if to show from the start he was going to refuse.

'What's up? Manolo, you bastard, how come we never see you these days?' he said.

'That's life, kid,' replied the Murcian.

'I get it,' said the other man.

'Look, Jesus, I'm in a spot of bother. Could you lend me three hundred pesetas?' He had known the King of Boogie for years, and although they had never been close friends, he knew he respected him.

'You don't say,' said the King of Boogie, folding his arms.

Despite his nickname, the result of a certain juvenile discotheque charm acquired twelve or fifteen years earlier (he had won boogie competitions in Piscinas y Deportes and other dance halls, competitions which were broadcast – he swore on his mother – by the famous radio presenter Gerardo Esteban, who had once shaken his hand), the difference in ages meant he no longer went round with the Murcian, whom he saw as an improbable but possible successor. 'What are you up to these days, Manolo, if I might ask? Where do you go dancing on Sundays, what girls are you seeing, kid?' he would occasionally ask him, although he never received an answer. In his day, girls wore very short skirts and carried shiny red, blue and green perspex handbags. Now he had heard that the youngsters danced rock 'n' roll. Sitting with the young married men in the Bar Delicias doorway on summer nights, the King of Boogie often stared into the distance, down to the Ramblas and the Barrio Chino, invisible beneath the layer of luminous dust rising from the city, and often thought of Manolo, but could never imagine him as being capable of having fun the way he used to do, or sneaking into the same dance halls. All this led the King of Boogie to suspect Manolo was a 'queer'.

'Well, well,' he was saying now, 'so that's it, Manolito.'

'Do me that favour, I'm flat broke,' insisted Manolo.

'I'm sorry, kid, it's the dry season for me too. Try the Cardinal.'

'I'll make do with two hundred.'

'It's strange to see you without cash . . .' Jesus argued.

'A hundred, go on,' Manolo pressed him.

The King of Boogie burst out laughing. 'Suck the old man off, that's your thing.'

Manolo frowned and clenched his teeth, then seized the other man by the lapels and jerked him out of his seat. 'Repeat what you just said!'

'Get your hands off me, you pansy,' Jesus protested.

Manolo spat at him between the eyes, still holding him.

The King of Boogie didn't react, but said: 'You don't scare me, you pansy: that's what you are, everyone knows it. Nobody wants to have anything to do with you!'

Manolo spat at him a second time, and then let him go, suddenly perplexed.

Deep down, he couldn't care less what Jesus or even the entire neighbourhood thought of him. What was important was that this confirmed the impression he had of being an interloper, of things falling apart, the feeling that events had begun to spin out of control without him realising it. The same was true of other people's feelings. With all this at the back of his mind, his hand, as though sensing some obscure warning sign, lunged at the dethroned King of the Boogie and gave him a violent slap. Something fell from Jesus's hand: a chewing-gum wrapper. Manolo recalled a strange habit the King of Boogie had: he was one of those who hate kissing whores on the mouth, and who after going with them insist on chewing flavoured gum.

Without giving him time to respond, Manolo turned his back and walked off. He would try elsewhere: first with his sister-in-law (a twenty-five-peseta note that stank of fish, but which he was sincerely grateful for), then with Sans, whom he had to go and find at his workplace (he was now cleaning trams in the depot in Plaza Lesseps, wearing tall rubber boots, a grimy cap on his ape-like head, and using a hosepipe) and finally the Cardinal, the only one he hadn't wanted to have to turn to. As he was running down the steps linking Calle Gran Vista with Calle Doctor Bové, he turned a corner and bumped into Hortensia. She seemed in as much of a hurry as him. The force of their collision knocked her against the wall, the sun blinding her lifeless eyes. He steadied her and mumbled an apology. On a flat roof below them at the foot of the steep hillside, a slovenly young woman with big black eyes was watching them with an indulgent smile as she bathed a little child in a yellow plastic tub. The Syringe, her hair dishevelled and carrying the faded school satchel she always used as a medicine bag, leaned back against the wall and raised her lifeless eyes to Manolo.

'Where are you going in such a hurry?'

'To your house,' he said. 'To see your uncle.'

'I'll go with you.'

She was wearing a pair of white high-heeled shoes Manolo had never seen before. As they walked round the tower, the sun was beating down on the back garden wall; Hortensia said nothing as she trotted beside him, head down, teetering unsteadily on her high heels. She was carrying the satchel carefully by the handle, walking with her arm hanging stiffly by her side as she used to in her schooldays.

'I went to give Luisa's boy an injection,' she said.

'Is that so?' said Manolo.

'Yes, that's the second one.'

'That's very good,' he said. 'It's a good job . . . and you like it, don't you?' He felt uneasy, but it was only when she invited him into the dining room that he realised why: the Cardinal wasn't at home.

'When I left, he was . . .' began Hortensia.

'It doesn't matter,' he said awkwardly. 'I'll come back another day.'

'Wait, let's look in the garden. Are you so pressed for time?'

He followed her out into the arbour, but even before they got there, they could see the empty wicker chair with the Cardinal's cane resting on it. Hortensia couldn't take her eyes off the Murcian. She removed the cane and sat down with a laugh, clasping her hands behind her head and stretching out, kicking her legs.

'Listen,' she said. 'You promised you'd taken me on a motorbike one day.' Beneath her weight the dilapidated chair creaked with an almost human groan.

Manolo had come to a halt some distance before he reached the arbour: he didn't need to go any further to see the old man wasn't there. 'Yes, one of these days . . .' He decided to wait a while, and sat on the ground, legs crossed, observing Hortensia curiously against the sun.

'Have you ever been in love, Manolo?' she asked with a laugh.

'No . . .' he said. When he saw her suddenly fix her attention on something in the garden (tilting her head anxiously as if she had discovered an insect in the long grass around her), it came to him yet again how extraordinarily similar she was to Teresa Serrat. As they swung in the air as if to chastise the sun, her legs only needed a beach tan to be Teresa's. Manolo studied her closely. Hortensia was good company and very pretty, and he began to wonder once more why, before he met Teresa, he hadn't fallen in love with her. They say love is irrational and blind, but he suspected this was another dirty lie invented to fool simple souls, because if, for example, he had met Hortensia at the wheel of a sports car, as he had done Teresa, falling in love with her would have been the easiest and most natural thing in the world.

Wouldn't that have been love? A great love.

Still swinging her legs, Hortensia laid her head back against the chair.

'You're not wearing the bandage any more,' she said.

'No, not any more.'

'Why?'

'It's healed.' He quickly turned his head aside and didn't look at her.

'Manolo, what's wrong with you? You seem so distracted these days. You're not the same.'

'Listen, Syringe, I've got loads of problems.' Collapsing on to his back on the grass, he added: 'I can't give you back the money yet . . . Did the old man find out?'

'Of course.'

'What did he say?'

'Oh, he hit me. Yes, he slapped me. And he's very angry with you.'

'I'll repay him,' said Manolo. 'I'll repay you every last cent. I don't want to be in your debt.'

'You're scared,' she said, bursting out laughing. 'How funny – I'd never have believed it! And you've become really dumb.'

'Child . . .!'

'The child works now, you know.'

'That's good . . .' he said, rising to his feet. 'Yes, that's really good. Well, I'm off. I'll be back another day.'

As he passed her, he stroked her chin with his fingers. He had expected her to accompany him but, no, Hortensia stayed where she was, sprawled in the wicker chair: Manolo could feel her metallic eyes on his back until he reached the gate. 'It's worse than ever,' he said to himself, thinking of the Cardinal's anger at him. But as he headed for the clinic, his spirits rose: after all, it was only in El Carmelo that he had problems and felt lost, and it had always been like that, so why worry about it?

Dina had just gone into Maruja's room and Teresa was sitting in the armchair like Hortensia, but in her attitude of self-defence, legs crossed and not looking at him. It seemed she had slept badly. 'I'm going to Blanes,' she said. The glossy pages of the magazine rustled in her hands. He understood immediately that something new was stirring in that small head of hers.

'What's wrong, Teresa?'

'Nothing. Except that poor Maruja is getting worse and I . . . I'm exhausted, on edge. I'm going to fetch Mama.'

'But she came the day before yesterday.'

'Well, let her come again. As soon as possible.'

She was flicking through the pages of the magazine so rapidly there was no way she could see or read anything, but that didn't seem to bother her.

LAST EVENINGS WITH TERESA

'Will you be back soon?' he asked.

'I don't know.' After a short pause, as though continuing a conversation with someone else: 'Besides, because of me you've run out of money.'

'What's that?'

'Are you deaf or something?'

You should have known, kid: no girl likes going out with a man who has no money, thought Manolo. He heard her muttering: 'I was thinking about it last night. We're idiots . . .'

'Stop talking nonsense,' he snapped, but without raising his voice. 'Come on, tell me what's wrong.'

Teresa had reached the back of the magazine, but quickly turned it over and began again from the front.

'With me? Nothing.'

Manolo walked up and down, head lowered and his left hand in a back trouser pocket. This was exactly the same gesture as on the previous evening in a bar in La Trinidad full of rowdy lorry drivers, when he had offered Teresa a bouquet of violets an old woman was selling, only to discover he had nothing more than a few coins at the bottom of the pocket. 'Don't worry, I've got some,' Teresa had said when she saw his embarrassment. 'This way I can pay for a change.'

'Look,' he said now, 'I don't see why you should get into a state about it. It doesn't matter . . . I mean, in fact I'm just waiting to be paid . . .'

'Of course it matters. Who do you think I am? A stupid spoiled child who doesn't know the value of things? Do you reckon I can agree to you spending all the time? I know about young men like you – you're too good, too naïve. You don't really understand what friendship is about. What annoys me is that I didn't realise until yesterday . . . I bet you've spent your holiday bonus.'

'I don't think that's why you're leaving. You're going because you're afraid.'

'Afraid of what? Well, Maruja is very ill, and that worries me ... Besides, I need to think.'

He folded his arms and sighed.

'You think a lot, Teresa.'

She laughed.

'How funny.'

Now she did seem to have found something really interesting in the magazine, because she focused all her attention on one page, saying: 'But let's be practical and talk frankly, because that's why we're friends, isn't it? Let's see: what is there between us? A friendship and nothing more, right? Go on, tell me.'

Listening in the next room, Dina the nurse immediately understood what was going on. She smiled to herself as she took her patient's pulse: Teresa was beginning to weigh up her friend's feelings. We women will always be foolish, she thought. Dina knew a great deal about love: she knew, for example, that the most dangerous statement a lover can make is to continually deny the existence of love, and refuse to allow oneself to be loved. And yet she also knew that something about this fellow, about his steady voice that seemed to have no past, his sharp, sarcastic eyes and his selfish, swift hands, suggested he desperately wanted to be loved. The Murcian himself must be aware of this to some extent, because recently, despite how kind and thoughtful he was with Teresa (more than once, Dina had caught them almost cuddling in the anteroom), he had always shown that serene indifference that made his friend's blue eyes fill with doubt and interest.

Now, as he walked towards Maruja's room, he added:

'Yes, nothing more than friendship. And, please, that's enough nonsense. Did you say Maruja is worse?'

With that, and disguising his racing heart with a more or less successful nonchalance (he never knew how his eyes gave him away, how they gave the lie to his harsh words), Manolo entered the adjoining room, leaving the door open. Dina was giving Maruja an injection. He knew the doctor usually called in around this time, but he had never seen him, as he and Teresa always left beforehand. Maruja did seem to have shrunk in the past twenty-four hours: her pallid, transparent cheeks had withered beneath the cheekbones; her forehead stood out, and so did her lips. Her frown appeared even deeper, as if the nightmare gnawing at her insides was increasingly terrifying.

'Is she very bad?' asked Manolo.

Without looking at him, the nurse pulled the needle out of Maruja's arm and pressed a piece of cotton wool on it.

'Leave the room, we're going to change her sheets.'

'But how is she?'

'She's got some sores on her back, that's all.'

'Is that serious?'

'Please, can you leave . . . the doctor is coming.'

By the time he returned to the anteroom, Teresa had vanished. Puzzled, he turned back to the nurse. 'She went to fetch her mother,' he muttered, and came to a halt in the doorway, as if waiting for Dina to confirm his words. But she was focused on her work. Carefully bending Maruja's arm, she slipped it under the sheet.

'Too bad,' she said. 'Go now and come back tomorrow.'

Of course, misfortune was signalling to him yet again: take, for example, what happened the next day with the latest motorbike he had decided to steal to bring in some money now Teresa was in Blanes. This occurred after he had convinced his sister-in-law to get his suit out of the laundry (so that at least if Teresa came back with her mother, they wouldn't see him dressed like a beggar). It was 18 July. As he was coming down the El Carmelo road at four in the afternoon, he overtook two local couples near Parque Güell. He could hear them criticising him in low voices behind his back; he stopped and, as though he had forgotten something, began to search his pockets. He took out all the money he had on him: small notes and loose change. 'This is impossible, you're a dead man.' He went into the park. The Interloper suspected this wasn't a sudden decision, but that it had been lying dormant in his mind for several days: if there was nothing else for it, he would steal a bike, but this would definitely be the very last time. The motorbike would go to the Cardinal, and with what he got for it he could pay debts and if he was careful he would have enough for the rest of the holidays with Teresa. The old man would be pleased, and agree to lend him more cash. He would also snatch a handbag (the last one, for real this time) to cover his everyday expenses.

A short way beyond the park entrance, next to a row of dusty hedges, cars and motorbikes with sidecars were parked higgledy-piggledy. The cries of children and birds came from among the trees. He was annoyed when several couples came in, walking slowly, almost religiously, arm in arm: he had already spotted the motorbike he wanted. It was a new, bright-red Montesa, staring at him out of the bushes with its baleful, waspish look. He had to wait more than three-quarters of an hour and smoked half a packet of Chesterfields (on the slate at the Bar Delicias) sitting on one of the big stone balls lining the avenue of palm trees, but then everything happened very quickly. Making the most of a moment when no one was passing by, he jumped on the motorbike, snapped open the padlock and started the engine. The frame folded under him like a trapdoor. He accelerated out of the park and rode at top speed down Calle Ramiro de Maetzu, then along Avenida Virgen de Montserrat. He kept his legs spread wide to avoid staining his suit: that was the only thing that bothered him.

His second target: a lady's handbag in a favourable spot (near Horta, a deserted unmade street flanked by building sites) – a big black bag bumping against the thigh of a slim, middle-aged woman also dressed in black, wearing dark glasses, who had come out of a doorway and was walking down the pavement. His engine idling, the Interloper slid behind her, close to the kerb. The street was filled with the sounds of pickaxes and labourers' voices. Manolo had already noted her slightly muscular legs in big flat shoes, her narrow hips, the masculine-looking back straining beneath the black blouse, and her hair done up in a bun, but now his eyes were fixed on something else: there was no one around. He drew closer to the woman, but when he was alongside her (a stern profile, no lipstick, a slight black fuzz on her top lip) and travelling at the same speed, she unexpectedly turned towards him. This complicated things: the bag now lay across her stomach, and so it was time to give the austere lady a glimpse of his trademark charm before she could cry out.

'Excuse me,' he said, with his brightest smile. 'Do you have the time?'

Calmly, her face a blank, she bent her elbow as she continued walking (fortunately, the bag swung like a pendulum on her arm) and glanced at her wristwatch, almost entirely concealed beneath the tight wrist of the blouse. Manolo's hand shot out and grabbed the bag, tugging hard. The woman gave a guttural cry of alarm, and the leather handle was caught for a few seconds in her watchstrap, but another tug freed it and in the blink of an eye he had stuffed it between his jacket and shirt. He accelerated away.

'Thief! Stop thief!' shouted the woman.

Manolo headed for Plaza de la Fuente Castellana, and then down Calle Cartagena. The Montesa responded instantaneously, but the woman's cries echoed in his ears for a long while.

Five minutes later, Manolo pulled up behind the Hospital San

Pablo and inspected the bag's contents: eyeliner, a perfumed handkerchief with an 'M' embroidered in blue on it (Margarita, Margarita), a purse with a few five-peseta notes and some loose change, a driving licence, a social security card, diary, biro, an old photo of a women's netball team (pleated skirts ruffled by the wind, faded knees and smiles in a bare field; a cross in ink above the head of a young, cat-like girl), a comb, a tube of aspirins, a paperback (*Souls in Torment* or something similar), only a single one-hundred-peseta note and another of fifty. Just his luck. Manolo left everything in the bag except the money and the perfumed handkerchief. He set off again, and then without stopping threw the bag over a garden wall. Someone would find it and return it. It was ten past five. As if accidentally, he would let Teresa see the handkerchief; oh, it's nothing, a souvenir from Margarita, the daughter of a Republican militiaman in exile, a love lost because of the war, a wound that never heals . . . No, how absurd (he threw the handkerchief away as well). Let's not get sidetracked.

He left the motorbike half hidden between two cars opposite the clinic. There were other motorbikes, and a young man in a checked shirt whose sidelong glances Manolo came to understand too late. This was one of the first consequences (at a bad moment) of him looking exclusively in just one direction: he no longer recognised his own colleagues. What distracted him above all was Teresa's Floride parked not far from there. She's back, he thought happily.

When he arrived upstairs in the clinic, the first thing he saw as he entered the anteroom was the grizzled head of a man leaning against the back of an armchair in the semi-darkness. He seemed to be asleep. Manolo walked past him without a sound and went into Maruja's room. Dina was reading a novel, seated beside the bed.

'How is she today?' Manolo asked quietly.

'Better,' the nurse replied, without raising her eyes from the book. 'Her father's here – didn't you see him?'

'Ah, her father. And Teresa?'

Dina didn't respond. He sensed there was somebody behind him, eyes fixed on the back of his head. He turned round. It was the grey-haired man. Manolo nodded a greeting, while the other man stared at him with weary eyes barely visible among the mass of wrinkles around his eyelids. His dark face seemed to be trying to avoid something, some troublesome light (his thick eyebrows had become stuck in the peasant reflex of avoiding the sun's reflections), and although he wasn't as tall as Manolo, he appeared to be staring at him from above. There was something about his look that Manolo didn't like. The man slowly shifted his gaze from the youngster to his daughter. Next to her head on the pillow the catheter lay like a small, evil snake. Maruja moaned softly; for a brief second her surprisingly thin, blistered eyelids drew back from the whites of her eyes, revealing the burning black of her pupils – her big, frightened pupils that did not settle on any of the faces in the room – and yet it was definitely a gaze, and it appeared to cost her a superhuman effort. She closed her eyes again. The elderly man coughed.

'You see?' said the nurse, as if speaking to a child. 'She's much better.'

Manolo went back to the anteroom and adjusted the blinds to let in more light. A few minutes later, Maruja's father joined him. He was wearing a very worn suit.

'Are you a friend of Señorita Teresa's?'

He was staring openly at Manolo.

'Yes . . . and of Maruja. It seems she's better, doesn't it?' he replied, to say something.

'God willing, because I reckon they're cheating me. Let's see if the boy is discharged next month ...'

He gazed at him with his weary eyes. Now that he was closer, Manolo could see he was exhausted and couldn't care less about anything. He saw him suddenly dip his hand into his pocket, probably to offer him a cigarette. Manolo felt so awkward he turned his back on him. Fortunately, at that moment Teresa appeared; she came in very determinedly and looked first in his direction (an indescribable gleam of happiness that quickly vanished from her eyes and didn't reappear until she was alone with him).

'Ah,' she said, 'so you've already met?' She introduced them: 'Señor Lucas is Maruja's father ... and this is Manolo, a friend.'

The Murcian held out his hand, and found himself clutching a chunk of lifeless wood holding a cigarette that must have been intended for him but which Maruja's father didn't remove in time, so that it was snapped in two.

'The young fellow here,' Maruja's father said, 'also finds her more awake. As I say, it's a matter of time. So,' he added, glancing towards the door, 'what about Doña Marta?'

'She's with the doctor, she'll be along in a minute,' replied Teresa. 'Papa is downstairs.'

Maruja's father began to head for the door, but then turned round, went into his daughter's room, said something to the nurse and came out again. He said goodbye to them all, then left, shutting the door clumsily behind him. Teresa came and stood very close to Manolo, lifting her head to look him in the eye.

'Hello there,' she said in her affectionate voice, slightly nasal as if she constantly had a cold; in it lay the moist promise of furtive caresses.

'When did you get back?' he asked.

'This morning. All the family has been here since three o'clock,' she added, not taking her eyes off him. 'Mama will be here soon. There's nothing wrong with Maruja, I was frightened for no reason . . .'

'But she's still very ill . . .'

'Well, yes . . .'

'And how are you feeling today?'

'Fantastic, as good as new.' She looked at his suit. 'Wow! How elegant!'

Hearing steps in the corridor, they moved apart a little, and Manolo instinctively adjusted his tie. He saw Teresa smiling at this, and at that moment the door opened and Señora Serrat came in, followed by some others. She was talking, and her voice dropped to a whisper as she crossed the threshold, as if she were attending a wake.

'Teresa arrived completely distraught, saying Maruja had taken a turn for the worse, that she had terrible sores on her back, that she was dying on us, and everyone was in such a state! I wanted to call before coming . . . But anyway, it's better it was a false alarm . . . Has Lucas left?' she added, looking at Teresa.

'With Papa.'

Manolo had gone over to the window, and stood there waiting to be introduced. Señora Serrat was accompanied by Doctor Saladich (tall, slow-moving, very attractive, with a hint of professional reserve in his fine grey eyes) and another woman who must be Aunt Isabel. She sat down at once, looking tired and bothered by the heat. Teresa went over to Manolo.

'Come,' she said, but her mother was already approaching them.

'Your father is waiting downstairs. He's insisting on finding the company chauffeur to take Lucas back to Reus. Those nerves of yours, daughter . . .' (then she noticed Manolo). 'Ah, you must be that young man . . .'

Teresa introduced him: 'He comes to see Maruja every day.'

Her mother didn't appear to pay him much attention (she didn't offer him her hand, because she was busy adjusting the green scarf covering her hair), but the other woman and the doctor did when Teresa introduced him to them. There was nothing remarkable in Señora Serrat's attitude (Teresa was trying to explain to Doctor Saladich her fears for Maruja the previous day), which was no more than a lukewarm glance, a glance that was not inquisitive about him, or at least not only about him, but included her daughter as well. Señora Serrat kept her face turned slightly towards Teresa, who was the person speaking at that moment, but in reality she was examining Manolo, the one listening.

'Nonsense, Teresa,' Señora Serrat suddenly said. 'Maruja is a lot better.'

Doctor Saladich wasn't so optimistic, but confirmed that Teresa's fears were unfounded. As they were leaving, Señora Serrat began a convoluted conversation with her sister and Teresa about what to do next: she was heading straight back to the Villa (she had guests) in her sister's car, while her husband, 'who of course won't be able to find the company chauffeur, because today's a holiday', would end up having to take Lucas home in the other car. 'Oriol was thinking of going to the farm sometime soon anyway,' she added.

Aunt Isabel suggested Teresa could take Lucas, and Oriol go with them to Blanes (but Oriol had things to do in the city). Teresa protested that she was tired out, and besides, she had to take the Floride to the garage for a repair. Still standing politely by the window, all Manolo gathered (the only thing that interested him in fact) was that Teresa would be free and in Barcelona.

'Do take care of yourself,' her mother ordered, although her voice lacked authority. 'You're as thin as a rake. Perhaps after

Maruja, you'll start . . . I'll convince your father you should come to Blanes for at least a week, to get some rest.'

'Oh no, Mama, that's so boring. And you know I want to be with Maruja – someone has to do it.'

'All right, all right,' her mother concluded, clearly not wanting to discuss the matter further. She took her daughter aside to have a few words. Manolo heard Teresa say: 'Mama, you have to give me some money.'

The two ladies said goodbye, and Saladich kindly accompanied them. By now it was six o'clock. Teresa collapsed into an armchair with a sigh, and kicked off her sandals. 'Ugh, at last.' She was wearing an old pair of faded blue jeans. 'What shall we do,' she said, though it wasn't really a question. They looked at each other.

'Are they all going back to the Villa?' he asked, and then, laughing: 'You really got them into a panic, didn't you?' He went over to her, took her hand, and pulled her up gently. 'Come on, lazybones.'

Teresa resisted with a laugh, planting her feet firmly on the floor: she could barely conceal her impatience. 'Manolo, were you annoyed yesterday when I left without saying anything?'

'No.' He tugged hard at her, and she ended up in his arms. They swayed for a while like puppets, laughing quietly, unsteady as if they had lost all their strength, and extended the pleasure of this movement until they banged against the door to Maruja's room. The smiles vanished from their faces, replaced by an expectant tension. Trembling, they kissed each other on the mouth.

'Dina is in there,' whispered Teresa. 'What a relief Maruja's problem wasn't serious, isn't it?'

'Yes,' he said. 'Come on, let's go.'

'Wait . . . I . . .'

'Let's go somewhere where we'll be on our own. The Tibet.'

'Yes. But ...' Smiling, she buried her head on his shoulder, and sighed. 'I don't want anyone to know about this. No one must know.'

'Know what?'

'What's going on between us. It'll be a secret just between you and me, all right?'

'Did you spend all the time at the Villa thinking?' Manolo asked warily.

Teresa hesitated.

'Please, don't come to any selfish conclusions.' (Confused, he blinked.) 'Please don't say anything.' She put a finger to his lips. 'Look, among my papers I found the letter a student friend of mine wrote from jail. If you knew what he says, the way it's written, it calmed me down ... We're cowards, Manolo, that's what I think, cowards because we never do things that are good and which give us pleasure. In his letter he mentioned Federico.'

Federico must be a beloved shadow. Manolo had already noticed that, whenever she referred to any famous beloved shadow, Teresa lowered her gaze with the receptive fervour of a studious schoolgirl: her fantasy world of emotions, sympathies and objects of admiration was not only much vaster and more generous than his, but also contained a mythical solidarity, forever sniffing a conspiracy – and that was dangerous. It was only later when they were in the car, which Teresa in fact couldn't manage to start (she hadn't been lying when she said there was a problem), that he detected the telltale signs, the outcome of her weighty reflections over those twenty-four hours at the Villa, the apparently trivial details that already bore a luxury label showing the price and the warning (Murcians: do not touch).

'Going out incognito like this is fun, isn't it?' Teresa said. 'But I want to introduce you to some friends who are dying to meet you. They're students.'

'Ah.' At this, the Interloper understood that things were bound to become more complicated, and that this was only logical, because he couldn't hope to live with Teresa in a bell jar, or as if this summer really was a magical desert island. So he had to confront whatever came his way, and even try to turn it to his advantage, especially since in his own territory, El Carmelo, a terrible vengeance was brewing. This was how the story of the latest stolen motorbike ended: looking round casually once Teresa had finally managed to get the Floride started to make sure the bike was where he left it (I'll come back for it tonight, thought Manolo), he seemed instead to see the Cardinal himself sitting on the kerb, laughing at him . . . in fact it was Maruja's father, doubtless still waiting for the car to take him to Reus, but he only just managed to prevent himself shouting for Teresa to stop. As for the Montesa, it had disappeared, together with the kid in the checked shirt.

Had that son of a bitch taken it? He really had got out of bed on the wrong side that morning. All these setbacks, scares, tiny alarms, came like road signs warning that there were sharp bends and crossroads ahead. It was during another hastily arranged evening at the beach (a little cove at Garrafa, with a snack bar and somewhere to park, the two of them lying beside the skeleton of an abandoned boat) when out of the blue another sign appeared, in the shape of a smiling young woman with plaits who came skipping towards Teresa, burning the soles of her feet. She was wrapped in a big red towel (an authentic Z on the yellow background of the sand: dangerous bend ahead) and caught up with Teresa as she was walking to the bar. Before that, she had been shouting her name until she almost lost her voice. She was with a young man who was lagging behind her. Watching from beside the boat, Manolo saw the two friends hug and kiss one another. They turned their heads in his direction two or three times, laughing and whispering: he thought he wasn't going to escape being introduced. Teresa's friend had a constant smile on her brown moonlike face, and didn't stay still for a moment, her body constantly wriggling in the towel. He couldn't hear what they were saying, but knew they were speaking in Catalan (he deduced this from the faces Teresa was pulling, which he had learned to interpret) and this and their increasingly loud laughter were enough to unnerve him. As if to confirm his suspicions, the breeze brought him the terrible word (*xarnego*) pronounced by Teresa's friend, and her laugh: the fearful, calculating Catalan sarcasm had surfaced again, embodied as a threat in this cheerful young woman (how mysterious that smile of hers). What can they be talking about: why doesn't Teresa call me and introduce me? Some other random words and sly questions reached his ears: 'Does he work?', 'On holiday?', 'Be careful, girl'. He saw a family resemblance between them and their surroundings. It was as if the elements were obeying their instructions: the red sun, already dipping towards the horizon, was shining directly in between the two dizzy little heads, its rays scattering on Teresa's blond locks, conjuring gentle illusions of dignity, something that might be called education or progress, a full life, infinite tenderness, which he could only earn using his intelligence ... Well, both of them were Catalan, pretty and rich. They parted with another kiss.

'Who is that?' he asked when Teresa returned.

'Leonor Fontalba, a friend from the faculty. She's very nice.'

'What were you laughing about?'

Teresa spun round as she flopped down next to him.

'We were talking about you,' she said. 'Does that upset your highness? Leonor is spending her holiday in Sitges. She's escaped with a friend. By the way, she says that tonight they'll all be in the Saint-Germain. Would you like to meet them? We could go for a drink. I'll introduce you.'

'Who are these people?'
'Friends.'
'What kind of friends?'
In the most natural way in the world, she told him:
'Left-wing students.'

Part Three

The nature of their power is as ambiguous as the nature of our situation itself: all that can be said is that they have conflicting ideas. Their first, youthful rebellion at university had something of the solitary vice about it. Unfortunately, at our university, where what Luis Trías de Giralt (in what was perhaps more than a slip of the tongue) called 'democratic hardloiners' did not exist, political awareness arose from a burning, doctrinal erection and lonely ideological masturbation. This gave rise to the lurid, murky, cryptic and fundamentally secretive nature of that generation of heroes in their first attempts to revolt. At the outset, no one appeared to be in charge. In 1956, they appeared out of nowhere, as if wound up like stiff clockwork dolls sworn to secrecy, a dagger up their sleeve and irrevocable determination in their leaden gaze.

Impressive and impressed with themselves, mysterious, important and self-important, they advance slowly and ponderously along the corridors of the Faculty of Letters with strange books under their arms, and who knows what overwhelming orders on their minds, creating as they go invisible waves of danger, slogans, cryptic messages and secret interviews, arousing admiration, uncertainty, sending shivers down female spines, together with furtive glimpses of a worthier future. Their noble brows, weighed down with terrible responsibilities and urgent decisions, penetrate lecture theatres like tanks enveloped in the smoke from their own guns; they demolish pockets of resistance, squash rumours and jealousies, crush opposing theories and adverse criticism, and enforce silence. It is then that sometimes can be heard, as at the climax of a concert, an unsuspecting voice confiding, in what seems to be one long, stammered, obscene word:

'... *pcithinkbelongstothepc.*'

Two or three of them are often to be seen at a remote table in the faculty bar, talking in low voices, reading and passing one another pamphlets. Teresa Serrat is always with them: active, forceful, lit like a screen from inside by her pink glow. Some right-wing elements insist the beautiful politicised blonde sleeps with her friends, or at least with Luis Trías de Giralt, and yet everyone knows that although this is a time of exploration both above and below, as yet there's nothing more to it than that.

Crucified between the marvellous march of history and their fathers' abominable factories, poor sacrificial lambs, defenceless and resigned, they wear their uneasy position as *señoritos* the way cardinals wear their purple gowns, humbly lowering their eyes. To their families they demonstrate a heroic resistance, a bitter distaste for wealthy fathers, disdain for entrepreneurial brothers-in-law, cousins and devout aunts, while paradoxically giving off a religious whiff of pampered, rich, mother's boys and cream tarts for breakfast. All this makes them suffer tremendously, especially when they're drinking red wine with cripples and hunchbacks in the Barrio Chino, shadowy bar-room figures presumably condemned by the Franco regime for a Republican, left-wing past. Caught in the crossfire, condemned to criticism from both sides, they remain aloof in lectures, unapproachable and impenetrable. They talk only among themselves, and then not a great deal, because they have urgent special missions to carry out. They try hard to cultivate expressive looks, cherish endless silences that they allow to sprout like trees in front of them. Like well-trained hunting dogs, they sniff dangers that only they can detect; they organise meetings and demonstrations, make plans on the telephone to meet, like star-crossed lovers, and lend one another banned books.

Only a few are among the chosen, and it's hard to categorise them. Luis Trías appears to be their leader. Tall, silent, his head tilted slightly to one side, intoxicated by his own rosy perfume, whenever he appears in the corridors and lecture theatres, he is like a human traffic light, controlling the movement of ideas and subversive conspiracies. But the masses wonder: is he genuinely well connected? The traffic light blinks, unfathomable, when Teresa looks at him.

In fact, it all began just as life itself does: the unrest and university resistance that in 1957 spilled out on to the streets with cultural and political demands, sowing the good seed that years later would blossom (written in honour of the memory of those martyrs still alive, some of them already seated in the director's chair of their family inheritance), had been germinating for some time in the minds of three enchanting young girls from the Faculty of Letters. One of them was Teresa Serrat, and another a fine arts student. Two years earlier, they began to attend lectures with a pair of trousers tucked under their arm, and afterwards met in an apartment on Calle Fontanella apparently owned by a pleasant, cultured former nun. There they donned the trousers, lit cigarettes, squatted on floor cushions and set their pulses racing as they discussed the new ideas as passionately as prostitutes at the imminent arrival of the US Sixth Fleet. Some time later, the increasingly numerous and excited attendees at the history lectures given by an associate professor recently returned from France were able occasionally to witness a miracle taking place before their astonished eyes. During the class, the professor's magic words, his exhaustive, dialectical analysis of some of life's realities, whirled about him (in reality, his detractors later claimed, he only ever talked about himself), like some marvellous exotic bird that used its beak to strip him of his clothes and dress him in different ones (or like the slow metamorphosis created by the waving of a magic wand), until, to his students' amazement, he was the very image of a Republican militiaman, clad in overalls and with a rifle, cartridge belt and all the rest. Naturally, those acquainted with the real nature of militiamen in the Civil War saw this as a remote, grotesque imposture. But for the most part a visionary shudder ran through the professor's students: the girls listened to him open-mouthed with their eyes closed; a well-known groper with a long, effective reach claimed he could hear them sighing, while others heard bells ringing – now is the time, release the doves, friends, I'm about to become a father. This is the story of a multiple adolescent birth, full of generosity and sacrifice, but also carelessness and confusion. Not all the resulting offspring would later be recognised by the father – that's life, we've all been young, so many things happen.

Events gathered pace: it was enough for Luis Trías de Giralt to pay a rapid visit to Paris for it to be rumoured on his return that he too had signed up. The news, which overnight made Luis the best-qualified person to take over the leadership of the nascent secret organisation, came in fact from one of the girls who went to the reunions in the apartment on Calle Fontanella, after she had spent a night of gin and reckless talk with the leader himself in the Bar Saint-Germain, where together they hatched vague connections with mysterious hidden powers. The University of Barcelona had to match the one in Madrid, which in these matters was always more serious, more consistent and audacious. *'In February '56, after a Student Congress in Madrid was suspended, the atmosphere grew heated, there was a clash, a shot rang out, and a young man fell to the ground, seriously wounded.*' Luis Trías, who at the time happened to be in Madrid (he was becoming a conveniently ubiquitous figure, evasive and surprising) was arrested and spent six months in prison.

Teresa received his letters and read them at the university, slightly apart from the others, but not so far not to be observed and envied. After that, the intrepid blonde and her friends took part in an attempted workers' strike that unfortunately failed. This was the first time the students had joined a workers' movement, and the fame of the four women in trousers grew in the lecture theatres with all the esteem, dignity and risk implied by what they had done. A special edition of *Les Temps Modernes* devoted to the *gauche* was passed from hand to hand. Astonishing news began to spread. At the same time, in the Faculty of Letters an Egyptian student began to come to the fore. Extremely handsome, looking like a prophet with legendary black eyes and full of apocalyptic pronouncements ('I've come to announce that this era of confusion is at an end'), he was classified as 'very well connected' even though no one ever knew who had decided this: it was thought to be a fifth girl plotter who had lately joined the small central committee. When Luis Trías de Giralt returned (as we know, he didn't come alone, but accompanied by the phantom of torture), he became the undisputed leader (categorised as 'extremely well connected') and began to be seen everywhere with Teresa Serrat, who during his absence had not only valiantly continued his work, but also remained faithful to him.

It was then they organised the many events that brought them glory and prestige. One day when the faculty was surrounded by armed police and they couldn't leave the lecture room even for their basic needs, they succeeded, thanks to a stirring speech the two of them made, in persuading all the male and female students to cast off their petit-bourgeois hang-ups and resolve to urinate on the spot, without any shame. This spectacle was seen as an act of solidarity, the details and delights of which many still recall. Their efforts culminated in the famous October demonstration, as a result of which the authorities closed the university for a week, several students including Teresa and Luis were reported to the police, and others expelled or arrested. It would be churlish not to mention the noble sense of dedication, verging on the reckless, that characterised the unselfish activities of Teresa Serrat and her friends. The precise nature of that generous dedication was and still remains a matter of debate.

Today, almost two years later, when everything at the university appears to have returned to normal, this generous democratic urge is still latent and is possibly more febrile than ever, although to be fair one must report a noticeable shift this urge has undergone within their youthful bodies. Put simply, it has descended a little further downwards to the obscure, moist regions of passion. Thanks to this, some have already started to fall from their pedestals (the Egyptian, who had been a precursor in every sense and was among the first to enjoy a large slice of female adulation, turned out not only to have no connections, but not even to be Egyptian), whereas others were confirmed, at least momentarily, in their leadership roles – including Teresa Serrat and Luis. Of the five young women, only one had the joy of connecting completely and utterly with the hidden power, even if perhaps only to regret it for the rest of her life. This was the fifth girl-incubator of myths, the sacrificial victim (of the Egyptian, it later turned out), swept away by the other storm, the underground movement that was also disturbing the surface. After abandoning her family and her half-completed studies, half a mother, half disenchanted, she ended up working in a *patisserie* in Paris. A student poet (who years later would become famous outside Spain for a book of poems entitled *I Put My Finger in the Wound*) said that from every drop of her spilled virginal blood, flowers of freedom and culture would grow.

LAST EVENINGS WITH TERESA

It is true that not all of them were equal to the challenge. Due to their reduced numbers at the outset, and their inveterate propensity for myth and local folklore, their names were silenced and eventually forgotten in subsequent chronicles (what did remain recorded was that they enjoyed a glorious, fruitful spring). That is not relevant, however, to our present account, where it is our painful duty to record a moment concerning Teresa Serrat that helps explain more fully the nature of the moral misunderstanding that led the beautiful university student into the arms of a Murcian *xarnego*. And also to do justice to them, in passing, because ten years later they would still be suffering the consequences; they would still be boring everyone with the weight of the sterile prestige they had won during those glorious days, dragging with them a great unfocused lucidity, a lamp lost in the sad night of renunciation and indolence, little by little falling apart in fashionable bars with a different integration on the horizon (with Europe, the benefits of which, if they ever arrived, they and their distinguished families would be the first to enjoy), going rusty like counterfeit coins, dribbling their futile political maturity, lazily determined to continue playing their former role as more or less prominent militants or conspirators who, thanks to supposed dogmatic aberrations, had been left in the gutter. Far from harming them, this too acts in their favour: it makes them martyrs twice over, veterans on two equally mythified, disappointing fronts. But youth dies when its wish to seduce dies. Weary, bored with itself, that glorious phantom of torment would over time become the phantom of personal ridiculousness, like a sad stuffed parrot, full of alcohol and rich girls' lipstick, the wretched leftovers of what had once been the imperishable spirit of contemporary university history. And with this, the fickle, multiple voices of a choir delivering its verdict: all that had been nothing more than a child's game, with chases, spies and wooden pistols, one of which suddenly fired a real bullet. Others put it more grandly and spoke of a noble effort worthy of respect. Others finally said the really important actors weren't those who had been in the limelight, but the ones in the shadows far above all the rest, whose labours had yet to be recognised. Whatever the case, if one accepts the noble impulse behind the events, there is nothing strange about the confusion between appearance and reality. What else was to be expected of those young university students back then, if even the ones who claimed to be serving the true, democratic cause in Spain were young men who carried their mythical adolescence around with them into their forties?

Over time, some came to be seen as frauds, others as victims, most of them as imbeciles or children, a few as sensible and generous (these were rewarded with a future in politics), and all of them as what they really were: shitty *señoritos*.

They usually met in the Saint-Germain-des-Prés bar, in the Barrio Chino. That night, after dinner, her eyes still moist from the sun breaking through the clouds, her skin still glowing from being so close to Manolo, Teresa Serrat was driving fast to Plaza Sanllehy to pick him up. Until that moment she had been dying to introduce him to her friends, but now all of a sudden the idea troubled her. It wasn't that she feared Leonor Fontalba's brazen coquetry, or some sly comment by a resentful Luis Trías, but the very fact of introducing him into this intellectual atmosphere, these nerve centres of theory (which she realised she was beginning to be really fed up with, now she thought she knew Manolo so well) which, depending on whether the group was depressed or in high spirits, would seek either to disconcert or dazzle him. Should she remind them that he was a worker – that is, a person who wouldn't appreciate any dialectical brilliance, a man who had other concerns? When such thoughts crossed her mind, she felt reassured and proud: she had complete confidence in Manolo and his natural power of seduction, his mineral, slightly cynical but respectful lack of concern, and above all in something she liked to define as 'the modern style of his attitudes', something that remained intact despite a few remaining primitive traces of the sullen gypsy that she often saw circling around his proud head. Besides, she would tell Leonor Fontabla, who on the beach had called him a *xarnego*, the aesthetic make-up of these modern attitudes of his was European rather than Spanish. Of course, it was not the same as that of certain uninhibited young people (whom she saw as neither youthful nor happy, but simply typical of Seville) that Luis Trías regarded as ideal for their Barrio Chino reunions, because their attributes were exclusively verbal: they might be loquacious and entertaining, but they had no physical presence, and were therefore harmless (this was what a strangely excited Luis maintained, insisting on how damaging the dark-skinned Egyptian had been). Manolo's power lay elsewhere – what do you expect, the power of Murcians is physical if it's anything – she would tell Leonor that as well. Aesthetically speaking, a Murcian can be more European than a Catalan; his impassive demeanour was only Iberian in the sense of being proud and self-assured, which wasn't a defect but quite the opposite . . . a pair of hands covered her eyes from behind, and she shivered to the roots of her hair.

'Manolo . . . Hey, what are you doing? You're very punctual.'

This wasn't true. She had been waiting for him over half an hour, sitting with her arms folded on the steering wheel, daydreaming and unaware of the passage of time. He got in the car, closing the door firmly and confidently once again.

'Of course, they're all very smart,' Teresa explained to him as she drove, craning her neck, her hands moving lazily on the wheel in a dreamy fashion. By now they were going down the Ramblas, and out of habit Manolo was keeping one eye on the motorbikes parked under the trees. 'But if you think they're being too silly or if they get boring talking about literature or our debates at the university . . .'

'I never talk politics,' he warned her.

'. . . you only have to give me a sign and we'll leave. I like them a lot, but I've seen more than enough of them. And these reunions in Encarna's bar aren't exactly a novelty for me.'

Manolo, who didn't know Teresa's friends (although he did know the bar, which he had frequented three years earlier, for reasons that, had she learned of them, would have greatly surprised Teresa), sensed that something decisive could happen that night, something that if he managed to take it by the horns would perhaps stand him in good stead. Because while it was true that Teresa appeared to believe in him, his position was far from secure. Until now, on his own with her, he had been able to keep up the pretence, to live up to that bizarre image she had so enthusiastically created of him, but he understood that things were bound to become more complicated, that the time had come to face risks that were still unclear to him, although they were beginning to make sense. No sooner had he entered the bar than the icy blast of danger hit him, the shock wave preceding the explosion (in his early days as a car thief, he had felt the same sensation). As he approached the others he promised himself not to say anything more than was strictly necessary: he sensed he would come under attack, premeditated or not, but didn't know which side it would come from.

The place was quite crowded. Teresa's friends had occupied two tables underneath the Dali-like portrait of an exuberant pink woman swathed in chiffon. In addition to Luis Trías, who was already on his fourth gin, there were two girls and two boys in the group. One of them was sheathing his sword to take his leave: he had managed to worm five hundred pesetas out of Luis. 'I'll give it you back tomorrow,' he said. His name was Guillermo Soto, he was tall and ungainly and had just returned from studying at Heidelberg. He had not heard of and was not interested in his friends' latest university skirmishes ('been there, done that'), while in return they saw him as decadent and a professional scrounger. Soto launched into a strange, rambling explanation about the loan, involving the disastrous afternoons in the sun that were fuelling his fiancée María José Roviralta's anxiety to get married. She was at the beach with her parents, who were supervising the construction of a hotel, and to rescue her he needed petrol for his car. As he left he shook hands with Teresa and Manolo without stopping on his way out, the five-hundred-peseta note still in his left hand (but he did notice the swift, unmistakable glance the Murcian gave the banknote, and in return Soto fixed his fierce, weary eyes on him, letting go of his hand and sketching a smile that blended affection with complicity, as if to say: 'There's more where that came from').

'You're crazy lending him money, Luis,' one of the girls said. María Eulalia Bertrán was tall and sleepy-looking, very elegant in a low-cut dress and covered in all kinds of ornaments, trinkets and strange objects: she wasn't so much dressed as furnished. She was listening as attentively as a bird of prey hypnotised by its own quarry to what Ricardo Borrell was reading from an open book on the table he shared with her. He was a delicate, pale young man, malleable and impressionable, who looked like a rag doll, and who years later got a new lease of life writing 'objective' novels. The other girl was Leonor Fontalba, whom Manolo already knew from the beach. Small and lively, she blinked and talked at lightning speed, all the while smiling with her dimpled, celluloid cheeks. The fourth member of the party was Jaime Sangenis. He was drunk, studied architecture, had the black beard of a movie villain, and wore a khaki military-style shirt. None of them could have been more than twenty. They were all very tanned from their summer holidays at key points on the coast (clear blue waters, conversation in French, catchy melodies: their conscience sleeping soundly in their bellies like a snake coiled up in the sun). To some extent they were only dangerous in the winter months, when from getting together so often, their vehement gossip and their habitual state of mind as a group – an odd mixture of intellectual effervescence and hidebound lives – led them to pronounce all kinds of moral judgements on their friends. The Murcian caused a sensation when Teresa introduced him, and he shook hands with them all. He noticed that the last handshake, from Luis, was needlessly long, warm and affectionate: maybe this was where the attack would come from.

They sat next to Leonor.

'You make a fine couple,' joked Luis Trías. 'It's really good to see you ... So you're the famous Manolo. Do you know Teresa hasn't talked of anything else for months?' (Teresa looked daggers at him.) 'Before you even knew her. Months and months ...'

'Yee ... aars,' stammered Jaime Sangenis.

'Centuries, I'd say,' added Leonor, leaning towards Teresa to whisper something in her ear. Manolo stared frostily at them. And what's this with secrets, as if we didn't have enough already.

'Tere, tell us, what crazy adventures are you mixed up in now?' asked a smiling María Eulalia, casting a sidelong glance at Manolo.

'Teresa,' he said, 'what are you drinking?'

'I don't know ...'

'How are things, Manolo?' asked Luis Trías.

'So-so.'

'How is Maruja?'

'Bad.'

'She's been like that for a long while, hasn't she?'

'Almost a month.'

'I wanted to go and see her, but Doña Marta told me the doctors don't encourage visitors. The poor girl was so unlucky, it was such a stupid fall ... absolutely incredible. I like Maruja a lot. Well, Teresa, what are you going to drink?' And then, turning to Manolo once more: 'I suppose you drink wine.'

Manolo looked at him, suspecting something. This Luisito was fighting with weapons he didn't recognise. He had to be careful. He smiled.

'For now I'd like a glass of milk.'

Luis patted him on the back.

'Like in the movies, eh? You're a hard man, kiddo!'

María Eulalia attracted Teresa's attention, pointing at Manolo. 'Hey, where did you find him?'

'Ah, that's a secret.'

'Haven't we met before?' asked Leonor.

'Yes, this afternoon.'

'No, I mean before that.'

'Goodness,' exclaimed María Eulalia, 'I was about to ask him the same.'

All at once questions rained down on the Interloper, all of them feminine (including those from Luis Trías) and childish, to which he responded by bestowing the phlegmatic frostiness of his smiles on all sides. His dark forehead was openly assessed, measured, examined in search of that telltale sign of talent or intelligence that, in an abuse of power, beautiful features often reveal only slowly. Manolo answered in monosyllables, rapidly and effortlessly regaining his longed-for silence (his favourite way of expressing himself). Gradually, the group's attention turned back to what Ricardo Borrell was reading as he sat hunched next to María Eulalia, who was busily appropriating him with an arm bedecked with bracelets and silk ribbons, folded like a wing.

'Encarna!' Teresa called out, rising to her feet. 'A Giró gin and a glass of milk.'

A booming, adventurous and warm voice was heard: '*Una llet, nena? Qui és aquest animal que beu llet?*' Drinking milk like a baby? Who is this strange creature that drinks only milk? Laughing, Teresa went over to the bar. Leonor smiled her full moon-smile at Manolo.

'You're right. Gin ruins the memory.'

'Is that so?'

'You bet. Didn't you know?'

The cavernous voice could be heard again, this time over Teresa's tinkling laugh. '*Ben parit, aquest nano. D'on l'has tret, lladre-gota?*' Well brought up, this little guy. Where did you steal him from?

'Do you always drink milk, or is this your little number?' asked Leonor.

'I don't do numbers, I'm not at school any more.'

Confused, Leonor smiled, then her round cheeks looked about to burst with merriment. Manolo suspected he had slipped up, and said with a smile:

'Milk is an antidote.'

'It's absolutely fabulous,' Luis Trías's voice came from beside him, and Manolo caught his inquisitive, penetrating look. He's all ears, the bastard, he thought. He turned again to Leonor Fontalba, who was still smiling blankly at him, as though inviting him to carry on, or to kiss her. In fact it was neither, and when she saw reflected in his eyes (a pitch-black wave engulfed her for the fraction of a second) the ambiguity that her celluloid smile was creating, she turned her head away. The Murcian corrected himself; it would take him time that night to understand many things: firstly, that her smile was not in fact a real smile, but nothing more than an accident, a strange effect created by her plump cheeks beneath the cheekbones. Years before, he had made the same mistake with a sad, mature foreign woman he had met on the Costa del Sol, the difference being that on that occasion the mistake (which he discovered all of a sudden one day when the German woman had no reason to go on smiling at him: she was accusing him of the disappearance of a certain amount of money) had in no way restricted his desire to please or spoiled his plans – far from it. As time went by, he came across so many similar fixed, glued-on smiles that he even came to think that, as with money, intelligence and a healthy skin colour, the rich also inherit this perpetual smile, in the same way that the poor inherit rotten teeth, defeated brows and twisted legs. This must be the case, because now he was also hearing random phrases he didn't understand in the slightest.

'. . . it was a real assassination, in June '53, a ridiculous . . .'

'. . . proconsuls of the new empire . . .'

'. . . a son of a bitch called Greenglass, do you remember?'

'. . . and a sinister old fogey by the name of Macarci . . .'

'. . . and those guys swear that all communists live in unmarried couples . . .'

'. . . as that imbecile joker Guillermo Soto says.'

'He's not such an imbecile as you think,' said Jaime Sangenis. 'He's right-wing, but a moderate.'

'Precisely,' Luis Trías responded. 'When you're on the right, it's best to be so a hundred per cent, as extreme as you can.'

'That's nonsense. It's like wanting the long-suffering middle class to become lumpen in order to speed up the revolution. Things have to be won wIth effort, my friend. What do you think, Manolo?'

At moments like this, Manolo stared at the portrait of the

woman swathed in chiffon while he worked out how to respond, and always answered cautiously:

'In this life, every effort brings its own reward.'

He knew this was a cheap lie someone had invented, and said it with a smile (although deep down he was serious) to deflect any suspicion. He suddenly realised that the woman in the painting was the bar owner in her younger days.

'Do you like it?' Leonor asked him.

'It's not bad . . .'

'It's horrible.'

The Murcian lit a cigarette.

'I mean the woman.'

'Oh, Encarna is a delight, even in that painting.'

'That's right.'

He couldn't understand how, if the woman in the picture was a delight, the painting could be horrible. When Teresa came back from the counter, she had taken a seat between Luis and Jaime, so that now Manolo was opposite her. She asked:

'Did you keep the cigarettes, darling?'

Luis looked askance at her. Taking out the packet of Chesterfields, Manolo tossed it on to the table. Some grains of sand fell out; Teresa gave Manolo an odd smile as she began to sweep them up into a small pile, which she left in the centre of the table: a public monument erected in honour of her happiness. Ricardo Borrell and María Eulalia were still sitting apart from the others. Every so often Ricardo's voice could be heard, reading or praising passages from the book. This was a volume of literary criticism currently being devoured in the faculty. María Eulalia asked them all to be quiet, and Ricardo read out a strange quotation, one of those phrases that will weigh heavily on an author all their life and keep them awake like a nightmare: 'In general, it has to be said that the nineteenth-century novelist wasn't very intelligent.'

'That's good,' added Ricardo. 'It was high time someone exposed Balzac and Co.'

'What rubbish,' exclaimed Teresa, who, worried at the direction the conversation was taking, was closely observing Manolo.

'Goodness, but they were all reactionaries,' said María Eulalia. 'Okay, so they were geniuses, but drunk on their creative power,' she added, glancing wild-eyed at Ricardo out of fear she might have said something crass (she forgot she had read it in the book) because occasionally it was difficult to communicate with him: Ricardo was so pure, so 'objective', that he seemed very *détaché* from other people's inner worlds.

'The two go together, sweetheart,' said a befuddled Luis Trías, downing his sixth gin.

'I have to say I find Rastignac more entertaining than Comrade Federico,' Teresa put in, apparently wanting to contradict the others for the sake of it. Unfortunately, her opinion was considered scandalously subjective and was therefore rejected.

'The fact you find it entertaining doesn't mean a thing, darling,' said Ricardo, unfazed by the alliteration. 'Besides, Rastignac isn't Balzac.'

Teresa suspected this affirmation proved what a pedantic bookworm Ricardo was, but said nothing; this was yet another subjective idea the others would have dismissed. She looked across at Manolo and saw he was examining his hands (that entire day she had seen he was worried by his worker's hands, as if afraid her friends would regard them as dirty or ugly), those powerful hands that had held her behind the wreck of a boat that same afternoon. How much better it would be to cling to them again and talk of simple things in that sweet, intimate space, their breaths intermingling, rather than wasting time here with these pedants! Sitting motionless, as disconcerting as a tree root or a suddenly decorative rock, with that mineral indifference she found so attractive, from time to time the Murcian returned her gaze through the smoky bar, the conversations and the music. They were brief affectionate, rescuing looks that contained just the right amount of reassurance to make her also feel secure. Rubbing the gin glass on his cheek, Luis Trías turned to her and said:

'I was looking for you.'

'What's wrong?'

'Nothing. I was just looking for you, that's all.'

'Is something being organised for the start of term?'

'Yes, but that's not why I was looking for you. For the moment you aren't needed.'

Teresa didn't seem to follow.

'So what for, then?'

'Nothing, as I said. I wanted to see you. I heard you weren't in Blanes, that you preferred to stay here . . .'

'Someone had to stay with Maruja, didn't they?'

'You don't have to justify yourself to me.'

'I'm not justifying myself, you idiot. I'm lying to you,' she said, standing up to go to the toilet. None of them could as yet suspect that relations between Teresa Serrat and the leader of the university resistance had undergone such a drastic change since that shameful night at the Villa. Teresa, who had elevated Luis to the role of student leader, now wanted to knock him off his pedestal, and was even willing to question his supposed political importance. The prestigious student's fall from grace had begun.

When Teresa returned, she sat next to Manolo, who by this time was absent-mindedly toying with his cigarette lighter.

'Do you want us to go?' she asked him.

'No, not yet,' he said.

Teresa saw that María Eulalia was motioning to her from the far end of the table, her braceleted arms waving above Ricardo's head as if she was about to fly off. 'I don't understand!' Teresa shouted at her.

'Why don't you have a fringe like I do? It adds depth to your look.'

At that moment Manolo put his arm round Teresa's shoulders (everyone saw it) and brushed the side of her head with his lips. To Teresa it seemed so natural: it was as if he wanted to defend her, to prevent her answering María Eulalia with something equally inane. Luis ordered another gin.

'Why don't we go to another watering hole?' said Jaime.

'Don't you want Ricardo to read you this?' said María Eulalia whenever one of them suggested leaving. 'Pay the lad some attention at least.'

'To hell with it,' said Luis Trías, who could only think of a young, perfect torso in a tight striped T-shirt lying on a red couch. He stayed silent for a long while, and when he broke the silence he seemed a different person.

'Do you know who's in Barcelona?' he said very seriously, and then added: 'Federico.'

'Have you seen him?' asked María Eulalia.

'Who told you?' Leonor wanted to know.

'I heard it from a reliable source.' Luis turned towards Manolo, stared at him, and even thrust his face forward, asking abruptly: 'Do you know Federico?'

So that's it, at last! thought the Murcian. It wasn't yet the low blow he had been expecting, but if it came, this was where it would come from. This was the second time in less than fifteen hours he had been asked the same question: Teresa had done so on the beach that afternoon. Lucky Federico, they all love you so much! Leaving the lighter on the table, he exchanged glances with Teresa (a glance that didn't mean anything, but was merely to see if the others were watching him), bowed his head slightly, fixed his eyes on Luis Trías, and said in a natural, rather forlorn voice:

'He mentioned you to me.'

Silence.

'Me?' said Luis. 'What do you mean?'

'Just that. We talked about you.'

Leonor leaned over to whisper something in Teresa's ear. Everyone saw her nod her blond head. Jaime patted Luis's back in commiseration. Beneath María Eulalia's loving gaze, the happy author-reader raised his voice once more:

'Hey, listen to this: "The author, whom the new techniques . . ."'

Manolo stood up. Everyone looked at him. Apparently indignant (in fact, he was bored), he had got up to go to the toilet. Still taken aback, Luis Trías shouted at Encarna for black tobacco, thumping the table with his fist.

'Encarna, it's really annoying you never have black tobacco. Shocking, in fact.'

'*Calla, macu!*' boomed her voice. Shut up, darling!

This led to an intense discussion about indignation and modern man. Luis was of the opinion that the Spaniard had lost his incredible capacity for indignation; he could put up with everything, was no longer indignant about anything. Sangenis agreed. Leonor pointed out that, as she saw it, in Spain there was still a certain capacity for indignation, but that it had to be admitted that it was no longer manly or national. As ever, she spoke rapidly and not entirely coherently:

'Man's indignation is naturally political. Put another way, man's natural indignation fundamentally is or ought to be political. However, when men waste their indignation on stupid, menial things like, for example, that madman in Pamplona who indignantly smashed a shop window because it was displaying a bikini – you must have read about it in yesterday's newspaper – or that other one who painted over Marilyn's cleavage on a cinema poster on Paseo de Gracia, did you see that? Or those who go to football matches to yell slogans, or you yourself just now (she was looking at Luis, who was already in a bad mood, and that night was beginning to have reasons to feel that way) with your blasted black tobacco . . .'

'Do you want to know something?' said Teresa, who had been served her third gin. 'You're so tiresome tonight, I've heard nothing but nonsense, it all sounds ridiculous to me . . .'

Her opinion, which isn't worth recording here because it was uninteresting, was, however, listened to with interest by the others, not so much because it came from her as from lips that were especially impetuous that night: it made them think of the Murcian and his own impetuous manner.

'What's wrong with you today?' exclaimed Jaime.

'Teresa has changed,' Luis ruled. 'She's acquired the blessed proletarian bloody-mindedness.'

'Why don't you stop drinking if you can't handle it, Luis?' said Jaime.

'That's precisely why I love your *xarnego*,' Leonor went on blithely. At that moment the Interloper was urinating in the toilet, cursing under his breath for having stained his trousers a little. 'Because in him indignation is always manly, always political.'

María Eulalia, meanwhile, whose accoutrements were getting increasingly spoiled as the night wore on, had almost succeeded in sheltering Ricardo beneath her hen's wing.

'Do you like the book?' she asked.

'It needs to be read very carefully,' said Ricardo. 'Will you lend it to me for a few days?'

'I brought it for you, sweetie – it's a present,' she said, clucking as she folded her wing over him.

Luis Trías was talking about someone called Araquistáin and

his influence in university circles. Manolo wasn't paying the slightest attention (he was looking down at Teresa's bare neck and the delicate shadow that swayed like a blue fishtail between her breasts) either to him or to his Araquistáin, whose name was a complete mystery. María Eulalia, who was half listening to Luis, let out a giggle that plainly had nothing to do with the conversation but more to a favourable, surreptitious advance of her knee or arm towards the impregnable fortress of objectivity that was Ricardo.

Manolo said nothing.

'Manolo, you're very important,' Luis said sarcastically.

Like hell, he thought. At around one in the morning, Luis Trías announced solemnly that he was going out for a while. Something urgent. He gave a brief nod to Jaime, for him to accompany him. When they came back half an hour later, Luis seemed calmer, and spoke with the authority and decision of the days at the university that had made him famous. He was carrying a yellow piece of paper the size of an envelope. There was some text printed on it, and from a distance Manolo thought it looked like an advertising flyer. Jaime and Luis sat at the end of the now deserted counter (Encarna had come over to their table and was joking with the group. 'You're well equipped,' she said, her sparkling eyes fixed on Manolo's tight trousers as she tried to recall where and when she had seen this boy before) and went on talking quietly until they came back and joined the others, looking concerned. Encarna returned to the counter with Manolo, who had ordered a *Cuba libre*. From there, with the music from the record player echoing in his ears, and while that huge woman, whose endearing, uterine voice deeply affected him ('*Ifellit meu*, I know you, baby, but I don't know where from'), was showing him the photographs of her splendid younger years on the wall, he listened to what they were saying at the table. Luis had asked them all to pay attention, but Manolo couldn't hear properly, and at first thought he was talking about trams. The others joined in, and there was a wealth of unfinished phrases, interruptions when they were being careful or were frightened, and the question under discussion seemed to make little headway. Manolo heard the word 'tram' several times and something that sounded like 'lipotype'. A lipotype that had been impounded, a leaflet it was urgent to print and distribute, a mistake somebody had made (whom Luis described as an irresponsible fool) and a fixed, unmovable date. The Murcian concentrated on what they were saying, although he sensed that the photographic biography of the bar owner with her Marlene Dietrich-style blond locks contained secrets and personal triumphs that were much more interesting and useful to him than those being aired at the conspiratorial table; but he would leave that for some other time. As he listened, he thought he was beginning to understand. Perhaps this was what he had been waiting for all night without realising it. He had a hunch.

'Pour it in that glass, please,' he said, pointing at a tall purple one. And that was what led Encarna to finally recognise him: 'It's almost three years since you were last here! Aren't you ashamed of yourself, *rei meu*? Where have you been?'

Regretting it bitterly, because he really appreciated this woman, Manolo said she had the wrong person (with weary astonishment, he again saw the image of himself sitting at this counter three years earlier: a well-groomed, sad young man, with a distant sense of indifference pouring from his black eyes – he had the harsh appearance of someone forgiving sins committed before he was born – on whose neck lay the fingers of a mature, affectionate prostitute and the gaze of a theatre director who claimed to be great friends with an American by the name of Tennessee. But that past was dead and buried). Behind his back he heard Teresa's beloved voice impatiently mentioning this 'lipotype'.

'It's not a problem, for heaven's sake. I'm sure there's more than one of them in Barcelona.'

'Who has one?' asked Luis.

Silence.

'Listen, Manolo might know of someone,' came Leonor's cheery voice. 'Didn't Teresa say he is ...' Her voice lowered to a whisper. 'It seems he knows Federico.'

'Hmmm!' said someone, probably Ricardo Borrell.

'Bah, enough fantasising,' said Luis. 'He's about as much one of us as I am of the papal curia.'

'That's where you're wrong,' said Teresa.

'Okay, that's enough. Down to business. You, Teresa, say you're sure there must be someone who can do this. Let's see: who?'

'I meant ...' she began. 'I meant I suppose that ...'

'Teresa, please,' snapped Luis. 'Try to be specific or simply shut up.'

It had probably already occurred to Manolo, but this was the moment when he decided to go into action. It seemed to him everything happened very slowly, but in fact it was very quick, perhaps too quick: he left the counter and went back to them, standing by the table and bending down to pick up a packet of cigarettes that had fallen under Luis's chair. 'Don't worry about that,' he muttered as he bent down (for a second he glimpsed Teresa's delicious legs: they were really worth it). After tossing the packet on to the table, he stood there immobile, holding the tall, surprisingly coloured glass full of Coca-Cola, tilting his head pensively and rubbing his neck (Teresa loved that gesture). He said with a natural, rather world-weary voice:

'Give it to me. I'll take care of it.'

Instantly, the leaflet was transferred from Luis's hands (as they descended, the Murcian's dark, swift fingers paused for an instant in front of the student leader's nose) into his own.

'This isn't a game, you know,' said Luis, shaking his head and raising his open hand as if expecting the paper to reappear by magic.

But Manolo wasn't looking at him: he was still standing there, handling the delicate glass with the dignity of a celebrant and perusing the leaflet (in fact he only noticed the headline: *People of Barcelona!*). He took a sip of his drink, folded the piece of paper and put it in his pocket.

'When do you need it for?'

'As soon as possible,' stammered Luis. 'But are you sure that you . . .?'

'There's nothing more to say,' Manolo cut in. He looked at Teresa. 'Are you coming? I have to be up early tomorrow.'

'Just a second,' Luis asked. 'I'd like to know where this is going to.'

The Murcian didn't hesitate.

'Do you know Bernardo?'

'No . . .'

'I don't have time to explain right now. Let's go, Teresa.'

Teresa stood up. 'We're all going,' said someone. Convinced of their own importance, and therefore lacking in humour and incapable of irony, it was as if they were hypnotised by someone else who might also be important. But Luis Trías felt obliged to insist a little more. He went over to Manolo. 'Don't you want to know how many we need?' he said, watching the Murcian's lips.

'Let's leave the details for now. Teresa will explain everything to me tomorrow. She can come with me. What's most urgent is settled, don't you worry.'

As they were leaving the bar, what he had feared from the start occurred, although by now it was all the same to him. The reasons for the lamentable incident were never clear, but what Ricardo Borrell deduced sometime later won general approval.

According to him, as they went out, Luis Trías had asked the Murcian if he was already sleeping with Teresa, and the poor kid, construing this as an insult to Teresa ('Don't forget that workers are very prudish in that respect. I mean they still have that ridiculous sense of honour, and turn everything into something personal,' Borrell explained), felt duty bound to slap Luis Trías.

But to return to what happened. As they were leaving the bar, there was nothing that led any of them to suspect what was about to occur. 'Can you really do it on your own, and you know someone . . .?' Luis had asked as they were saying goodbye to Encarna. All the others thought this was a really unnecessary question. Luis and Manolo were slightly behind the others as both of them insisted on paying (in this the Interloper was roundly defeated), but they heard Luis's final words, filled with an irony that nobody apart from the Murcian was able to perceive.

'I'm sorry,' he said with a smile, looking at his lips again, 'but you still don't seem very clear about it . . . and in this kind of thing we have to take every precaution, don't we? So tell me, who is this Bernardo?'

They didn't know if Manolo had answered him; they couldn't hear anything more because by now they were all out in the street. When they reached the second corner on Calle Escudillers, Ricardo also fell behind, leaving the warmth of María Eulalia's wing to go and urinate in a dark doorway. Teresa, Jaime, Leonor and María Eulalia were in front. Ricardito was taking time to rejoin them, and María Eulalia suddenly said in a tone of utter distress: 'Oh, what an interminable pee!' But Ricardo was already back with them, and she was breathing a sigh of relief when all of a sudden he turned and started to run back towards the bar. He didn't get there in time: Luis and Manolo were squaring up to one another on the street corner.

'You don't seem clear about it,' Luis was saying to Manolo.

The Interloper stared at him as if he was a Chinese hieroglyph, utterly perplexed.

'What do you mean, kid?'

Ricardo was just about to turn the corner, with the others close behind him, when they heard the disturbing scrape of soles on the pavement, and Ricardo saying, 'Come on, don't be such animals, let it go,' but before they arrived they saw a shape hurtling backwards towards them, landing at their feet. It was Luis Trías, and it looked as if he had simply tripped. 'What's going on?' asked Jaime Sangenis. Luis was rubbing his chin, and didn't want anybody to help him up. His head was definitely to one side now. Manolo emerged out of the darkness, not looking at anybody.

'Are you coming or not?' he asked without stopping. This was obviously aimed at Teresa, and they all glanced at her. The Murcian carried on walking towards Calle Escudillers; for a moment the others had no idea what to do. They knew that these things happen when you drink more than you should. What of course they couldn't know was that this slap in the face by the Murcian was the first in a series of tremendous slaps that the prestigious leader was to suffer, as if he had abruptly fallen from grace, all of them for no apparent reason, and coming out of nowhere. Misfortune can sometimes engulf a person without any obvious cause.

Manolo carried on down the street, hands in his pockets and head lowered. The footsteps he was hoping to hear rang out at last behind him. He slowed down. When she caught up with him, she hung on his arm.

'Are you annoyed with me as well?' Teresa wanted to know.

'I'm not annoyed at anyone. But let's get out of here. These things always end badly.'

'But what happened? Did Luis say something about me?'

For the first time, he was tempted to tell her the truth. But what he said was: 'That's between him and me.'

Teresa staggered slightly.

'I'm also quite drunk, you know,' she said, closing her eyes. 'But I'll take you home, to your blessed Monte Carmelo. Tell me, though, who is this Bernardo?'

Manolo didn't reply. But he had to pause, because Teresa had gone limp, as if she had fallen asleep in his arms. Her tousled blond head nestled against his chest as they stood under a streetlamp. Manolo brushed back her silky hair and stroked her cheek. Teresa cooed like a dove. Looking at her exhausted face, like a child's overcome with sleep and unfathomable emotions, the Murcian smiled under the yellow lamplight: a sad smile, with the sudden taste of ashes in his mouth. As they walked slowly down a narrow alleyway towards the quays, he wanted Teresa to wake up for a while before she took the wheel. But she rubbed herself against him like a little cat, hung her arms round his neck and forced him to stop once more. She kissed him and said: 'I'm happy.' By now they were in the darkest part of the alleyway. From somewhere came the sound of clapping and a guitar being played. Manolo thought it would just be a quick smooch because Teresa could barely stand, but her moist pink and white mouth was unexpectedly hot, a sweet wet sponge dabbing at him, and so he pulled her close and avidly returned her kisses. With a bluish, clear gleam in her eye, she backed away slowly until she was leaning against the wall, trapping his hands for a moment. His fingers discovered something that drove him wild: as he slid them up and down he found there was no brassiere strap, leading him to imagine yet again her vibrant nudity, the tremulous freedom of her small breasts beneath the blouse. Now she drew him to her, thrusting her childish, schoolgirl thighs forward in a glad, deliciously obscene gesture. She allowed his hands to caress her thighs and move upwards; suddenly her senses were filled to overflowing with an amazing taste of honey. 'No, not here ...' she murmured as she felt his burning mouth on her shoulders, her neck. She flung her head back and then returned to him out of the shadows, offering her trembling lips with a sibilant rush of breath. Her eyes seemed to be imploring him (she had just made up her mind) to take her somewhere, to be loved and to be his until death ...

Whoa, *xarnego*, you'd better stop there, he told himself. Her submissive, frustrated gaze pierced him, but he put an arm firmly round her shoulders and led her to the car. There, pressed against his chest, she calmed down and smiled happily, her head still spinning. A cold breeze was blowing. Stroking the strands of her blond hair, he pushed aside his constant, lacerating foreboding for the future. He felt desolate again, without knowing precisely why.

Evoking that intense summer years later, they both recalled not only a general impression of light pouring over every event, with its golden variety of reflections and false promises, its multiple mirages of a redeemed future, but also the fact that at the centre of their mutual attraction, even at the core of their sunlit kisses, there had been dark recesses where the cold of winter and the mist that would obliterate the mirage were already beginning to encroach.

'Are you being sincere with me, Manolo? I'm afraid sometimes . . .'

'Afraid of what?'

'I don't know. Is what's happening to us true?'

And yet the collapse of the myth took place without affecting her growing love for the Murcian. Teresa became aware of his real character at the same moment (three evenings sufficed) as she came to fully realise she had been seduced not by an idea, but by a man. At first it was a feeling of mental imbalance, the need to review her ideas about the astounding world we live in, and the discovery of previously unsuspected connections, the shocking intertwining of reality and illusion.

One Sunday afternoon of sunshine and showers towards the end of August, Teresa insisted they went to a popular dance in El Guinardó. By chance they had sheltered from the rain in a bar from where they could see the Salón Ritmo across the road, where crowds of young men and women were thronging to enter. Manolo happened to say this had once been his favourite dance hall.

'Why don't we go in?' she asked, a delighted glint in her eye.

'You won't like it, the place is full of riff-raff,' Manolo tried to warn her, but Teresa insisted so much ('It's raining and we don't have a car, what else can we do?') he had no choice but to satisfy her whim. At that moment the heavens opened. Manolo took off his jacket to protect her as they crossed the street. Laughing, Teresa pressed herself against him. A fat, pink-faced man was at the ticket booth, smoking Ideales. Teresa asked him for one.

'Don't be so cheeky,' Manolo rebuked her with a smile.

'Be quiet, you. We're going to have a great time, you'll see.' Boys 25 pesetas. Girls 15. 'Discrimination,' laughed the young student. Refreshment included in the price. Featuring today: Orquesta Satélites Verdes with their singer Cabot Kim (Joaquín Cabot), the Maymó Brothers (Afro-Cuban rhythms), Lucieta Kañá (juvenile singer of Catalan *cuplés*) and other leading artistes. 'It looks good,' said Teresa, who from the outset seemed strangely excited. Special appearance by the Trío Moreneta Boys (the stirring notes of the *sardana* and modern rock combined in a single tune). 'Fantastic!' exclaimed Teresa as they went in. 'I'm not going to miss that.'

The hall was crammed and noisy, with not a centimetre to spare on the dance floor. Youths in their Sunday best, with sardonic eyes and impertinent expressions, were going round in tight groups, bothering the girls, leaning over to look down their cleavages and whisper sweet nothings. Almost all of them were from Andalusia. Teresa caught many meaningful glances in her direction; it was only Manolo's presence beside her that saved her from being besieged in a way that, had she been on her own, would doubtless have gone far beyond admiring looks. By chance that day she was dressed with an almost Sunday-style simplicity (white pleated skirt, high-necked blue blouse and a broad black belt) that would have fitted in well were it not for her groomed rich girl's hairstyle and her skin pampered by a sun-filled life of leisure – two assets that instantly gave her away even though she would have liked to pass unnoticed. In the boxes and seats ranged around the dance floor stiff clusters of girls stood chatting to one another, while on the small stage at the far end the garishly dressed Satélites Verdes were playing, accompanying their singer (too much of a crooner for most of the audience), a youngster with a pencil moustache and a nasal, almost monk-like voice. The locale had once been a Workers' Cultural and Recreational Society (the Weavers' Union Social Club) that, with its massed choir, its library and its theatre, had disappeared with the Republic. The décor was solemn and antiquated: four walls splendidly adorned high up by a frieze of flowers, bunches of grapes and plaster roundels each with a portrait inside, with underneath an illustrious name (Prat de la Riba, Pompeu Fabra, Antoni Clavé), the glory of Catalonia, the heroes of that much-missed workers' paradise of *orfeó i caramelles*, Orpheus and sweets, whose stern profiles seemed to pour scorn on this Sunday invasion by illiterate Andalusians. On the first-floor balcony, along with the musty smell of the wooden audience boxes, there still floated a melancholy phantom of the family atmosphere that had once reigned here but was now relegated to one corner: the storeroom for drinks and odd bits of junk. This had been the library and billiard room, and now contained the mangled but still surprising remnants of Dostoevksy and Proust translated into Catalan, alongside Salgari, Dickens, *Patufet* and Maragall, together with tarnished trophies and ancient Weavers' Union banners, all sleeping the sleep of oblivion.

It was incredibly hot in the dance hall; the air was filled with an overpowering smell of armpit. Teresa tried to curb her generous enthusiasm. Oh, Sunday dances, the world is yours! Uncultivated, teeming islands, violent skies, primordial impulses, trampled tenderness, gardens without fragrance where love flourishes even so: tomorrow belongs to you! Clinging to Manolo's arm as though they were a married couple, or sitting with him at the back of a box, body relaxed but head in the same vigilant, wide-awake attitude she had in the cinema (imbibing an atmosphere peopled by phantoms) and revealing her bare throat, Teresa took in every last detail of the spectacle, praising the couples dancing tirelessly in each others' arms as if she were looking down on a teeming anthill. Manolo recognised some well-known figures from his neighbourhood, the same ones who on Thursdays went to the Salón Price to dance with housemaids, and also to Las Cañas, the Metro, the Apolo, as well as to the Iberia, Máximo, Rovira, Texas and Selecto cinemas: small, sweaty Murcians in striped shirts with stiff collars and stifling double-breasted jackets, poignant would-be dancers who never found a partner even though they went round and round the dance floor peering up at the boxes, their eyes devouring the young girls sitting on their chairs like sphinxes. Their scornful silence or flat refusals of the boys' invitations ('Want to dance, girl?' 'No.' 'Why not?' 'Just because.' 'Well, fuck you, you consumptive.' 'Dwarf, cheeky lout') were of course, as Teresa told Manolo, unfair and infinitely more cruel than the insults the girls received. Perhaps that was why, given that today Manolo didn't seem to share her wish to have fun (this surprised her: she only twice succeeded in getting him to take her on to the dance floor, and then reluctantly), Teresa was hesitating about saying no to a short young man who was following them round, bent on making Manolo remember a night on the town they had shared a long time ago. Teresa asked Manolo to introduce him, and wanted to know where he came from and what he did. He turned out to be from the distant suburb of Torre Baró, and said he was an electronics expert.

'Would you care to dance?' he asked very politely.

Teresa had not yet decided (she saw Manolo smiling ironically, his mind elsewhere), but just then something happened that pushed her to accept gladly: the three of them were standing in a corner of the hall while everyone was waiting for the band to strike up the next tune (Domin Marc had just finished and the Trío Moreneta Boys had been announced), when a sudden commotion ran round the dance floor. Female protests could be heard, a few couples seemed agitated, and many heads turned to look at them. Apparently some joker had been going round pinching girls' bottoms. Teresa laughed as if this was the most natural thing in the world.

'How funny, what a great idea!' she said.

She was standing opposite Manolo's friend, whose head only reached up to her chin, and yet he gave the impression of being slim and erect, with an agile body that gave off a strong fragrance of cologne; he was wearing a tight checked jacket, had slanting, sad eyes and wore a toupé smothered in brilliantine. Teresa was looking at him kindly, still unable to make up her mind, when she felt her buttocks being pinched in a masterful way: slowly and artfully. She didn't say a word, but, red as a beetroot, whirled round, just in time to see the hunched silhouette, with slouching, timid shoulders, of a man slipping away chuckling among the dancing couples. Next to her she heard a girl's voice saying to her friend:

'I know him, his name is Marsé – he's a small, dark guy with frizzy hair who's always groping people. Last Sunday he pinched me and then gave me his phone number, to get in touch if I wanted anything from him, the cheeky so-and-so.'

'And did you call him . . .?' the other girl asked.

Teresa didn't hear the reply because the gallant little fellow was still staring at her, goggle-eyed, and insisting: 'Shall we dance, Teresina?'

This electronics expert is so delightful, so charming, she thought. The band was playing again, and Teresa, her buttocks still smarting from the pinch, and possibly actually stimulated by the murky but admirable labour of molesters like Marsé, or perhaps simply carried away by the atmosphere, surrendered to the tiny Murcian from Torre Baró, plunging headlong with him into the raging sea of pushing and shoving, elbows and sweat. Outdoing themselves, the Trío Moreneta Boys were playing their latest hit, a bolero ideal for dancing in a dimly lit hall. But in the confused sea of heads circling slowly round, Teresa saw none of the healthy joy, free from bourgeois complexes, that she had been expecting: the couples held each other tight without speaking, with strangely serious expressions on their faces. A grotesquely romantic and restrained air of respectability floated around them, even more pronounced than at a ball organised for eligible rich debutantes.

Teresa kept her eyes on Manolo above the bobbing heads, saw him striding away looking bored, and suddenly realised she was sinking definitively. Even though at first she found it amusing, the situation soon became horrible: she hadn't been aware that her flimsy, elegant skirt and the fact that she wasn't wearing a brassiere were bound to arouse outlandish dreams in her partner. The result: the electronics expert turned out to be a frenzied molester, a desperate fifty-handed octopus whose mouth was panting in the darkness, glued to her left breast, unable to say a word as he pushed at her with his belly, sweating and shoving her. She tried to resist out of pure politeness until, crushed by the other couples in the middle of the dance floor, they were left standing still, with him swaying (Teresa could sense his small, rough hand crawling over her back and buttocks like a spider), his body arched like a poised tango dancer. He reached the desired erection, and she felt him rubbing it against her thigh. Where was the spontaneous joy of popular dances? A smell of armpit and a furtive, depressing arousal: that was all.

Around them, the other couples had stopped dancing and turned towards the stage to listen to the Trío Moreneta Boys. Hands were feeling desperately for waists and breasts; strange, laborious flirtations in the shadows. Teresa still tried to laugh, but it was for the last time that day. All at once she stiffened: the little electric tadpole was squeezing her so hard her feet were off the ground. She had lost sight of Manolo some time ago (can he have gone, leaving me in the hands of these savages?) and, suddenly fearful, believing she had been left on her own and wouldn't be able to escape, she glanced furiously at her partner, who was in a lamentable state of dissolution. What she glimpsed when she saw his tiny eyes (many years later she would still recall those diminutive, congested, sad-looking eyes staring up at her like those of a beaten cur: it was the first time reality truly impinged on her), she came so close to a nervous crisis that she struggled free from his grasp and began to push her way through the couples as if she couldn't breathe. Everything was a lie: the crooning Trío, Manolo's worker friends, popular dances... The other couples looked at her and smiled, but no one seemed to want her to leave the dance floor.

'Look at that stuck-up hussy! She's dumped him,' she heard one girl say. 'Poor lad. That's not done.'

She finally managed to reach the corner where she had left Manolo. No sign of him. She stood there bewildered in the darkness. 'Manolo,' she murmured faintly: he could be any of the shadows around her. As if in a nightmare, strangely lit sweating faces loomed over her, swaying to a cha-cha-cha rhythm. A daring hand tugged at her fine golden hair, and lips crudely pushed against her delicate ear, drooling obscene comments.

'Are you looking for me, blondie?'

'Princess, you're good enough to eat.'

'Don't be in such a hurry, sweetie – you'll drop your knickers.'

A stocky girl with bright red lips defended her, shouting insults at the louts. Legs quivering, feeling ashamed and furious at the same time, Teresa looked desperately for Manolo all over the hall, and even on the first-floor balcony, where several couples were dancing entwined in the shadows. In one of the corridors she thought she saw Manolo entering a room, and hurried after him. Inside, a yellowing bulb covered in a wire mesh, an old friend of flies, dimly threw a bleary light on beer crates stacked near some mildewed shelves covered in broken glass and cobwebs. On the floor in the centre of the room lay dust-covered books and old magazines, piled up as if for a bonfire.

'Manolo, is that you?' whispered Teresa.

The smell of damp was overwhelming. A stifled cough came from behind the beer crates. Teresa stumbled over the heap of books (she thought she heard a joyful female laugh) or, rather, over a volume that lay some distance from the pile. It had red covers and was lying on top of a photograph, yellowed with age, that showed a venerable white beard: Madame Bovary and Karl Marx slid across the floor in a passionate embrace, fleeing the repository of science and knowledge waiting for the fire or the rag-and-bone man. Sighs from a corner, and now Teresa could clearly hear the lewd giggle mocking her, mocking her bewilderment, her fear of reality. Something moved behind the crates: a dark girl with big dreamy eyes and braids went scurrying off, straightening her skirt. She was looking at Teresa slightly flustered, but didn't blink or seem embarrassed, taking refuge once more behind the stack of crates. A young red-headed lad in a waiter's jacket sat up, a bottle of brandy in each hand.

'Are you looking for something?'

Another hearty laugh from the girl with braids, who now had her eyes fixed on her friend. Teresa lowered her own eyes, glanced one last time at this strange couple rolling around at her feet amid an overpowering smell of mouldy velvet, stammered an apology, turned on her heel and ran out. She went back to the balcony overlooking the dance floor. The lights had gone up. Leaning over the guardrail, she could see all the hall and the boxes. Manolo had vanished.

'Maybe he took offence. I'm stupid, so stupid . . .'

When she turned round she got another shock: the tiny electronics expert was behind her, hands in his trouser pockets, a ghastly grin on his face. He stood there waiting, respectful, humble, definitely smitten. Teresa ran off again and bounded down the stairs. She finally reached the foyer, where the cloakroom and bar were situated.

Manolo was standing at the bar counter, drinking a beer. Her first impulse was to run to him and throw herself into his arms, but she forced herself to calm down and approached his back slowly, eyes on the floor. When she reached him she stood on tiptoe and gave him a kiss on the cheek. Manolo turned round and smiled affectionately at her: 'Tired of dancing already?'

Feeling better, Teresa nodded, looking at him in that meek way she had learned to assume, when all at once her strength left her and she leaned her head on his shoulder. 'Please, never do that again, don't leave me on my own!' She asked him to get her out of there at once.

'What world do you live in, child?' he joked when Teresa explained everything to him. 'I told you this wasn't a place for you.' He hugged her and stroked her head gently until she was calm once more.

They ended their outing in the Cristal City Bar, among respectable, discreet courting couples who at nine o'clock had to be home, and ended up kissing on a mezzanine inaccessible to Murcians on the loose and furtive prowlers, sitting in front of two gin and tonics, each with its insipid slice of lemon.

Over the course of the next few evenings, Teresa's emotional state underwent a slow, subtle change. Other breaking points: happy warm nights in Monte Carmelo, people out on the street, good-looking young men in T-shirts, romantic strolls in the moonlight, slogans for workers' rights in the famous Bar Delicias... For some time now, Teresa had felt a burning desire to experience this effervescent liveliness, but by the time she took possession of Monte Carmelo, that mythical land (as Florida must once have been for the Spanish conquistadors), it was too late. Until now, the neighbourhood had for her been no more than a blurred circle of shadows admired from afar: Manolo had always refused to take her there and introduce her to his friends. But there was one name she was very familiar with: Bernardo.

To avoid having to talk about certain adventures (that was what he preferred to call them, although Teresa employed a fussier, almost biological term: cell meetings) that she disingenuously imagined for him but which he had never in fact taken part in, Manolo had decided that whenever he mentioned Bernardo it would be in the same mysterious fashion he had heard the students employ when they referred to Federico. As a result, in Teresa's mind Bernardo had become another prestigious clandestine leader, the inaccessible and impenetrable possessor of the greatest secrets.

'Do you know Bernardo? Have you heard of him? Bernardo could explain how it works better than me,' the Interloper would often say to Teresa, when her curiosity caught him out.

'Will you introduce me to him one of these days, Manolo?'

'That's a bit risky,' he would argue.

Teresa therefore respected Bernardo without knowing who he

was, partly due to her attraction to Manolo, and partly due to her own extravagant moral perceptions. But these were as generous as they were misguided; Teresa's moral realism did not arise, as she supposed, from any analytic effort, but from love, and so she still had disappointments in store for her.

One night when she took Manolo back to the top of El Carmelo, as they were saying goodbye she suggested they have a stroll round the neighbourhood. At first he refused, but his desire to embrace her behind the bushes on the far side of the hill, as well as to talk seriously to her about something that had been going round in his mind for some time (the possibility of getting a good job thanks to Señor Serrat) led him to change his mind.

'Okay, let's walk round the other side, so I can show you Valle de Hebrón.'

They left the car on the main road. Manolo put his arm round her to shield her from the gaze of some locals taking the air on their front doorsteps and led her to Calle Gran Vista. Beyond the Bar Delicias, some children were playing in the middle of the stream, and by the light from a doorway two little girls were holding hands and singing:

> *The yard in my house*
> *Is very special,*
> *When it rains it gets wet*
> *Like all the rest . . .*

Teresa went over to the girls, squatted down and sang with them for a while. Her excitement grew to fever pitch. It was a warm, starry night; the hazy green-tinged moon was drifting lazily over the flat roofs, and there was a red glow at the edges of the sky. All that was missing was a radio, a loud radio out on a terrace somewhere, blasting out a simple, tacky melody into the night.

From the open ground at the end of Calle Gran Vista, the road leading to El Guinardó park began. She and Manolo sat for a while on a ruinous semicircular stone bench, then walked hand in hand down the slope through the fir tree saplings in the park. The metallic chirrup of crickets filled the air. Teresa lay down on the grass. That night her lips were welcoming, her yielding eyes filled with generosity and tenderness. Maybe, thought Manolo, this is the moment to come clean with her, the moment to tell her I'm out of work, that I see the future as very dark, and that possibly her father, if she asked him, could help me find a job with responsibility and prospects ...

'Tere, listen, your father ... your father ... could your father ...?'

It wasn't indecision, but her ardent mouth and tiny pointed breasts with their strawberry nipples that made him stammer in this way; the twin universe he was cupping in his hands, a universe promising all the sweet, pleasant rewards of future dignity and prosperity ... He stood up to put his thoughts in order. Teresa was peering at him from the ground with dreamy eyes. He went back to her, still not sure: it was true he could make her his and be her lover for a while, perhaps even for months on end; but where would that get him? What did that huge word 'lover' really mean? What modern girl, university student or not, but rich and with newfangled ideas, doesn't have a lover nowadays, without it meaning anything? Then so long, been good to know you ... it was lovely, but farewell, a fleeting passion, an ephemeral sexual encounter, too bad, that's life. No, kid, your idea of bedding Teresa was a mistake. Because of course you can possess a creature as adorable as her, so cultured and respectable (though her moral defences aren't as solid as the respectability her class might expect), but that won't mean you possess the world that goes with her: distinction, cultural values, elegance and decorum.

Just look, you only need caress that pretty golden mane of hair, those pretty silken knees, you only need hold in the palm of your hand this twin universe of strawberry and mother-of-pearl to understand they are the luxury product of an intense social effort, and that you have to deserve them thanks to a similar effort: it's not enough to extend your trembling talons and grab them ...

Teresa got to her feet, went over to her friend, and hugged him from behind. 'How pretty it all looks from up here, doesn't it?' she said. There was an intense scent from the firs and pines all around them. In the distance shone the lights of Montbau and Valle de Hebrón, and along the main road they could see a line of headlights as cars entered the city one after another, as if in a procession. Laughing, Teresa let go of Manolo and skipped round him. 'I love your neighbourhood,' she said. 'I'll buy you a *carajillo* brandy in the Bar Delicias.'

'Here we call it a *perfumado*,' he corrected her, with a smile.

'All right, a *perfumado*, then,' she said. 'I want a *perfumado* from the Delicias.'

Manolo followed her slowly, going over what he wanted to say, grinning, floating as if in a dream, kissing her time and again, nibbling her neck, smothering his face in her blond locks (your papa, your pa ... pap ... pa ... pa could pos ... sibly ...) until she escaped with a laugh and had him chase her. Manolo ran after her, stumbled, caught up with her, lost her a second time. You're driving me crazy, little one!

'I want a *carajillo*, I want a *perfumado*,' she insisted. 'Take me to the Delicias, then we can come back here for a while,' she suggested, smiling irresistibly.

She ran off up the hill until she reached the road. She paused for a while to look back at him, then set off again towards Calle Gran Vista. Manolo followed her more hesitantly, head down and hands in his pockets. The noise of the crickets exasperated him. When he came to the first houses, he quickened his step. He couldn't see Teresa anywhere. Then it happened: he heard her scream – she must have been fifty metres in front of him. The street was so dark he couldn't make anything out, but he could guess where she was and began to run. He found her clinging to the wall, covering her face with her hands and her back towards the shadows on the far side of the street. Her shoulders were heaving.

'What happened?'

Sighing, Teresa tried to regain her composure, hands on hips. She seemed more indignant than frightened.

'There,' she murmured, 'in that doorway ... There's a man ...'

She pointed to a dark corner, one of the arcades in the Casa Bech retaining wall on the hillside, where people lived. The slanting light from the only streetlamp did not reach as far as the arcade, but it did reveal a little of the stranger hiding there: a pair of old shoes partly obscured by the muddy turn-ups of a pair of over-long trousers.

'He scared the life out of me, the lunatic,' Teresa murmured. 'He must be crazy, because he jumped out of the darkness and stood in front of me with his arms spread and ... everything undone, laughing as he stared at me ... I can hardly believe it!'

There was the sound of heavy breathing in the darkness, and the stranger's feet moved. Manolo flew to the spot and thrust his hands forward until he felt the sticky collar of a shirt (his fingers rubbed against a face with three- or four-day stubble and a big nose that seemed familiar). There was an unbearable stench of wine.

'Come on out, you louse! Let me see you!' he shouted, and tugged the man out.

The person who emerged, shaking like a rag doll in the dim lamplight, was none other than Bernardo Sans, or rather what was left of him after two years as the target for Rosa's infernal conjugal death rays.

'Aren't you ashamed of yourself, you pervert, a family man like you!' said Manolo, shaking him.

Suddenly blinded by rage, he started to punch his former friend. Sans's aberrant behaviour was no secret in such a distant, ill-lit neighbourhood like El Guinardó: it happened quite often, and Manolo was aware of it. But he beat Sans so badly (in reality he was driven by a sense of revenge that went far beyond what the insult to Teresa might have aroused in him) that she was taken aback.

'Don't hit him any more, let him go.' Manolo carried on punching him. 'He doesn't deserve to live!' he shouted. 'I told him long ago. I warned him! Pervert! Look what's become of you!'

Up against the wall, completely drunk, Sans was giggling sadly, protecting his face with his arms. 'I didn't know!' he groaned, then mumbled: 'I didn't see you, I promise I didn't see you.' Eventually, stumbling, almost crawling, he succeeded in escaping, and ran off.

Manolo was still shouting at him: '*Trinxa*, animal! That's what you get, you animal, for scaring defenceless women like that! Get out of here! Die, why don't you, you don't deserve to live!' He went back to Teresa, who was staring at him in astonishment, put his arm round her, and explained: 'Neighbourhoods like this . . . I told you about it. The streets are dark, decent girls can't go out on their own at night. It happened to my sister-in-law as well. One night she came home almost in tears . . . Did he do anything to you?'

'No, no . . . Is he from here? You seemed to know him.'

'I could have killed him. He didn't used to be a bad guy,' Manolo muttered thoughtfully. 'No, believe me, he wasn't a bad kid. But his life got difficult, things went badly for him . . . but he has no one to blame but himself. I always told him, I warned him. Now he's done for, he's taken to drink and behaves like an idiot. One day he'll be found with his head smashed in.'

'But,' said Teresa, 'if he's a friend of yours, why did you punch him like that? He didn't even touch me.'

'Didn't I tell you? He deserved it... He had it coming,' Manolo concluded angrily.

Of course, he was careful not to tell her that this dirty-minded human wreck was the famous Bernardo, the other anonymous El Carmelo hero. However, events conspired against him, because when they got back to the car, Teresa still wanted a drink in the Bar Delicias (though not as enthusiastically as before, simply saying she needed it to get over the shock). By the time Manolo caught on and tried to avoid it, she was already inside. And there was Bernardo, seated at a table in the corner, still breathless, bleeding from the nose and as paralysed as a terrified rat. Even then it was possible Teresa would not have suspected the truth, had not Manolo's brother also been there. Everybody in the bar turned to watch her enter: two bus conductors who were talking to Manolo's brother, leaning on the counter; four lads playing dominoes, and an old man sitting by the entrance.

Manolo's brother came over to them. He gave a wary smile, head bobbing in the air. He was around thirty, tall and hunched, with a dark, heavy, expressionless face and big, yellowing teeth; placid, slow, peasant-like, prone to effusive greetings and now wearing greasy overalls. He delighted in quick jokes ('It was so very dry that the trees chased after dogs, ha, ha, ha'), but, paradoxically, would launch into lengthy tales punctuated by digressions that few could follow, which meant everyone in the bar usually stayed away from him. Precisely for this reason, frequently finding himself left on his own with more to say, he had a strange disjointed way of telling things. He often seemed to have begun a story somewhere else, to somebody else who had turned his back on him without awaiting the end, and so he would suddenly loom up, looking for company, anxious to continue. Since this happened quite frequently, the result was a series of never-ending instalments spread evenly between several acquaintances, none of whom were apparently interested in either the beginning or the end. Tonight, however, Teresa *was* interested in how his story ended, because he happened to be talking about Bernardo. Manolo found himself obliged to introduce her.

'A friend,' he said. 'We're not staying.'

But his brother insisted she drink a glass of *calisaya* liqueur ('It's very good for women,' he explained, although quite why this was so remained a mystery), which Teresa gratefully accepted. She found Manolo's brother friendly; his stolid face reminded her somewhat of a horse, and yet she found it hard to take her eyes off her unbuttoned assailant lurking shamefully in his corner. She felt sorry for him as he wiped his bloody nose with the back of his hand. Manolo's brother had gone over to the two conductors drinking beer at the counter. He began telling them something, but since they still had their backs to him he turned to Teresa and continued:

'... and it's obvious he's been given a good hiding this time, just take a look at him, go on, he's completely drunk, but don't think he's dangerous, it's just that his wife is a battleaxe. This useless fellow here ...' (pointing to Manolo) 'my brother, can tell you. He and Bernardo' (he pointed to Sans, and Teresa's ears pricked up when she heard the name) 'always used to go round together, when things were good, when work was respected and there was a bit of dignity. The thing is that Bernardo had bad luck with that Rosa, she's a sergeant-major. Rosa is his wife,' he concluded, keen to explain.

This marked the end of his tale that night. Teresa imagined

the beginning must also have contained other equally surprising revelations, but it was impossible to recover it now – it was probably already fading from the two bus conductors' memories. At any rate, the terrible suspicion was plain: could the great Bernardo that Manolo had spoken about so much, and whom she had compared to Federico (that wandering, mythical Parisian shadow), be this human wreck dripping blood in his corner? Her doubts grew when she caught a furtive glance from Manolo trying to discern her reaction, and she once again felt the nausea and sense of disappointment she had experienced days before at the Sunday dance. At that moment she saw Bernardo get up to leave: could this poor fellow staggering along, his face thrust stubbornly forward like a blind man or a dangerous lunatic, this moral and physical ruin, really be the militant worker, Manolo's comrade, the one who worked with him in the shadows . . .? Had that hunched back, those shuffling feet, that crushed El Carmelo spectre not seemed so frightful, she would have burst out laughing. And someone so irresponsible, this future sexual delinquent, was the one who would be printing the students' leaflets? It was as she had always suspected: Monte Carmelo was not the place she'd imagined, Manolo's brother wasn't a car salesman, but simply a mechanic, there was no working-class consciousness here, Bernardo was a product of her own revolutionary fantasy, and Manolo himself . . .

Without really knowing what she was doing, she ordered a *perfumado* (which produced a loud laugh from Manolo's brother) as she gazed enquiringly at the Murcian, bemused and depressed by what had just happened. But in her friend's black eyes she saw only adoration: no secret power, no imagined heroic dangers, no other emotion apart from devotion to her. She rushed out and headed for her car. Close by, a radio was blaring out a delightful but inopportune melody – *you're not needed any more, and the charming local kids are no longer playing in the moonlight.* Manolo went after her, watching with an almost paternal concern, as if she really was a little girl taking her first steps on her own and could fall at any moment. He was worried about Teresa's reaction and the flood of questions that was bound to engulf him at any moment. But Teresa remained stubbornly silent. Walking rapidly, with an air of offended dignity, she merely allowed him to accompany her down the road. When she reached the automobile, she got behind the wheel and sat still, staring straight in front of her, thinking things over. Manolo slid catlike into the car as though he didn't want to disturb her thoughts, peered at her profile for a while without saying anything, then brushed her temple with his lips.

'That's enough, Manolo, please,' said Teresa. 'Did you think I was so stupid?'

'I tried many times to tell you what it was like here, that you shouldn't have too many illusions . . .'

'Be quiet. You're a fraud.'

Teresa turned and stared at him, her face harsh. Manolo held her blue gaze. At that moment he was more in love with her than ever. It seemed to him that in the space of a few minutes Teresa had become a woman, an adult woman who could just as easily sink a dagger into his chest as make room for him for ever in her bed and in her life. He thought it over: what if I speak plainly to her this once, here and now, and confess I am nothing and no one, penniless and jobless, a ridiculous sneak thief from the city slums, a disreputable wretch in love? . . . Wait, stay calm.

'All I want to know,' said Teresa, her voice trembling, 'is what is happening with the duplicator and the leaflets you promised us.'

Manolo ran his fingers through his hair: he had completely forgotten the strange commitment he had made almost without thinking, and he couldn't come up with any excuse.

'Get out,' Teresa ordered him.

'What?'

'I want you to get out of the car . . .' Suddenly her voice gave way completely. 'Why aren't you honest with me? I think . . . I think that's the least I deserve.'

He was about to say something, but Teresa had already opened the car door and was rushing out. She slammed the door shut, leaving him in the car, and stood on the road, arms folded. Behind her the crickets were chirruping once again, and the lights of the city twinkled in the distance.

'It's so ridiculous!' she exclaimed. 'I wish Maruja would get better and put an end to all this, then I could leave and to hell with the summer, the holidays, these drives, the lot of it! I'm sick and tired of it!'

'I'm sorry,' he said. 'I'll explain. Come on, get in.'

She didn't move. Manolo opened the car door.

'Come on, woman, get in.'

'When you've got out, if you don't mind.'

She was staring into the distance, chin on her chest and a forlorn look that accentuated still further her top lip's enticing, disdainful pout. Manolo contemplated her awhile, strangely aroused by this new Teresa who even so was still holding the dagger up above him. He loved seeing her angry like this, and told her so.

'Go to hell,' she murmured, moist-eyed.

When he realised she was about to burst into tears, Manolo leapt out of the car and went over to her, but she dodged past him and got behind the wheel once more.

'Tere, listen . . .' he pleaded.

She switched the engine on, but didn't set off immediately: she seemed to have problems with the gears (she couldn't find first) or was pretending to, perhaps expecting him to do something.

Manolo understood he shouldn't let her go without offering some kind of explanation. It's clear, he thought dimly, that, for her, love and the political conspiracy are still one and the same thing. Then he had an inspiration.

'Fine, have it your way,' he said, extending his hand to her hair. She jerked her head away. 'Tomorrow I have to go and collect your friends' blasted leaflets. You'll come with me, won't you? I'll be at the clinic at ten in the morning, waiting for you. Do you hear me? At ten.'

Teresa gave him one last sad look, then the car sped off, with that youthful, mad roar that always made the Murcian shiver.

He set off slowly down the road. When he arrived home, he took a pair of white trousers out of the wardrobe and asked his sister-in-law if she could please iron them for the morning. Then he flopped on to his truckle bed (his brother was calling and insulting him, but he ignored him) and went over the details of a plan in his mind.

Teresa, meanwhile, called the clinic as soon as she got home: no change with Maruja. She took a shower and, barefoot, in her underwear and with her pyjama top unbuttoned, she sat alone, head down, at the dining-room table. Her father had gone to Blanes in the late afternoon. Vicenta served her dinner, but she hardly touched it. She put on some Atahualpa Yupanqui records, drank two neat gins with a lot of ice, and went to bed with a third glass, her head throbbing with doubts and conjectures. She asked herself a hundred serious questions about Manolo, until to her surprise she discovered she wasn't being honest. The tantalising shadow of self-criticism hung over her: the change starting to occur in her ideas took her aback. She was angry with herself, her behaviour towards Manolo seemed ridiculous, utterly stupid – she recognised that his political identity had stopped being important to her a long while ago.

LAST EVENINGS WITH TERESA

Admit it, she thought, lying on the bed in her blue-painted bedroom, unable to sleep (her abdomen was throbbing to a guitar rhythm), sweating from the gin and the music, surrounded by dolls, records and books, gently rubbing her cheek against her bare shoulder. When will I learn to control my emotions? Freedom, the political opposition, militating in the party ... After all, what is the opposition? What does it mean to be a militant in a cause? And what exactly does it mean to be a communist? Teresa's thighs are honeyed; a motorbike roars through the quiet San Gervasio night. Deep down, she thinks, I'm alone. Until yesterday I lived in a world of phantoms. Solitude, generosity, sentimentality, curiosity, interest, confusion, enjoyment. She could list all these emotions because she thought they held the key to explain Manolo's behaviour and her own: each of them in their own way was battling against destiny. But she was still curious. What can the idea of freedom mean to a poor lad like him? To sit beside me in the Floride as we travel at more than a hundred and fifty kilometres an hour, or kiss my mother's hand courteously; making love on the beach with a rich tourist: perhaps all of that is simply a way to gain time, to steal time from poverty, misfortune and oblivion. Yes: a man trying to gain time, a man battling against destiny, that's Manolo, that's what we all are. But what is his idea of freedom? A sports car. A rapid, gleaming convertible. A white Floride for everyone (don't step out of line, stay in it) instead of a world where a Floride for everyone is possible. An error of perspective – it's not her fault, she thinks – and somehow it doesn't matter; in other words, it's normal. He is intelligent, attractive, generous, but untrustworthy, shameless and probably a liar: he defends himself as best he can. But what do I know of the strange effects poverty has on the mind? What do I know about cold, hunger, the real horrors of oppression someone like him must suffer? I haven't even asked him what his daily wage is. If we obstinately refuse to talk about how much a person earns and only about the way he behaves (well, comrades, I affirm that a man's behaviour depends on his daily wage), why, even today I behaved like a stupid little *señorita* throwing a tantrum in front of her chauffeur. I forced him to get out of the car, I wanted to interrogate him instead of helping him, when he is so considerate, so good-looking, so kind and patient with me! . . . Has he ever asked me for my ideological credentials? No. And yet he's promising the leaflets tomorrow; it's very possible all this is no more than a load of nonsense. I couldn't care less. A hundred useless questions and a hundred useless answers about my Manolo: whatever is true or false, whatever his class consciousness may be, his vision of the future, the real question is . . . (Oh, Mama, I still can't sleep!)

The big question had been reduced to: how far will he go for me?

The street looked like a riverbed: mud, weeds and pebbles. In less than a year it had sunk, as if impetuous flood waters had rushed along it. Teresa wondered what had become of that young worker with the innocent smile who had never heard of Bertolt Brecht. Tall chimneys rose into the sky, smearing it with smoke. The lower slopes of Montjuich were visible at the far end. They walked in silence along the ruined pavement, beside the long factory wall behind which the dull thump of machines beat like a pulse. There was no one in sight: that street had never led anywhere. It was around eleven in the morning, and the sun was beating down. For Manolo, the noise from the factory brought back a wintry memory of his earlier visit here, and the disturbing image of Teresa's knees wrapped round a stranger's legs. He recalled Maruja's laughter, her arm in his, the heavy suitcase filled with cutlery ... A group of children came running out of a doorway, chasing him with toy pistols. At the end of the street, Manolo came to a halt.

'It's here,' he said, pointing to a small entrance. 'I'll probably meet them on the roof terrace. It's best if you wait for me here, or in the car – whichever you prefer. They don't like me bringing strangers ... But if you see it's taking me too long, come up. Got it?'

Teresa was watching the children playing on the other pavement and didn't reply; but she had heard him. Out of the corner of her eye she saw Manolo going into the building. Now that she was on her own, her heart began to race. Since they had met at the clinic half an hour earlier, she had only deigned to speak once to her friend. She was not so much angry with him as bewildered: he seemed so determined about the leaflets, so completely and guilelessly dedicated to winning back her affection and trust. Besides, that morning something had happened in the clinic that still haunted her: when they were standing together beside her bed, just as Manolo was extending his hand to remove a stray lock of her lovely hair (which had been cut very short), Maruja suddenly opened her eyes in alarm. Feverish, she fixed them on Teresa for a few seconds, as if pleading with her. Dina was also present, but neither she nor Manolo appeared to notice anything, or to think it was important. And yet it had been more than a simple nervous twitch of the eyelids, more than the chance, blind roaming of those broken doll's pupils, those two veiled lenses. Teresa could have sworn (at least at that moment) that Maruja had wanted to tell her something, and that her lips even moved, that this was a direct, personal appeal for her understanding as a *señorita*, a sudden flicker of lucidity that was somehow begging her to trust the lad and not let him get involved in any more crazy schemes ... Or had that simply been Teresa's impression? When they left the clinic and were getting into the car, she was about to tell Manolo about it, but he cut her short by asking her to drive him to Pueblo Seco. On the way, he was the only one who spoke: how wonderful the summer was, with the streets watered, the air almost perfumed, the elegant neighbourhoods looking asleep and empty. Oh, Teresa, the city is ours ...

'What's wrong?' he wanted to know. 'Are you still angry at me?'

She was driving rapidly, distracted and with that strange rebellious attitude of hers (he could see her leaning back in her seat, arms stretched out rigidly from the steering wheel, head down, glaring at everyone and everything: that must have been how James Dean died), paying attention to the traffic but dismissive of it. She was concealing behind a mask of indifference her great curiosity and the musical vibration in her stomach that had continued from the previous night. The Interloper had appeared in battledress: a long-sleeved black shirt with pockets, trainers and a pair of tight, brilliantly white trousers that really suited him. What was he up to? When they reached Avenida Paralelo, he told Teresa to take a street on the left and to stop at the entrance to it. When she recognised the street, it was another surprise.

'Here?' she had asked, puzzled.

'Yes. This is where we leave the car.'

That was the only time she had spoken to him. Why do I resist being let down so much, when perhaps that's how I'll discover the best in him? Teresa asked herself. She began to peer inside the entrance. There was a dark, narrow staircase, with an iron rail and a single door on each landing. She could only stand being on her own for five minutes (he had calculated fifteen) before, feeling for the walls and the iron railing, she silently climbed to the top floor, the third. From there, a dozen steps led up to an explosion of golden light: a small, rotten wooden door that the sun's rays were filtering through like an old sack; two coin-shaped holes let in incandescent blades of light. Trembling, Teresa slowly climbed the steps, approached the blazing light and peered through one of the holes. Blinded at first, she was gradually able to make out the floor of a dusty flat roof, washing hanging on lines, and a pretty child with blond curls running around naked. Sitting with their backs against the parapet at the far end were five young men in T-shirts, idly reading magazines and comics. Teresa's eye was caught by the one in the middle, who was stroking a small black cat on his lap; he was sunbathing bare-chested and had on a pair of dark glasses. Next to him two girls in swimsuits were stretched out on towels, their faces smothered in cream (their chins raised determinedly, as if posing or preparing to give a kiss). Teresa recognised them at once: they were the girls she had seen in San Gervasio one afternoon, asking for Manolo. On the ground around them lay cheap novels and illustrated magazines, beer bottles, a bucket of water and a small portable radio blaring out a dance tune. Sometimes Teresa's view was almost completely blocked by the little boy's blond head as he came and went from the bucket to the door, waving his wet little hands.

The young man in dark glasses seemed to be staring at someone Teresa couldn't see (it must be Manolo) and to be speaking to him now and then in what, to judge by his expression, wasn't exactly a friendly manner. He was gesturing rudely for the other person to come closer, but Teresa couldn't hear what he was saying above the music. Then she recognised Manolo's voice right by the door, and caught sight of his back. The sun was glinting on his white trousers. She pressed against the door to get a better view, excited by her impunity, the opportunity she had to see without being seen (strangely also drawn by a gentle warmth she felt deep inside her: a shaft of sunlight). There was a short pause on the radio that allowed her to hear the words Manolo spat out:

'I've not come to ask for anything that isn't mine, and if there's one thing that disgusts me, Paco, it's your sisters' lies.'

'What a bastard,' she heard one of them say. 'He comes here making demands instead of paying what he and that Cardinal's crazy niece owe?'

The two Hermanas sisters laboriously raised their oily faces to look at Manolo. 'Can't you see he's only come to insult and provoke us,' shouted one of them. The music on the radio boomed out once more: a military march. Over the noise of the brass band, Teresa heard them mention a relationship between the accused and someone called the Syringe. The younger sister was talking about a party at the Cardinal's house:

'May I be struck down on the spot if it's a lie: the girl was completely naked under her slip' (which sounded a bit odd to Teresa) 'and this barefaced liar had her on his lap. I remember it well – that was when he openly denied having touched a single piece of cutlery in the case . . .'

The youngster in the dark glasses got up slowly; the cat jumped off his lap and landed on the ground, hissing, back arched fiercely. 'I told you I'd smash your face in if I saw you here again, Manolo,' he said.

A sudden breeze blew the hanging washing close to the back of the Murcian's head, while the pretty little boy, his pink bottom exposed, clutched his legs and tugged at the white trousers with his tiny hand. As Manolo stooped to push the child away, he suddenly stared straight at the door (directly at her spying blue eye, she could have sworn), but it was only an instant. Then the little boy fell daintily between Manolo's legs; and he bent down smartly to set the boy back on his feet with that dazzling, affectionate smile of his. This meant their positions changed in a way she couldn't see: she had moved away from the hole because the stab of light almost brought tears to her eyes. By the time she looked again, another lad menacingly tossed aside the comic he had been reading. Above the sound of the music, she heard Manolo's voice repeat two or three times the words 'leaflets' and 'lipotype' (was this a joke, or didn't he even know how to pronounce it?) together with her name, 'Teresa'. But the others paid him no attention: they appeared not exactly uninterested or surprised, but increasingly annoyed.

'He's off his head,' one of the youths said. They exchanged impatient glances, and the fellow in dark glasses waved his hand to calm them down.

Teresa was fascinated. She heard wings beating close to her – a dovecote perhaps – then saw Manolo approaching the group, still waving his arms: he had taken his hands from his pockets but still had the same indolent air about him, calmly goading them. What's he going to do now? she wondered. He was obviously demanding something that, to judge by the faces of those listening to him, was extremely insulting. Teresa pressed closer to the door and the finger of light, just in time to see one of the girls get up (how dreadful, that pear-shaped behind) to move the little boy out of the way. There's going to be trouble . . . Shall I push open the door and come out? He told me that if he didn't appear . . . but it hasn't been more than ten minutes, Teresa told herself, glancing at her watch. She didn't want to come to any conclusion about what she was witnessing at this vulgar home-made beach (no, of course this wasn't a clandestine cell, the very idea! It looked more like a gang of hooligans or unemployed workers) on this distant roof in Pueblo Seco, with its depressing backdrop of factory chimneys, flat roofs with washing hanging out to dry, and a sky smudged with smoke: she was determined to stick to the facts. As a result, she watched this extraordinary spectacle without taking sides (except perhaps for the proud black and while silhouette she could see), observing details and their immediate consequences, such as, for example, the light hurting her eyes, although perhaps a little less intensely than before, because at that moment a fluffy cloud was obscuring the sun.

But something odd was going on: her sight was suddenly blocked again by the little boy's profile with his golden curls and lipstick-stained cheek, and she understood that the faces he was pulling were the horrified reflection of what he was looking at. When he moved away (his mother's hand tugged at him sharply), she saw Manolo was cornered and that a scuffle was imminent.

She could clearly hear him yelling, 'I won't allow you to talk of Teresa like that; don't even mention her name!' together with the music on the radio and the furious, calculated insults from the lad with the dark glasses, followed by the sound of Manolo's fist striking something, a moan.

'He's crazy!' shouted someone.

Doubtless reacting to a threatening gesture that Teresa couldn't see, the others took a step back and looked at each other enquiringly. The one called Paco had thrown himself on Manolo; close to the door she could see part of a bare back, a whirl of arms and shoulders. She cried out, pushed and kicked the door, but to no effect. Through the hole she saw Manolo defending himself, his shirt torn, his dark, muscular abdomen doubling up under the blows (she flattened herself against the door, arms spread wide, pushing with her sun-warmed stomach and her hands, but still couldn't open it – couldn't open it). She saw him retreat, then trip over one of the girls' legs and fall backwards. They all leapt on him. Making a supreme effort, twisting his sweaty, powerful neck and raising his head, he turned towards the door and shouted, 'Teresaaaa . . .!' in a voice that pierced her soul. She thought she would die. Sobbing, she carried on pushing vainly at the door (it seemed to her that years went by), and by the time she finally succeeded in getting out on to the roof and had run to Manolo, the others had left him and he was lying face down, next to the transistor, which was playing listeners' requests.

Teresa's sudden appearance took them all by surprise. They moved away and began to collect their things. Without even looking at them, she shouted, 'Leave him, that's enough!' and threw herself on him. Manolo was having trouble breathing; with her help, he turned over, opened a swollen eye and peered at her with a forced smile. One of his eyebrows was cut, and the side of his face was covered in dust and blood. His hair was dishevelled, his white trousers badly stained, and all the buttons were gone from his torn shirt. Trembling, Teresa helped him to crawl a little (incomprehensibly, because he didn't seem to have the strength left to do anything, he surreptitiously picked up the radio and took the music with him) and propped his back against the parapet. When she raised her eyes and looked round, all the others had disappeared.

'Manolo, what have they done to you? Why did they beat you up like this?' she murmured, not daring to touch his face. 'What is this madness all about?'

'They were insulting you and your mother . . .'

'But why, who were these people . . .? And why did we come here?' She had taken out a handkerchief and was wiping his face, stroking him and pushing strands of black hair from his face. The transistor, which he had craftily left very close to Teresa, was playing its role to perfection, transmitting a gentle love song. 'Look what they've done to you . . .! Please, speak to me, say something . . .!'

'They . . . they had it in for me. But they're the only ones who could help you, do you see?' Raising his head, Manolo blinked at the sun, the intense physical effort covering up his racing thoughts: he still had to get through, if not the most dangerous part (the beating he had taken had been far worse than expected, thanks to that bastard Paco), but the most delicate, sensitive moment. 'I wanted . . . I wanted to see if I could get that lipotype for your students.'

Teresa's amazement only increased, until she exclaimed joyfully:

'Oh, my God, Manolo! What are you saying? Are you crazy?'

'No . . . as you saw, I tried. It was worth it . . . But I can't work miracles. I promised to help you . . . it was just for you . . . for your cause.'

'I knew it, I knew it, but don't try to talk now, forget the students, the leaflets, everything...! Lipotype, lipotype... that's what my love calls it.'

She collapsed on top of him, embracing his bare chest, her hair swirling round his throat. 'What do they matter to us?' she said. 'Lipotype,' she repeated, half laughing, half crying, like a *femme-enfant* (next to them, the radio had begun to play a favourite song, dedicated by a soldier to his girlfriend), while Manolo let himself slide very slowly down to the floor, saying: 'Come here, lie down beside me, that's it, hold me tight... Now listen, Teresa.'

'Don't say a word, you don't have to tell me anything,' she said, turning his face towards her. 'Does it hurt, my love?' she touched his mouth and swollen eyebrow with trembling fingers. 'It must be really painful. Let's go home, I'll take care of you...'

She tried to help him up.

'Wait,' he said. 'It's good here in the sun. Besides, I have to explain everything to you, I have to.' He secretly increased the volume on the transistor:

> *Last night I talked to the moon*
> *and poured out my troubles.*
> *I told her how much*
> *I want to love you...*

'I have to confess that...'

'There's no need,' she interrupted him. 'Nothing matters to me, nothing, do you understand? I love you, I love you, oh, so much!' She smothered his face with kisses, barely touching him so as not to hurt him, which made it even more exciting.

'I'm in a real mess, Teresa,' he said all of a sudden.

'What's wrong?' She looked at him in alarm. 'Have you done something bad?'

'No, no... I don't have any work.'

'No work?'

'None. I mean: I've lost the job I had . . .'

'Ah,' she said with a sigh. 'I thought it was something serious.'

Relieved, she clung to him. By now they were both practically lying flat on the ground, up against the parapet. Her head was on Manolo's chest; he looked defeated, his eyelids drugged.

'It is for me. How could I look you in the face without a job?' the Interloper took it upon himself to explain. 'You're my angel, Teresina, my child, but what would your parents or your friends say?' he added, slipping his hand between her knees.

'It doesn't matter,' Teresa groaned. 'None of that matters to me. Look what they've done to you.' She leaned over him, her hair brushing Manolo's split lip. 'And it was all our fault, mine and my friends'. No, darling, this is the end of it. Don't you see: you could be arrested for unlawful assembly and seditious propaganda. You've already done enough, more than you should, more than the university deserves.'

'That's nothing,' he replied indulgently. 'Over time you and I will do great things, you'll see. I'll be whatever you want me to be, I'll become whatever you wish, because I love you.'

'Do you really love me? Swear it.'

'I love you more than anything in the world, I adore you, my child – I need you.'

Teresa's lips hovered over his mouth like a glow-worm. Then she said:

'This is what we're going to do, my love: we'll take care of you, I'll help you find that job you need. All I have to do is talk to Papa – he knows heaps of people. You'll see, it'll be very easy. Leave it to me.'

'Tell him I've got lots of commercial experience and that . . .'

Teresa leaned over and kissed him again. The atmosphere was saturated with:

LAST EVENINGS WITH TERESA

Last night I talked to the moon:
she told me so many things
that maybe tonight
I'll talk to her again ...

Intoxicated by so much sun and music, they lay in each others' arms for a long while, as though asleep. Blinded, dazzled by a superior reality, the last phantom fled from Teresa's little blond head as she nuzzled the Murcian's chest: her tender, valiant friend was as alone and lost as she was – that was the truth of the matter. How weak I feel now, but how happy, she said to herself. It was curious: she would never have thought it could be like this, she had never met anyone like him, living alone and constantly struggling the way he did, she would never have imagined that his neediness was his strength, the clearest expression of his truth. She thought tumultuously: until recently I didn't think I was so alone and lost, but things haven't turned out as I thought, as everybody said they were, as I've been taught at home and at university. Yet he has managed to convince me that is how we are, and that is how things are, that's how they happen.

They heard someone trotting across the roof: the little boy was running towards them, naked. He arrived, picked up the radio, gazed at them a moment with his huge, liquid eyes, and then ran off.

... as he let himself collapse, oh, so slowly, at the feet of the elegant stranger, his knees bending little by little, his strength ebbing, head down on his chest, hands grasping for support in mid-air as he crumples silently in the stifling heat of the workshop, overcome with sleep and tiredness and the threat from his brother increasing every day – 'I don't support scroungers' – how strange and alien the city appeared back then, my love, how suspicious people seemed, how sly their voices sounded, their Catalan accent, the lit-up streets, the two friends who on Thursdays take her to Plaza de Cataluña, the three of them arm in arm, eating ice creams and laughing, the conscript's shy smile and his shaven head (later when his hair grew back, I saw it was as golden as the sun). I can recall the first kisses in the dark corners of the garden, the gunpowder smell of the rockets, the disinfectant in the swimming pool water: it was the same romantic moon as at the party but shining on different trees, different kisses. She was younger then and sillier, and all the time the only thing she could think of was the barracks smell that came off his safari jacket and his gentle way of speaking and his bright-blue Canary Island eyes that had seen so much sea, and how scared she was she might lose him, how she gave herself, how she deceived herself and was deceived, how stupidly we cling to other people simply not to be on our own all our lives; tell me, what else could I do? Remember that often on the beach with Doña Isabel's children she didn't even have the heart to get them to play, still less to go for a swim; she thinks how she stayed quite still in her black uniform and white starched cap, sitting awkwardly on the sand, trying not to show her legs, for month upon month after he had gone for ever, she thought she could see a kind of mark, a sign in her knees, the shadow of the hands of the soldier who would never again embrace her in La Ciudadela park, a few metres from the barracks, and she was overcome by the obscure shame that the *señora* would see what he had done etched on her skin. Every so often she would call the children to wipe their noses or to tell them not to get too close to the water, and above all not to disturb her master and mistress sunbathing in their hammocks. Meanwhile, in Monte Carmelo you are still falling to the workshop floor, slowly doubling up, covered in a cold sweat; you're about to faint and we will never know if it's real or one of your ruses to touch the stranger's heart. Here, on the other hand, everything was always completely clear, here the high, luminous midday was always filled with honest laughter and gossip about marriage, the family, holidays, business and the intimate secrets of absent couples. Taking advantage of her being distracted, drowsy from the sun or from considering the consequences of all those crazy nights, the little ones get dangerously close to the sea. 'Señora ... the children ...' First thing on Sundays, she would go to Blanes in the car with the *señora* to attend Mass together, and then it was worse, having to separate from you after the sweetest sleep, because to have you in my bed, to feel you next to me while you're sleeping is the only true, beautiful thing in my life. But these are the things that can't be seen, the things she wouldn't be able to explain to the *señora* if she had to, because she has always been like a mother to her. The rest of the family and a guest or two have also come down to the beach to bathe, and she, accustomed to looking on, stares at the men's big, lethargic, suntanned bodies, at the *señorita* and her girlfriends stretched out on towels. Occasionally they all seem friendly, they really show an interest in the maid – she's so hard-working, so pretty, she styles her hair better than Nené Villalba, oh yes, much better than Nené Villalba, no question (Nené hadn't come that day) – and they ask her: do you have a boyfriend? No? How is that possible: boys today are a disaster. They talk and look at her, but don't see her. They're the same as those women who, in front of a looking-glass in a shop window, can't see beyond the mirror and take their own image away in their minds; they're only concerned with themselves, they're constantly listening to their own love story that seems to have no beginning or end, I reckon, because in the end what do I care: I have you. And for a moment she lays her head on the sand, her back to the others, and murmurs to herself, 'Maybe he'll come tonight,' because she never knows when he will arrive, climb in through the window, take her violently in his arms ... Sometimes he looks tired and has dark shadows under his eyes, and only comes to sleep. The sun, the sea, the knees that give her away: the *señorita* looks at her with real affection, but she doesn't know anything either. It all began badly, and that was how it was bound to end, because before this summer, a long time before she first saw him at the party (out in the street, looking so handsome leaning on the car, smoking and wondering how he could approach us), a long while before he collpased and fell on to the filthy workshop floor, at a time when yours truly was learning how to lay the table and still sounded frightened when she answered the telephone, he was already up to his tricks to avoid being sent back to his village in Andalusia. There he goes, climbing Monte Carmelo hill with his beach bag on his shoulder. Night fell while he was at the top, standing very still and looking down at the city at his feet. No doubt when his brother saw him arrive from Ronda so unexpectedly and said, 'Why did you leave Mother on her own?' and he answered, 'I didn't leave her on her own, she's with a man,' there was no way of knowing whether he was telling the truth, but his first lie came when he added that he had only come to pay his brother a visit and to meet his sister-in-law and their children, and that he would be leaving soon. He would have let himself be killed rather than go back to Ronda. After a few days his brother told him he couldn't keep him there scrounging, and that there was no room for him in the house. 'I'll work, I'll help you in the bicycle workshop,' he would say. 'There's not enough work for two, the business is in trouble ...' It was his sister-in-law who took pity on him, and thanks to her that first winter he had a mattress next to the children and a plate of food on the table. Entire nights away from home – on the Ramblas, just imagine! – spending hours leaning on the counter of a bar

LAST EVENINGS WITH TERESA

in the Barrio Chino, according to him making friends, though he never said much about that; it must have been some shady business, you don't know him yet, Teresa. He bought his first suit. No good asking him where he got the money: 'I know how to earn a crust anywhere and anyhow,' he always says. He only appeared at the workshop for a while in the afternoons, and at the house at mealtimes, until one day his brother got fed up and told him he couldn't put up with him any longer. Now just look how he staggers and falls: it's midday and he's pumping up a bicycle tube, naked from the waist up, sweating in the workshop's stifling heat. His brother is going on at him as usual – 'I don't support people who won't work' – but he isn't listening. He's thinking about the strange things happening in the workshop of late (there's a brand-new motorbike in for repairs, but there's nothing to repair), and it's at that very moment that the longed-for solution to all his problems crosses the threshold: a well-dressed, friendly and educated man with an ivory cane, distinguished, lovely white hair, holding his niece by the hand – a little blonde girl. As soon as he enters, he starts arguing with the brother (calmly, without raising his voice, but firmly and with an authority that catches one's attention – he'll tell you if you ask), about a motorbike sold without his permission. Alarmed, the mechanic doesn't know what to reply, and the stranger threatens to demand the money he's owed him for a long while. His annoyance doesn't prevent him noticing the dark back of a lad working at the rear of the workshop, and he asks who he is. 'My brother,' says the mechanic, and takes advantage to change the topic of conversation. 'He escaped from our village and now there's no way to get him to go back. He's a pain in the neck!' He, meanwhile, was looking at the stranger over his shoulder, glancing at him out of the corner of his eye – he says it was like a revelation: that noble, distinguished client must be the wealthy recipient of the stolen motorbike his brother was hiding in the workshop – but if you ask him for more details, he'll tell you he saw only friendship in the man's eyes, understanding and even gentleness, because suddenly the bicycle wheel fell from his hands and he realised he couldn't breathe and that he was going to hit the ground like a sack. He'll tell you he was fainting due to the heat and exhaustion, that his legs wouldn't hold him up any more, that he couldn't avoid it ... He heard the thump of his own body on the floor just as he thought he could grasp the stranger to steady himself, and just before he passed out, he says he had time to feel the first friendly hand he had encountered in the city on his back. The girl's, I said – silly me – but no, it was her uncle who had kneeled down to come to his aid. 'That's hunger, poor boy,' said the man, lifting him in his arms. The mechanic replied, pointing at him: 'It's play-acting, I know him.' (But listen, *señorita*, how could he have heard them if he was unconscious?) A white, fragrant hand that gave off the scent of cologne was patting his cheeks to bring him round. The mechanic said the lad wasn't even his real brother, but only his half-brother, and that he felt no obligation towards him, but the man attacked him for having been so cruel and inconsiderate, and sent him to the bar for a glass of brandy, telling the girl to go out and play in the street. He says that when he came round, the kind gentleman invited him to go and eat at his house, and the next day as well, and forced him to take a shower and wash himself with a good Palmolive soap, and that from then on he was great friends with the girl, spending whole days at their place and of course he began to get to know all those in the gang of shady characters who turned up in the evenings with suitcases full of clothes, transistors, cameras, electric razors, and I don't know what else, not to mention the motorbikes that ended up in the workshop, bikes that he and his brother stripped overnight. At first he was only allowed to assist; he was too young. But he didn't stop until he was the one in charge: after managing, thanks to the gentleman, to get his brother to stop threatening to throw him out, he began to accompany the others in their night-time escapades as the lookout while they did the work. There were three of them: one from Pueblo Seco, another from El Guinardó, and one called Luis Polo, who ended up in jail; that was in summer, and they broke into dozens of foreign cars. He says, laughing, thanks to the great interest the gentleman showed in him from the start, he finally managed to get his brother not only to leave him in peace but to be pleased with him: he earned a lot of money, and had a second summer suit made that was cream-coloured and double-breasted. What a fortunate fainting fit, he himself admits, even bragging about it many nights as he told me the story, laughing with that self-satisfied laugh men have when they think they've made an easy conquest, when they're deceiving someone in someone's arms. Some aspects of his life in El Carmelo were so brazen, so cynical, so outrageous that she, listening to him talk as she stroked his head nestling against her stomach and in that bed bathed in moonlight, was even envious, but above all fearful, the fear she always felt for him, from the very first day, not only because of his lies and antics. Because his thieving and the fear of seeing him in jail is what most terrifies her, yes, but it's not that: there's something else in him, I can sense another crime, whose atonement could ruin his entire life ... My God, what a black cloud, what an unending night. Hold me in your arms and never let me go, my love, you're always the first to fall asleep, but I have a feeling that tonight ...

Despite everything, the slow crumbling of the myth brought its compensations: Teresa saw, touched, and then believed.

As for Manolo, a week later the only visible sign of the fight on the Pueblo Seco rooftop was a tiny, diabolical scar on his eyebrow. Roaming his neighbourhood, lying in wait for friends to borrow a miserable amount of money in order to get by, barely surviving, always with the feeling he was leaving part of himself in different corners of El Carmelo (and already suspecting the power of retention or salvation that the Syringe's ashen gaze was exerting on him), he still managed one evening when he went to the house for her to dress his wound to get her to lend him a hundred pesetas behind the Cardinal's back. On this occasion it cost him a kiss (supposedly fraternal) and the formal promise to take her out on his motorbike the following day. When he left, the banknote in his pocket, he headed straight for the Bar Delicias and organised a game of cards with a twenty-peseta stake. He played behind closed doors until half past two in the morning, and was in luck: the hundred pesetas became four hundred. The next morning he gave his sister-in-law a hundred – making sure he did so with his brother looking on – and with the rest bought himself a white shirt and a bottle of cologne, then went to the public baths on La Travesera. That same evening, when he entered the small, deserted bar on Vía Augusta where Teresa was waiting for him (since the start of September they no longer met at the clinic, and he hadn't seen Maruja for three days), she flung her arms round his neck and said:

'Make sure you dress up tonight. We're invited for dinner at my friends' house.'

'The two of us?'

'Naturally. It's about your job. Aren't you pleased? Then you won't be able to say I don't look after you.'

'I've never said that. Did you talk to your father?'

'Not yet, he's at the Villa. What I have done is sound things out. This morning I spoke to Alberto Bori, someone I met at university. He now works in advertising and book distribution. I'm not quite sure what he does, but it has something to do with the Library of Business Management and Administration, one of Papa's dodges . . .'

'A dodge?'

'Well, one of his business schemes . . . Papa works with commercial editions and suchlike . . . I don't know what exactly, and I'm not interested.'

'That's where you're wrong. You should be interested.'

'Well, the thing is, Alberto knows far better than me what Papa does, and he can tell us. Besides, he and his wife are close friends of mine. Look, this is what we'll do . . . I'll pick you up at nine at the Roxy cinema bar. Don't be late. How's the money situation?'

'I've got just about enough to pay for the drinks,' he said defensively.

'I'll give you some . . . And don't give me that look of offended dignity, because I'll be angry. It's a loan.' She nestled in his arms with a smile, ran her fingers through his hair, saw his features tense as he thought this over, then gave him a quick, impulsive kiss: she had managed to re-establish the intimate link between the ideal and her desire. 'Listen, why don't you come as you are, in your blue jeans and your . . .?'

'No way. I can still present myself to your friends with the respect they deserve.'

Teresa gave a tinkling laugh.

'You're turning out quite a little bourgeois.' Her tone of voice changed as she added: 'Promise me you'll be very nice to Mari Carmen. It's important.'

'Who is Mari Carmen?'

'Alberto's wife.'

'What if I brought her some flowers?'

Teresa stifled another chuckle. She lightly touched the scar on his eyebrow and brushed back a lock of his black hair.

'I love you so much,' she said. 'No, darling, you don't have to take her anything. Simply bring yourself. They want to meet you, and we'll have fun, you'll see. We ought to go out sometimes with friends – it feels like centuries since I've seen anyone. Don't you feel that? Sometimes it's as if . . . I don't know, as if you and I lived on our own in a different, unknown city.'

'And once summer is over . . .?' he murmured, looking her in the eye.

'The same. I'll be at the university, you at your job. I'll go and wait for you to come out, and we can take walks in the rain . . .'

The Bori couple were expecting them at half past nine. They were received with great glee, and celebrated as if they had just returned from a long pleasure cruise: there were glimpses of curiosity, of complicity even (between Teresa and Mari Carmen there was quickly established, first with kisses and then whispering, that singsong sound of running water and reeds that newlyweds produce), but no direct question about the progress of their relationship; the couple only wanted to know how the two of them had met. Manolo had already observed, not without a certain sense of exclusion, that what most aroused the interest of Teresa's friends was how they had met, where, when and by what coincidence they had encountered one another. While he was talking to Alberto Bori, something Mari Carmen said to Teresa in an undertone ('I can tell you're happy just by looking at you, Tere. Does your family know you're going out with him?' to which there was no reply) made him think that the night could end up like an intriguing image in his private album. But he was mistaken. What was strange was the unrelenting sense of distance his imagination gave him, the fact that a frugal but formal cold collation (salad, slices of roast beef, French cheeses and good red wine served in fascinating clay mugs, on a low marquetry table) for the first time failed to produce in him that disturbing sense of luxury and respect he had always associated with Teresa and her world. A recent photograph of the Bori couple, leaning on the guardrail of a ship (in half profile, their faces lifted to the sky as if observing an imaginary bird, their eyes filled with emotion, swept along on a whirlwind of intimate vanities and vague artistic aspirations), reminded him of the careless tourist attitude the Moreau family had, and that other moment of negligence that had struck Maruja down. There was an aura of unreality that enveloped (or protected) them, like a pane of glass that no sound or cry for help could penetrate, and which not only defended but embellished them. He had not been there long when he decided darkly: kid, these people won't lift a finger for you.

The Boris lived in the Barrio Gótico, right by the cathedral (its spires, illuminated at night, filled the window like a fantastic backdrop) in a comfortable, luxurious loft apartment that nevertheless looked somehow chaotic: on one side, ceramics and abstract art, *engagé* literature, Picasso reproductions (a large *Guernica* presided over the supper), as well as engravings by the young Spanish realist school; on the other, a surprising profusion of pamphlets and catalogues of publications about sales systems and administrative control, with reference books strewn on armchairs (one volume, *Marketing: 40 Practical Examples*, keeping captive a pair of spectacles for short sight; another, *Young Executives*, nestling by Teresa's tropical legs on the couch).

'Don't pay any attention to the state of the room,' said Mari Carmen. 'Alberto is impossible. We got back from Cadaqués three days ago, and in half an hour he had turned this place into an office.'

The couple had no children; both came from well-to-do families, but considered themselves independent and happy in their loft. They had lived for some time in Paris, and both of them worked. Alberto was a thin, attractive and very tall young man, who spoke rapidly and engagingly, and wore glasses. A left-wing intellectual with a passion for literature, he had reluctantly turned to advertising in the publishing industry. Mari Carmen was twenty-five, had got married, very much in love, before completing her literature degree; by the time she did finish it, when all her girlfriends were getting married, she discovered she couldn't follow suit because she already had a husband. A trivial observation, perhaps, but not entirely so: for anyone who has few important things to do in their life (as was the case with Mari Carmen), to get these two events the wrong way round, or to do them at the wrong time, can be fatal: not only did Mari Carmen go about lost and seriously depressed for a year, but it threatened her marriage. Not knowing what to do, she finally decided to look for work among her husband's acquaintances, and joined the translation department in a publishing house. She was a delightful pale little woman, with an all-encompassing gaze, her hair cut short like a boy's, no make-up, still with a Parisian air about her. That night she was wearing a thin black polo-neck jersey; her flat, sunken chest and timid shoulders suggested fits of exquisite boredom. This twofold world, the double-sided aspect or rather the cultural schizophrenia reigning in the loft (*Guernica* and marketing) soon surfaced in the conversation.

'It's a shame Manolo doesn't know any languages,' Mari Carmen told Teresa. 'I could get translations for him. Easy texts of course.'

'Well, a travelling salesman isn't a bad idea,' said Alberto, spreading a piece of Camembert on bread with a knife. 'It would be a great place to begin.'

'Something in the administration department would be better, don't you think?' objected Teresa. 'I'm sure he could start on the basis of seven or eight thousand a month. I'll see what Papa says . . .'

'It depends on what Manolo can do,' said Alberto, looking at her. 'For the moment, a salesman seems more suitable to me.'

'You may be right,' Teresa conceded.

Mari Carmen laughed. 'Do you think so?' she whispered. 'You wouldn't see much of him. Doesn't that bother you?'

'No, the thing is he needs to work, for the moment in whatever he can, you see? It's all he ever talks about. If you knew how he goes on about it! He's in such a mood!'

Mari Carmen smiled enigmatically at her, chewing slowly, her ears filled with solemn organ notes (music by Albinoni on the record player all through the meal). Manolo wasn't saying much, but kept his eye on Alberto Bori.

'Of course,' the latter was saying, 'looking good is important for selling books, well, for selling anything really, but it's not essential . . . Your hair's a bit long, maybe. What do you think, Mari?'

'It's fine as it is. Don't listen to him. Alberto's just jealous,' she said, studying Manolo.

'I'm being serious, Mari.'

'Good, so am I! You don't understand about men.'

She exchanged a sly, rapid look with Teresa, and they both laughed.

'That may be so,' said Alberto, 'but I do know booksellers' mentality. I've nothing against his hairstyle, but it won't help him in his job.'

'You're the one most concerned here, Tere. What do you think?' asked Mari Carmen.

Teresa laughed. 'If you touch a single hair on his head, I'll kill you both,' she said, downing what was left of the wine in her mug. So you too, sweetheart, are joining in the joke, thought Manolo. To get the job, he was happy to have his head completely shaved.

They talked about friends still on holiday and those starting to return. They talked about Paris. And about advertising and its strange rituals.

'The way things stand in this country,' Alberto said, glancing at Manolo, 'the future is in advertising. It's a monumental bore, one of the biggest scandals of our time: I spend the day dealing with cretins. But it's well paid, Manolo. And don't think you need to know anything special; it's a job anyone can do, you included. Just imagine ...' He went on to outline some of his publicity ideas, which were apparently meant as a joke (Manolo couldn't grasp his sense of humour): an extraordinary system of night-time billboards on major roads that would rise up as vehicles went past thanks to an automatic contact. Something really striking, like castles or balloons suddenly appearing in the middle of the countryside, he said, or advertising on restaurant plates, the roofs of apartments, in public urinals, on whores' backsides, and so on. 'They're ideas that come to you if you wrack your brain a bit,' he concluded. 'The problem is, Spain isn't ready for businesses on such a scale, ones that are so European.'

The women laughed. The Interloper tried hard but in vain to see what was so funny: they all seemed like excellent ideas to him. Besides, he was keen to get back to the question of his employment.

But a mysterious fluttering around the Bori couple, a constant evasiveness produced by boredom, seemed determined to ruin the evening. Mari Carmen decided they had to do something. A lot of wine was consumed, and after the meal they set off in two cars (the Boris had a Seat) for a drink at Bagatela on Avenida Diagonal. There, Teresa slipped three hundred-peseta notes into Manolo's pocket as she gave him a kiss, and later suggested they all go to the Tibet 'which Manolo discovered'. As they were driving through the upper neighbourhoods they passed decorated, lit-up streets filled with people strolling around or dancing to the sounds of loud orchestras.

'It's the Fiesta Mayor, the patron saint's day celebrations,' Manolo explained.

Teresa, who was driving ahead of the Bori couple, pulled up and suggested they explore the liveliest streets. In Plaza Sanllehy a big marquee had been erected, with dancing and stalls. They bought ice creams and paper hats, danced, and walked round the area. Eventually they sat on the terrace of a small bar and ordered *Cuba libres*. It was a short street called Calle del Laurel, tree-lined and covered over with bunting and coloured lights. The orchestra stage stood in the middle, against a convent wall, and locals were sitting in their doorways watching the couples dance and the passersby. Manolo waited in vain for the question of his job to come up again. Teresa was really enjoying herself, but Mari Carmen, who at first also seemed very lively, even at one point dancing with a stranger who timidly invited her to do so, fell into an inexplicable depression as the night wore on. Once, when Manolo approached them from behind (he had just shown

Teresa where the bar toilet was), he saw Mari Carmen glance furiously at her husband, and heard her say:

'Do you mind? We all know you, Alberto. You'll always live in an unreal world; you're a cynic, you have no intention of doing anything for that boy . . .'

Later, with Teresa nestling on his shoulder as they sat at a table, he watched the other couple dancing. At first, Mari Carmen had her back to him; her husband was dancing with his eyes closed – they were hardly moving, holding each other tight, they even seemed to want each other – but they turned round slowly until it was Alberto who had his back to Manolo and she was facing him: expressionless, completely empty eyes, atrocious – the icy gaze of a woman who isn't there for her husband, the dance or for anything. The gaze of a stuffed bird of prey or a statue was peering over Alberto Bori's shoulder.

'Listen,' Manolo said to Teresa. 'Do those two love each other?'

Teresa shrugged.

'He loves her. He'd be lost without Mari Carmen. But her . . . Well, Mari Carmen is a bit disappointed, if you follow me.'

'No.'

'Alberto is someone who had a lot of promise at the university; he had talent.'

'But he earns a very good living, doesn't he?'

'It's not that, darling.' Teresa closed her eyes drowsily, head on his shoulder. 'It's not a question of just earning a living. Alberto is an intellectual . . .'

'Does she cheat on him?'

'Oh, I don't know, my love, don't put words in my mouth.' She laughed. 'Kiss me instead.'

When the orchestra finished, the Boris disappeared inside the bar for a while. Something must have happened, because when they reappeared they said a very awkward goodbye.

'We're leaving, it's very late,' said Alberto.

Beside him, facing the other way and with her arms folded as if she was cold, Mari Carmen was looking at the orchestra and the very few couples still sleepily dancing, almost without moving. Her shivering, fragile shoulders conveyed something of how ridiculous, meaningless and boring all this must now seem to her – the couples stubbornly clutching one another, the music reduced to the asthmatic beat of the drums – and she must have felt so intolerably depressed that she hardly even said goodbye: a vague wave of the hand and a listless *chao* as she walked towards their car without looking at them or unfolding her arms, hunched over elegantly and skirting round the dancing couples as though protecting her chest from some threat or infection. Teresa got up and followed her. Alberto Bori extended his hand to Manolo, who looked straight at him, trying to convey an impression of self-confidence.

'Okay, so you'll tell me what there is . . . Don't forget, I really need that job. I'm having a hard time.'

'Of course. I'll give you a call . . . Better still, I'll call Teresa.' For some reason, Alberto Bori could not sustain the Murcian's frank gaze. 'See you soon.' As he was leaving, he bumped into Teresa. '*Chao*, Tere. Have fun.'

Teresa sat next to Manolo and kissed him on the cheek.

'That's from Mari Carmen. She says sorry for disappearing like that . . . How did you leave it with Alberto?'

'That he'll call me. But I don't trust him much. Shall I tell you something? I only trust serious people . . . Your father, for example.'

'Don't think badly of Mari Carmen. She often gets depressed – it always ends like this when we go out. But she's a very good person. Alberto as well, you'll see how . . .'

'He's a shit. I saw it in his face.'

'Don't say that, sweetheart.' Teresa leaned her cheek on his chest. 'And I thought you'd got over your bad temper!'

'Who's bad-tempered here?' he said, smiling and nibbling her ear. 'Come on, take me home, I'm exhausted.'

'Oh, no,' she exclaimed, 'just when we're enjoying ourselves so much . . .! Besides, I can stay out all night tonight. I told Vicenta that perhaps I'd stay over and sleep at the Boris' place . . .'

She looked at Manolo with her clear, trusting blue eyes and cuddled up to him. The night air was turning cool: a sudden breeze stirred the leaves in the trees and the canopy of bunting and garlands. 'I'm cold, my love . . .' she murmured, as if in her sleep. 'Don't go . . .' Manolo was burying his face in the back of her neck, when suddenly something in the air told him rain was on the way. He sensed obscurely that the summer, that golden isle of theirs, would soon be coming to an end. All around them, the celebrations continued.

Half an hour later, Teresa took him back to El Carmelo. She stopped the car at the top of the road. Manolo gave her a kiss goodbye.

'Please,' she said, 'don't go yet . . .'

He said he was sorry, but there was something he had to do, and he wouldn't even wait for the Floride to pull off. As he turned the corner to his brother's house, he saw an acquaintance.

'Ramón,' he called out. 'Are you going to the Delicias?'

'Yes.'

'Is there a game tonight?'

'I don't know . . . I'm going there now.'

'I'll be with you all right away, I just need to change.'

His brother wasn't at home. His sister-in-law and the children were sleeping together, dead to the world. Without a sound, Manolo changed in the darkness, and left in his jeans, pulling on a polo shirt. He was hurrying along head down, so that when he reached the road he almost collided with the automobile parked there.

'What are you still doing here?'

Her hands on the steering wheel, Teresa stared at him.

'I was waiting for you. You wanted to fool me, didn't you?'

'Don't be silly . . .'

'Where are you going?'

'For a walk. I can't sleep . . . And you listen to me: go home, it's very late. If your parents find out . . .'

She gave a sad smile. Her eyes were glistening in the darkness. 'You're scared,' she said. 'I'd never have thought it possible.' Lowering her head, she moaned: 'How do you expect me to believe you?' Manolo got into the car and gave her a tender embrace. As he buried his face in her fragrant hair, he knew he was beaten.

'All right, all right, I'll stay with you. I'm here, don't cry . . . I was only going to the bar. And do you know why? To play cards for a while, I'm on a lucky streak and I need money . . . there, now you know.'

'Is that true? You're not deceiving me?' Teresa threw her arms round his neck. Feeling weak and exhausted, he pressed his mouth to her bare shoulder.

'Yes, that's where I was going. What else can I damn well do while I'm waiting? You can't be responsible for my problems . . .'

'Everything will be all right, Manolo. Don't think about it tonight. Please stay with me. Please . . .!'

She lay back in the driving seat. The perfume of her body and the feverish gleam in her tearful eyes drove Manolo wild. He gave her a lengthy kiss, and the salty taste of her tears mingled with the softness of her lips.

'It's cold here,' she murmured. It was past two in the morning.

'Yes, let's go.'

Determined now to embrace whatever the night had to offer, they prolonged their adventure as long as they could in the same street festivities they had explored earlier. They sat at the same marble table beneath the leafy trees and danced slowly once more, staring into each other's eyes, oblivious to everything, including the increasingly lethargic, ragged music from the orchestra. All of a sudden a few raindrops fell, a shower that lasted only a few minutes. People ran laughing for cover in the doorways until the rain stopped and everything went back to how it was before. Together with the other couples, they enjoyed the end of the celebration, throwing packets of confetti and streamers at one another, hugged, danced the last waltz and were the last to leave. People were slipping away, the locals were going indoors, the musicians packing up their instruments. As tradition demanded, the youngsters in the organising committee carried their chairman down the street on their shoulders, then piled up the folding chairs by the platform, covered the piano and switched off the lights.

The small bar closed and so, arms round each other's waist, Manolo and Teresa walked slowly down the street through a multi-coloured jungle of streamers hanging from the streetlamps and from the canopy of bunting and garlands swaying in the breeze, treading on the soft carpet of confetti. The street had returned to its usual sad yellow gaslight, but still offered glimpses of an innocent, youthful dream, a remnant of the tender, passionate atmosphere that had filled it for a few short hours, a promise reluctant to be swept away and obliterated by the coming of autumn. They carried this promise with them: the last revellers examine them curiously (this pair of lovers at odds with their surroundings, in the same way as their clashing attire) as they walk slowly away, treading carelessly on the white flakes on their way to the car parked on the corner. But before they reach the Floride, the first gust of autumn wind makes them shut their eyes, and the white wings of confetti rise and spread around them, completely obscuring them, leaving them lost.

This was the early morning of 12 September; Manolo would remember the date from the roses and kisses strewn in their wake, the sad state of abandonment everything was left in. They still had confetti in their hair and shiny spirals of streamers etched on their retinas when they reached the gate to Teresa's garden. The stars were fading; a reddish glow stretched along Vía Augusta. Grey clouds were gathering menacingly in the sky over Tibidabo.

'It'll rain tomorrow,' said Manolo. They stared into each other's eyes. To him it seemed as if the finger of destiny was about to anoint him; they went through the gate and crossed the garden. Teresa opened the front door with her key. 'Vicenta's asleep,' she told him in a whisper. Hand in hand they advanced through the darkness until they reached the living room. Teresa switched on the lights. At that moment, the telephone rang in the hall. Afraid it might wake Vicenta, Teresa ran to pick it up. The telephone was on a small table between a tall plant with shiny leaves and the staircase banister.

'Hello . . .?'

'Is that you, Tere?' a sleepy, whispering female voice said. 'Did I wake you? I'm sorry.'

'No, no,' Teresa replied, recognising Mari Carmen's voice. 'I was reading . . .' A silence.

'Yes, I woke you, and I'm sorry.' Despite this, there was no note of apology in her voice, something more like the satisfied cooing of a dove. 'This is no time to call, but you know that annoying my girlfriends in the middle of the night is my speciality.' A fresh silence, whispering, distant laughter. For some time, all Teresa could hear was Mari Carmen's urgent breathing.

'Where are you, Mari?'

'Where do you think? At home in bed. Have we really not woken you up?'

'No, Mari, don't worry . . .'

'Alberto didn't want me to ring you . . .' She gave a nervous laugh, as if she were being tickled, then her voice sounded further away, and Teresa could hear the muffled sound of sheets being tugged, of bodies shifting in bed. She turned to Manolo, who was waiting for her in the living-room doorway, and signalled for him to come over.

'What a pair of lunatics!' she said when he was beside her, covering the mouthpiece with her hand. Trying not to laugh, she motioned for him to listen with her, and they pressed their faces together in the almost completely dark hall. Mari Carmen's voice came on again, as though from a deep well.

'Are you still there . . .? I'm sorry, Teresa. First things first. Did you remember to tell Manolo I was sorry for the way I left?'

'Yes, of course.'

'Good. Another thing: does your Manolo have a phone?'

'No.'

'It doesn't matter . . . Stop that, you idiot!' she added, laughing, and then again to Teresa: 'It's Alberto, fooling around the whole time. We've been having fun together . . . Listen, I've got good news, and I'm glad I couldn't resist calling you. Your Manolo has a job, for certain. Get him to call me the day after tomorrow without fail. I've just woken several people up and I suppose they'll still be cursing me, but your great love can start next month. Definitely: you know I keep my word.'

'You're an angel, Mari,' exclaimed Teresa, looking at Manolo.

'As I wanted, in the sales department. Fantastic, isn't it? But he's got to prepare himself: he should do some correspondence courses at least, whatever he can, because he'll have to familiarise himself with everything as quickly as possible.'

'Yes, of course, we'll all help him . . .'

'Alberto thinks he could start at a basic five or six thousand . . .'

Teresa could feel Manolo breathing up against her neck. A fresh silence at the far end of the line, then whispering, laughter and muffled scuffling sounds, while Manolo's hand slid down her stomach to her hips, obliging her to turn round slowly. Teresa felt a tremendous sense of well-being, partly as a result of the apparent conjugal harmony reaching her from the far end of the line. At the same time, though, she had a nagging doubt: what did Mari's sudden enthusiasm towards Manolo mean? And her voice as if she was rolling around on a bed of leaves . . .

'Are you there, darling? I'm sorry – it's this monster, his hands are all over me, he won't let me talk . . .'

Laughing as well, Teresa lifted her elbow above Manolo's head to move the cable, still keeping the earpiece close to them, then twisted to accommodate his caressing hands, leaning back against the wall. In the dark, the plant's big leaves gave off an intense fragrance. She couldn't move, and allowed his mouth to brush her lips, hearing her skirt rustle and him shifting surreptitiously until his body was pressing against hers – apparently so that he could hear Mari Carmen better.

'Well, Tere,' they heard her say, her voice struggling with something; in the background they could make out Alberto purring. 'Don't forget to tell your friend, and get him to call me the day after tomorrow here or at Alberto's office. *Chao*, darling, be happy. And don't do anything crazy, right? Alberto is telling me to tell you that love does wonders for you . . . One of these days I'll call you so the two of us can have a good chat. Bye.'

'You really are a pair of wonderful lunatics,' whispered Teresa. 'Thank you. See you soon.'

'Good night, darling.'

The cable was caught between Teresa's back and the wall,

and so without moving, she changed hands with the receiver and felt for the hall table. As she moved, her body was squeezed even closer to Manolo's. She replaced the receiver, but the cable became entwined around Manolo's arm, and they struggled for a few moments, laughing.

'Did you hear what she said?' asked Teresa, barely able to contain her excitement. 'Did you understand? We've got the job!'

Neither of them realised they had been gasping for breath for some time. Manolo lightly touched her hair with his lips. He didn't want to say a word. So it was true: the finger of destiny had anointed him, and what he saw beyond her silky tresses and perfumed bare shoulders, in the shadows of the hall, was no longer a glossy sticker in his album jealously kept since childhood, but a qualified young man entering a modern office with a briefcase and the confidence that came from carrying one (he recalled a job offer read in the newspaper: wanted – dynamic, elegant young man, earnings on a par with Europe, immediate promotion to higher positions), while somewhere a telephone was ringing – but he didn't have to answer it, let an assistant do that ... Teresa's arms wound round his neck, and her yielding body in the shadows, her drowsy eyes, were another drug. He scrutinised her face determinedly. Finally freeing his hand from the telephone cable, he reached out to her shoulder, lowering first one strap of her dress, then the other. She raised her open mouth to him and fell into his arms, moving her legs apart and readying herself to slide down to the floor. Bending over slightly, Manolo held her up, accepting with pensive tenderness what she was offering him. In some strange way, Teresa's virginity had until now been the surest guarantee of him being able to gain his longed-for entry into the golden castes and upper echelons of dignity and work; now that he had succeeded in winning her trust and that of her friends, now that the two of them loved each other heart and soul, nothing stood in the way of him making Teresa his. But curiously, that telephone from his future office had carried on ringing for some time, not merely in his imagination but right there, next to them. It was Teresa, stretching out her hand in the darkness as if in bed asleep, who eventually picked up the receiver, murmuring almost at the same time, 'Who can it be now?' and 'Hello', while he, already foreseeing the irruption of dreadful reality, let go of her just as the hall light went on and (a depressing sight for both of them, the harbinger of winter) the old housemaid Vicenta appeared in her purple dressing gown, grey hair dangling in an untidy plait, staring at them, astonished and reproachful.

Her small, sleep-laden eyes announced the same as the call from the clinic: Maruja had died.

In the pale light of five in the morning, the clinic's illuminated windows offered a stupefied silence. As every year, the grey, mauve and ochre colours were by now visibly, reluctantly coming to the fore on Paseo de la Bonanova, and it was almost certain that today the sun would not manage to force its way through the clouds. Beautiful and perplexed, two youthful faces came and went from a third-floor window, their golden brows looking vulnerable. Somewhere, a patient with a fever who couldn't sleep was groaning weakly. The two of them looked out at the garden, where the fronds of the tall palm trees hung like claws beneath a leaden sky, then took in the streetlamps still shining on the Paseo, the wooden benches, the trees, a tram crawling like a glow-worm along its rails. At the same time, they could sense behind them white uniforms going to and fro, especially in Maruja's room, through whose half-open door came a confused babble of voices, the hasty delivery of the last rites (it seemed the priest had also arrived late). Above all, they noticed the absence of the constant background hum that had always accompanied whatever was said in the small anteroom, from the first afternoons when they flicked through magazines, an ethereal sound like the buzzing of telephone wires, evoking distances already dimly imagined in childhood. Today all of a sudden the noise had vanished, giving way to a deathly silence and, later on, to an ominous congregation of professional Catalan voices from the funerary chamber.

'*Han avisat a son pare?*' Have they notified her father?

'*Sí, doctor.*' Yes, doctor.

'*I al Señor Serrat?*' And Señor Serrat?

'*Sa filla ho ha fet. Diu que ja vénen.*' His daughter did. She says they are on their way.

As the night nurse had explained, news later confirmed by a dismayed Dina when she appeared, wearing a transparent plastic raincoat speckled with raindrops (this was how they learned it had begun to rain, reinforcing the unease they felt on seeing the Mallorcan nurse out of uniform and in everyday dress, looking strangely diminished and threatening), poor Maruja had not suffered, and had not been aware of anything. At four-thirty that morning, she had lapsed into a deep coma, and at ten minutes to five had gently slipped away in her sleep. Even though her state had always been a source of concern, nothing in recent days had suggested such an abrupt outcome. In fact, the previous afternoon when Señora Serrat called as usual from Blanes to ask the nurse for news, Dina herself had told her that Maruja seemed to be slightly better and that the sores on her back had almost healed ... That morning when she suddenly fell into an alarming state of lethargy, Doctor Saladich was called, and he instructed them to ring Señor Serrat's home in Barcelona. Unfortunately, it appeared his home telephone was constantly engaged (at this point, Teresa instinctively felt for Manolo's hand) and then, when the line was finally clear, it took a long while for anyone to answer. Propping her small blue umbrella against the wall, Dina had finished by saying that Maruja had died attended by a young doctor, who was one of Saladich's assistants, and two nurses.

Manolo and Teresa stayed at the window for a long while, still holding hands. All around them, stealthy banks of fog were closing in on their timeless summer isle: Señor Serrat and his wife arrived a little after ten in the morning, and later, Maruja's father appeared in a rental car from Reus, accompanied by two farm workers, two bewildered countryside shadows in their tragic Sunday best. Maruja's brother (a dark-skinned soldier with thick lips and a flat nose, a small, sad shaven head and a khaki uniform that thanks to the drizzle gave off a penetrating smell of hens) came in from Berga that afternoon, shortly before the burial.

This was an intimate, rapid affair, perhaps because of the drizzle that had begun to fall that morning and accompanied the three cars of black-clad mourners all the way to the Sudoeste cemetery. The clouds, the wet asphalt, the streets and faces, all merged with the rain, falling like grey ash from the sky. Señora Serrat was doubly disturbed. She had wept as the coffin was carried out, and then argued in a low voice with her daughter when Teresa insisted on wanting to travel to the cemetery in the same car as Manolo (nobody in fact had seen him get into it; he was already there when Señor Serrat distributed everyone), together with the two farm workers from Reus. Señor Serrat himself went in the first car, with Maruja's father and brother. Even though Teresa got her way and accompanied Manolo to the cemetery, the deep concern, alarm even, she saw reflected in her mother's face led her to suspect she knew something, that perhaps she had talked to Vicenta and was aware of certain details about her relationship with the Murcian. Already earlier that afternoon, and especially over lunch, Señora Serrat had been very interested in knowing everything Teresa had done in the previous days, what time Manolo had arrived at the clinic, who had given him the bad news, and so on. If she didn't take her interrogation any further it wasn't for lack of wanting to, but because Lucas was present: it had to be remembered that this fellow Manolo had been Maruja's fiancé. After that, Teresa didn't give her the chance to speak to her on her own. As for her father, he had been very busy, cold and distant since his arrival (it was difficult to know exactly where his grief ended and his bad temper began), but no doubt he was storing up questions for when it was all over – that at least was what certain glances he gave the young couple appeared to indicate.

Teresa was wearing her white raincoat, with a hood. Standing motionless on the black earth in Montjuich that was so sodden it was impossible to walk across (some planks had been laid in the mud to transport the coffin to its burial niche), she and Manolo watched the employees at work. A few metres in front of them, Señor Serrat, his shoulders scornful, his hands clasped behind his back, was talking to Lucas and his son beneath an umbrella one of the farm hands was holding aloft. When Señor Serrat noticed this, he took it from him, but then thought better of it, handed it back and instead stepped to one side (he was wearing a grey overcoat) so that Lucas would be protected. An embarrassing situation arose when it seemed no one wanted to use the farm worker's umbrella (it was true that what was falling from the sky wasn't very troublesome) until finally Lucas and his son resignedly shielded themselves beneath the black silk. Someone had produced cigarettes, and everybody was smoking: the smoke rose through the drizzle in a dense blue cloud. Teresa couldn't take her eyes off the workman sealing the niche. Manolo stood beside her in silence, the lapels of his brown combat jacket raised, his wet hair plastered on his forehead. Señor Serrat turned his head and observed them for a moment. Teresa felt Manolo's hand reaching for hers, and slipped a hand out of her coat pocket to take his. Her shoulders and neck still almost as painfully tense as they had been for hours, she didn't look at him but burst into tears.

She had not done so earlier, not even in front of the dead body in the clinic bed, gazing at that face still reflecting a nightmare, some remote inner vision that had finally consumed her – terribly emaciated (her nose and teeth unrecognisable, a new physiognomy), pale as wax, framed by her short black hair that had been combed back. There too she and Manolo had felt for each other's hands, and yet she had been unable to weep (she thought he was crying, and squeezed his fingers tenderly). Nor had she done so when she saw Maruja's father approach them with his unbearably timid steps as though wanting to ask them something; or when she saw the black, red-rimmed and fearful eyes (the same as Maruja's) of the soldier gaping at her knees. He kept the sticky khaki beret in his hand, not daring to move because of the noise his big studded boots made. But now Teresa did weep, disconsolately: hot, abundant tears that she shed for her friend, but also for herself and for Manolo, out of a confused sense of guilt, the unfairness of destiny, this sudden return to mud, grey weather and rain.

When it was all over and they were walking back to the cars, they saw Señor Serrat detach himself from the group and head towards them. They stopped and waited for him, but before he reached them he was reluctant to cross a large patch of churned-up earth and came to a halt, motioning to his daughter to go to him. Teresa obeyed, skirting the muddy patch to reach her father. She listened to something he said to her, and stayed with him, her blond head bent and hidden beneath her hood. When the Interloper saw she wasn't coming back to him (they had decided to walk rather than get into a car), he went directly towards the two of them, hands thrust in his combat jacket pockets as he splashed through the mud (he sensed that was no longer important). Señor Serrat had taken out a handkerchief and was blowing his nose. He cast a glance at the men waiting for him by the cars, then at his daughter, and finally at Manolo, who had just come to a halt on the far side of a puddle.

'Well, my boy,' said Señor Serrat, 'this looks like the end. Our poor Maruja is no longer suffering: it will happen to all of us one day.' Carefully, as if it was a very delicate object, he was slowly folding and refolding the handkerchief, eyes lowered. 'I know you loved her very much, but don't let grief overwhelm you. You're very young, you'll get used to it and eventually forget her.' All at once he extended his hand, a sad, affectionate smile on his face. 'Farewell. I'm sure we won't ever have occasion to see one another again.'

Manolo no longer heard him: his half-closed eyes were struggling to retain a distant light. The others were also peering at him as they stood by the cars: long, solemn-looking faces, the blurred silhouettes of a tribunal in the rain – a real farewell. It was very quick: looking away from Señor Serrat, Manolo held his hand out to Teresa across the puddle, not to say goodbye but reaching for hers so that she would follow him (his gesture was suspended in mid-air for the fraction of a second in the tender blue gaze).

'Teresa,' he said in a serene, gentle voice. 'Come with me, I need to talk to you.'

Slowly, but without a moment's hesitation, her face concealed beneath her hood, Teresa took his hand and jumped over the puddle. They said goodbye briefly to the others, and walked off down the path to the exit. The Murcian knew Teresa's father was looking at them, and couldn't resist turning his head back. It was a chilling sight: through the grey, glistening drizzle, on Señor Serrat's thin lips he could make out a blurry, indulgent smile full of consideration (he even gave a slight wave of the hand before getting into the car), a benevolent, casual, terribly obsequious smile.

The following afternoon, Teresa did not appear. They had agreed she would pick him up in her car at half past four in Plaza Lesseps. When it was gone five, Manolo called her home, but no one answered. That night he called again several times from the Bar Delicias, always with the same result. Then he remembered the Bori couple. They weren't at home either. He told himself they were probably dining out. The next morning he telephoned Teresa again. No one at home. The Boris. Mari Carmen came on: no, she hadn't heard from Teresa, they must be at the seaside Villa; yes, it was very odd she had left without a word ... By the way, she was very sorry, but she couldn't tell him anything yet about the job, perhaps it was best to wait until Teresa reappeared ...

That afternoon he went to the Serrats' house on Vía Augusta. All the windows were closed. Bending over a rake in the garden, an old man with a pink shiny bald head turned to look at him. Manolo greeted him from the gate and asked if there was anyone at home. The old man said there wasn't, and asked what he wanted. Manolo replied that he had a message for Señorita Teresa. The gardener told him the Serrats and their daughter had gone to Blanes the previous morning, and wouldn't be back until towards the end of the month.

That night, not knowing what to do, Manolo called Mari Carmen again and told her he needed to speak to her urgently. She apologised: they were eating out, she had finally convinced Alberto it was cheaper for them to have a bite to eat somewhere and ... Manolo butted in and suggested they could meet after dinner in a bar. 'Wait a moment,' Mari Carmen said unenthusiastically, and he could hear her talking to Alberto. There was a silence, until finally she agreed and chose the time and place: at eleven in a café opposite the cathedral. When he was on his way down Vía Layetana to meet her, wondering how the Boris could help him (doubtless all he could get from them was the Villa telephone number, and not even that was certain), his eye was suddenly caught by a yellow and red flash (the tips of Teresa's scarf and hair) and the outlines of a car speeding round the next corner: a rapid glimpse of the Floride's gleaming white bodywork. Perhaps Teresa had persuaded them to let her come back to Barcelona, and at that very moment was looking for him. He started to run, but by the time he rounded the corner the car had disappeared. He could have sworn it was Teresa.

Forgetting the Boris, he set out on a frantic search of all the bars in the port area they had been to together, imagining she must have thought the same. It took him more than an hour and a half: he asked in the Saint-Germain (the booming, endearing voice tried to keep him there by introducing him to a new waitress, a girl with an angular, fervent face who claimed to have known him for years), in the Pastis, the Cádiz, in Jamboree. Although by now he had given up hope of finding her, he looked in all the Plaza Real bars. Suddenly, he remembered the Tibet and hailed a taxi. Of course, if she was in Barcelona, where else would she wait for him but in the Tibet, near El Carmelo?

The taxi driver, a little red-haired man with a Valencian accent, craned his neck over the steering wheel and began to say that winter is almost upon us, what can you do, in no time at all that's another year gone that we'll never see again ... He was driving exasperatingly slowly, no doubt thinking of his offspring: two moon-faced girls in plaits, with smiling faces, their cheeks pressed together as they stared at him from a studio photograph stuck to the dashboard with a message from them written at the bottom: 'Don't go too fast, Papa!'

When he saw this, Manolo shouted: 'Forget your girls and get a move on, Papa – it's growing late.'

The taxi driver protested in a sing-song voice: 'What's wrong, lad? I'm in no hurry to get to the cemetery.'

Manolo threw himself forward and yelled in his ear: 'And I don't have those little beauties waiting for me at home, so get this shitty taxi moving, come on!'

The driver glanced at him in his rear-view mirror, saw he wasn't joking and accelerated.

Teresa wasn't in the Tibet either. By now it was past one in the morning. Tired and cursing his fate, Manolo called the Boris. After making him wait quite a while, someone picked up: it was Alberto; they were already in bed. Manolo apologised for not turning up for their meeting, but he thought he had seen ... Alberto Bori interrupted to tell him quite coldly that he should please ring in the morning. No, for heaven's sake, they hadn't seen Teresa and didn't know anything about her.

One last try: the small bar on Vía Augusta they had been to the previous week. It was deserted, but as soon as he entered and saw the way the waiter was looking at him (a lad from Almería that Teresa had really liked), a familiar blue wave swept over Manolo: the young lady had left a note for him the previous morning, before she set off. 'She seemed to be in a great hurry,' added the waiter. It was a card inside an unsealed envelope, which read: 'I'm leaving for the Villa in a few minutes. As soon as I can I'll write explaining what's going on. Don't do anything before you receive news from me. I love you, Teresa.'

The next morning (sun and wind, with big clouds scudding towards the south) he decided to steal a motorbike to go to the seaside Villa. With a bit of luck, he would find a way to see Teresa. There was no way he was going to wait for news from her; he shouldn't and wouldn't. He needed to see her. Besides, how crazy clocks were, how the hours and days went by, how threatening the solitude in this city filling up day by day with Catalans as busy and noisy as automobiles, at the same time as it emptied of bright, festive tourists. No, impossible for him to wait, and he heeds the warning from a local policeman ('Hey, you, why don't you look where you're going? Or you'll end up under the wheels of a car'). Yes, wake up, Manolo, wake up ... At six in the evening, after looking everywhere, he had to make do with a Vespa he saw outside a mansion on Paseo Maragall.

He escaped by a whisker from being taken to the Horta police station only because the stupid scooter wasn't locked and he managed to put it in gear at the first try (or possibly because its owner was in skirts: Manolo saw the priest running after him, cassock up above his knees, his arms whirling, as withered and skinny as a skeleton, wearing gold-rimmed glasses, and shouting, 'Hey boy, there – that's my scooter, that's my scooter!', but the cassock thwarted him).

Manolo had to abandon the Vespa ten minutes later when the petrol cable snapped. He was already at Badalona. His nerves, impatience and bad luck meant he couldn't find another motorbike until almost eleven that night (this time outside a chemical factory in a wretched alleyway; at least it meant no priest would come running after him). It was an old, ruinous Rieju, an asthmatic camel about to give up the ghost, its insides full of rust and dirty grease. Sitting astride this wreck – probably one of the last still on the road – the Interloper sped as fast as he could along the coastal highway. There was little traffic at that time of night, but despite his best efforts the journey took him more than an hour; the ancient Rieju was on its last legs. By the time he got beyond Blanes and was gliding along the track to the Villa with the sound of the sea in his ears, he realised he had arrived too late.

The Villa was quiet, with no light in the windows or out on the terrace. The night was darker than many others he kept lovingly in his memory, and the big house looked more imposing, its outline less well defined and austere than he remembered, close and yet at the same time distant in the darkness. He hid Grandma Rieju in the pine wood. Everything around him was asleep, lulled by the chirruping of the crickets and the murmur of the waves. A white sea mist was floating in the depths of the wood, enveloping it in an unreal beauty. Manolo walked under the tall eucalyptus trees in the garden at the back of the Villa;

he came to a halt at the wall where ivy grew up to the terrace. Almost invisible among the leaves, a uralite drainpipe also rose up the wall. As he thought he recalled from a conversation with Maruja, Teresa's bedroom gave on to the terrace, next to the children's bedroom, which was exactly above Maruja's room. There was only one window on this side of the house, the one he had so often climbed through. Manolo took a good look at it: it had changed somehow, and was now half hidden by the ivy, its shutters closed and seemingly stubbornly mute, with a hermetic defensive look. He turned hurriedly away, picked up a stone and threw it on to the terrace. He did the same several times, without luck. What if Teresa's room didn't give on to this terrace? It was a shame he had arrived so late; he had been hoping to find Teresa still up, in the garden, for example ... Manolo stepped back a little, lost in thought, then sat on the ground and leaned back against the trunk of a pine tree. He dug his fingers into the wet earth, not knowing what to do next, shaken by an ardent mouth calling to him from the dripping shadows of the ivy: Maruja's window, and inside a pair of bare arms spreading to welcome him, feverish eyes helping her gather strength in bed, the way she gave herself, her rhythm ...

Maruja is the kind of woman whose breasts you don't remember as beautiful; you remember their shape, their tremulous weight, as well as the slightly sour, harsh line of her mouth, her dark back retreating timidly to the shadows. Manolo could recall a taste of eucalyptus or mint in her saliva, the purring sound in her throat when she kissed, as well as a deep-seated cold shudder when he saw her shrug her slight shoulders in front of the mirror, or her languid footsteps as she crossed the room, naked and shy. He could see her climbing up to El Carmelo one windy winter's day, in her tight, unfashionable checked coat with a maroon velvet hairband. But above all he saw how she blinked fearfully in a whirlwind of dust on Calle Gran Vista, surrounded by children armed with stones, wearing masks that left only their small curious eyes visible, saw the trembling sweetness of her hand on her chest as she closed the lapels of her coat, the submission in her tightly closed legs, the delightful way she tilted her head when she came into the Bar Delicias and stood there waiting for him, unashamed of being a fallen housemaid . . .

All of a sudden, Manolo jumped up (that's what you get for sitting in front of this window, as if the poor thing was still waiting inside for me) and cursed himself for sensing obscurely that deep inside he had also begun to house many of the seeds of Maruja's unnerving conformity. He had often criticised her for it, but now this memory would feed on him too, silently devouring him. He was beginning to suspect it had been stupid to come here, that it would have been better to wait for news from Teresa. Disheartened, he directed his steps to the long, deserted beach, dimly lit by the fading blue starlight. It was cold, the waves broke with a dull thump along the shore, spilling their white foam and then drawing back, their echo gradually diminishing. He recognised the night breeze on his skin, and the beach, and yet he was surprised that only two months had passed since he began to go out with Teresa – he could have sworn it had been years, as if she had devoted much longer to him than he did to Maruja. His time with Teresa had an emotional density lacking with Maruja; he tried to recall the moments when possessing that boundless time had been more complete, more real. He discovered how naïve and gullible he had been, how he had been deceiving himself when he thought he was so clever. To think that Teresa could have been his a long time ago! Oh, how blind, what a fool he had been, he told himself, remembering her in his arms, on the beach or in dark streets (my God, that sweet, beseeching look of hers the night they left Encarna's bar and were entwined leaning against the wall) or on the slopes of El Guinardó park (her nasal child's voice calling to him from the grass) or the unforgettable morning on the Hermanas sisters' roof, cuddling and caressing one another beneath a magical sun ... But he had always pulled back, and thinking it over now, perhaps that restraint, born of a more powerful desire than that of mere physical possession, had not been completely in vain: to judge by the passion Teresa had shown in the days leading up to poor Maruja's burial, she had been his more than ever. So he had respected her, but what good would that do if he wasn't given time to consolidate their relationship? It could end up being a useless, stupid sacrifice, one of those you pull your hair out over for the rest of your life, one that might not have the crass, sanctimonious respect of most formal engagements, but was just as pitiful.

Oppressed by his solitude on the beach, the Interloper felt cheated, mocked and above all disconcerted by a change that had begun to take place within him and which he was only now discovering to his amazement. He had not respected Teresa whenever he had the opportunity in order to gain some reward: there was something more, an outside influence that had become part of him, an unclear emotion combining dignity and credulity that had infected him, that had gradually stuck to him. He had never been what might be called a 'good lad' and would probably never have the chance to be one, unless he married Teresa – so why on earth had he behaved like one, for what reason; and why, let's see, why had he allowed himself to be drawn into a situation of respectability and dignity that would get him nowhere? Why had he signed up so quickly and naïvely to the sacred laws of good behaviour, by virtue of what moral precepts, what agreement or accord, what rules of prudence, decorum or social norms had, in less than three months, converted the Interloper into such a hypocrite towards Teresa? What could have made him so inconsiderate towards a girl in love with him, a generous girl in need of tenderness, or caresses . . .? Cursing and full of self-loathing as he recalled Teresa's kisses, he felt growing within him an immense love for her and her frustrated desire to have sex. He remembered with a real sense of loss the night when Maruja died, and he and Teresa had their heads together over the telephone, enveloped in that burning cloud: at that moment, himself an ardent flame, he had decided to make her his. But oh! That night had come too late: he had wasted too many hours pursuing the white gazelle of dignity, of a radiant future . . . However, there was still time to put things straight, to return to being the determined brute and convinced liar he had always been and should never have left off being. How ridiculous of him: if you drop your guard they eat you alive, and so, patience, shuffle the pack, he resolved, furiously kicking a mass of rotting seaweed the waves had spat on to the beach.

Although in the city for the past four days he had lost all notion of the time, or even when it was day or night, here he was able to calculate (his wandering and the wait on the beach seemed so ingrained and familiar) it must be past three o'clock. Since he had come here and had nothing better to do, he would wait until day dawned. If the weather was good, Teresa would probably come down for a swim. He went into the wood, jumped over the fence and tried to sleep in a hollow filled with earth and pine needles. The cold and the sound of the sea made this impossible, and so he went back to the garden, protected from the breeze, where he curled up on a swing seat covered in a fringed awning.

A day of radiant sun dawned. The mist quickly melted into the pine wood, as if a wind was greedily swallowing it. He felt stiff and thought he was still dreaming, but when he moved his arm from in front of his face, the sight through the piercing rays of sun of a tall, black-haired young man coming towards him holding a tennis racquet and with a towel over his shoulder acquired an unexpected, cheerful reality. In the early-morning silence, the gravel path in the Serrat family garden crunched beneath the stranger's white tennis shoes. He had an athletic body, broad shoulders and was wearing a blue short-sleeved shirt with its soft collar raised; his shorts revealed a pair of tanned, muscular legs. He was headed straight towards the Murcian, but with his head lifted to the sun, shielding his half-closed eyes with his hand. Realising the stranger had not yet seen him, he quickly slid off the back of the swing and rolled until he was hidden behind a thick clump of geraniums. Before reaching the swing, and offering Manolo a sudden reflection of himself (the same straight, dark hair, the same energetic, arch profile), the young man turned on to a path leading to the tennis court. Shortly afterwards, in similar attire and also carrying a racquet, Señor Serrat appeared and followed the same path as the youngster. Manolo backed away until he found a safer hiding place among the pines from where he could continue to spy on the garden. No sign of life from Teresa. He waited. He heard the ball striking their racquets, the admiring or disappointed shouts, often feigning a delighted despair (these came from a breathless Señor Serrat, whose slow game obviously couldn't match that of his young rival) that ended with a smattering of mutual praise.

At around ten o'clock, Senõra Serrat appeared, accompanied by a new plump young housemaid, who laid a tray with coffee and toast on a low table shielded by a parasol. Señora Serrat's voice rang out cheerfully and clearly through the mid-morning air, momentarily establishing a happy link, a leisurely harmony with the merry voices from the tennis court. Then a rustic-looking man appeared with a hosepipe; the mistress of the house spoke briefly to him, entered the house through the French windows, came out again, went back in. All this is such nonsense, thought Manolo, a tremendous summer-vacation bore that Teresa's absence makes even more unbearable. Around noon, as he ran his hand over his face, Manolo could feel it was unshaven and suspected he must look awful. You won't get anywhere like this, he told himself. Thirsty, tired, his bones aching, he decided the best thing would be to return to Barcelona and wait for news. He didn't care about the noise the motorbike made (let Teresa know at least how close he had been), and soon afterwards came out on to the main road. The tiny, fearful Seat 600s kept obediently to his right. He couldn't even reach a decent speed. Two hours later, gasping its last and all its joints creaking, the Rieju deposited him in Barcelona. He abandoned its carcass behind the Hospital San Pablo, and set off on foot up Calle Cartagena.

That same afternoon a letter arrived for Manolo in the Bar Delicias. A young boy delivered it to his brother's house. It was from Teresa. On the envelope was written simply: Manolo Reyes, Bar Delicias, Carretera del Carmelo. Inside were three sheets of paper covered in small, pretty, neat handwriting, clearly copied from a longer draft as it contained only one crossing out.

The opening letter 'D' in 'Darling' had been written with resolve, rage even, although the stem was adorned with a playful curlicue. Then came: 'Forgive the delay: I don't know your address, and I thought I'd be back in Barcelona by now. My parents insisted I stay here at the Villa until I return to university at the end of the month. Clever move!' Several similar comments suggested there would follow an outraged analysis of the reasons for her parents' tedious decision, their 'clever move', and yet instead Teresa launched heroically into a charming, impassioned description of her present (volatile) state of mind and some sleepless nights: she spoke of 'eager expectation' and 'horribly cold sheets', before finally revealing the cause of such fevers and hallucinations: 'I've been in bed for two days with a temperature, delirious' (this musical adjective danced fleetingly before the Murcian's eyes wrapped in a pink Empire-style nightgown). 'Today is the first time I've felt strong enough to write to you. I caught a cold in the rain, and Maruja's sudden death and not being able to see you made me so miserable I arrived here and went straight to bed. At first I felt utterly lost and demoralised . . .'

Teresa went on to insist they mustn't despair, because nothing had happened apart from the irritation of this brief separation. Even more vexing perhaps was her parents' attitude ('which can hardly come as surprise to us'), which confirmed there was a sickness at the heart of her family that had somehow shaped her since childhood, and of which she had become increasingly aware since she met Manolo: 'Their reaction is yet another example of my ridiculous upbringing; they think they're protecting their shameless, wayward daughter but they don't realise it's too late. I could die of rage and shame. What must you think of me, of all of us? If only you knew how bored I am, Manolo, how much I miss you!' And this was why, she added, the Villa seemed empty, even though they had visitors, distant, unwelcome relatives ('a vain, pompous cousin from Madrid, who is waiting for me to get better so he can thrash me at tennis') – she felt as if a shipwreck had thrown her among strange people with outlandish customs. She repeated how lonely she was, and then a sudden warm sea breeze, the blue wave he associated with Teresa, the longed-for return to the tropical island: 'Yet what makes me miserable isn't the hostile atmosphere here, it's your absence, Manolo. The most dreadful loneliness would be a paradise, the cruellest tragedy a blessing, the most deadly disease a nuptial bed, the worst misery and suffering a caress, compared to the unbearable pain of not seeing you for days, my love, my love, my love, of being without your lips, your hands, for what seems like an eternity . . .'

Despite his delight and awe (what a difference an education made, how good she was at expressing her feelings), Manolo let his impatience get the better of him and skipped a few lines in search of something more concrete. After this impassioned section, in which someone with a more cultivated mind than the young Murcian would instantly have recognised certain literary borrowings, the tone descended to a more practical, informative level. Teresa described a tedious conversation with her parents 'during which we all showed great restraint' but the real problem was never broached. This conversation took place in the evening after poor Maruja's burial, and 'although no one mentioned any names, I felt sure that dreadful gossip Dina, that floozy from the clinic, had blabbed about us, and Vicenta as well. And of course, Mother completed the picture. I don't think I'm exaggerating when I say that even before she met you my mother was afraid you'd defile her daughter's virtue. Blessed virginity, what nonsense people spout in your name! And if you remember that my parents think I'm virtually a Marxist, I needn't mention the follies and amorous adventures they see me as capable of.' And yet she insisted the subject of her feelings never came up: 'They simply decided Maruja's death had come as a terrible shock to me, and they must now take proper care of me. Papa says I respond too emotionally to things, that I'm still a child, and that all the excitement this summer has left me in a state of nervous exhaustion: in short, I need rest, and what better place for that than at the Villa; a change of air, or rather of ideas. In fact, your name never came up.'

Here, Manolo reflected that this was typical of Señor Serrat's attitude: Teresa maintained that her father had never before shown so much interest in her, 'in my way of thinking', not even when she was arrested during the student demonstrations. Apparently they had discussed the university and the political winds blowing there. 'It's terribly funny. I don't know if you realise how unusual that is for my father.' She went on to explain how he'd never taken any serious interest in such matters before she met Manolo; on the contrary he liked to make fun of 'my friends, especially Luis Trías de Giralt, rather amusingly, I must admit: believe it or not, Papa is a dreadful tease'. As for 'our relationship', she wrote further on, no one had raised their voice or made a scene. 'But let's not deceive ourselves, let's stick to the facts: my parents aren't as afraid of what their crazy daughter with her radical ideas might have done up to now, but of what she might do in the future. It isn't a question of morality, although there's a lot to say about that, because I assure you that even the most virtuous and respectable members of my world consider the offence of losing one's virginity before marriage, and for pleasure, far less shocking and irreversible than to make a bad marriage.'

There followed a few indignant but (in Manolo's view) unnecessary reflections about the 'outrageous sense the bourgeoisie in this country have of their own self-worth', as well as a curious analysis of the conflict raging within her family with regard to her ('they confuse my love for you with my progressive ideas, because their daughter has turned class traitor'), aware, no doubt, that she herself had been labouring under the exact same confusion when she first met and befriended Manolo. And on that point, she ended with a pompous declaration of principles: 'As for me, Manolo, love has replaced solidarity' (here was the one crossing out on the page: the word 'solidarity' must have given her pause, because she had crossed it out and then, unable to find a suitable alternative, had rewritten it) 'or rather through love solidarity has found its rightful place in my heart – a place of equal importance, since I also love my country – but free now of conspiracies, romantic ideals and other nonsense . . . Forgive my ramblings, darling, but it does me good to order my thoughts.' Otherwise, she went on, she spent long hours in her room reading or contemplating the sea from the terrace. 'How tedious, how meaningless everything seems without you! If you only knew how desperately I need you, if I could only see you, tell you how I feel right now, have you here by my side, even for a moment.' She repeated that her course didn't resume until October, and after that all would be well ('nothing will ever keep us apart again'), but in the meantime . . . What were they to do? Wasn't there some way of seeing each other before then? And now, in dense lines of blue ink, she confessed she'd tried not to think about him, but in vain. Three suspension points (sloping downwards) stifled a surge of passion: 'You're the only real man I've ever met, you've taught me how to live, made me feel like a woman . . .'

Then the farewell and below that a puzzling postscript, hastily scrawled and blurred in places, perhaps where a tear had caused the ink to run (or was it sea spray: a few grains of sand in the envelope suggested she wrote the letter, or at least the postscript, on the beach). It took a while for her words to become clear to Manolo: 'Be rebellious, proud and brave always. One night I dreamed I saw you beneath the pines when you came to see Maruja, gazing up at my balcony. Did you ever notice how splendid and verdant the ivy is? I lie awake at night thinking of you, longing for you, my love, while the ridiculous bourgeois family I'm ashamed to be a part of, sleeps. Yours ever. Kisses. Teresa.'

Ecstatic with joy, Manolo carefully folded the letter, slipped it into his breast pocket and left the bar. It was half past three on a hot Saturday afternoon and the sky was persistently blue.

Yielding to the tentative, ambiguous invitation in her postscript, Manolo resolved to meet her that same night. He was convinced that once he saw her, everything would be as before. Her letter also confirmed that his strategy of being sexually respectful had paid off: Teresa had been faithful, and was waiting for him – she was waiting for him! He spent the rest of the afternoon in a state of excitement that gave him the focus of a madman: there was too much at stake for him to take any foolish risks, such as travelling there on a stolen motorcycle. His first idea was to take the train, but he didn't have the money for that, and besides the nearest stop was Blanes station, a three-mile walk from the Villa. Then he remembered the Cardinal's old Derbi motorcycle. He knocked on his door just after six.

'My uncle is out,' said Hortensia. Manolo strode inside and carried on through to the garden, the Syringe trailing after him. As he headed towards the shed at the far end where the old man kept the Derbi, he explained he needed it to make an urgent trip.

'Is it far? Why don't you take me with you?' she asked. 'You promised . . .'

'That's impossible,' he said. 'Some other time – today I'm in a big hurry.'

He had to stoop inside the low-ceilinged shed. Paint pots and garden tools were rusting away in the damp. The Derbi was up on its stand, on some oil-stained newspapers spread over the floor. It looked in good shape. Manolo made to unscrew the cap on the petrol tank.

'It's full,' the girl's voice said behind him. 'I filled it myself.'

Manolo detected the abrupt, disgruntled tone in her voice, and he turned slowly, a vague weight on his shoulders. The Syringe was holding a pair of red slacks, folded – she must have had them ready in some strategic spot in the house and had grabbed them as she came to the door. She flashed him a pleading look: 'Shall I get changed, I'll be quick . . .?' she asked. He thought it over and said:

'Tomorrow. I promise. I already told you, I'm in a hurry today.'

Hortensia flung the trousers on the floor, turned round and said as she began to walk away:

'If you want to borrow the Derbi, you'll have to wait for my uncle and ask him. So there!'

Manolo caught hold of her arm. 'Wait a minute,' he said laughing. 'Wait a minute, my little wildcat.' He did some quick mental arithmetic: it wasn't sensible to show up at the Villa until well after dark, which gave him time to take the girl for a spin and settle this trivial debt once and for all. Come to think of it, he was happy to do so today of all days: on the eve of great and joyous events, of the rendezvous that promised to secure his passage into the world of adults, there was something gratifying about satisfying the Syringe's childish, innocent whim. 'All right, princess,' he said with a grin. 'I'll take you. But be prepared to learn what speed means.' Hortensia stifled a yelp of joy, and wanted to put on her red slacks, but Manolo said there wasn't time, and besides she looked more grown-up in her lab coat, and prettier, too.

What followed was quite simple. Manolo was taking Hortensia for a spin in order to have the Derbi, but also because of the need he felt that day to please her, or in some strange way to please himself, he realised, because he couldn't avoid the agreeable sensation that something was about to happen. As he drove at breakneck speed up and down Paseo del Valle de Hebrón, Hortensia's arms were wrapped tightly about his midriff, and he could feel her cheek pressed against his back: her small, firm breasts and her neglected heart hammering through his thin cotton shirt conveyed all the tenderness of a frightened little animal.

'Hold on tight, girl, hold on tight,' he yelled.

Hortensia remained silent throughout: she clung to him. Eventually, terrified, with the stinging wind making her eyes water, she begged him to take her home as she was feeling dizzy. Reluctant to leave the Derbi out in the road, he wheeled it through the back gate into the garden. Pale and unsteady on her feet, Hortensia tripped as she went towards the shed to retrieve her unworn red trousers. Manolo caught her gently by the elbow, and her lonely, quivering young body rubbed up against him in time with her irresolute, clumsy steps. She remained ominously silent. The bleak, neglected garden, already assailed by night, suddenly made Manolo sense the familiar dark snare close around him; this is the end, the saddest of farewells, but I'm getting out of here ... Wishing he could break Hortensia's silence, he searched his mind for a few kind words, but his head was empty, the gentle banality of language seemed devoid of meaning, lacking that blithe glibness with which he usually treated the girl: unless he saw in something a sign, a mark of destiny lighting up his boundless, shimmering future, his mind refused to work, his lips to utter a word. However, he came back to reality as he recalled Teresa's letter in his breast pocket, which Hortensia's trembling shoulder was causing to rustle together with his cigarette packet, and this restored his euphoric sense of an urgent mission. Inside the shed, he stooped to pick up the girl's trousers and as he turned to give them to her, he saw her dull eyes peering at him through the gloom. Her figure in the doorway, immobile against the dim light outside, was in fact that of Teresa, but only her outline (why isn't your hair shiny, child, why the cold stare?). That was enough, though, and Manolo tried to rescue the situation by giving her a frown that was halfway between concerned and affectionate. He tapped the girl's burning cheek with that wretched assurance that evolves with youth and finally destroys it, but then, finding himself suddenly enveloped by the scent of bitter almonds and at once aroused and grateful to the girl, and for his own good fortune, he leaned down, drew her to him and kissed her on the lips.

As if this were a magnificent stage set, the veranda lights came on across the garden. They could hear the old man's mellifluous tones calling Hortensia from inside the house, but they hesitated before they emerged into the gathering darkness. 'Come on, let's ask him if he'll let us have the Derbi,' she murmured, tugging at Manolo's hand.

Bewildered, he let her lead him. The night breeze brought him to his senses, and he let go of the girl's hand as they stepped inside the house. They found the Cardinal in the dining room.

The Cardinal pondered. 'No, I think not,' he said. 'Out of the question.'

'A friend of mine is seriously ill ... in Moncada,' lied the Murcian.

'No, no and no.'

'Look, I have to see him. Don't be so mean!'

'No, I said.'

As well as refusing to lend him the Derbi, the Cardinal demanded Manolo pay back the money he owed, the money he'd recently wheedled from Hortensia, 'by whispering sweet nothings in her ear, and false promises of marriage'.

'That's a lie,' protested Manolo.

The old man was on the couch reading a newspaper, while Hortensia, cheeks still flushed, went back and forth along the corridor with bundles of clean laundry (she'd already balanced the ironing board on two chair backs in a corner of the dining room next to the standard lamp) until finally she left everything where it was and sat down on the table to listen. Her hair was swept up in a loose bun. Her uncle rose to his feet, flung the newspaper to the floor and set off unexpectedly on one of his solemn, devout pilgrimages around the house. Manolo followed close on his heels, brushing the elegant, purple skirts of the Cardinal's dressing gown like a humble acolyte seeking a special audience. The Cardinal toured the downstairs and first floor, adjusting a painting here, a candelabra there, blowing the dust off a figurine, straightening the drapes of a curtain, the position of a chair, a vase, some cushions. Amid his wild gesticulations and the endless soliloquy of a sentimental cuckold, the old man refused all discussion with Manolo, seeming to listen only to an inner voice.

'A close friend, you say, in Moncada . . .? Liar,' he repeated, as if to himself.

The urgency he saw in the young Murcian's eyes had the name of a girl on it, he was sure of that. But that wasn't the worst of it; for a man like the Cardinal, who had wide-ranging ideas about life, and had come to a painful recognition of his own mistakes (he often said he was born in the wrong century, the wrong country, religion and gender), had also come to certain conclusions that were no less accurate for being so bitter, namely that the real cause of the recent misfortunes afflicting an intelligent youth like Manolo boiled down to the dual maxim he often repeated: 'How little we love those who love us, and how we like to go too far.' As for the young girl who had turned Manolo's head, the Cardinal had nothing against her personally, but insisted one must live with a person for a while, if only to allow oneself the pleasure of going back to them, for which it was first necessary to abandon them. And therein lay the problem:

'Son, women don't understand how necessary these comings and goings are in a man's life.'

'Stop giving me a hard time and lend me the Derbi, Cardinal. Always the same spiel!'

'No, no, and no,' the old man repeated, and carried on warning him about life's dangers, just as he'd been doing for years, without success. 'You're heading for such a beating out there, they'll have to scrape you off the floor,' he prophesied. 'But of course, no one wants to be cured of the disease of youth.' It didn't sound as if he had drunk a lot, and yet he was staggering and waving his arms and hands about the way drunkards do to ward off loneliness.

Perhaps because she'd seen it all before, the Syringe didn't follow them on their ramble round the house. But afterwards, when her uncle, prey to a sudden fatigue, slumped back in his wicker armchair and laid his head on a bolster (in his bizarre and complicated rearrangement of furniture, he had moved a bed without a headboard out into the arbour, beneath the illuminated wooden framework where all the sky's fading light seemed to have accumulated), Manolo caught her standing behind him, staring at something on the floor. She thrust her hands deep into the pockets of her white coat, stretching the fabric as far as it would go, and had let down her hair once more and put on a pair of high heels. However, he would only recall these details later on; when he pulled the cigarettes from his shirt pocket to offer the Cardinal one, the Syringe was still wearing that empty smile, and he only saw her when she sneaked up behind him, then stooped to look at the floor, before quickly moving away. The Cardinal, meanwhile, went on stubbornly refusing to lend him the Derbi, and Manolo threatened half-heartedly to leave the house and never return. Even so he renewed his offer, only to receive another rebuff ('A cigarette? No! On your knees, on your knees, thankless child!'), and then in a friendly gesture plumped up the bolster for him, turning it over.

'Away with you, hypocrite!' the old man said, swiping at the air (years later in an ironical twist of fate, the lonely old Cardinal would adopt the lad's habit of plumping up pillows for patients in Modelo prison, as he did his daily rounds of beds in the sick bay; a final poignant homage to their exhausted, emaciated and no longer angelic bodies). The Murcian made one last sing-song entreaty, but the Cardinal was deaf to all but his inner music, and so, realising his sly attempts at kindness had got him nowhere, the Murcian decided to leave.

He thought Hortensia must be ironing, but as he crossed the dining room he saw her standing by the table, facing away from him, head bowed. She wheeled round, hands behind her back, as if she was hiding something, and followed Manolo with teary eyes before lowering them to her own cheeks that seemed suddenly to have puffed up. Before Manolo reached the hallway he turned round:

'What's the matter, Hortensia?'

Outside in the arbour, the evening breeze ruffled the Cardinal's silvery hair as he sat slumped in his chair. 'Don't go, my boy,' they heard him say. Clearly there was nothing more to be had from him.

Without fully understanding, yet sensing the coming storm, Manolo darted into the hallway. He could feel the Syringe's ashen eyes fixed on the back of his neck, but continued without looking round. As he opened the front door, he heard the old man's cries from the garden:

'Manooooooolo!' a ridiculous, coquettish, tortured echo, so distant it might have come from a well or the depths of a ravine, yet no doubt audible to everyone this side of the hill, even up in Monte Carmelo: 'Manooooolooooo . . .!'

Goodbye, maestro, goodbye you endearing old bastard. It had all been for nothing, and he had wasted his energy and precious time. Yet Manolo was determined to reach the Villa, on donkey back if need be; he wouldn't allow anyone or anything to keep him here. He would see Teresa, renew their interrupted courtship, find a job, and later on Señor Serrat would use his influence (how could he refuse: a little blond Interloper bouncing on his knee, the follies of youth, Murcia is beautiful despite everything) to give his prodigal son-in-law the helping hand he needed . . .

No doubt his bold contemplation of these limitless horizons prevented him from seeing the punctual and inevitable setting of the sun. And by the time he glimpsed the ticking bomb inside Hortensia, it would be too late: she had followed him out of the house, slipping like a shadow down the road, tailing him to Plaza Sanllehy where, inevitably, she saw him pick out this motorbike and jump astride it. She sat crouched in a doorway some twenty metres away, chewing her nails and staring intently at him. When he saw her, Manolo instantly realised (his hand darting to his breast pocket) that he had lost the letter: he must have dropped it when he pulled out the cigarette packet, and of course that brat had read it . . . There was no time, he had to make a quick getaway if he didn't want the owner of the motorbike to catch him, and yet he remained transfixed by the girl, his leg hovering in the air, foot poised centimetres from the kick-start lever. What could the Syringe be thinking? The same jolt caused by the answer to this triggered the neurons that sent a signal to his foot; he automatically twisted the throttle and the engine roared beneath him. He gave the Syringe one last glance. Later on it occurred to him he ought to have said something to her, anything, told her to wait at home for him, that he'd be back soon and tomorrow he'd take her for another ride, or better still to the cinema, anywhere she wanted. Maybe if he'd waved or smiled, it would have been enough, who knows, but he didn't do or say anything, except to open the throttle and speed towards the coast, leaving her hunched in the doorway with that glowering catlike expression on her broad, moist face and in her vindictive ashen eyes.

Beneath the midnight sun an abandoned rubber swan floats in the still, private waters. Filled with air, it glides along the silvery trail of the moon, spinning round and round, graceful and nonchalant, pushed by opposing currents and surface ripples as it obeys strange, distant commands from the open sea. A gentle breeze propels it towards the jetty, where it bobs against the salty flanks of a moored motorboat. Yet an inhospitable and oddly Arctic atmosphere reigns over the Villa and its surroundings, bleaching the deep-green pines and the sandy beach. Hours before, the setting sun had disappeared in its red cloak behind a gap in the nearby hills, its last rays falling slantwise over the Villa like a fan, the way light shines through a door left ajar. The breeze rose as night fell. Like elegant guests preparing to venture into a drawing room, the garden's silver fir saplings quiver, eager and excited, as they are bent towards the glittering surface of the sea.

The Interloper arched his back and squeezed the sides of the burning metal tank between his thighs. He raced along, the wind sending the air ballooning beneath his shirt, eating up the distance and the night, past signs he didn't read (except for: Costa Brava, with an arrow pointing ahead). This time he was riding a brand-new, hot-blooded Ducati. A luxury model, a crimson and chrome monster, a glowing, mythic flame, the plaything of champions and rich kids (early on he had dreamed of owning a Ducati just like this), as capricious and skittish as a filly.

Clenching his teeth against the wind's fury, he opened the throttle all the way, clinging on for dear life to his spirited steed, his heart pounding to the Ducati's exhilarating, carefree momentum. He was speeding down Avenida Virgen de Montserrat, overtook some cyclists returning from work, a grey Dauphine and a Seat that was hogging the road. It was driven by a white-haired man with one hand on the wheel – next to him an enormous German shepherd dog and a young girl laughing with her head thrown back (Manolo observed these details because for a while he was forced to ride level with the Seat) – apparently unwilling to let Manolo overtake. But Manolo not only passed the Seat, he cut in dangerously close in front, so that the driver had to slam on his brakes.

He crossed Paseo Maragall without looking and carried on down Calle Garcilaso to Concepción Arenal. There he slowed and turned left before accelerating again towards San Andrés. For a while he sped through wasteland where some kids had built bonfires, slowing to cross La Rambla de San Andrés beneath a traffic policeman's suspicious gaze. Soon he hit eighty again, but when he reached the army barracks he slowed down, preparing to turn right past Carretera de Vich on his left. There, to his astonishment (he thought he'd consigned it to oblivion), the black Seat caught up with him again, no doubt also heading for the coast, and no less eager to arrive than he was. As the car swerved towards him on the bend, the dog barked, and the uncle's hand must have remained on his pretty niece's knee, forcing Manolo on to the pavement alongside the barracks' wall. He overtook the Seat a second time shortly before they reached the bridge over the River Besós, from where he could see the lights of Santa Coloma.

Three kilometres of wide, straight, quite busy road lay before him. Shifting his weight slightly, the Interloper moved out into the left lane then and zigzagged in and out between the snout-like front of a bus and the back of a *roulotte* (with lace curtains in the rear window, a real home), before finally overtaking a cart piled high with maize. As there was little oncoming traffic, Manolo stayed in the outside lane to pass two vehicles driving nose to tail. He took advantage of his acceleration to overtake a huge, panting lorry festooned with sidelights that appeared to be floating amid blue swirls, protecting the cyclists in its wake the way a mother hen does her chicks. He rode flat out towards the bridge, defying the cars coming towards him. The angry grille of a Seat 600 drove straight at him, swerving at the last minute as he knew it would. The Ducati reached a formidable hundred and fifteen on the clock, the whole machine quivering like a nervous girl, but without any superfluous spasms or untimely euphoria. One pothole and you're done for, Manolo, he told himself. Behind him in the rear-view mirror streetlamps and car lights flashed and vanished swiftly, swallowed up by a black, hollow vortex hurling them into the void.

He rode with a fury and recklessness that left the weekend drivers aghast. Hortensia also became no more than a blur in the cold memory of the rear-view mirror, together with the heartbroken old man, the workshop, his family, their house, the entire neighbourhood. The bewildering speed of events over the past few days, beginning with Teresa's sudden disappearance and the way time had gone crazy, the urban labyrinth, the relentless search, the surprise letter with its joyous invitation, Hortensia's kisses, the hunger (he hadn't eaten a proper meal in weeks, possibly months), even the smell of burning rubber when he was forced to brake behind a ridiculous Seat 600, was to provide him with food for thought for years to come. Yet the thrill of speeding along like this couldn't explain everything. It didn't encompass the reality of his initial impulse, born of darkness, summer and celebration: some silky details, some touches of a warm inner thigh – in short, the powerful network of the hidden forces playing around the Murcian's proud head.

Fine skeins of moonlight lay over the Villa's towers, a murmur of waves, complete solitude and impunity at the end of his sixty-five-kilometre journey. Everything else was uncertain. Teresa: probably awake but not expecting him. Place (chosen, it seemed, by Madame Moreau): *une chambre royale sur la Méditerranée.* Time: midnight or thereabouts.

Everything would be as before, apart from the murmur of the sea (growing louder, more threatening). He would steal beneath the tall eucalyptus trees in the garden, trample the bed of leaves by the chain-link fence of the tennis court, approach the ivy-grown wall below the terrace. His hands would shake uncontrollably (calm down, kid) when he first touched the glossy green cascade lit by the moon, groping amid the ivy's cold, damp leaves for the hidden drainpipe and a branch sturdy enough to help him climb. The Interloper froze, hesitated, ducked to avoid a moth's funereal wings, and in one of those unfortunate tricks memory can play, he saw Maruja's face hover over the pillow, announcing her imminent fall (in the rear-view mirror he caught sight of a bewildered nun walking backwards, extending her arms and no doubt yelling as she sank oddly into the asphalt as if into quicksand), but then his hand would at last grasp the rough sinuous branch and he would begin his ascent. In his mind's eye, moonlight glistened on each shiny leaf. He leapt on to the terrace. A parasol, a small table and two hammocks (one red, the other yellow) yawning at the foam-crested waves. The moon slid alongside him, helping him open a path through a strange constellation of threats and insults (shocked, indignant faces continued to peer from car windows, shouting at him) as he crept over to the French windows with white shutters that opened into Teresa's room. Little white flowers like snowflakes flowed from a large hanging basket that stood guard at the entrance. Inside, a blue lunar landscape and at the far end, along the wall, he could glimpse the smooth ridge of a sheet draped over a female body. He pushed at one of the French windows, which as it opened reflected part of the terrace with the two hammocks (why did he also see a distant motorbike headlight?). *Crash!* went a wave as it broke against the jetty, a gust of wind swept the hair from his brow, and the French window screeched. But he was already inside, greeted by a somnolent hush. He felt as ethereal and sinister as a bat. Four steps on a parquet floor, two on carpet, two more on parquet, followed by a lunar landing on the white ridge of the bed. Journey's end.

She would be wearing: a mauve Empire-style nightgown (please!) and a black velvet band in her blond hair. She was fast asleep on a small drop-down bed, facing away from him, half lying on her front. The sheet was drawn up just above her waist, and her posture vaguely reminded him of the easy, buoyant way with which she swam in shallow, warm waters, one arm arched above her head, the other brushing her hip, her head gracefully raised, drinking in an imaginary sun. Wings timidly folded, the mesmerised dark bat leaned over her, drawn to the bronze gleam of her shoulders. He studied her doe-like neck pulsing with bold, intrepid life even as she slept, and all at once was enveloped by the pink effluvium of sleep: a noontide cherry blossom fragrance. Yet how frail, how defenceless and childlike she looked! Seeing her virginal face outlined against the white pillow, he found it easy to imagine the strict supervision to which her mother subjected her during the day (even now, he could sense the delicate presence of Señora Serrat floating in some corner of the bedroom), the parental wall of fear and misgiving created no doubt by the anti-bourgeois sentiments issuing from their daughter's hazy red lips – sullen and brazen in their childish petulance.

But more to the point for the Interloper, exactly where in the Villa would her parents and their guests be sleeping? Near or far from their daughter-turned-traitor, he wondered, recalling her letter. Manolo's speculations about her Catalan relatives' vigilance (including the dark, handsome tennis player he had spied that morning in the garden, the cousin from Madrid, who might be wide awake, practising heaven knows what new serve he wanted to teach his cousin) were important not so much because he feared they might overhear (do politicised virgins moan with pleasure? In the end, they must do, like all the others) but because of a failure to protect or love Teresa in childhood which somehow, for the Interloper, would favour ejaculation. It excited him to think of her parents asleep in the marital bed (if possible hung with yellow mosquito nets) while he set about making a woman of Teresa, gently and with the greatest sense of responsibility, as if acting on behalf of the family, to everyone's benefit.

Just at that moment, Teresa moved her knee. Now (he had left the French windows ajar) the shutter threw stripes of moonlight across her hip. Her breath grew ragged and she shook her tousled blond head restlessly, wishing in her sleep for a more crowded, less dull, beach, and to judge from her smile her wish was fulfilled. Oh, Teresina, how happy you are, for if your dreams are sweet, how much sweeter your awakening, thought the expert in nightmares, the orphaned creature of the night as he gazed at her tenderly. Teresa moaned. Brushing her hip, her swimmer's hand, fingers splayed, still had need of his friendship, his protection in this mad world. And so Manolo clasped it gently in his as he kneeled down next to her bed, and a light blinded him (the same one as when that damned Seat slammed on its brakes a second time before they reached the bridge, forcing him off the road and boxing him in, the Ducati intact – thank God – and in the car window the shocked expressions of the German shepherd, the uncle and his niece, on whose pretty knees his hairy hand still rested). This made Manolo reflect he shouldn't go around with young girls, take off his clothes or climb into bed and embrace Teresa ... Her awakening would doubtless be delightful, untroubled, prolonged through their honeymoon in the south. But what if she rejects me? he thought (my, if only they could see you now). Another screech of tyres, more distant than before, and a whispered prayer (Teresa, my love, my April rose, princess of Murcia, lead me to your Catalan family!) as he kissed her hair tenderly. His hand ached to touch her, but perhaps it would be a good idea to control his urges before he woke her (how you've changed) so as not to startle her.

Teresa was alone in her room in the Villa, while everyone else slept, cocooned in their lofty cloud: which meant he had nothing to fear ... except himself. Around her, a pleasantly childish untidiness: strewn about the floor were clothes, magazines, records, a stuffed bear, glass eyes gleaming in the darkness, a doll, a pair of tennis shoes. His other knee rested on Marilyn Monroe's enticing red lips (a shiny brand-new copy of *Elle* magazine, whose horoscope section Teresa had no doubt read that night), but he preferred to fix his gaze on the elegant vase on her bedside table with its five roses. An enchanting touch, the roses. Did they influence her sleep, framing it in one particular spring? He couldn't resist the urge to breathe in their scent before making Teresa his, and as he did so, his senses brimmed with cathedral-like solemnity, a prenuptial blessing (Teresa de Reyes at the altar, all in white, joyously, shamelessly pregnant), which unleashed a demon in him that made him want to kiss the bride. But since he was no scoundrel, no vulgar opportunist, all he did was squeeze her hand gently to wake her. His unusually timid response was also unnecessary, for once again Teresa would make things easy for him: she pulled her hand free, seemingly oblivious to the sensitive, thoughtful, curiously selfless (my, how you've changed) intruder, gave a sleepy sigh and turned over to face him: a flicker of eyelids and then the blue gaze of her open eyes stared at him in surprise.

Teresa sat up abruptly in bed, apparently unconcerned by the startling transparency of her nightgown. How simple things would be under the shelter of her doubly amorous gaze: the blue lakes of her eyes, the budding violets of her nipples. For the briefest of moments the lovers would bring to life an innocent, joyous Christmas-card scene of angels embracing, foreheads touching, adoring and awestruck, the same messianic glow that emanated from the maiden's lap. *Shhh!* went Teresa, a finger pressed to her lips. She smiled, moaned, stammered a kind of nervous, exhilarated telegram:

'Lunatic . . . you came . . . surprise . . . if they find out.'

He would caress her hair, her glowing shoulders, draw her to him. 'I got your letter. Are you pleased to see me?' was all he could say.

There was a look of controlled fear in her eyes, less because of the ardent desire she could sense in his hands and mouth (a flame as yet unfanned, but which she was more than willing to be consumed by) than due to the uncanny silence the Villa was immersed in. And then something happened which the Interloper wouldn't understand straight away, so well intentioned was he at this stage: Teresa wrenched herself free from his embrace, leapt off the bed and blundered about the room briefly before making a dash for the door, as though in a desperate attempt to get away. A defenceless, half-naked, terrified Teresa narrowly escapes the clutches of a faun (as he thought), barefoot, hair flying, delicately pinching her skimpy nightgown between forefinger and thumb to keep it from getting tangled between her thighs. A fleeting, jerky sequence of images that, conveniently edited by someone with a more malicious imagination, such as the Cardinal, might have delighted Manolo, eliciting a stifled laugh from the outcast faun he had once, without any great conviction, dreamed of being, trampling on the flowery beds of residential neighbourhoods as he pursued wealthy young nymphs, a scenario which that night in the Villa, given Teresa's apparent attempt to flee, promised to have either a more timid variation or a tender culmination.

Had the intervening days not deposited Manolo in this bedroom in such a state of eager excitement, turned him into this naïve, fearful, well-mannered suitor, a sad, anxious shadow of his former self, and had Teresa's experience of love that summer not turned her into a realist, opening her eyes to their respective social and sexual circumstances – if none of that had occurred, then something resembling a vaudeville show might have taken place that night, to the huge delight and satisfaction of the powers of evil. But he wouldn't lift a finger to stop her, and would remain at the foot of the bed; in all fairness, nobody could accuse him of knowing or even suspecting for a moment Teresa's true intention, which obviously was not to escape his grasp but to make sure everyone in the Villa was sound asleep and that there was no danger. This was why she would cautiously open her bedroom door and lean out to inspect the shadows on the stairs and in the hallway, one naked foot in the air, hitching up her nightgown, before slowly, carefully closing it again (and turning the key, oh yes, turning the key); then she would wheel round with a smile and lean back against the door. All at once she would rush off again, this time to the bathroom, where she would switch on the light before slipping inside (through a crack in the door, he would see the busy, joyous movement of her arms in front of the mirror as she speedily adjusted her hair, her rosy cheeks, her nightgown), only to reappear almost at once in the doorway, triumphant and glorious, just like him after one of his mad motorbike rides. Motionless, smiling shyly against the light, she fixed him with her gaze for a while, then ran over and flung herself into his arms.

She was no longer wearing her black velvet hairband.

'Teresa, are you being honest with me? Sometimes, I . . .'

'What?'

'I don't know . . . I thought you were going to leave me. Are you afraid?'

'No.'

'Have you really been unwell?'

'I'm all right now.'

Everything was all right now. Now there were only delicate bows, soft silk ribbons that melted in the heat of his fingers, and the ever so faint and sweet imprint of her underwear elastic on her skin. The fragrant lilac mist enveloping her body showed off her giddily thrusting hips, her little ivory breasts, before slipping to the floor where it floated about her naked feet, on tiptoe at that everlasting, intimate frontier between the invisible and the visible. Was she not perhaps smaller, more fragile, more firmly attached to her obscure habits and conventions than he had imagined (for example, her natural, spontaneous habit of sweeping her blond hair from her face before turning her moist lips towards him, in the same casual way she might drink from a public fountain), but also remoter, and somehow resilient, inviolable, as if her beloved face, receding beneath twilight waves of sun and cloud, were plunging ever deeper into a different dream, a different realm even more distant and forbidden than that of the Villa – into the impregnable, hereditary chambers of her caste, whose defences when he awoke the next day (if indeed he woke up beside her), would prove even harder to overcome than the ones in this bedroom. There would also be a hiatus, a length of time without memory that nothing could fill, a few decisive minutes that would whisk them from the calm autumnal peak where they stood in each other's arms, still resisting the final, two-pronged attack of winter and the voice of reason, to the pillow on which she would lay her head, and where his hungry mouth, after drinking from her eager ruby lips and closing her weary eyes, would briefly stray around her neck and shoulders before descending, fleeing, voyaging for ever between soft golden hills towards the south.

And then to stretch out on golden sands, on a shore swept by a torrent of sighs and idleness, breathless passions melting all summer long: even the swan, swept along now by brisker winds, overtakes the languid foam crests and lazy wavelets of a slower pattern of currents, and he tells himself he will learn like the palm of my hand, my love, the cultural map of your luminous skin so we may swim together another summer, and I will pierce the mysterious, generous motion of your sweet, sun-kissed hips, and remain faithful to you until I die. Beyond that, farewell odourless girls of my neighbourhood, breasts swathed in sheets of fear and foolish hope – I'm out of there! Now, hair blowing in the wind on a ship's prow, on the steps to the aircraft, on the terrace overlooking the sea and the moon, now, our blond, blue-eyed children conceived on yachts and ocean liners, on express night trains, between candelabras on grand pianos, beside private pools or with breakfast in bed served on tiger skins, no longer on stormy nights that cloud eyes and misshape hips weary of their own weight, no more, but yes, now, yes, together between beautiful, slender, solemn thighs emblazoned by the sun that ripen in winter like golden lizards, like the labels of far-flung hotels adorning our suitcases, like precious scars from ancient, youthful adventures on the islands, and that music, can you hear it? We already know the origin of that music, and the pleasant evening awaiting us in the family garden, waving our tennis racquets and handkerchiefs in the air, and presents wrapped in tissue paper tied with red ribbons that remain unopened to this day, but now, yes, now this crystal glass is yours and mine, this rhythmic, coupled flight of longings and doves and kisses on fine linen sheets on the garden lawn, and dignity and respect and more, much more, little one, you drive me to distraction, now it is ours, Teresa my love, now . . .

'Documents.'

Before the harsh, clipped voice, what swooped down on him this time, forcing him to veer off the road, slam on his brakes and fall off the motorbike, wasn't a car's headlights but two angry, sinister Sanglas motorbikes, with their leaden riders, booted, helmeted, belted and brandishing notebooks. No doubt they'd been giving chase since he turned off towards Besós bridge, had caught up with and escorted him, before ruthlessly boxing him in when a lorry and a slow-moving car in front made it almost impossible for him to get away. He careered along at the foot of a grassy bank, then lost his balance and toppled on to his right side. He realised too late why everything at the Villa had gone so smoothly, apart from the murmur of the sea (increasing, threatening, the roar of the Sanglas bikes) and that they had barely given him time to leave Barcelona: he was in Paseo Santa Coloma, the bridge in front of him, and to his right, a few metres below the road, the river bank with its reedbed, the railway tracks and a hazy row of cheap dwellings.

He stood up, the Ducati juddering between his thighs, engine still purring, brushed the mud and grass off his trousers, letting its unsullied headlamp light up the dismal wasteland. With a limp, defeated gesture, he silenced the final throbs of his faithful companion, which died beneath him with a spluttering sneeze. He didn't even bother to respond when the officer demanded to see the motorcycle papers and made to jot down the number plate. To their left, cars zoomed past almost melodiously, their lights and sounds still harmonising with his fading fantasy. The officer clicked the top of his ballpoint pen repeatedly, to no avail. As if he could read in his face the disappointing solution to some mystery, Manolo studied the man's clean-shaven cheeks, trim black moustache, and eyelids drooping with boredom. The other officer propped his motorcycle on its stand and walked towards them along the roadside. He gesticulated furiously at the vehicles to move along, as if by waving his hands he was trying to reimpose an authority momentarily dented by this loutish motorcyclist. Knowing all was lost, Manolo remained silent, apart from informing them politely where he was going in such a hurry.

'To see my girlfriend,' he said, causing the officer to snigger.

And as he waited for them to complete their stupid paperwork and take him away, he stroked the Ducati's chrome headlamp (farewell, old friend), suddenly recalling another evening with Teresa, a balmy, tranquil night brimming with promise, and yet which also resounded with the same mocking laughter, a foreshadowing of this scene of bewilderment and despair.

This was long before Maruja died, when Teresa's Floride was in the garage. At the end of a long stroll, the lovers found themselves on a bench on Gran Vía waiting to hail a passing taxi to take them home. He had his arm around Teresa's shoulders, and once in a while his mouth brushed her face, descending to taste her deliquescent pink lips. Above their heads the stars danced serenely in a slate-black sky, and the street was deserted and quiet, apart from the sound of ripping silk made by the tyres of a passing car. And then, between two kisses, he became aware of the shadowy, cynical onlooker, the broad sardonic smile that never believed in his chances of success, a hazy presence comprised of everyone and no one, neighbours asleep behind their windows, prying eyes peering from passing cars, people near and far, present and future friends, the trees, streetlamps and benches lining the avenue. All of a sudden this disdainfully cynical attitude, this generalised disbelief in him took concrete shape in a young policeman, rifle slung over his shoulder.

'Documents,' he had demanded, looking at Manolo. Oddly, with his amiable face, freckles and blue eyes, he looked more like a young Swiss man. 'Documents, please.' Apparently (Teresa explained later in the taxi, a hint of intrigue in her voice), the previous evening someone had tossed a firecracker into a nearby newspaper office, and the whole area was under close surveillance. Teresa had handed over her identity card (Manolo apologised for having left his at home), and as the officer strained to examine it in the poor lighting, a colleague of his appeared out of nowhere, also carrying a rifle slung over his shoulder. This second policeman looked hard at them for a while, head tilted to one side, brain working overtime (as if he wanted to establish who they were, especially Manolo, without having to check their documents), until his thick Andalusian lips muttered something like: 'Lationsip!' His mistrustful gaze slid from the Interloper's jeans and polo shirt to the *señorita*'s snow-white slacks, sandals and silk blouse – a serene glow, obviously above suspicion. Manolo was puzzled by the word, which sounded more like an invocation. The officer stepped forward, smiled sardonically, and growled:

'Your relationship with the young lady, dammit!' A real Sherlock Holmes (Teresa would say laughing, much later) with a southern accent.

Indignant, Manolo looked down, and then, just as on this occasion, he replied fiercely, 'She's my girlfriend,' to someone who smiled incredulously and gave him a scornful look tinged with condescension. And then, just as now, Manolo suspected that what he would find most humiliating, would cause him the greatest pain and suffering, would not be to end up in prison one day, or to have to give up Teresa, but the brutal conviction that no one, not even those who had seen him kiss Teresa so tenderly, would ever take him seriously, believe he was truly capable of loving her or of being loved in return.

Perhaps that was why he now gave up without a fight, held out his wrists blindly, instinctively. He wasn't even surprised to learn at Horta police station an hour later that there was a warrant out for his arrest.

That odourless flower Hortensia had reported him.

The morning quivers to the vibrations of a tram carrying swarms of people to the beach on its running boards. It's Sunday. From the city's outskirts endless columns of vehicles flow slowly towards the coast. Noisy, jostling crowds fill station platforms and bus stops. On Calle Trafalgar, men and women form long, animated queues. Cheerful youths cram into metro carriages, pushing and pressing against each other, while above them the sun beats down on the empty, eviscerated city. In El Ensanche, deserted streets are sunk in the slow-burn torpor of summer that blinds the solitary passerby, enveloping him in the echo of his own footsteps. The desultory blast of a distant ship's horn reaches him through avenues and side streets, like a breath of cool air amid the sun's corrosive heat. In his mind's eye, he sees flags floating in the wind, writhing on their poles like parched tongues, licking the splendid bronzed surface of yet another blue sky, the youthful flanks of more passing clouds, while close to he can hear radios droning on balconies, trams grating as they return empty, and taxis cruising aimlessly.

Turning a corner, he suddenly found himself on the Ramblas. The first thing to attract his attention were the vast numbers of foreign tourists. He sought the shade of the trees as he descended the avenue, and the proximity of greatly missed outdoor cafés. Manolo halted briefly along the way and, as if his ears had suddenly popped, he heard the clink of spoons and glasses, birds twittering in the trees, leaves rustling in the breeze. He slipped into the side streets, where for the first time he rehearsed the long, brisk strides that would give the impression that somebody somewhere was waiting for him, that this Sunday still held something in store for him ...

What follows are Luis Trías de Giralt's recollections of that same Sunday, when he was more or less exiled in the Bar Saint-German, having lost his taste for conspiracies, the admirable mental faculties that had brought him so much prestige now reduced to a sad collection of cynical predictions and obsessions. Luis maintained it was the hottest, most depressing day of that summer, at a time in the morning when anxiety and remorse from Saturday night still haunted him. He seemed to be floating in the harsh, ignominious glare of his friend Filipo's red polo shirt, when all at once behind him he heard the unmistakable feline tread, the muffled squeak of rubber soles, and felt a pair of eyes boring into the back of his head.

Luis had not seen him enter, but since hangovers always gave him a heightened sensitivity to what was going on behind his back (a fact that could only be explained by his natural propensity to interpret the silent language of looks), he knew instantly that it was him. Yet when Luis turned around, all he could see was a blurred outline close to his face, and for a split second he didn't recognise him. Apparently absorbed in the contemplation of the picture that depicted Encarna wreathed in damp chiffon, the Interloper stood there, hands in pockets, an old corduroy jacket slung over his shoulder. Filipo was also looking at him. They heard the waitress ask what he wanted. 'A beer,' he replied. Apart from her, they were the only three people in the bar.

Luis Trías studied him closely, focusing almost painfully on the details: what had they done to his hair? The particles from the sun's glare filtering in from outside mingled with a strange nocturnal pulsation emanating entirely from the Interloper, something that had adhered to him down at the docks or in some seedy boarding house, or wherever he was living. The collarless white shirt he wore was too small for him, the cuffs buttoned pathetically above the wrists; his basketball shoes had no laces, and on the thighs of his jeans were two large white patches, the result of friction and countless washings, which when he moved (he was slowly approaching the bar for his beer) gave him a lithe, menacing air. Yet what stood out above all was his brutal, degrading haircut: the starkly shaven neck and sideburns evoked a particular kind of harsh disciplinary regime. His face oozed a cool disdain as he once more surveyed Encarna's portrait: an air of weary, gaunt impatience floated round his head and slumped shoulders.

'Don't you remember your friends?' Luis called out to him, proffering his hand as he suppressed the memory of a certain punch. Manolo stared straight at him and came over. Luis didn't notice any flicker of surprise on his face; he had obviously recognised Luis when he walked in, but didn't want to be the first to say hello, probably because after all this time he could only have one, obviously naïve reason for being there: to ask about Teresa.

'Hey, Manolo,' said Luis. 'It's been a while. Two years, isn't it?'

'Yes, two years.'

'So, kiddo, what's new? How was it in . . .' He smiled, softening his tone. 'Well, I mean to say, not good, I suppose.'

'I've been travelling.'

Swaying a little on his stool, Luis Trías burst out laughing. He nudged his friend Filipo discreetly in the ribs and for some reason decided that this latest disingenuous lie from the Murcian warranted his first gin of the day. He ordered one for himself, with plenty of ice, and another for Filipo.

'Do you want one, Manolo?'

'No, thanks.'

Luis clapped him on the back, laughed again and said:

'You needn't pretend with me – I know you've been in prison.' He paused to see the effect his words had on Manolo, but the Interloper seemed unfazed: he simply looked him straight in the eye.

Luis asked:

'When did you get out?'

'A few days ago,' Manolo replied blankly, raising his shoulder slightly to stop his jacket slipping.

'There's no shame in it, kid,' declared Luis, and a glimmer of his old superior attitude showed itself when he added playfully: 'Somebody once said that, morally speaking, to rob a bank is the same as to found one.'

'I didn't rob any bank – stop messing with me.'

'And if it's any consolation to you, I was locked up for a spell four years ago: admittedly not for the same reasons as you. But to tell you the truth, these days I can't see any difference. In the end, you and I both wanted the same thing: to sleep with Teresa Serrat. Isn't that so?'

Luis gave a splutter of laughter and nodded wistfully. This was the first time he had mentioned Teresa's name in front of the Murcian, and now he waited in vain for him to ask about her, to admit why he was there. Instead, Manolo remained impassive; except that his eyes were burning with a strange intensity, focused on a single object like an animal on the prowl. Luis asked him what he was doing, whether he had a job, where he lived.

'I told you, I just got out,' Manolo muttered, holding the other man's gaze, and despite Luis's insistence, all he got were vague answers, an oblique reference to a possible future employment. Suddenly the Murcian said: 'Who told you about me?'

'Teresa,' Luis replied hastily, and then, a note of triumph in his voice: 'Do you want to know Teresa's reaction when she heard?'

'Sure,' said Manolo.

Luis Trías dropped a hand on his shoulder. 'She laughed, kid. Seriously. I think she's still laughing.' He fell silent and waited for Manolo to ask him more questions. Manolo didn't open his mouth, but from his expression and general demeanour, he still appeared ready to listen to anything.

And so he found out what he wanted to know, what he no longer dared ask: how in early October, alarmed by his silence, Teresa had gone to Monte Carmelo, where she was told of his arrest; how for a while she'd refused to see anyone, except a cousin of hers from Madrid, with whom she went around a great deal; how months later in the faculty bar she had told Luis the whole story, laughing and searching for her words, as if it was an old half-forgotten joke that was still hilariously funny; how, that same winter, word had gone round the faculty that Teresa had finally lost her virginity, and how the following year she graduated with top honours, and soon struck up a close friendship with Mari Carmen Bori, with whom she currently frequented certain intellectual circles that he, Luis Trías, could no longer abide; how, incidentally, if Manolo knew Mari Carmen and her husband, it might interest him to know they had split up, and Mari Carmen was now living with a painter; and finally, how Luis himself, having abandoned his studies and gone to work for his father, was finally living at peace, if not with his country, at least with himself, with his few drinks and his small circle of friends; he didn't miss or resent anyone, he was non-politicised and forgotten, although he sincerely wished the new intake at the university greater wisdom and better luck ...

'Still, it was fun,' he concluded.

Fleetingly in sympathy with the spirit of an already distant summer, connected for a brief instant with the giddiness of silk and moonlight, the Interloper's gloomy expression acknowledged none of this, not even the parts referring to Teresa. He must have thought to himself, reflected Luis Trías, that he had only come here to confirm something he already knew, and that this confirmation could not affect him in the slightest because, right from the outset, from the very first evening he came in here with Teresa, defying them all with his lies and swagger, it had been cruelly, irrevocably branded on his sardonic face.

Manolo made to pay for his drink.

'You're leaving already? Have another beer and we can talk some more,' said Luis Trías. 'On me.'

'Thanks, but I'm in a hurry.'

Luis laid his hand on Manolo's shoulder again.

'What are your plans?'

'I'll see. Goodbye.'

And, wheeling round, hands in his pockets, the Interloper strode out.

Translator's Note

Translating Juan Marsé's novel in 2024–25 is like opening a time capsule. It contains all kind of clues as to what life was like in Barcelona during the decade of the 1950s (the main action of the book takes place between June and September 1956). First published in 1966, the Catalan society depicted in the novel is deeply traditional: at the top are the Serrat family, land and property owners whose spoilt only child Teresa gives the novel its title. They live in splendid mansions in the city and keep summer villas on the Catalan coast. At the bottom of the social scale are their maids and the men and women who look after their country estates.

Outside this society, and posing perhaps the greatest threat to it, are the *xarnegos*, poor immigrants from the south of Spain who have been coming to Barcelona since after the end of the Civil War in the 1940s. They live on bare hillsides outside the city in neighbourhoods such as Monte Carmelo, in makeshift houses from where they catch only glimpses of it in the distance:

> At dawn from the top of Monte Carmelo you can occasionally glimpse a distant, unknown city rise out of a dream-like mist: strips of fog and lingering nocturnal shadows still float above it like the ghostly sprinkling of dust . . .

Manolo Reyes, the hero or anti-hero of the novel, known in Spanish as the *pijoaparte* (which after much debate I have translated as the *Interloper*) is one of these immigrants, the son of a cleaning woman in a marquis' palace in the Andalusian city of Ronda. Like many of those drawn to the thriving Catalan capital, Manolo must take whatever jobs he can find, often indulging in petty crime.

This is one of the aspects of the novel that takes us back in time. In Barcelona during the 1940s and 1950s, immigrants from Andalusia were regarded as foreigners from a different culture with less refined customs and habits. As often happens, they were treated with suspicion, if not outright hostility. Pointing out how things have changed in Spain since then, on the fortieth anniversary of the book's first publication, Marsé himself said that if he were to write the novel these days, he would have made the main character an immigrant from the Maghreb.

Teresa's relationship with Manolo is based on a complete misunderstanding. She thinks he is so secretive and elusive because he is involved in clandestine political activity for the Spanish Communist party, beginning to reorganise after the defeat in the Civil War. She sees him as a 'working class hero' involved in all kinds of conspiracies to bring down the Franco regime, already in power for more than fifteen years. She contrasts this with the politics that her university friends (especially the student leader Luis Trías de Giralt) indulge in, talking of proletarian revolution when they do not even know anyone from the working class.

Unlike other novels which feature strikes in Barcelona and protests against the Franco regime, Marsé here makes little direct political comment (although some of the student leaders are said to have been in jail and tortured). Instead, he concentrates on a bitterly sarcastic attack on the university-educated *señoritos* (rich kids) who import their ideas from France (Sartre and Simone de Beauvoir) but who are useless when it comes to any kind of action, on even the most intimate level, as Teresa learns to her dismay.

This issue of sexuality is another aspect of the novel that roots it firmly in its time. Catalonia is just starting to open up to foreign tourists, who offer the kind of guilt-free sexual behaviour not available to the repressed locals. It is even more of a problem for an upper-class daughter like Teresa, desperate to show how modern and free she is by losing her virginity, when her *xarnego* friend has his own concept of right and wrong in sexual matters.

This is Juan Marsé's third novel, begun in 1962 and first published in Spanish by Seix Barral in 1966. The novel became hugely controversial when it won the coveted *Biblioteca breve* prize in 1965, with many in the Spanish literary establishment of the time seeing it as poorly written and without any ideological premise. According to Marsé, the Franco censors prohibited the book because of its content, but then apparently ignored it.

It is tempting to see Marsé as the interloper in the Spanish literary scene: he left school at fourteen and became an apprentice in a jeweller's workshop. As a writer he was self-taught, not being part of the Madrid scene of writers following the fashion of writing objective 'social realist' novels. Marsé lived in Paris doing menial jobs for two years in the early 1960s and has said that meeting the Spanish exiles living there (see, for example, the Alain Resnais film *La guerre est finie*), confident that the Franco regime would be swept away by pressure from the masses was what inspired his bitterly ironic take on the pseudo-revolutionaries portrayed in *Teresa*.

Among the many challenges for the translator attempting to convey Marsé's style and vision of Barcelona in the 1950s are of course the different registers, from the educated upper classes to the poor marginalised southern immigrants. But perhaps the greatest challenge is in properly conveying the contrast between reality and Manolo's fantasy world, often described in cinematic terms. This is especially true when the two are mixed up together, with a paragraph beginning with a character speaking that then morphs into what they are thinking or imagining.

This gap between reality and imagination is also crucial to the sarcasm with which Marsé describes the would-be student revolutionaries, as well as Teresa's perpetual wishful thinking. Marsé further delights in physical descriptions of people and places that immediately capture the period; one small example, Señor Serrat's moustache:

> ... he looked like a member of that distinguished clique of meticulous, anonymous and identical middle-aged men who apparently wished to proclaim for ever their youthful support for the victorious Nationalists thanks to a carefully groomed and curiously trimmed military moustache.

With *Last Evenings with Teresa* Marsé became known as one of Spain's finest contemporary writers. His later novels return time and again to the post-war years in Barcelona and memories of childhood, but perhaps never offer such a comprehensive view of a specific world and time. However, despite its appearance as a time capsule, the story of Manolo Reyes and his epic battle to make reality match his dreams is as timeless as all great literature.

Nick Caistor